Praise for Richa
The Illumii

An impressive saga, set at a blistering pace, teems with excitement and suspense. A fascinating, richly detailed historical thriller, worthy of Dennis Wheatley at his best. *Daily Mail*

Extremely enjoyable historical yarn, almost induces the reader to cheer. Will please many who like their reading with a Scarlet Pimpernelish flavour. *The Guardian*

A stirring love story and a compelling, richly-detailed historical thriller. *TV Oracle Teletext*

Richard Rees's research is as meticulous as Frederick Forsyth's, or George Macdonald Fraser's. *Press Association News, London*

This is big-screen stuff. The formula is right. Plenty of suspense, action, historical detail, and a love interest to boot. No mega-name of the period has been left undropped. A good yarn, a good read. The research must have taken many painstaking hours, the author has managed to recreate the atmosphere of those turbulent times to brilliant effect. *Country Quest*

A splendid period adventure novel and a cracking read, fast moving, never fails to hold the reader's interest. *North West Mail*

THE
REIKEL
CONSPIRACY

Also by Richard Rees

The Illuminati Conspiracy
Twice Upon A Thanksgiving
Dear Abigail
Somebody Wants to Kill Me

THE
REIKEL
CONSPIRACY

RICHARD REES

ISBN: 978-1-0902676-3-4

Front cover design: Paul Simpson, www.artychoke.com

Book design: Dean Fetzer, www.gunboss.com

*To my son, Huw, my daughter-in-law, Claire
and their family, Lowri, Adam, and Imogen.*

Author's Foreword

In researching the historical facts for *The Reikel Conspiracy*, I discovered the involvement of the part played in it by the famous brigantine, *Mary Celeste*. Delving deeper into this unexpected development – the vessel's abandonment in mid-Atlantic and disappearance of her crew, which has remained a mystery for almost 150 years – I was able to obtain copy transcripts of the Gibraltar Admiralty Inquiry at which the Captain and crew of the *Dei Gratia*, the brigantine that found the deserted *Celeste*, were questioned in great detail by Solly Flood, a British Admiralty advocate who suspected them of having been involved in a cover-up, possibly murder, in order to falsely claim salvage on the vessel, and by Henry Pisani, a Gibraltar advocate they chose to represent them. But the transcripts contained only the *replies* of the witnesses, with few or no full-stops or commas to show where one sentence ended and the next began. Consequently, in chapters 49 and 51, the questions put to them, especially by Flood, and the punctuation of their replies, are based on the suspicions and fractious temperament of the British Admiralty advocate, as reported in the newspapers of the time.

Richard Rees

New York

Tuesday, November 5, 1872

The New-York Times

MARINE INTELLIGENCE

NEW-YORK, MONDAY, Nov 4

Cleared
Steam-ship: Minnesota. Morgan. Liverpool
Brig: *Mary Celeste*. Briggs. Genoa

The New York Times gave only the barest information for vessels departing or entering New York port. Type and name of vessel. Surname of captain. Port of destination or origin. That was all.

The name and age of the *Mary Celeste's* captain was Benjamin Spooner Briggs, 37. He was from Marion, Massachusetts. Also on board were nine other souls: Briggs' wife, Sarah, 30; their little daughter, Sophia, 2; First Mate Albert Richardson, 28, from Stockton Springs, Maine; Second Mate Andrew Gilling, 25, a Dane; the crew: Volkert Lorenzen, 29, his brother Boz, 25, Gottlieb Goodschaad, 23, all from the island of Fohr, Northen Prussia, Arian Martens, 35, from the nearby island of Amrum, and the ship's steward, Edward Head, 23, from Brooklyn, New York.

One Month Later, Wednesday, December 4, 1872

Mid-Atlantic, some 600 miles off the west coast of Spain. Second Mate John Wright of the brig *Dei Gratia*, nineteen days out of the same port, New York, spotted an approaching vessel on the grey horizon, some four miles off the port bow. Training his telescope on her he saw she was a brig, focused on her tattered sails, and called his captain, David Morehouse, to view her. Joined by First Mate Oliver Deveau and the rest of the *Gratia*'s crew, they watched the vessel loom nearer.

The name on her bows read *Mary Celeste*.

Her deck, silent and empty, exuded the eerie feeling of a ghost-ship. Her unmanned wheel was turning aimlessly from port to starboard and back to port, as her rudder obeyed only the movement of the sea. Her forehatch cover was off, lying alongside the foremast – the recent high seas must have poured into her open hold. Her foretopsail hung by its four corners. Her main staysail lay loose across the top of the forrard deck-house. Only her lower topsail jib and foretopstaysail were set, the rest were furled. Her standing rigging looked to be good, but most of her running rigging had been carried away.

The vessel drifted slowly closer, until she was no more than a hundred yards away.

Captain Morehouse raised his hailer: 'Brig ahoy! Brig ahoy!'

There was no answer from *The Mary Celeste*.

Morehouse tried again: 'Brig ahoy! Brig ahoy!'

Still no reply. Just a strange deathly silence, broken only by the creaking of the *Mary Celeste's* rigging, the dull flapping of her sails, and the wind whistling across her empty decks.

- 1 -

Five Weeks Earlier, Thursday, October 31, 1872, New York

After two years in Europe, Colleen had forgotten how small the Church of Saint Francis Xavier was. As her cab turned into West 16th Street, the one-storey building with a simple wooden cross on the roof apex, looked crushed in the middle of a row of four-storeyed brownstone houses, and decidedly plain compared to the grandeur of the churches she'd attended while she was abroad.

Descending from her cab, she looked toward Fifth Avenue, struck by how much busier and noisier it was than she remembered. Endless crowds of people crossing in both directions at the intersection, continuous streams of wagons, coaches, hansom-cabs, the familiar "Yellow Bird" and "Red Bird" omnibuses, all rushing in both directions, as if there weren't enough hours in the day. West 16th Street, by comparison, was calm, three horse-drawn wagons, two men pushing hand-carts, a score or so pedestrians, all using it to get to and from Fifth and Sixth Avenues.

Covering her hair with a black lace headscarf she'd bought in Venice, Colleen paid the cab driver and entered the church, finding its hushed, hallowed atmosphere a soothing relief after the noise of the hectic world outside. It looked just the same, nothing had changed.

She gazed down the two aisles, separated by rows of plain wooden pews, remembering standing there in her white wedding gown before the high altar, below the marble statue of the Madonna and Child with Michael alongside her, looking into each other's eyes and promising to love each other until death did them part.

Until death do us part. What empty words they had been.

She turned her face away, noticing as she did so that the frescoes depicting the Stations of the Cross lining the chapel's walls were still richly coloured, showing no signs of fading. No, she sighed inwardly, nothing had altered here, while *her* life had been irrevocably changed.

The church was almost empty. A dark coated man, three women, heads covered, kneeling apart in prayer, and a solitary priest in the far corner of the left transept standing before a statuette of Mary and the Christ Child, below which was a side altar.

The priest was a stranger to her, but after being away so long this was no surprise. Young Jesuits were always being sent to Saint Francis Xavier for the kind of pastoral training only to be found in a city like New York. In months, they were gone, called away to missionary fields as far away as South America or China, following in the steps of Francis Xavier himself.

Wearing a black cassock, the priest was placing a lighted candle in a holder in front of the altar and preparing to kneel, but at the hollow echo of her footsteps as she started down the aisle he remained standing, waiting for her to reach him.

Colleen was immediately struck by his paleness of face and fairness of hair, almost albino white, both accentuated by his black robe. He was about the same height as Michael, five eleven, slim, a lean face. In his early thirties and very handsome, she thought. Despite his priestly vocation he was sure to flutter a few young female hearts.

'May I be of help?' The whispered voice was foreign. His slate-blue eyes were regarding her with detachment, evincing no response to her femininity.

'I'm hoping so,' she replied, 'but having been abroad for two years, I'm afraid I don't know your name, Father...'

'Reikel.'

'You sound German, Father?'

The Jesuit merely inclined his head. Colleen could feel the unseen barrier with which he surrounded himself. There was an alienation about him, as though his inner being was with some distant entity that only he could see. The young maidens of Saint Francis Xavier needn't waste their dreams on this priest, she thought. The man was irrevocably wedded to the Church.

'What part of Germany?' she persisted.

'Berlin.'

'Berlin. I spent a month there. A beautiful city. But not the best place for Catholics at the moment, I'm afraid,' she added, remembering the refugees fleeing the country, crowding the railway stations and platforms, and the way those wearing crucifixes had hastily removed them and stuffed them in their pockets when armed soldiers appeared, pushing people aside as they looked for anti-Protestant offenders to arrest.

'The Lord will restore the vine,' the Jesuit replied, a steely edge entering his whisper. 'in the meantime, Miss…Mrs?'

'Lowell,' she stated, she no longer used her married name, it belonged to the past. 'Colleen Lowell. Miss.'

'You wish confession?' His slate-blue eyes pierced into hers. His gaze made her feel uneasy. This, and her concern for her father, his bad reaction at being drawn deeper into the Tweed Ring investigation, caused her to rush her words.

'My uncle was a member here. Perhaps still is. I believe he's now in Europe, I'm hoping you have an address for him? Or a forwarding address? I called on my aunt but the house is closed up, and I thought I would try Saint Xavier, being he was so devoted to this church. That he might still be sending contributions?'

The white-haired priest stayed silent, looking deep into her eyes. As if he was trying to reach into her very soul, Colleen thought, and a cold shiver ran down her spine.

5

'The name of your uncle?'

She was certain the whispered question contained a sinister tone. Embarrassed by the family connection, she was suddenly hesitant to answer it. But she was here on behalf of her father and couldn't back out now.

'Sweeny. Alderman Peter Barr Sweeny. How long have you been at Saint Xavier's, Father?'

'This is my eleventh week.'

'Then you won't have met him personally.'

Because of his downfall as mastermind of "The Tweed Ring's" corrupt reign over New York, and the extent of their systematic rape of the city's finances, over $200,000,000 stolen during the years they were in power, she again felt discomfiture about being related to Sweeny as she added, 'Even so, I'm sure you must know his name?'

'Only that,' the priest replied. 'But not his address.'

Colleen was beginning to feel agitated – and also strangely uneasy – in this man's presence. His whispered voice, his cold penetrating gaze, were peculiarly disturbing.

'Is Father Hudson still Rector?'

'He is.'

'Then if I might please see him? He may know—'

'Miss Lowell, to repeat, we have no knowledge of where your uncle is. During my third week here, Father Hudson's secretary was taken ill, I was given his place. One of the letters requiring to be answered was from Police Headquarters asking the same question. Father Hudson informed me it was a routine request and instructed me to reply in the usual manner – we have not heard from Mr Sweeny since he left New York.'

Now regretting she had declared her relationship to Sweeny, Colleen turned to go. 'Thank you, Father. I'm sorry to have troubled you.'

Reikel watched her walk swiftly out of the church, feeling no guilt at having denied any knowledge of where Sweeny was now.

That must remain sacrosanct between himself and one other person.

His own shadowy Black Knight protector.

- 2 -

The Vatican, Rome

From a first-floor window, Pope Pius IX, the two hundred and fifty-fourth inheritor of the covenant made by the Christ to Simon Peter, looked down at the Piazza Pontifico and the Vatican gardens beyond.

He glanced at his gold pocket watch. After a lifetime of the strictest discipline it was certain, despite the personal danger to him in returning to Rome, that God's chosen strategist would be on time.

Turning away from the window, Pio Nono looked around "The Room of the Popes", one of the Appartamenti Borgia's five Tuscan styled halls. Once magnificent – its frescoed walls and ceilings painted by da Udine and del Vaga – the room was in need of restoration, but it would have to wait, Pius brooded, until the problem of Satan's appointed usurper, Victor Emmanuel, had been resolved, and Holy Church was again the Church Universal.

Universal! Righteous anger welled up in Pio Nono's papal breast.

Universal throughout the rest of the world, maybe, but no longer in mother Italy, her country of birth. Not since two years ago, September 20, in the year of our Lord, 1870, a day imprinted into his memory. The oppressor's guns bombarding the Aurelian Gate, creating breaches on both sides of the Porta Pia for his Piedmontese riflemen to pour through, violating Holy City with their presence, leaving *Pius* no alternative but to order his papal troops to lay down their arms and surrender.

Since then, he, the appointed Vicar of Christ on Earth, Successor to the Prince of Apostles, Servant of the Servants of God, had suffered the indignity of being held prisoner in the Vatican, while around him his Church in Italy was being plundered – her holdings: churches, seminaries, monasteries, made the illegal properties of the State.

Adopting the strategy of silent protest, Pius had hoped to stir passions around the globe, and inundate the usurper with floods of outcries from foreign governments. But after twenty-two months he had to accept it had failed.

It was now time for action. Which was why he had forced his shaky eighty-six-year-old legs down two flights of stairs from his private rooms, holding on to the walls all the way. Because within God's Holy Church, action meant one Order, and it was only into this room that its Head could obtain secret access into the Vatican.

A nearby clock began to peal the hour.

On the second stroke, Pius heard the expected click. A panel of winged cherubs, painted by Michelangelo, opened into the room and Pierre Beckx, Father-General of the Society of Jesus stepped out of the cobwebbed passage, into the Borgia "Room of the Popes".

Wearing a black suit instead of his habitual black cassock, Beckx' decline of body in the two years since they'd last met was immediately evident to Pius. His lined face was an ill shade of grey, making him look older than his seventy-seven years.

Pius extended his hand. With obvious stiffening of his bones, the Head of the Jesuits lowered his frail body on to his knees and kissed Pio Nono's pontifical finger ring.

'Your Holiness.'

Looking down at Beckx' snow-white head, seeing it for the first time without its black calotte, Pius thought: We are both getting older and frailer in God's service. I pray He will grant us time to resolve this attack of The Evil One, and enable me to bequeath my successor a Church restored.

'My friend, my very good friend.' Pio Nono helped the Jesuit General to his feet, feeling, as he did so, the absence of flesh on his bones.

9

'I thank you, Holiness.' Beckx' voice had lost much of its deep timbre, further evidence of bodily ill-health. 'As you see, my frame is no longer active, but my mind remains vigorous and at your Holiness' command.'

Hearing the familiar steel still in Beckx' voice, Pius searched the gnarled old Jesuit's eyes and saw the fire burning deep within them, their gaze as inflexible as ever. He gave an inward sigh of relief.

'Your journey from Fiesole was without incident?' he questioned.

'Completely, Holiness,' Beckx replied, explaining how he had travelled openly by train from Florence to Rome, mingling with ordinary people in a 3rd class carriage, then by cabriolet to the corner of Borgo Santo Spirito.

Pius pictured the dark, narrow street with its entrance facing the south-east corner of the Piazza di San Pietro, and the dark grey building, numbered 5, which, until their recent expulsion from Rome, had been the Society of Jesus's headquarters. 'Nor a problem entering your premises?' he asked.

'None, Holiness. It was unguarded. And the locks unchanged.'

Not for the first time since he was appointed Pontiff, Pius gave silent thanks for the life of the soldier-cardinal, Rodrigo de Borja, later the Borgia Pope known as Alexander VI, who had searched ancient parchments and discovered the ancient Mons Vaticanus catacombs where the Christian dead from Nero's Circus had been buried and over which St Peter's Square had been built, and then extended its many passages to link the Borgia owned 5 Borgo Santo Spirito to the Vatican.

Not that he approved of Alexander's reasons for doing so, Pius tempered his gratitude, using it as a secret access for his many mistresses into his bedchamber, and his illegitimate daughter, Lucrezia, to entice men he wanted removing, into the Appartamenti with unholy promises, then disposing of them by pouring poison from one her jewelled finger rings into their gold goblets, and returning the bodies to the tunnel to rot in a lime-filled pit.

With Alexander eliminating those who built the tunnel and leaving their corpses in the same lime pit, it remained a Borgia secret. But when Alexander's great grandson, Francisco de Borja, was elected Jesuit Father-General, he made Borgo Santo Spirito his headquarters, enabling him to gain access to the then pope and act as papal advisor in secret, without inciting the jealousies of cardinals of other Orders living within the Vatican, all anxious to be granted that privilege. The tunnel had thus remained a Jesuit-Papal secret, used by succeeding Father-Generals to gain covert access into the Vatican, and the incumbent pontiff's ear.

Including today, when it was needed most.

'Holiness, may I have your permission to be seated? My limbs no longer have the strength they once had.'

'But of course, my good friend – forgive me. But first...' Pius indicated to the window.

Beckx joined him. Both men looked down at off-duty Piedmontese soldiers ambling along the carefully laid-out paths, as though Holy See's private gardens were there for their sole pleasure.

'Their guards are on every gate,' Pio Nono stated. 'No one is allowed in or out without an authorised permit. This applies to everyone, irrespective of rank, resident or working within Holy See. Even then they have to satisfy each checkpoint as to their credentials, and explain their reasons for wishing to pass through their impertinent barriers.'

'A violation of Mother Church's supreme authority,' Beckx declared.

Despite a Jesuit ruling that every emotion, other than spiritual, should be kept under control, Pius detected a note of anger in the Father-General's voice and was uplifted by it. Taking hold of Beckx' bony elbow, Pius led him to an ornately carved high-back chair, rested his own stiffening frame on a replicate chair, and began.

'My good friend, this crisis facing Holy Church is why I summoned you to Rome. Although it is our certainty that God will, in His Own time, reap vengeance against this anti-Christ, this so-called King Emmanuel, the evil perpetrated in the meantime could soon become irreparable.'

Pio Nono paused to give effect to his words. Beckx waited, his eyes fixed on the pontiff.

'And there is worse to come. Three days ago, I was informed that before the end of the year, the usurper is to present yet another Act to the Assembly, the purpose of which...the purpose of which...'

Righteous anger caused Pius to choke on his words.

'The purpose of which,' Beckx took over, his face impassive, 'is to apply its provisions as in all previous Acts, allowing him to illegally add every last one of our properties here in Rome, including Holy See, to the forty thousand and more already stolen across the rest of Italy by his evil regime.'

Meeting Pius's surprised look, Beckx continued. 'Like your goodself, Holiness, I too have my sources within the Assembly. The question is: what action do you propose? We have already allowed two years to elapse, making only passive protest. Now, with barely six months before this new Act is made law, I fear we may already have left it too late.'

Hearing the tone of criticism in the Father-General's voice, *Pio Nono* justified himself.

'My friend,' he mildly admonished, 'bear in mind that by fleeing Rome instead of remaining incognito in the Vatican, you yourself deprived me of your spiritual insight, thus forcing me to consult with others, none of them gifted with your unique wisdom. Many suggestions were made, including my abandoning Rome altogether and re-establishing the Vatican in another country, in particular the United States of America, where its freedom of religion under its constitution offered a certain permanence. But our American Church is still young and full of new ideas which do not coincide with our own, whereas I and your goodself are of the old school, traditionalists, who see Rome, and only Rome, as God's Holy City on Earth. After much contemplation and prayer, I came to the conclusion that it was my sacred duty to remain here, to be seen by the rest of the world as the Church's figurehead, refusing to submit to temporal authority, and the only way I would leave Rome would be either by death or by force.'

Beckx was swift to respond. 'Even so, Holiness, I fear that when this new Act is passed, force is what this arrogater will use.'

'Which is why I sent for you.'

Rising to his feet, Pius paced the room, hands clasped in front of his long white cassock. 'To the problem here in Rome, we must now add the worsening crisis in Germany, with von Bismarck emulating Emmanuel by increasing his Kulterkampf policy of persecuting Holy Mother Church and her people, across his entire Second Reich—'

'Banishing the Society of Jesus from his borders,' the Father-General interjected, his voice evincing no emotion. 'Forgive my presumption, Holiness, but as I have already intimated, despite the seclusion of Count de Ricasole's villa, I still retain my sources.'

'As I see,' *Pio Nono* rejoined. 'I trust you will also agree that despite this further setback, it is still necessary for me to continue my line of peaceful resistance. As Supreme Pontiff of the Church Universal, there is no other course of action open to me. Whereas you...'

Pius looked into Beckx' eyes. In them he saw the cold steel of resoluteness. Total commitment.

Hope rose within his breast. 'My friend, you have already formulated a policy?'

'Four months ago, Holiness. And not just formulated, but put into action.'

13

'Four months? Without my blessing?'

'I deemed it necessary. If Holy Church is to survive.'

'And of what form...' Anticipating the answer, Pio Nono hesitated to ask the question. 'Of what form does this policy consist?'

'Counter-revolution, Holiness. There is no other option.'

Pius heard no fear of rejection in Beckx' voice, and realised he spoke the truth. There was no other option. Counter-revolution had come to the salvation of Holy Church before. It could do so again.

'But such a strategy will require financing, which we no longer have.'

'On the contrary, Holiness. Our Church in America has richly blessed us. A munificent contribution, more than enough to put my policy into action, is but days from being on its way. All that is required is for you to bless its journey. And pray for the protection of its courier.'

A silence filled The Room of the Popes as Beckx awaited Pio Nono's judgement.

The Holy Father raised his hand, made the sign of the Cross and intoned:

'Benedictus qui venit in nomine domine.'

Blessed is he who comes in the name of The Lord.

- 3 -

Paris, France

Brains Sweeny sat back in his armchair as the Paris-Naples train pulled out of Gare de Lyon, took a gold cigar case from his inside pocket, chose a corona, smelt it, showed it to the black cassocked priest sharing his luxury saloon and anterooms.

'You don't mind, Father?' he questioned, raising his bushy eyebrows.

Father Guilamo Cottone smiled, the whiteness of the young Sicilian's teeth accentuated by his dark skin and black hair. He was a handsome devil, Brains conceded, but looks weren't everything. It was money that got you places.

'Not at all, Mr Sweeny.'

He couldn't object, not after I'd already selected it, Sweeny smirked to himself, it was, after all, a fait accompli, as the French said. Proud of the few phrases he'd picked up since hiding away in Paris, Brains lit up. Drawing on his cigar, he contentedly exhaled a long, thin stream of smoke.

'Next destination, Florence.'

'With God's grace,' the young Jesuit replied.

'Sure,' Sweeny agreed, pulling a Paris-Mediterranean Company's timetable from his pocket. 'We'll be stopping at Dijon at three-fifteen in the morning. After that, the next stop is Macon at six, then it's straight through to Modanne, arriving there...' he looked up '...one-thirty in the afternoon! Seven and a half hours! That's a helluva — apologies, Father — that sure is a long time to go without a break. We'll get off at Macon and grab a quick breakfast there. What do you say?'

Father Guilamo smiled. 'That seems sensible, Mr. Sweeny. I will wake you up. I shall be rising at five for prayers.'

'Sure, Father, much appreciated. But make it five-thirty, if that's okay with you.'

The young Sicilian inclined his head and Sweeny returned to his timetable. 'According to this, we're stopping only forty-seven minutes at Modanne,' Pulling a face, he looked up again. 'That gives us hardly enough time for even a bite there. You'd think they'd make it an hour.'

'Modanne is a border post,' Father Guilamo explained. 'Italian time is forty seven minutes ahead of French time. It is only a fleeting call for customs men to come on board.'

'You mean, no stopping?'

'I regret not.'

Brains studied the timetable. 'That means the first real stop after Dijon isn't until Turin at six-thirty in the evening!' He swiftly calculated. 'Fifteen and a quarter hours!' he protested, 'I'm sure glad you thought of bringing that luncheon basket, Father.'

'I journeyed on this train from Naples to Paris,' Father Guilamo replied. 'I can still feel the hunger pangs.'

'Lucky for me you did,' Sweeny growled. 'If this is how they treat you on French railways, I'll be glad when we finally get to Florence. I wired the top hotel, booked their best two rooms. The Hotel De La Ville on the Piazza Manin. Hope you like it. It's nob class according to Baedeker.'

The young Sicilian acknowledged his host's generosity with a slight incline of his head.

'I confess I am looking forward to it. Luxury such as this is far beyond my province.'

'Yeah?' Sweeny questioned, looking surprised. 'I thought you said your uncle was rich? And owns the biggest villa in Palermo?'

'He does,' the young priest confirmed, with no trace of boast. 'But before the usurper Victor Emmanuel occupied our island, I rarely stayed with him. I lived in a small casa next to my church in Bagheria. It had only two rooms and a kitchen.'

'Gee, that musta been rough,' Brains sympathised, thinking of his West 34th Street mansion back in New York. 'But speaking of this King Emmanuel, it sure is a crime what he's doing to Holy Church. It's strange God ain't struck him down dead for all the evil he's committing.'

'God moves in mysterious ways,' Father Guilamo said gravely.

'Ain't that a fact,' Sweeny agreed, chewing his cigar. 'Just look at the way He brought us together, sitting next to each other in Notre Dame Cathedral.' The New Yorker pronounced the "Dame" as he would back home. 'It just goes to prove what the Bible says is true. The Almighty really does take care of His most generous givers.'

Shaking his head at the wonder of it all, Sweeny continued. 'If it wasn't for my writing to the Father-General offering a contribution to Holy Church to try to put an end to this Emmanuel guy, I wouldn't be on this train with you to meet him. I've been hearing about Father Beckx for nearly twenty years now, but I never thought I'd ever get to see him face to face.'

The young Jesuit glanced out into the darkness beyond the window, then looked back into the salon. 'God's predestination, Mr Sweeny,' he stated, sitting forward earnestly. 'We are both part of His great plan. This is why He brought us together. Why he ensured our meeting in the cathedral. When God so intervenes, we have a duty to respond by demonstrating our willingness to follow His divine guidance. Before your meeting with the Father-General, kneel and ask God to direct your path. He will reply in such a way that His purpose for you will be so clear, there will be no doubt as to the contribution you must make.'

A silence filled the carriage as both men dwelt on their own thoughts.

Predestination! Guilamo thought wryly. More like preparation. Within hours of knowing that Brains Sweeny, the man who had been instrumental in swindling $200,000,000 from the city of New York, was in Paris, Guilamo was on his way there to seek him and and gain his early confidence. His next brief had been even simpler. All he'd had to do was convince the East Sider his money would be repaid fourfold. From that moment on he'd been on edge to start the journey. Human strategy plus clinical planning, rather than divine guidance, was the secret taught in Saint Ignatius's Spiritual Exercises. During his 10-year training as a Jesuit novitiate, Guilamo had mastered the lesson well.

Predestination! thought Peter Barr Sweeny. It made one feel good inside to know that one was part of some great eternal plan. Not that predestination was enough. When the Almighty sent the main chance your way, you had to grab it with both hands. Okay, so what if his scheme was revolutionary, as long as they could agree terms, it would make New York's haul seem like chicken feed. And if they were unable to agree, then what the hell! Nothing would be lost. From what he'd heard about Florence, it would be well worth the journey just to see the sights. Besides, his meeting with the Father-General wasn't for another two days, the vessels weren't due to leave New York for five days after that. Allow thirty days to cross the Atlantic, then if the second and more important meeting he and Guilamo had also arranged broke down, it still gave him plenty of time to wire Kaufmann, for him in turn to wire Gibraltar and have both ships to revert back to Marseilles as first planned.

The Jesuit maxim "The end justifies the means". Brains ruminated, was very true, no argument about that. But paramount to his success, past, present, and future, was the secret he'd drummed into Kaufmann before skipping New York:

Never let the right hand know what the left hand is doing.

And that, Sweeny smirked to himself, was even truer.

Drawing on his corona and exhaling, Brains watched the smoke drift up to the carriage ceiling.

New York

Brooding in his high-backed chair by a roaring fire, Jacob Kaufmann was worried that something might yet go wrong, even at this late stage.

Usually when he felt this way, just the sight of Gerda – sitting at her wood inlaid desk, writing encouraging letters to their many frightened relatives back home in Germany, anxious about what was going to happen to them – confinement camps or even execution – as von Bismarck increased his persecution of Holy Church, was enough to reassure Jacob that the risk was well worth it.

She was a solid, large-bosomed woman, Gerda, and being portly himself this was how he liked her. This evening she was wearing his favourite outfit: a maroon silk blouse with a high collar and a voluminous dark grey silk skirt, her hair pulled back and fastened at the back in a bun. From her tight grip on her pen it was obvious that the strain of the last few weeks was getting to her. This made the reality of the situation even more acute to Jacob. He did not want to lose Gerda. Nor their beautiful mansion.

Take their drawing room, big as a ballroom, the very epitome of their success since arriving in New York as children with their respective parents. Everything in it chosen by Gerda, walls half panelled in walnut, surmounted by maroon brocaded wallpaper, and large oil paintings in heavy-moulded gold frames. A thick carpet matching the blue velvet curtains spread from wall to wall. Two huge crystal glass chandeliers hung from an embossed ceiling, with a heavy gold-framed French mirror above the white marble fireplace. As for their furniture, every item was proof of their social standing: red, green, and purple sofas, chaise-longues and chairs, some velvet, others silk, some plain, the rest striped, interspaced with solid, ornately carved display tables on which rested china ornaments and figures, mostly Dresden and Meissen.

Desperate though the situation facing Holy Church was, to lose all this because of Sweeny's insatiable greed would be a tragedy.

He checked his gold watch. It was nearing time to attend the *Dei Gratia's* loading.

'Gerda.'

Gerda looked up. 'Ja, Jacob?' Kaufmann loved her guttural accent.

'I will be staying at the Astor for the next few days. My paperwork has fallen behind and I must complete it before Tuesday.'

'Is that when the *Maria Celeste* leaves?'

'Yes, mein schatz.'

'And it will then be all over?'

'Almost. It would have been,' Jacob gave a heartfelt sigh, 'had the Venango not gone up in flames. But after the *Dei Gratia* has sailed in her stead, all our fears will be at an end.'

'And then you will retire, Jacob?' she prodded. 'As you promised?'

'Completely, Gerda. After this, there will be no more buying or selling of diamonds, not even for my most personal clients.' Kaufmann felt an inner comfort at the thought.

'You have been careful, Jacob?' Gerda prompted, her brow furrowed in worry. 'You are sure there is nothing to connect you to Herr Sweeny?'

'*Nein,* mein schatz. My books show no record of our transactions. The purchases were spread evenly over the last twelve months and always in small amounts, using exchanges in ten different cities right across America, and never once in my name.'

'Gut!' Gerda gave a sigh of relief. 'And Vater Reikel?'

'Today is his last day in Saint Xavier. He will also be sailing on Tuesday.'

'Gut! And the *Maria Celeste's* crew? Did he find the men he was looking for?'

'Each dedicated to the Fatherland we once knew. But continue your letters, mein liebling. Our relatives will need all the moral support you can give them.'

Visibly relieved, Gerda returned to her correspondence.

Kaufmann sank back into his brooding, remembering last evening's final meeting with Reikel, the Jesuit's face so emotionless as he rechecked every detail.

Kaufmann reviewed them once more in his mind, making sure he'd left nothing out.

Check one: both vessels and their cargoes cleared for Genoa.

Check two: both vessels with one extra barrel on board.

Check three: wire Sweeny when both vessels had left New York.

Check four: both vessels to call into Gibraltar to confirm no change of orders.

Check five: both vessels arrive Genoa, unload their cargoes.

All correct...*except his new checklist now differed from Reikel's.*

Check six: Genoa. Unload just their *legitimate* cargoes.

Check seven: both vessels depart Genoa for Palermo with the extra barrels *still* on board.

Check eight: wire Sweeny in Palermo and let him take it from there.

Well might the Jesuit priest think he was in control, quoting his maxim: "The end justifies the means."

Jacob preferred the one he'd learned from Sweeny.

Never let the right hand know what the left hand is doing.

- 4 -

East River, South Street, New York

'Martens! Watch that barrel!' came the warning shout.

Captain Briggs swivelled around. James Winchester, his shipping agent, who'd given it, was neatly dressed, but not dapper, long sideburns, goatee beard, and looking down into *The Mary Celeste's* hold. With him was a large, portly man with a German accent, who had accompanied him on board. Winchester hadn't introduced him, but Briggs had heard his agent address him as "Jacob". Judging by his clothes, he was wealthy: black overcoat with a velvet collar, shiny black leather boots, black silk top hat, and a light grey cravat fastened with a jewelled gold pin.

'That barrel!' Winchester insisted.

Briggs crossed to the hatch and peered down to see Martens, one of the new all-German crew, acknowledge the warning. He and Goodschaad, one of his compatriots, rolled the barrel into a corner of the hold.

'Anything wrong, Mr Winchester?'

'Nothing, Benjamin,' his agent replied. 'It was just that he was handling it on his own. We don't want any breakages, not with alcohol, especially with you not allowing any liquor on board. The smell would fill the ship and give the men ideas.'

Very true, Briggs thought, and sensible of Winchester to warn the crew to be extra careful, right from the start.

His own refusal to allow drink on his vessels had been instilled in him by his father, Captain Nathan Briggs, a strict disciplinarian, under whom he had served his apprenticeship, and whose Articles of Agreement always contained the clause: "No grog on board".

Briggs glanced back into the hold. Under the eye of Second Mate Andrew Gilling – a 25-year old Dane who Briggs had met for the first time only an hour earlier, when he and the *Celeste's* new crew, all chosen by Winchester, reported to him on deck – the four Prussians were working in pairs: the two Lorenzen brothers stacking in one corner, Martens and Goodschaad in the other. All four were fair-haired with piercing blue eyes.

Turning away from the hold, Briggs' gaze followed the second net-load of barrels as it lifted from the wagon standing on the quayside and swung across the deck, stopping over the open hatch. On First Mate Albert Richardson's command, the gantry operator coaxed his draught horse backwards, allowing the net to descend gradually into the hold. Despite the keen wind blowing up the East River, the horse was sweating, steam rising from his powerful muscles, the snorts from his nostrils clearly visible in the thin air.

He was a good man, Richardson, Briggs said to himself, pleased at having been allowed to choose his First Mate. A small, wiry man, twenty-eight, clean-shaven – unusual for a seaman to be beardless, Briggs mused, he himself was rather proud of his dark beard and moustache – Albert hailed from Maine, and had served on board Briggs' last vessel, Sea Foam, proving himself to be an excellent sailor with a steady nerve. With a forty-day passage in front of them, Briggs' first voyage on the *Celeste*, it was good to have someone on board he could depend on, especially as they would be surrounded by so many foreigners.

A sudden gust of cold air swept over the deck. Swinging his arms across his chest to warm himself up, Briggs looked towards the galley, where the only other American member of the crew, Edward Head, the 23-year-old steward and cook from Brooklyn, was making a hot brew.

Worried about his wife and little daughter being out in this chill wind, Briggs crossed to the ship's rail and looked down at Sarah standing on the pier, supervising the unloading of items from home. But with little Sophia wrapped up warm in a shawl in her arms, Sarah was more concerned about the safety of her melodeon and wasn't noticing the cold, watching its careful transfer from a removals cart on to the gang-plank.

Whenever she sailed with him, the organ always came along. Briggs smiled fondly, doubly grateful she was joining him on the voyage. Not only would he have her company, but there were also the evenings to look forward to – singing hymns in their cabin after his day's work was done. When not at sea, Briggs attended his father-in-law's Congregational church back home in Marion, Massachusetts, and was a firm believer in giving proper praise to God for all His many blessings before turning in for the night.

Dark haired, pretty, and petite, Sarah was his cousin and childhood sweetheart. They'd been married ten years earlier by her father, Reverend Leander Cobb: Briggs was twenty-seven, Sarah only twenty-one. She'd made him a good wife, often sailing with him on his voyages, mostly to Mediterranean ports. Even their honeymoon was at sea, on board a schooner, Forest King, his first command.

She was also a wonderful mother. Briggs looked down fondly at his wife and child. Today was Sophia's second birthday – Sarah had used Head's stove to bake a cake with two candles, and this afternoon, her brother was coming over from his home in Boston to spend a few hours with them. The three of them were taking Sophia for a coach ride in Central Park before returning to the *Celeste* for a birthday tea.

Still leaning on the rail, Benjamin looked past Sarah at the teeming activity of South Street.

New York was only 250 years old, yet already it was second to London as the busiest seaport in the world. South Street's cobbled surface, stretching from Battery Park to where the East River turned at the great bulge of Manhattan at Corlears Hook, was the city's most maritime street, its counting-houses, warehouses, rum-holes and grog shops all fronting on to the river.

Sloops, schooners, square-riggers, and brigs from every part of the globe were crowded side by side in both directions, as far as the eye could see: two-masted and three-masted vessels, bowsprits and jib-booms jutting out over the two-miles-long quayside, moored alongside pine-planked slips which, supported by open piling and projecting some 200 to 300 yards out into the river, were themselves extensions of the many side streets and alleys leading into South Street.

Lifting his gaze, Briggs looked up in awe at the towering girders of the new Brooklyn Bridge growing high above him, right alongside the *Celeste's* Pier 50 mooring, between Roosevelt and James Streets. It was a stupendous engineering feat, Benjamin thought. All work had been halted twelve months ago because of the city's lack of funds after the The Tweed Ring debacle, but with construction now resumed the noise was deafening.

Gazing across the grey waters of the East River towards Upper Bay, from where, in five days' time, they would take their last look at New York, and giving only a passing glance at the grand mansions of the wealthy on Brooklyn Heights on the other side of the East River, Briggs' thoughts returned to his new vessel, further evidence of God's blessing upon his and Sarah's lives.

A couple of weeks earlier and seeking a new command, Winchester had offered him *The Mary Celeste*, a brig he'd recently purchased. Her previous name was Amazon. As to why Winchester had changed it, he hadn't explained. To Briggs' mind, her new name: "Celestial Mary", was distinctly Romish and offended his Protestant ear. But he'd kept his opinion to himself because Winchester had also given him a one-third share of the vessel, even advancing him a loan of the $3,600 required to buy it. Briggs wasn't sure why. The only explanation he could think of was that Winchester must feel that by being a part-owner, it would give him greater incentive to safeguard both vessel and cargo.

Whatever, Briggs could hardly believe his luck – correction, he thought: divine favour – and immediately wired Sarah to join him. She and Sophia had arrived in New York the previous Sunday, and been with him over a week now.

Briggs glanced towards the main hatch, where another net full of barrels was descending into the hold. At the pace everyone was working, loading should be over by late tomorrow afternoon, leaving Sarah and him free to enjoy the next three days. More sightseeing on Saturday. Church on Sunday. And then on Monday evening, the eve of their departure, they'd been invited to a farewell dinner at the Astor House, by their good friend David Morehouse, of the *Dei Gratia*–

Dei Gratia – "God's Grace", Briggs thought. Another Romish name. What's more, recently renamed, just like the *Celeste*. And she was also carrying a cargo for Winchester. And destined for the same ports: Genoa, Italy, then to Palermo, Sicily, to pick up return cargoes for New York. Strange coincidences, but no more than that, surely, since it was he who'd gotten David the contract in the first place?

'I'll be off, Benjamin!' Winchester's voice interrupted Briggs' thoughts. Turning, he saw his agent already standing at the top of the gang-plank, with Jacob down on the pier waiting.

'Going so soon?' Briggs was puzzled by the brevity of Winchester's stay.

'Yes. All seems to be in good hands. See you in my office, ten o'clock Monday morning. I'll have the crew-list and Articles of Agreement for you to take to the Harbour Commissioner.'

'Very good, Mr Winchester.'

But as the two men merged into the clamorous bustle of South Street, faces lowered, muttering to each other – almost as if conspiring, Briggs thought to himself – the barrel incident flashed again into his mind's eye, and for some reason he began to feel uneasy.

- 5 -

Five Days Later. Tuesday, November 5, 1872

It was obscene. Michael Callaghan looked down at the corpse. Okay, so life was cheap on Lower East Side, and after two years on the Detective Squad he should be immune to violent killings. But this one was different. The dead man's naked body, corpulent and turning grey, was sickening enough, but what made it so gruesome was the way he had died. His attacker must have crept up behind him and in one sudden movement, placed his hands on the man's shoulders, his knee in the base of his spine and snapped it in two, leaving the body doubled up the wrong way, buttocks bent back to the shoulder-blades, and the legs taking the feet past the top of the victim's head.

Instructing Patrolman Hagan to stay with the corpse, Callaghan re-climbed the stone basement steps. It was a typical East Side alley, bleak, narrow, a dark forbidding slit between two five-storey warehouses. He crossed to the other officer – in this part of town, cops always went about in twos.

'Name?' he asked. 'Just for the record.'

'Murphy.' Not turning his bull-neck, the man stayed legs astride, twirling his nightstick at the growing crowd of ghouls, as a threat to the more curious not to come too near.

'Who found it?'

The stick stopped in mid-spin and pointed to a ragged male wretch sitting hunched against the warehouse wall. Seeing the empty gin bottle held upside down in his hand, Callaghan knew what to expect.

'Bring him here.'

'Can't stand,' Murphy declared. 'Someone slipped him a bottle and he ain't stopped drinking since.' As if to confirm this, the man slid slowly sideways, releasing the bottle which clattered across the grey cobbles.

'What did I tell yehs?' said Murphy, twirling his nightstick with added flourish.

'Couldn't you have stopped him?' Callaghan asked.

'T'was me duty to protect the corpse,' Murphy retorted, 'not take care of drunks.'

Callaghan sighed. 'Did you question him?'

'Just t'ask how he found the body.'

'And?'

'Went t'sleep there after the Shamrock.' Callaghan knew it: a nearby grog shop on South Street. 'T'body was underneath him when he woke up. Slept on it all night, hadn't even noticed it. He came out of t'alley like a banshee out of Hell. Me and Pat was passing at t'time. I stayed with the deceased. Pat ran back as fast as he could, minding the weight of him, to tell Sergeant Kelly.'

'Was the body naked when he found it?'

'Like a newborn baby, says he. But not as pretty, says I. Tis the work of a madman, so it is,' Murphy added knowingly, walking purposefully toward the advancing crowd, slashing the air with his nightstick.

Callaghan agreed. No sane man could have committed so vicious a crime.

A cold gust of wind blew in from the East River. He shivered, pulled his overcoat collar up over his ears, and returned his thoughts to the dead man. At first glance, the motive seemed to be robbery. His brief examination of the body – smooth skin, soft hands, manicured nails – indicated the victim was wealthy. But why remove all his clothing? Assuming the man had been wearing expensive items – gold watch and chain, diamond fob, gold rings, and maybe jewelled

– and that his overcoat, suit, shoes, even his shirt, necktie and tiepin had also been worth stealing, that made sense. But why his underclothes and socks? No East Side thug would bother. Quick escapes were their pattern, ensuring that very few were caught.

Maybe it was all just a cover-up, to conceal the victim's identity? Except that someone close to him, a relative or friend, was bound to report his disappearance to their local precinct station, who would forward his details to the Bureau of Inquiry for Missing Persons at Headquarters. They in turn would check with the city morgue, and within two days – three at the most – the body would be identified.

But there again, a lot could happen in two to three days. Maybe that was the killer's aim? Not to conceal, but to delay identification? If so, then once the victim's name was known, someone would stand out as the likely suspect. His wife's lover perhaps? Provided his wife was years younger and in better shape, Callaghan reflected, glancing at the portly body – plotting together to inherit the dead man's money? Or a business associate wanting him out of the way? But whatever the reason, the killer needn't have got rid of the poor sod in that way. He'd either hated his victim, or, as Murphy had opined, he was insane.

Still, the place to start was Missing Persons.

'Murphy!'

The patrolman only half-turned his head. Callaghan had met similar insubordination during the War. It was time to be firm.

'Find a sack or something. Cover the body – straighten the legs first – then see if you can find someone amongst this crowd who can identify him. Hagan can check with the nearby shipping-offices and warehouses.'

Without waiting for a reply, Callaghan started down the alleyway. Passing through the crowd, he rumpled the hair of a bare-footed urchin and gave him some pennies. 'Gee, tanks mister!' Other bare-footed urchins crowded around their pal.

'And where d'hell yehs going?' Murphy yelled after him.

'To arrange for the morgue to pick up the corpse,' Callaghan replied over his shoulder, exiting the alley into South Street, resounding, as always, with the noise and hectic activity of vessels of every flag being loaded and unloaded, boxes, barrels and lumber cluttering their East River piers, forcing longshoremen, seamen and passengers alike, to pick their way between them and the dray horses hoisting cargoes in and out of the holds.

The body had been found in an alley between Wall Street and Old Slip, near pier 12. Being loaded alongside the pier was a shiny horse-drawn cart from Stewarts – the city's most fashionable department store, six-storeys of white marble built by Alexander Stewart, a poor immigrant lad from Ireland who'd worked hard and struck it rich. The symbols on the crates showed that this cargo had come from the Orient. The aroma of spices carried across the street to Callaghan, and no doubt the rest of the cargo would appeal equally well to the city's pampered society ladies.

Behind South Street lay the city's overcrowded tenement district with street names like Rag Picker's Row, Murderer's Alley, Cockroach Row, Cat Alley, which until twelve months ago was known as "Tweed's Town", where Boss Tweed and Brains Sweeny had terrorised the polling-stations to ensure their re-election as City Aldermen. It was home to New York's rapidly expanding immigrant population, and marked by tightly packed rows of ancient buildings and clapboard houses, all in varying states of decay.

So what in the hell had the War against the South been all about? Callaghan asked himself, remembering back to all the blood he'd seen shed, friend and foe alike. The North had said it was to free slaves; yet all the time they had their own form of slavery: poverty, keeping the underprivileged shackled to their crowded hovels. Still, he thought, now that The Tweed Ring had been caught out and the extent of their fraud exposed, maybe the election of some honest politicians would repair the damage.

There were many vessels out on the East River; one – a brigantine with furled sails being towed against the current to Upper Bay – caught his attention. Near the prow stood a woman with a small child in her arms, encouraging the little one to wave New York "goodbye" as the brig headed out for the grey Atlantic Ocean beyond the Bay.

'Want a better look?' A gnarled old seafarer standing alongside Callaghan was offering him a brass telescope. Training it on the vessel, Callaghan focused on the woman.

Medium height, an attractive oval face, dark hair escaping from under her bonnet, she was wearing a heavy overcoat, as was the child, a pretty little girl no more than two years old, also bonneted and shawled against the biting wind coming in from the Atlantic. They continued to wave, seeming to look right at him. On impulse, he waved back and returned his hand to the telescope. The vessel was extremely trim, looking fit for anything the Atlantic had to offer.

A fine brig, Callaghan thought, reading her name, *Mary Celeste*, on her bows.

- 6 -

Callaghan entered New Street.

It was polling-day in the presidential election between General Ulysses Grant, the incumbent Republican holder of that office, and the Democrat nomination, New York's own Horace Greeley, owner of the Tribune newspaper and New Yorker magazine. Declared a public holiday, downtown was crowded.

Callaghan crossed the street. The First Precinct's offices were on the first floor of No. 54, above the fire station known locally as "The Eighteen Hose".

Except for Police Headquarters on Mulberry Street, the First was the busiest station in New York. With a huge tenement population, half of whom were Irish, it took a force of one captain, three sergeants, two detectives, and eighty to a hundred men – depending on injuries sustained in the course of duty – to control it. Its triangular boundary, from the Battery to Fulton Street, then along Fulton to the East River, and down South Street back to the Battery, held not only the immigration clearing-house at Castle Garden, but also the consulates of most other countries, and a major part of the representative wealth of the USA: the sub-Treasury, Assay Office, the Stock Exchange, money brokers, bullion dealers, diamond merchants, shipping offices and national and foreign banks.

Today, in an effort to prevent any vote rigging of the recent Tweed Ring years, most of the uniformed police were guarding the polling stations. The First had asked for cover and Callaghan had been seconded to them from Headquarters.

He reached No. 54, stone steps and black iron railings leading up to a black front door with blue lamps on either side. The hallway was brown and peeling.

Taking the wooden stairs to the first floor two at a time, he entered the grimy office where only the desk-sergeant was on duty. Kelly's copper badge was so highly polished that the bald-eagle on top of the shield had been almost rubbed away.

'Well?' Kelly questioned. 'Was it like Hagan said or was he exaggerating as usual?'

'Worse.' Callaghan described the method of killing.

'To be sure and that was no way to go!' the desk-sergeant exclaimed, 'not if he'd stood up in Harry Hill's and said he was a Republican and a Protestant. Any clues to the body's identity?'

'None. Any new missing persons reports?'

'Not unless Greeley's read *The Times* and decided to cut and run.'

Producing a folded copy of the newspaper from under the counter, Kelly opened it at page 8, for Callaghan to read the main block-letter headline:

NIGHT BEFORE ELECTION

> Politicians were busy at the various Assembly headquarters as bees in a hive. Ballots were being folded, and all the artful dodges and tricks to be practised at the election were being perfected at the Greeley headquarters. But all interest in the national election seems to have faded as all the parties agree that Grant will surely be elected.

'What with the front pages declaring Grant ahead in most places voting yesterday,' said Kelly, "tis enough to make the poor man go into hiding. That's all he needed, on top of his wife.'

Greeley's wife, Molly, had died five days earlier, after a long illness, leaving him to face the election grief-stricken. It was thought he might gain a sympathy vote as a result, but that was not to be according to *The Times* prediction.

'Have you voted?' Callaghan asked.

'Me? Wouldn't waste me shoe-leather,' Kelly disdained. 'Democrat. Republican. Boss Tweed. President Grant. Senator Colfax. What's the difference? They're all in it only for themselves.'

Callaghan agreed. Retaliating to *The Times'* exposure of The Tweed Ring, their Democrat rival, New York's Sun, had uncovered a fraud they were calling "The Credit Mobilier Scandal", by which Senator Colfax, a leading Republican, had pocketed huge bribes from the construction of a Union Pacific railway line. In an effort to influence voters in the race for the White House, the Sun had brought it all to the nation's attention, demanding Grant's resignation. But to no avail, it seemed. Greeley's appearance: tall, plump, bald, wispy beard, round pink face, spectacles, had been fully exploited by Republican newspaper cartoonists, especially *The Times*, and it looked as though Grant's "war-hero" tag was going to carry the day.

But Kelly was right, Callaghan agreed. Was no one clean in politics anymore? As for Brains Sweeny, the City's Chamberlain and mastermind behind The Ring's countless frauds, he was the lowest of the low. Pure evil, as Callaghan personally knew only too well. If it wasn't for the hope of finding a clue, an overlooked detail on police files, an associate of The Ring willing to trade information in exchange for a lighter sentence, leading him to where Brains had flown the coop to, he would escape from it all on one of his brother-in-law's brigs, as he'd done before when Colleen walked out on him.

The thought made him remember the brig sailing down the East River, and the woman and child waving goodbye to New York.

Where were they bound, he wondered? Turning to the "Shipping News", he checked "Cleared Vessels" and saw her listed:

Mary Celeste. Briggs. Genoa.

That was the one. Bound for Italy. Under the command of a Captain Briggs. The woman and little girl he'd seen on her deck were probably his wife and daughter. On days like this, Italy, his mother's native country, would be just the place to go to. Maybe Rome, he'd always wanted to see it. Or Florence? Once there, perhaps he'd stay. There was nothing for him in New York anymore–

Except the hope of finding where Sweeny had fled to, Callaghan dismissed his thoughts. And make the shyster pay for all he'd done to them.

Colleen and himself, their lives ruined.

His father, Tom, dead. His mother widowed.

Their newspaper stolen.

All because of Brains.

He turned for the door. Just the chance of finding the evil chiseller was more than enough reason to stay. It far compensated for all else.

'Where yehs off to?' Kelly called after him.

'Headquarters, to check "Missing Persons",' Callaghan replied as the door shut behind him.

'Best of luck,' yelled Kelly. 'Yehs'll need it.'

- 7 -

Callaghan turned down Exchange Place into the deafening bustle of Broadway, crowded with people taking advantage of an Election Day off.

With the horses back on the streets after the distemper outbreak, the avenue echoed to the rumble of densely packed traffic. Omnibuses, hackney-carriages, wagons, carts. As for people, they were everywhere, all, it seemed, in a hurry; their mixed appearances making New York's fast growing immigrant population apparent: Irish, Germans, Jews, come to the USA to escape persecution or famine in Europe. During his own thirty-year lifetime, the city's population had grown from below 400,000 to over 1,000,000. Soon there'd be no damned room to breathe.

Callaghan reached Trinity Presbyterian Church, on the corner of Rectory. Surrounded by three-, four-, five-storeyed buildings, its towering spire easily made it New York's tallest building.

Reaching out to a God who wasn't there, Callaghan thought and just as swiftly dismissed it.

A yellow omnibus drew up. He got on, sitting, as it headed up Broadway, between a large, fur-wrapped woman and a stern-looking man in a dark overcoat and stovepipe hat.

The avenue epitomised New York's rapid transformation. Only a few years ago it had been mostly residential, but now, stretching all the way to Bleeker Street, there was nothing but top-class hotels like the Astor House, and fashionable shops like Stewarts, with its lines of waiting carriages and uniformed footmen contrasting with ragged-dressed young girls plying the pavement outside, trying to earn the price of a loaf of bread by vending hot corn, with their cries of, "Here's your nice hot corn, smoking hot! Smoking hot just for the pot!".

'Bleeker Street!' The shout brought him back and he descended from the omnibus.

This far uptown the traffic was not so frenetic and he walked the two blocks east to No. 300 Mulberry Street, the city's new five-storeyed Police Headquarters. The Detective Squad occupied Rooms 5 and 6 on the ground floor, with The Bureau of Enquiry for Missing Persons in the next room, but none of the "John Does" fitted his murder victim. His next call was the Telegraph Office in the basement, to check whether a Missing Persons report had come in, fitting the body's description. None had, and he headed back upstairs to discuss the case with his chief.

Captain Irving, Chief of Detectives, was a burly man, face half hidden behind a moustache and beard. Replacing Captain Kelso – a personal friend of Boss Tweed's – when Kelso was made superintendent two years ago, there were rumours Irving had paid $5,000 for the appointment, The Ring's rate for a police captaincy, and today his mind seemed to be elsewhere.

Callaghan concluded his report and waited, the large wooden clock on the wall loudly ticking away the seconds as Irving continued to look past him through the window and into the distance.

Callaghan coughed. Irving's eyes returned to the room and focused on him.

'The post-mortem?' Callaghan repeated.

'What the hell d'you want a post-mortem for?' Irving demanded.

'To confirm the cause of death.'

'Damn it, Callaghan. I've got enough work on helping the DA prove the case against Tweed, without going through stupid procedures and form-filling. What the hell does it matter how the guy was killed, it had to be for the money. We don't need any blasted sawbones telling us that.'

Despite his apparent detachment, Irving had clearly heard the gist of the report.

'I think there's more to it.'

'And what gives you that idea?'

'A hunch. The way he was killed. And the fact he was completely naked.'

'Hunch nothing. It's a typical assault by East Side thugs and we've not a cat-in-hell's chance of catching them.'

'What about identifying the body?'

'What about it?'

'How much time do I give it?'

'Zilch. Just file your report and forget it.'

Callaghan gave it one last try. 'But what if he's got a wife or children worried about him?'

'Then they'll report it to their nearest precinct,' Irving spoke slowly and finally, 'and that's Missing Persons' problem. Now, if you've finished, I've got more important work to do.'

Two weeks earlier, the Grand Jury had dismissed all charges against Mayor "Elegant Oakey" Hall, one of the Tweed Ring's four leading players. With Sweeny and Comptroller "Slippery Dick" Connolly having skipped the country, there was only Boss left. City officialdom was said to be divided over Tweed's fate. Half wanted him locked up, the rest were praying for him to follow Sweeny and Connolly and make a run for it.

Suspecting that Irving's true motive in assisting the DA was to cover up any evidence of his own bribe, Callaghan got to his feet.

'Ten gets you one that though Oakey got off, Boss is a sure-fired certainty to be found guilty.'

'Get out,' Irving growled.

- 8 -

The Mary Celeste rode at anchor, sails furled, on a shallow flat off Staten Island. The gale-force wind hurtling in through the six-mile gap between Sandy Hook and Coney Island had forced Briggs to shelter in the confines of Upper Bay and wait for the wind to drop, before venturing out into the open sea.

Pretending to be tidying his desk, Briggs glanced towards Sarah seated on the bed, darning a tear in Sophia's play-dress. Their small daughter was standing by her side cuddling her doll, "Sarah Jane", and turning over the pages of a photograph album placed on the bed.

With deliberate casualness, Briggs took a key from his pocket, unlocked his desk drawer, and for the umpteenth time read David Morehouse's brief letter spread open inside. Sarah sighed and looked up. Briggs closed the drawer and locked it, saw sadness in his wife's deep brown eyes and sat beside her and placed an arm around her shoulders.

'What is it?' he asked, but his mind was with David's note. 'Is it Arthur?' Arthur was their six-year old son, who'd been left at home with Grandma Briggs to start his education.

'Yes,' Sarah replied, tears welling in her eyes. 'I do hope he'll be all right.'

Briggs drew her head onto his shoulder. 'Don't worry,' he said, doing his best to reassure her. 'We'll be back home before you know it. And Ma Briggs will enjoy looking after him.'

At the mention of Ma Briggs, Sophia looked up, pointing a stubby finger at a photo of a stately lady sitting on a studio chair, wearing a dark voluminous dress and staring fixedly into the camera.

'Gamma Bis, Gamma Bis,' she lisped, searching her mother's face for confirmation.

Sarah gave a half-smile and stroked Sophia's hair, 'Yes, darling, Grandma Briggs.' Brushing the tears from her eyes, she gave her husband a brave smile. 'You're right, Benj, I'm sorry to be so maudlin. I realise Arthur needs the schooling, but I miss him.' She straightened her shoulders. 'Still, I'm looking forward to seeing Genoa and meeting up with David and Desiah again. How lucky you were able to get them an alternative cargo, and to the same ports as ourselves. Desiah would have hated Curaçao.'

Briggs removed his arm. 'Yes, it was fortunate.' He stood up, restless. 'I think I'd best check on the crew.'

'Benj, what is worrying you? Is it that letter? You've been on tenterhooks ever since you received it.'

Briggs forced a smile. 'Winchester wishing us God's-speed? No, Sarah, it's not that. It's just the frustration of being stuck here, especially with so much resting on this voyage.'

Sarah clasped her husband's hand. She knew his ability to repay Winchester's loan of $3,600 to buy his one third share in the *Celeste*, depended on the success of the trip.

'Then be of good faith, Benj,' she reassured him, 'and God will bless your endeavours. The weather will soon lift and we'll be on our way.' She smiled. 'And now, if you must, go and check your crew.'

But as he left, Sarah's smile faded. Picking up Sophia, she held her tight for comfort.

She'd known Benj too long not to realise when he was lying.

Out on deck, Briggs leant on the stern rail and looked across Upper Bay at the night lights of New York in the near distance. He thought again about David's letter, still agonising over his dilemma.

What ought he to do? Sail, as David was begging him to? Or obey his instinct and turn back?

Were the storms raging out in the Atlantic, preventing the *Celeste* from sailing, a sign from God he should choose the latter? Or should he venture out when they dropped? What's more, with four foreign seamen he knew nothing about? And although his new second mate, Gilling, would be able to translate his commands, he was still at a loss to understand why Winchester had taken on an all German crew without consulting him first, particularly with him now being a partner in the vessel?

A sudden strong gust of wind blew in from the Atlantic, churning the waters of Upper Bay, rocking the *Celeste* and chilling the air.

Engrossed in his quandary, Briggs didn't even notice it.

- 9 -

Fiesole, Italy

Father-General Beckx ended his prayer to a statuette of the Blessed Virgin for the success of Father Reikel's holy mission. Old bones creaking, he rose from his knees in a dark corner of his sparsely furnished room on the ground floor of Count de Ricasole's villa, where he'd sought refuge after fleeing Rome, and thought back to his final meeting with the German priest, just four months past.

Sitting at his rough-hewn desk as Reikel stood before him, Beckx declared, 'They are anti-Christs. Victor Emmanuel and von Bismarck. The mark of Satan is upon them. Evinced by their evil deeds and their persecution of Holy Church.'

Taken into the Father-General's presence directly on his arrival, Reikel awaited his superior's permission to speak. The vaulted ceiling gave the room a monastic feeling. The window screens were closed, shutting out the mid-morning sun, intensifying the sombre effect of the umber walls.

'In the twenty-one months since I arrived here – thanks be to the Blessed Saint Ignatius for his protection during my journey from Rome...' Wearing a black cassock and black calotte, a crucifix hung from Beckx' neck. He raised it to his lips and kissed it.

'Amen,' Reikel responded, crossing his breast.

'During this time,' Beckx continued, 'Satan's attacks have greatly increased.'

Hearing the restrained anger in his superior's voice, Reikel was uplifted. The spirit still burns within him, he thought, despite his decline in body, so bent and broken since their last meeting, the day Victor Emmanuel entered Rome. With reverential pride in being summoned by his Father-General – a vanity kept under the subjugation of a Jesuit priest – Reikel studied the man who had sent the message to Genoa, commanding him to travel day and night without rest to Fiesole.

Despite his age, the General's deeply-lined face evidenced a sharpness of intellect that before Victor Emmanuel's subjugation of Holy See made him Pio Nono's secret confessor and advisor. Among the clergy who had taken refuge inside the Vatican, there were many so jealous of the Belgian's special relationship with the Holy Father, they still whispered he was the power behind the papal throne, maliciously calling him "The Black Pope" behind his back.

'The Evil One is constantly on the rampage,' Beckx declared. 'Forever warring against Holy Church's supreme authority.'

Because Satan is never off the offensive, Reikel thought to himself. The invasion of Rome, happening just weeks after Pius took Beckx' counsel and placed the matter of his own infallibility before the Vatican Council, had been no coincidence. It was Lucifer's response to its confirmation. Then daring to challenge God's rule by having Victor Emmanuel confine Pio Nono, Heaven's appointed Bishop on Earth, as a prisoner in the Vatican.

Blessed Pio Nono, who nine weeks earlier, had stood, arms outstretched, identifying himself with the crucified Saviour as 533 voices – less only the misguided American cardinals who walked out in protest – unitedly declared: Placet! – "It pleases!" – confirming Papal Infallibility as part of the dogma of Holy Church, sealed by God Himself with an accompanying clap of thunder and a bolt of lightning that flashed into the conciliar hall, bathing Pius's white-robed figure in a holy glow.

'And now that The Adversary has deceived von Bismarck into emulating Victor Emmanuel,' Beckx continued, 'other countries will seek to follow. It is time for the Society to act.'

Reikel agreed, mind and soul. Had he himself not suffered greatly at the hands of both men.

When Emmanuel's army entered Rome, he had been forced to flee the Congregation, leaving behind the result of three years' work. Travelling rough across Italy, he had finally crossed into Germany, then to Berlin, eventually reaching the seminary where he spent ten years as a novitiate, and been given a post as a tutor.

But the old Germany had greatly changed in the seven years he'd been away. Renamed "The Second Reich" by its new military Chancellor, the Protestant Prince Otto von Bismarck, it was now the supreme military power in Europe and at war with France. Within months of Reikel's arrival in Berlin, the people were glorying in Bismarck's victory over the armies of Napoleon III, with Paris occupied and the provinces of Alsace-Lorraine annexed by The Reich.

The one exception to the mood of patriotism sweeping the country was that of German Catholics, who were steadfastly refusing to obey Bismarck's diktat that Germans owed their first allegiance to the State. Loyal to Holy Church, they were being persecuted for their faith, with von Bismarck enforcing his Kulturkampf policy by closing down all Roman seminaries and churches, forbidding Catholic teaching and confining the more rebellious bishops and priests in prison camps.

Rather than openly dissenting, Reikel had assumed command of the Berlin seminary's ejected priests and novices, forming an underground resistance and distributing tracts telling German Catholics to stand fast, even to the ultimate punishment, death, in the certain knowledge that Heaven would be their eternal reward.

Bismarck retaliated by ordering Reikel's arrest, blaming him for inciting unrest. Again he was forced to flee a country, back to Italy, finding refuge for himself and his band of priests in a deserted castle on a lonely promontory east of Genoa, where the Father-General's messenger had found him and brought him to this secluded villa in the hills above Fiesole.

'As I wrestled in prayer,' Beckx continued, eyes piercing Reikel's, 'our founder, the Blessed Saint Ignatius, appeared to me in a vision. His face shone with the glow of one who sits at the right hand of the Saviour in glory, but his expression was stern.

'"For twenty months, without retaliation," he accused, "you have allowed The Prince of Darkness to rule over the affairs of man. During this time, all you have done is to kneel and pray. Prayer has its place," he stated, "but I formed the Society of Jesus to be active, to be in the fore-front of repelling the attacks of The Evil One. Must I remind you how we combated the attacks of the Anti-Christs, Luther and Calvin, reversing the spread of their evil blasphemies against Holy Church? Did you not absorb my teaching?" he stressed. "In my Spiritual Exercises I constantly lay emphasis on the necessity for zeal. I therefore come to you now as our militant Lord's envoy, bearing His command for you to wage a holy war against these evil allies of Satan".'

The Father-General's gaze held Reikel to his every word.

'As our holy founder's image began to fade, I was emboldened to say that a counter-revolution would need to be financed, and all that we owned had been taken from us. "Find one among you to sail to the New World," Blessed Ignatius replied, his voice growing fainter. "There, in our Church of Saint Francis Xavier in New York, he will find a man whose first loyalty is to Holy Church. In him resides God's key to the wealth that will ensure the downfall of these Satanic usurpers".'

Beckx took in Reikel's pale face, its fine ascetic features, the slate-blue eyes which, at their first meeting, had gripped his own with a contradictory mixture of icy coldness and sudden flashes of intense fire, and waited until he felt the very room charged with tension before he continued.

'With this, the vision of the Blessed Ignatius ascended above me and passed through the ceiling back to his rightful place at the side of our militant Saviour in Heaven. In that same moment, Father Reikel, you came into my mind. I recalled the reports of your organised resistance in Berlin before you were forced to flee that city to seek sanctuary, and I knew, without a doubt, that you were the one our glorified Saint had chosen to undertake this most holy of missions.'

Reikel fell to his knees and bowed his white-haired head in silent prayer.

Aware of the German priest's fervency to the Society of Jesus, his implacable possession of a Jesuit's commitment and zeal, and knowing his order could not be refused, Beckx prompted him as he remained bowed in prayer. 'The very fate of Holy Church rests in your hands.'

Reikel lifted his face. In his gaze, Beckx saw the intensity he was looking for.

'The Celestial Mary be praised,' he declared. 'I leave it to you to decide your course of action. Join the church as a member of the congregation, or as a priest, if you think that best. And should you deem it necessary, choose someone you can trust to accompany you, one who will protect you from harm. But be cautious. Keep your mission veiled, as did our Lord when He attended the Feast of the Tabernacles in Galilee, not openly,' Beckx quoted, 'but as it were in secret. Apply deliberation to your every thought. Discretion to your every spoken word. Strategy to your every move. And in so doing, our Heavenly Father will surely bless your quest.

'Finally,' the Jesuit Father-General instructed, 'ensure that all telegraphed messages end with the code-word Opus Dei – the work of God. And also never forget that in the furtherance of God's work...' Beckx deliberately paused, '...the end justifies the means.'

To further emphasise the maxim, Beckx repeated it in Reikel's own tongue: 'Der Zweck heiligt die Mittel.'

Still on his knees, Reikel bowed low and kissed his superior's sandaled feet. Under his black hair shirt, his jagged iron crucifix pressed into his breast. The sharp pain sent a surge of ecstasy through his body as he identified with his militant Lord, and the agony He must have felt as His hands and feet were pierced, nailing Him to the Cross of Golgotha.

Placing both hands on his head, Beckx gave him his final blessing:

'Benedictus qui vadit in nomine domine.'

Blessed is he who goes in the name of The Lord.

- 10 -

It was eight that evening before Callaghan signed off duty. It had been a long, gruelling day, quelling clashes between rival gangs of Republican and Democrat supporters. But the real trouble came in the afternoon, when news began pouring in from around the country, sealing *The New York Times'* prediction of a Republican landslide. Realising they had lost the election, a Democrat mob that had grown outside the Sun's offices since midday, looted the surrounding buildings and set them on fire, then, with a cry of "Let's gut it", had set off for *The Times*.

The succeeding battle left the First with a number of injured, but the fight took the steam out of the rioters, and as darkness descended they were now licking their wounds inside grog-shops and gin-palaces.

Callaghan reached Broadway to find it a solid mass of horse-drawn traffic with myriad coach-lamps dotting the length of the avenue, and fusing into a massed blur in the far distance. There was no point taking an omnibus, he decided. It would take hours to get home. The only way was through the side-streets.

A yellow cab unloaded a male passenger. He ran to it. 'Greenwich. Carmine,' climbed in and fell into the seat, and a wave of exhaustion sweep over him. What a hell of a way to seek avengement, he thought, and in that moment decided to resign from the force. Face it, Callaghan, there was no point hanging on any longer. The chances of finding Sweeny were what? Zero. As for the $200 million stolen, he'd probably already managed to get it abroad, or it was so well hidden it would never be found. As for the "John Doe", he shrugged him off. What did it matter if the stiff ended up in Potter's Field? Mausoleum, cemetery or lime pit, the dead didn't know where they were buried. Good, bad, believer, atheist, it was the same end for all. Oblivion. Total. Absolute.

He studied his reflection in the cab's darkened window. Had he changed that much since Colleen left him? Hardly at all in physique: five-eleven, broad shouldered, 150 pounds. His waist may have thickened, but no more than an inch or so since the War. The fine sabre scar across his left cheek Colleen used to trace with her finger, was now almost invisible. Yet the face mirrored in the window was that of a stranger, hard and so without feeling it was difficult to recognise.

He studied his eyes – it was said they were the window of one's soul. If so, then heaven help him, because the eyes looking back at him out of the darkness were emotionless, devoid of joy. The eyes of a man who saw the world for what it was, harsh, uncompromising, uncaring, where only the tough survived.

Colleen was sitting at her writing bureau in her bedroom, trying to decide the ending of a novel she was writing, a catharsis for her pain. Her two years as far away from Michael as Europe, had done nothing to cure the ache in her heart. Yet, her worry about her father kept breaking into her thoughts…

The more he was being dragged into The Tweed Ring Investigation, the increasing likelihood he'd be indicted because of his past involvement with Sweeny, the more he was taking to drink. This was why their family attorney, Sam Phelps, had wired her London hotel, advising her to return home, and why she was determined to find Sweeny and get his sworn affidavit, clearing her father of being knowingly involved in any fraud…

Her mind returned to her manuscript and she flicked back through how the heroine, a spirited daughter of a New York society family, had volunteered, despite her father's protests, for a basic course in nursing run by the city's doctors and was then posted straight to the battlefront between North and South, then paused at the part where the young nurse first met the hero as one of a wagon-train of wounded. He was a Northern Army cavalry captain, dark, rugged and handsome, with a sabre scar across his left cheek telling he was a man used to seeing action, yet there were tears in his eyes as she prised a dying, Southern boy-soldier from his comforting clasp.

The memory of his tears remained with the nurse throughout the long, hard day of helping the surgeons and scrubbing-up after each operation. Coming off duty, she'd searched for him and eventually found him lying on the hard planks of a commandeered molasses warehouse, left to die.

Sensing her presence, he opened his eyes. Vivid blue.

'Would you like a blanket?' she whispered. 'Or some water?'

Despite his obvious pain, he grinned up at her and she felt her heart miss a beat.

'Champagne and two glasses,' he replied.

'We're right out of champagne, I'm afraid,' she responded, thinking how brave he was and going along with him. 'But I can find us some whiskey. What are we celebrating?'

'Our engagement.'

Her heart missed another beat. 'And when did that happen?'

'A moment ago. Didn't you feel something pass between us?'

Oh yes, I did, the nurse in her novel thought. I shall remember this moment for the rest of my life. What's more, soldier, you're not going to die.

Using her female wiles to persuade an elderly army surgeon to operate on him, she assisted to open the suppurating wound and remove a bullet lodged near the lung, then nursed him four days and nights without sleep. Only on the fifth day, when his fever subsided, did she crawl exhausted to her bed and slept twenty-four hours without waking, but dreaming of the officer, that he would recover, and they would fall in love and marry and live happily ever after.

Colleen looked up from the manuscript.

Well, Michael did recover. They fell in love. He went back to the War. And survived.

A month after peace was declared, they married.

And for four years had been blissfully happy.

But as for ever after…

She hurled the pages aside.

'Colleen!'

Her father was calling up from his study. By the sound of his slurred voice, he'd been at the whiskey again.

Finding Sweeny was getting to be more and more urgent by the day.

She rose to her feet and headed downstairs, realising she had to face it.

She was going to have to swallow her pride.

Michael was now her only hope.

- 11 -

Although Colleen was no longer there to greet him, Callaghan was usually glad to get back to Greenwich. Its slow, backwater village atmosphere, the way it refused to succumb to New York's insatiable growth, usually lifted his spirits. Tonight, it had no effect on his mood.

Entering his mews-house, he crossed to the dresser, lit an oil lamp, poured a large whiskey and knocked it back, feeling the spirit burn away at the ache in his stomach, then put a match to the fire. Too tired to cook, he went to the kitchen, and cut himself a hunk of bread and cheese, took them into the sitting-room, flopped into his high-backed chair by the now blazing hearth and as he ate, returned to his thoughts in the cab.

Where not only the tough survived, he brooded, but the corrupt, too, remembering back to the day Sweeny started to ruin his and Colleen's lives.

It was strange how one always remembered the small things first.

The slanting rays of an afternoon sun lighting up a myriad of tiny dust specks floating about the room. And the expression of horror in his father's voice as he reacted to Sweeny's ultimatum.

'But my loans aren't with the Bowling Green Bank.'

'They are now.' Squatly built, large head covered with thick black hair and walrus moustache, Sweeny kept his black silk top hat on. 'And the deeds.' His voice evinced his gloating satisfaction. 'I bought them from your bankers this morning. Paid top premium for them.'

Called "The Man in Black" by *The Times* because of his habitual black attire, Sweeny was born on East Side of Irish immigrant parents and educated at a Catholic School. After reading for the law, and then admitted to the bar, he was elected ward boss of the large East Side, 20th District, at the age of only thirty-one and was religiosity and evil combined, according to *The Times,* with evil predominating, inventor and manipulator of The Ring's fraudulent empire on his corrupt side – hence his East Side "Brains" moniker – yet on the other, Saint Xavier's most ardent worshipper and donor.

'Not *both* sets!' His father's despairing voice begged Sweeny not to confirm it.

'Business and home. You got until midnight to redeem them, or I foreclose.'

Callaghan strode towards him. 'Midnight! You know damn well it's impossible. You have to give us more time. If you don't then by all that's holy, Sweeny, you'll pay for it.'

Pulling a revolver, Sweeny backed towards the door. 'Forget the threats, Mikey,' he snarled, 'I'm acting within the law. Lay a finger on me and I'll have you behind bars so fast, your feet won't touch the ground. Still, you've got until midnight. That's a whole six hours.' And with that, Brains hot-footed it down the stairs and drove off in his black coach waiting in the street below.

Tom failed to redeem the loans. *The Despatch* was taken, he and Michael's mother, Elisabetta. were evicted from their home, their furniture distrained by a clause in Sweeny's "small print". Too distraught to remain in New York, they left for Savannah to stay with Michael's sister, Francesca, and her ship-owner husband, Jonathan.

Meanwhile, Callaghan was on the end of another shock, when Sweeny's coach pulled up outside his mews house. Making no attempt to hide his loathing, Callaghan met him out on the cobbles.

'Aren't you going to ask me in?' Brains sneered.

'Over my dead body.'

'Anytime.' Sweeny drew on his cigar and slowly blew out the smoke. 'Just say the word.'

'That's the pleasantries over. I take it you're here for a purpose? A writ you want to serve?'

'I did your da a favour, Mikey. You gotta admit *The* Dispatch's style was getting stale. Once we've got some different political articles written, you won't recognise it.'

Callaghan fought to control his anger. Sweeny's reason for stealing the paper was clear. Under sustained attack from *The Times'* campaign, The Ring were known to be looking for a reputable daily to refute the allegations. But one thing was puzzling Callaghan. *From where had Sweeny found out about the mortgages?* They'd been a closely guarded family secret.

'You should hear our new chairman's plans for it,' Sweeny cut into his thoughts. 'But then, Ed's likely already told you about them. Or waiting until he can tell you and Colleen over dinner.'

Ed. Edward Lowell. Colleen's father. Sweeny's wife, Sarah Augusta, was his first cousin by marriage. Callaghan felt himself go cold.

'Say, I'm sorry, Mikey,' Brains feigned self-reproach. 'Now I've gone and spoilt it for him. But thank him again from me for the tip-off about the loans. Can't stop, other matters to see to.'

Too stunned to move, Callaghan watched Sweeny get back into his coach and mockingly raise his top hat as it moved off. The rumble of wheels jerked him out of his daze. He stormed back into the house. Colleen was standing in the sitting-room, face white, having clearly heard every word.

'Did you tell your damn father?' he demanded.

'No, Michael. I swear.'

He simmered down a little. 'I'm not saying you told him deliberately. Maybe it slipped out.' His voice hardened again. 'But one thing's for certain. Your father went running to Sweeny with the information. No surprise there. He's been his lapdog for years, getting kickbacks for signing pieces of paper pushed under his nose, and never bothering to read the print.'

'Michael!' her tone should have warned him. 'Knowing how you feel after all Uncle Peter's done, I'm going to forget what you've said. But I deny saying anything to Father about the loans, and his company appointments are few, merely attending monthly meetings and signing minutes.'

'Knowing they're written by a fraudster like Brains,' Callaghan scorned. 'He must shut his eyes every time he picks up a pen.'

'Michael!' her voice was dangerously tense now. 'So far, nothing's been proven against Uncle Peter. *The Times'* allegations are no more than hearsay. Yes, I'll admit he's ruthless, his treatment of your parents was unforgivable, but Father says he has no reason to doubt his integrity.'

'Doesn't he! Then he must be stupid as well as blind. But there again, what else can he say? With a fat income coming in from all the contracts awarded by The Ring, enabling him to live in luxury, surrounded by staff, and not caring what happens to *my* mother and father—'

'Michael!' Colleen's face paled, her voice was cold. 'You've gone too far. Either you accept my word I said nothing to Father, or I'm leaving.'

'That's fine by me.'

Colleen stood a long moment searching his face. He avoided her gaze. When she spoke, her tone was distant. 'If it's fine with you, Michael, it's fine by me. I'll send Mary for my clothes.'

Those angry words had been the last to pass between them.

After a restless night he awoke to an empty bed. Staring up at the ceiling, his heart still full of bitterness, he stuffed clothes into a valise and took a train to Savannah, to find his mother responding to the family atmosphere, looking after her two grandchildren for Jonathan and Francesca to rebuild their shipping business, ravaged by the Northern blockade of Southern ports during the war. But his father was locked into a shell, blaming his "selfish ambition" for placing Callaghan's mother in such a vulnerable position. 'All lost,' he kept saying. 'Home. Furniture. Newspaper. Because of my damn signatures on two pieces of paper.'

Meanwhile, Callaghan was feeling his own pain over Colleen, and turning to drink in a vain attempt to forget her. Realising he must find some other way to put her out of his mind, he turned to his brother-in-law when they were sitting on the veranda one evening.

'I'd like to sail on one of your brigs, Jon. As one of the crew.'

'A seaman! Are you out of your mind! Have you any *idea* how hard the life is?'

'Hard is what I need right now.'

'But why, for pity's sake? Is it to do with Colleen?'

'Let's just say I need to see new places. If you won't take me, I'll find someone who will.'

Jonathan gave in, finding him a berth on his brig Nyack. Sailing from Savannah to Havana, to Caracas, Rio de Janeiro, and across the southern Atlantic to Capetown, he headed back to Savannah four months later a hardened seaman, but with his mind cleared, realising how much he'd wronged Colleen, and anxious to get home and ask her forgiveness.

Two days after his return, his father suffered a heart attack. 'Michael,' he whispered, as Callaghan held him dying in his arms. 'Forget Sweeny. Make it up with Colleen, before it's too late–' His father's last breath rasped out, and Callaghan dismissed his words and once more blamed Colleen.

But he charged Sweeny even more. What Brains had done was tantamount to murder and he began plotting his revenge. The day after the funeral, he returned to New York, a plan in his mind, and went to sound it out on *The Times'* Chief Editor, Louis Jennings, an old acquaintance.

In his mid-thirties, Jennings was English. An acerbic writer and trenchant investigator, he had needed no persuasion from George Jones, founder and owner of *The New York Times*, to lead the campaign against The Ring.

After receiving Jennings's condolences about Tom's death, Callaghan began his reason for calling. 'I hear that James Watson, the County Auditor, has just been killed in a sleigh accident.'

'I can't say I will shed any tears, old fellow,' Jennings' English accent and affectations were deliberately pronounced to hide a penetrating mind. 'He was a Ring man through and through.'

'How about O'Rourke applying for the position?'

Matthew O'Rourke was *The Times'* best undercover freelancer, who'd infiltrated himself into Tammany Hall by pretending to be an ardent Democrat. 'Michael, what an excellent idea. He's ideal for the role. A few months in the Treasury and we should have all the evidence we need.'

'And I can get myself into the Detective Squad at Headquarters. It will give me a chance to probe into places a reporter can't get access to, and also pick up on any inside gossip.'

'Even better. But how can you ensure you'll be sent to Mulberry Street, and not end up as a roundsman?'

'Police Commissioner Smith. He was one of my father's best friends.'

'General "Baldy"? The old warhorse?' Jennings smiled. 'Michael, you've just made my day.'

He pulled out a whiskey bottle and two tumblers out of a desk drawer, half-filled both glasses handed one to Callaghan, raised his own and proposed: 'Here's to the demise of The Ring.'

A week later, Detective Callaghan was at Companies Registration Office checking through files of firms awarded city contracts, searching for a familiar name he could link to The Ring, a person on whom he could apply pressure to talk, when one leapt up at him off the page.

Patrick Oates! His father's trusted ex-bookkeeper! Named as a director of a Ring company! Realising immediately he was the one who'd betrayed them to Sweeny, Callaghan flicked through the rest of the files. Oates' name appeared on the lists of three other companies.

He sat there a while collecting his thoughts, feeling a mixture of remorse, trepidation and joy.

Finally, he walked out of the office and headed for Greenwich, his legs feeling like lead.

The butler closed the study door behind Callaghan. Lowell was sitting at his leather-topped desk.

A tall man with a goatee beard, and inherently wealthy, he was unused to hard work, but prior to the newspaper fiasco, he had always been genial, approving his daughter's choice of husband.

Today he remained seated, glowering at Callaghan. 'What in damnation are you doing here?'

Callaghan hesitated. His prepared speech was for Colleen.

'Well?' Lowell snapped.

'I've found out it was Oates who gave Sweeny the information, sir. I'm here to apologise.'

'Apologise!' Lowell shot to his feet. 'I should damn well think so! Only Colleen persuading me otherwise, stopped me from suing you for defamation.'

'I wouldn't have blamed you, sir. My behaviour was inexcusable. My anger got the better of me. I spoke without thinking. I'd like to see Colleen, if I may, to try to explain.'

'Explain! Do you think, for *one moment*, she'd listen to you!'

'I was hoping she might. If you'll tell her I'm here, perhaps she'll–'

'I can't. She took off on an extended tour of Europe over a week ago, when she heard you were back in Greenwich. Said she never wanted to see you again, and I can't say I blame her. I'm afraid your visit has all been in vain.'

Callaghan went numb. Europe! That was one hell of a way to go, just to avoid him. And even further proof of how much she must hate him.

'Sir, if I wrote her a letter, would you send it on?'

'Don't waste your time. She told me that on no account were you to be told her destinations.'

Callaghan glanced at the door to the drawing room as he heard the sound of china breaking.

'The maid being clumsy clearing away my mid-morning tray,' Lowell said. 'Now, if you'll excuse me, we've nothing more to discuss.'

Still in shock, Callaghan turned to go, then felt he was under an obligation to his father-in-law to warn him. 'Sir, I hear *The Times* is planning a new campaign to bring down The Ring that stands every chance of success. I hope you won't take offence, but maybe you should consider resigning your chairmanships–'

Lowell's face darkened with anger. 'Michael, you'd best leave. But first let me tell you that until Collen told me, I never knew Peter had made me chairman of your father's newspaper. I straightaway refused it. As for my other appointments, no evidence has ever been laid against any of the present administration. Which, by inference, applies to my association with them.'

He strode to the door and flung it open. 'Let yourself out.'

From that day, Callaghan's determination to see Sweeny behind bars had been his driving force.

Continuing his investigations between his routine detective work, he spent every waking hour pursuing clues. But the breakthrough came from O'Rourke. Copying every ledger he could lay his hands on and handing them over to *The Times*, Jennings was now in possession of such explosive facts and figures, that the case against The Tweed Ring could finally be proven.

With the dexterity of a financial juggler, Sweeny had created a litter of stocks and bonds for every project under New York's sun: City Improvement Bonds, Brooklyn Bridge Revenue Bonds, Central Park Improvement Stocks, City Streets Improvement Bonds, Croton Aqueduct Bonds, the list was endless. Nor was there any money in any of these funds. The Ring had syphoned it all off.

On July 22, 1871, *The Times'* new campaign hit the streets. The main headline read:

THE SECRET ACCOUNTS: PROOF OF UNDOUBTED FRAUD BROUGHT TO LIGHT

Next day, Dick Connolly came to *The Times* and offered Jennings $500,000 to drop his exposé.

Realising he at last had The Tweed Ring on the run, Jennings published Connolly's offer in his next issue, added an open refusal, and continued printing facts until public opinion rose to such a pitch that Mayor Hall had no option but to appoint a committee to examine the books. Composed of men such as Judge James Emott, Robert Roosevelt, it secured an injunction against all four Ring members from acting further on behalf of the city and, on October 24, fully endorsed the extent of the fraud. The District Attorney was instructed to commence criminal proceedings.

By then, Connolly had flown, leaving Tweed, Mayor Hall and Sweeny to face the music.

Papers were issued on all three. Callaghan volunteered to serve Sweeny's.

West 34th Street

Sweeny's mansion was in darkness. No glimmer of gaslights or oil-lamps shining behind closed curtains. All the way from ground floor to attics, the building exuded an air of sudden desertion.

Too damned late! Callaghan swore to himself, crumpling the warrant into a ball and stuffing it in his pocket. Swigging some whiskey from a hip-flask, he slouched off towards the gates.

From behind the mansion came a clatter of hooves and rumble of wheels.

He spun about and saw four black horses and a black coach hurtling down the drive at him. Eyes rolling, nostrils flared, the horses bore down on him as the coachman flicked his whip, urging them on. He flung himself aside. Sweeny was sitting inside the coach, recognisable by his squat shape. Brains saw him, his evil eyes bore into Callaghan's, then he smirked through his walrus moustache, raised his high-crowned black hat, and doffed it with an exaggerated flourish.

Images of Colleen, his father and mother, flashed through Callaghan's mind, resurrecting all the pain and rage of the last two years.

He exploded into action. The coach was slowing down, forced into executing a ninety degree turn into West 34th Street, making for Fifth Avenue. Callaghan ran after it, drawing level with the window to see Sweeny glaring at him through the shut glass, his ugly face now showing alarm.

The coach straightened and increased speed. Bolted on to its frame between window and door was a pull-up grip. Callaghan grabbed it with his left hand, using the coach's momentum to increase his stride, wrestling the door-handle open with his right. His feet slipped from under him. Holding on with both hands, arms outstretched, shoes scraping the floor, his body in danger of rolling under a rear wheel, he fought to get back up.

Above him the coach window lowered. Sweeny leered down at him, a silver-topped cane held high in his hand, and whipped the stick across the back of Callaghan's right hand. Despite the pain, he clung on. Brains struck again. Fearing his fingers being broken, Callaghan let go, but clung to the pull-up grip with his left hand, legs trailing, banging against the spinning spokes of the wheel. He felt his fingers slip. Seconds more he'd be crushed. Using his last strength, he pushed himself off the metal grip, tumbling away from the coach and missing the iron rimmed wheel by inches.

Getting to his knees, the coach thundered away from him and reached the end of the street, then turned into Fifth Avenue and headed north out of the city.

Since then, and with the help of the Canadian police, Sweeny's escape route was traced across the Canadian line to the house of a Jesuit priest in the village of Pont Neuf, near Quebec, where he'd hidden until passage could be arranged to Dublin, Ireland, a voyage that had taken six weeks…

Only for him to disappear again.

Four months went by with nothing more being heard, when the Irish Garda received a tip that he was hiding in an isolated monastery deep in the foothills of the Slieve Bloom Mountains of County Laois, only to find he'd been smuggled out of the country days earlier on a fishing-boat.

But to where – that was the question?

This was partly answered when *The Times'* correspondent in Paris wired Jennings that a New York couple on vacation there thought, but couldn't swear on it, that they'd glimpsed Sweeny walking along a boulevard in the company of a young priest…

- 12 -

That was but five days ago, Callaghan continued to brood, staring into his drawing-room fire.

A rat-tat-tat on the mews-house door-knocker broke his thoughts.

He crossed to the door, opened it, and stood still with shock, unable to move.

'Hello, Michael.'

A moment passed before he was able to reply. 'Colleen.' His voice sounded far away, as if it wasn't his.

'May I come in?' She gave a slight shiver of cold and pulled up her fur collar around her neck.

'Of course.' He moved aside. She brushed past him, intoxicating him with her nearness and the familiar scent of her perfume. It was as if time had rolled back for him, and past sorrows were no more than a dream.

She stood by the fire warming her hands and looked around the room.

'I like the way you've rearranged it, especially the dresser. It looks well in the alcove.'

'I tried to imagine how you would have done it,' he said, with quiet candour.

'Oh, come, Michael. You always had taste.'

'Mostly learnt from you.'

'Did it work?' Her green eyes were probing and serious.

'Did what work?'

'Changing everything about. Did it erase the memories?'

He didn't answer, his pulse racing, his mind teeming with questions.

She glanced at her portrait in its ornate gold frame on the far wall. Painted on their return from honeymoon, her happiness at the time seemed to radiate from it. 'You kept it?'

'Yes.' His pulse beat was starting to slow down. 'If I can't have you, I'll settle for that.'

She turned to him with a steady look. 'I'm not here to resurrect the past, Michael. Too many hurtful things were said. But may I sit down?'

His heart sank. Trying not to show it. he indicated to her favourite chair still close to the hearth and gave it one more shot. 'I kept that there, too. Same reason.'

She didn't respond.

He sat opposite her and forced his voice to sound calm. 'When did you arrive home?'

'Last week. Father's not well.'

'I'm sorry to hear that. What's the matter?'

Their conversation sounded so polite in his ears, more like strangers than ex-lovers.

'His heart. The strain of being dragged into this dreadful Tweed Ring affair.'

Having being instrumental in exposing them, Callaghan stayed silent.

'It's all so unfair. He's innocent. After you saw him, he took your advice and looked deeper into the contracts. When he saw what was happening, he resigned every one of his chairmanships. Until then, he genuinely believed Uncle Peter wasn't guilty, despite what you–'

'How did you know I'd talked to your father?' he cut across her.

'He wrote to me,' she fabricated, crossing her fingers. She'd been in the next room, heard every word. She not sailed for Europe until a week later. But this was not the time for confession. With every enquiry having failed, Michael was now the only one who could help her find Sweeny.

65

Otherwise, nothing on earth would have brought her here.

'Did he also tell you about my finding out it was Pat Oates who—'

'Yes. But that's all water under the bridge.'

'Colleen, I'm so sorry I reacted the way I did.' His words, pent-up for two years, came out in a rush. 'After Sweeny lied about your father being the one who told him about the loans, I lashed out without thinking. I shouldn't have let him get to me. Nor been so stupid as to accuse you of—'

'I don't want to talk about it, Michael. It happened too long ago.'

Callaghan was unwilling to give up. 'Please, just let me try to—'

'Michael!'

He saw how set her face was, the flash in her eyes, and with it went all hope of a second chance.

'That you could suspect me, let alone accuse me, was enough. It's over.' Seeing his reaction, as if he'd been struck in the face, she tried to remedy her harshness.

'But now that I'm back, maybe we can try to be friends again?'

A renewed glimmer of hope in his eyes prompted her to hastily add: 'Except, I ask you to respect that I want nothing more. The sooner we legalise our separation, the better.'

Okay, Callaghan thought, feeling his neck stiffen, if that's how you want it. 'Fine,' he said, switching to an attitude of indifference. 'I take it you mean divorce?'

'Yes, despite the Church's teachings. And amicable. I want nothing from you.'

'Don't worry.' His amusement was genuine. 'I've nothing to give. Is that all you've come for?'

'No. Being back in this room, I got side-tracked.' Her phraseology was still from the war years, he noted, not of accepted society. It was part of her charm and he still loved it. He still loved her. But if she was so indifferent toward him, he was damned if he was going to show it.

'In that case, whatever it is you want, fire away.'

She gathered her thoughts and leant forward in her chair. 'Very simply, Father tells me you're now with the Detective Squad at Police Headquarters. I also heard from another source that your department's still after Uncle Peter. Or rather: *Sweeny*, after what he's done to my father.'

'So now you know how I felt.'

'I also did at the time,' Colleen said, meeting his gaze.

'Yes, so I since realised. But why do you want him?'

'To sign an affidavit clearing Father of what was going on.'

'Sweeny! Sign!' Callaghan scorned. 'You're not serious, surely? He's never signed anything in his life.'

'Perfectly serious. Though all attempts to find him have so far failed, should they succeed, then knowing him, there's no hope of extraditing him back to face trial, so he's got nothing to lose.'

'Maybe, but if you're hoping he'll put his name to an affidavit, you don't know what makes Brains tick. He enjoys watching people suffer. He'll just laugh in your face.'

Her eyes flashed. 'I can at least try! It's better than doing nothing, watching Father slowly kill himself.'

'I'm sorry,' his apology was genuine. 'I can't help. The only thing I can tell you is that *The Times'* man in Paris wired Louis that Sweeny's been there. Acting on it,' he elaborated, 'the guy went ferreting, but all he came up with was a postal address in Montmartre. Mulberry Street asked the Paris police for help but they say he's our problem. Our Embassy's got more to do than try to find him. Besides, he may only have been there a few days and moved on again. So it looks like we've reached yet another dead end.'

Colleen looked back at him, her eyes steadfast, determined. 'Montmartre? Do you have the address?'

'I can get it, but it won't do you any good. As I said, it's only postal–'

'Still, it's a starting point,' she persisted. A sudden thought struck her. She quickly weighed it up. It meant they would be together for weeks, maybe months on end. Something she would never have contemplated less than a moment ago. Even so…

Intently studying his face to check his reaction, she asked: 'Michael? How much would you give to find him?'

'You know the answer to that,' he said, trying to read her questioning eyes. His heart leapt, hardly daring to hope he was right. 'What's more, I think I can guess what you're about to suggest.'

Colleen smiled her reply. It lit up the room for him. 'Are you willing? Father will gladly pay for us both.'

Callaghan felt like springing out of his chair. Just hours ago his life had been at a cross-roads. Now this. And though it would probably end up as a wild-goose chase, at least they'd be together. Besides, who knew, the Montmartre address might lead to something? It couldn't achieve less than he'd accomplished so far, getting nowhere in New York.

'Strangely enough,' he said, trying not to show his exhilaration, 'I'm thinking of resigning the force. Should we find him – no,' he corrected, anxious to give weight to her idea, 'when we find him, I'll make damn sure he signs your affidavit first – before frogmarching him to our nearest Embassy and leave the extradition legalities to them.'

'That sits fine with me.'

The army phraseology again, Callaghan thought. Unladylike, unique, absolutely charming.

'As for when we get to Paris,' she continued, already thinking ahead, 'we could write him a letter, keep watch on the address, and pay whoever comes to collect it to tell us where it's being forwarded to? I'm sure that for the right money…'

'Miss Lowell, welcome home,' Callaghan said. 'It's a great plan. As for us being in Paris–' he grinned at her at the thought of it and

Colleen's heart missed a beat, just as it had when he smiled at her that first time, in the old warehouse reeking of molasses.

'On a business-like basis Michael,' she reaffirmed, with a firmness she no longer felt.

'Absolutely platonic,' Callaghan agreed, crossing his fingers.

- 13 -

Her mooring lights gleaming, *The Mary Celeste* rode at anchor off Staten Island, surrounded by other vessels all waiting for the Atlantic storms to abate.

In their cabin, Sarah Briggs, aware of Sophia sleeping soundly beside her, snuggled closer to Benjamin for warmth and saw his eyes were open, staring at the dimmed oil-lamp swinging from the ceiling.

'What is troubling you, Benj?' she whispered. 'It can't be the loan. You've borrowed before and it has never caused you concern.' Raising her face, she voiced her innate suspicion. 'Be honest with me, Ben. It's that barrel you told me Mr Winchester made all the fuss about. That's it, isn't it? You suspect him of something nefarious? Smuggling contraband, perhaps?'

Even in the dim light she could see his reassuring smile was forced.

'Of course not,' he replied. 'Mr Winchester's honourable. He'd never get involved in crime. It's just the frustration of being stuck here when we should be twelve hours out into the Atlantic.' He kissed her on her forehead. 'Try getting some sleep. Tomorrow the wind may have dropped and we'll be on our way.'

In the galley, 23-year-old Edward Head put away the washed supper plates and from his sea-chest removed a leather-bound book, inkpot and pen. Placing them on the table, he sat on the bench and in the dim light of the oil-lamp swinging overhead, wrote on the flyleaf:

The Diary of Edward Head
145 Newell Street, Greenpoint, Brooklyn.
Steward on-board the brigantine 'Mary Celeste'
Voyage across the Atlantic

He added his dedication:

To my dear wife of two weeks, Emma

Allowing the ink to dry, he turned the page and began:

Tuesday, 5 November 1872.

After leaving East River this morning bound for Genoa, Italy, we were forced to anchor off Staten Island, because of the storms out in the Atlantic. I have been out on deck looking at the lights of Brooklyn, trying to imagine which is yours, Emma, and wishing I could fly across the water to be in your arms for just one more night before we hopefully set sail tomorrow.

But as I cannot, then dedicating this diary to you makes me feel nearer to you, my love.

First, let me tell you about my shipmates. The Captain, Benjamin Briggs, is a strict but fair man, and according to the First Mate is an excellent seaman. His wife is also on board, her name is Sarah Elizabeth, and she is the kindest of women. They have their daughter, Sophia Matilda, with them, a pretty little thing, just turned two, who calls me "Edad". One day, Emma, you and I may be fortunate enough to have a little girl just like her.

The First Mate, Albert Richardson, is twenty-eight. His wife's name is Frances, but he calls her Fanny. During the recent war, when only eighteen, he served with the Maine Volunteers.

The Second Mate, Andrew Gilling, is twenty-five. I've not spoken to him much, so know little about him, except he comes from Denmark. All four seamen are German. Their names are Volkert

Lorenzen, who's twenty nine, married with a two year old daughter; his brother, Boz, twenty-five, who's engaged; Gotlieb Goodschaad, twenty-three. They come from the same village, Utersum, on the island of Fohr, off Northern Prussia, and are all friendly fellows, unlike the fourth, from the island of Amrum, also off Northern Prussia. His name is Arian Martens.

Head paused again as he thought of the words to describe Martens.

He's thirty-five, a strange, silent man, with hair so fair it's almost white, like an albino, and cold blue eyes that normally show no emotion, but can suddenly pierce right through you, and is always on his own, seeming to prefer his own company.

Head paused again as he thought uneasily about Martens.

There was no doubt about it.

The man gave him the shivers.

- 14 -

Fiesole

Pierre Beckx re-read the telegraph from New York, just delivered by messenger from Florence. Straining his eyes in the flickering candlelight, it was dated November 4, 1872, and read:

> *Cargo valued $100 sails tomorrow arrives 5-6 weeks. Similar cargo follows 10 days. Opus Dei*

Beckx noted the figure, added six noughts, and drank-in the resulting sum: $100,000,000. With a further $100 million to follow, it confirmed all rumour of Peter Sweeny's immense wealth.

By his success in organising the shipments, Father Reikel had fully justified Beckx' decision in entrusting him with the mission.

The Father-General brooded. With Sweeny arriving tomorrow, the news could not have come at a more critical time. Only yesterday, Count de Ricasole had informed him that the wording of Victor Emmanuel's evil new Act was almost complete. If passed, Holy Church would be illegally, satanically robbed of all her remaining properties, even the Vatican, The Holy See of Saint Peter, God's powerhouse on Earth.

If this was to happen, not only would it leave them without authority in Italy, but throughout Europe, and would have a devastating effect on their missionary program for the rest of the world.

But with the advance donation Sweeny was bringing with him to tomorrow's meeting, votes could be immediately purchased. The evil Act would be vetoed. And the downfalls of both Victor Emmanuel and von Bismarck could then be planned.

Gripped by rare excitement, Beckx prised himself out of his high-backed chair. Leaning on his stick, he dragged his feet across the floor to the long, shuttered windows. Opening them with shaking fingers, he stepped out into the cool of the late evening, and gazed down the Arno at the distant red domes and rooftops of Florence.

Cradle of the Italian Renaissance, its churches were still full of religious paintings by Raphael, Michelangelo, Leonardo da Vinci, Donatello and others; works that belonged to Mother Church, but which – through armed might – were now the property of the State.

Beckx permitted himself a rare smile. How true was Blessed Saint Ignatius's saying: That while The Society of Jesus lives, the Church of Rome will never die.

Victor Emmanuel would soon be discovering the truth of that saying.

Counter-revolution.

Meticulously planned.

Jesuitically controlled.

Leaving nothing to chance.

- 15 -

Florence

In the dining-room of the **Hotel De La Ville**, Sweeny dropped his knife and fork on to his empty plate and pushed it aside with a satisfied sigh. He chose a tooth-pick, leant back in his ornate chair, unfastened his bottom waistcoat button, and looked across at Father Guilamo. The young Sicilian was wearing the same black suit he'd exchanged for his cassock just before approaching the Italian border at Modanne.

'That was some meal, Father.' Brains picked between his teeth and swallowed the findings. 'I doubt Delmonico's could've done better.'

'It was excellent, Mr Sweeny,' Father Guilamo agreed. 'I am grateful to you for your generous hospitality.'

'The pleasure's mine, Father.' Brains dismissed the priest's gratitude with a flick of his hand. 'And my thanks to you for showing me Florence. All the sculptures and paintings! Those guys certainly had talent. Especially that Michelangelo. That David statue of his must have taken weeks of carving – though it could have done with a fig leaf for women not to stare at it.'

He reflected a moment, his face hardened. 'But it's now back to business, and our meeting tomorrow with the Father-General. I've ordered the coach for three. That give us enough time?'

'Ample, Mr Sweeny.'

'I'm looking forward to getting down to detail. After seeing what this Victor Emmanuel's doing, it's high time he was sorted out. It's a sacrilege that all the churches we visited are now owned by the State.' Brains brooded as he thought about it and remembered another injustice. 'Not only that, but we also had to apply for permits to get inside them, and then pay at the door. Churches are for the faithful to make confession, not money-making attractions. Don't you agree, Father?'

'I rather think you are rather preaching to the converted, Mr Sweeny.'

Brains gave a low, growling chuckle. 'Yeah, sorry, Father.'

Without asking the young priest's permission, he selected a cigar from his gold case, sniffed it and lit up. 'But come tomorrow, whatever the General's got planned, I've got some ideas of my own. Just leave it to Peter Barr Sweeny. After taking over New York like I did, sorting out this Emmanuel guy is gonna be a doddle.'

Brooding on his cigar, Sweeny exhaled smoke rings and watched them drift up to the ceiling.

- 16 -

'Message f'Callaghan!' Callaghan looked up from writing his resignation. Framed in the doorway, Haggerty, telegraph's messenger-boy, a thickset youth with long arms, was wearing his usual smirk.

'Here!' Callaghan called out.

Haggerty ambled across the room. 'S'from Brennan,' he slurred. Richard Brennan was one of the telegraph operators.

Callaghan sighed. 'Haggerty, if Darwin had only known of your existence, he could have saved himself twelve years of controversy.' He picked up his paper-knife and pointed it at the boy's middle. 'Now,' he threatened. 'You've got two seconds.'

'Don't know anyones called Darwin,' Haggerty pugnaciously grunted. 'Two wires just come in for Missing Persons. One's from the Fifteenth, other's from the Eighteenth. A priest from Saint Xavier's gone missing, and a broad's reported her old man missing. Brennan says the description fits your John Doe.'

'Name?'

'Reikel. Father Karl Reikel.'

Callaghan sighed again. 'The husband, Haggerty.'

Haggerty consulted a crumpled note in his hand. 'Coughman,' he pronounced slowly.

Callaghan took the paper. 'Kaufmann, Haggerty. It's German, not asthmatic. Address?'

'Twenty-fifth Street, east of Madison.'

'Number?'

'Forgot,' Haggerty's smirk returned. 'Ask Brennan.'

Callaghan sat pondering, then decided: what the hell. Might as well see it through. It would be only a slight diversion on his way to The Times to get Sweeny's Montmartre address. He could finish the letter in Jennings's office and post it to Mulberry Street before going on to Colleen's.

It was a sunny but piercingly raw day as the omnibus headed uptown. Callaghan got off at the corner of 25th Street, raised his collar against the harsh east wind, and walked one block east to Lexington, past solid brownstone mansions built on land which, only twenty years earlier, had been vacant lots and fields.

Kaufmann's grand house was on the north-west corner of 25th and Lexington. Reaching the pillared front entrance and climbing up to the double front doors, Callaghan rang the ornate bell.

After a long pause one of the doors slowly opened, revealing a dark-suited butler. His look of disdain increased as Callaghan introduced himself. He glanced at the detective shield, then, in an aloof Boston accent, pronounced, 'If you would wait here a moment,' and closed the door.

Callaghan checked his watch. Two minutes passed before the man returned.

'If you will follow me, Mrs Kaufmann will see you.'

With slow dignity, the butler led the way through a huge hall with a carved sweeping staircase of marble, past exotic plants in large vases, statuettes on pedastalled columns, into a vast drawing room. Callaghan almost closed his eyes at the clash of colours, the brocaded maroon wallpaper, the vivid blue carpet, matching velvet curtains, chairs and sofas of almost every hue. *The Rainbow Room*, he thought.

A large, heavy-bosomed woman, with her hair tied back in a bun and wearing a grey silk blouse and skirt, was sitting at a writing desk in the far corner. Although she must have been aware of his entrance, she continued writing for at least a minute before looking up.

'The policeman, ma'am.'

'Thank you, Robert,' she dismissed him in a pronounced German accent. First generation, Callaghan decided. Born in Europe.

'You have news?' Her question to Callaghan was imperious. But he sensed it was all an act.

'Possibly, Mrs Kaufmann.'

'*Vat* do you mean, possibly?'

Arranged on a side table were a number of silver-framed photographs. Callaghan's gaze fixed on one – a large man with a walrus moustache and beard. He picked it up. 'Mrs Kaufmann, is this your husband?'

'Naturally.'

The face staring at Callaghan was unquestionably that of his "John Doe". Mrs Kaufmann was watching him with eyes of trepidation.

'Mrs Kaufmann, I regret I have grave news.'

Some ten minutes later, she'd stopped shaking and was sitting by the fire, sipping a glass of cognac Callaghan poured for her.

'I'm afraid I must ask you some questions, Mrs Kaufmann,' he apologised. 'You didn't report your husband missing until eleven, Tuesday night, at least thirty-six hours after he met his sad end. Why the delay?'

'There vas no delay, *vat*soever.' Her voice was subdued. 'My husband had urgent matters to attend to that required him to stay in town a number of days. He stayed at the Astor House and vasn't due to return until acht o'clock, Tuesday evening. Jacob was most punctilious, but I vaited until gone zehn, and then sent my maid to the nearest precinct to make enquiries.'

'I see. May I ask Mr Kaufmann's occupation?'

Callaghan noticed the slight hesitation before she answered.

'Diamond merchant.'

'And his office?'

'Somewhere near the corner of Front and Wall Street. But I'm afraid I do not know the exact address,' she added hastily. 'Nor do I have a key.'

Unlikely, Callaghan thought. So, why was she holding out? Whatever her reason, the corner of Front and Wall Street was only a stone's throw from where Kaufmann's body was discovered. Having now discarded the "wife's-lover" theory, he was about to ask about a possible business partner, when Mrs Kaufmann questioned:

'*Ven* can my husband's body be released from the morgue?'

'Whenever you can arrange it, Mrs Kaufmann.'

'Gut. I'm sure Vater Hudson vill attend to everything for me.'

'The Rector of Saint Francis Xavier's?' Callaghan queried, with increased interest.

'Ja.'

'The same church as Brains Sweeny?'

Again Mrs Kaufmann hesitated. 'Ja. Regrettably, Mr Sweeny did attend Saint Xavier's.' She now rushed her words. 'A terrible witness to those outside the faith. But I am glad to say ve did not know him. His pew was on the other side of the church.'

Callaghan saw her hands trembling and realised it was from fear not shock over her husband's death. Recalling Haggerty's other report of the missing priest from Saint Xavier's, he decided to pursue this connection. 'Do you know a Father Reikel, Mrs Kaufmann? I believe he's with your church.'

The woman's resulting panic was unmistakable, showing in her eyes and the wringing of her hands as she tried to control her shaking.

'Vater Reikel?' she repeated. Her voice sounded strangulated inside her throat.

'Yes. Karl Reikel. His name suggests he's of German descent. Like Mr Kaufmann and your goodself. If so, you would have had things in common.'

Gerda Kaufmann took a moment to reply. When she did, it was so whispered, Callaghan was hardly able to make out the words.

'Ja. Ve knew him, but only slightly. He had been at St Xavier's three months and vas a very dedicated priest. As soon as he arrived from Berlin, he opened a soup kitchen for the needy on East Side.'

'Mrs Kaufmann, forgive me, but you seem to be referring to him in the past tense. As though he's moved on.' Callaghan paused. 'You don't happen to know something about him we don't?'

She was slowly recovering her composure. 'Only that he seems to have gone missing. It vas announced in kirche on Sonntag morning, when prayers were made for his safekeeping.'

'I see.' Callaghan decided to alter his line of enquiry. 'Was Mr Kaufmann born here?'

'Nein. In Deutschland.'

'When did he arrive in this country?'

'At the age of five, with his parents.'

'Was his father a diamond merchant, too?'

'Nein; an official with a Deutschen bank.'

'Then Mr Kaufmann built up his business from nothing?'

'Jacob was very industrious.'

'And very successful…' Callaghan swallowed '…judging by your home.'

'It was purchased from the proceeds of some excellent investments Jacob made.' Gerda's tone was suddenly wary again. 'He vas…how do you say it?…an kluge…an astute man.'

Carefully watching for her reaction, Callaghan asked his final question. 'Mrs Kaufmann. Did your husband have any dealings with The Tweed Ring?'

'Nein,' she refuted indignantly. 'Nein.'

But Callaghan again saw fear in her eyes.

Callaghan followed the black-robed Father Murray into the library.

The last time he was in St. Francis Xavier's was for his wedding, but this was his first into the inner sanctorum. Replacing his copper detective badge in his overcoat pocket, he glanced around.

It was a dark room, spartanly furnished with a long wooden table, plain and bare, surrounded by a number of simple chairs. Its walls were shelved with black and brown leather-bound books, interspaced with black and white engravings depicting Jesuitical images of Heaven and Hell, Hell predominating: stark visual reminders in accordance with the teachings of Saint Ignatius Loyola of the dreadful eternal punishment awaiting those who chose not to side with God.

Callaghan looked away.

'Do you have news of Father Reikel?' The Jesuit asked in a refined New York accent.

Guessing, he was in his early thirties, lean, thin-faced, grey eyes, clean-shaven and bald, with narrow strips of prematurely grey hair along the sides of his head.

'I'm afraid not,' Callaghan said, then told him of Kaufmann's murder.

At the conclusion, the priest closed his eyes, lips moving in silent prayer.

'What a sad reflection of today's violent society,' he said, opening his eyes and shaking his head in despair. 'Mr Kaufmann worshipped here twice every Sunday, and attended our monthly Alumni Sodality meetings. I know Father Hudson is extremely committed, but I am sure he will find time to call on Mrs Kaufmann to pray with her and render his consolation. And should Mr Kaufmann have committed any venial act since his last confession, special mass will be said for his sin to be purged and his soul delivered from purgatory.'

'That should console her,' Callaghan said dutifully, then checked on Gerda Kaufmann's statement. 'Father, to your knowledge did Mr Kaufmann know Brains Sweeny?'

Murray was momentarily silent, clearly disturbed by the question. Small wonder, Callaghan thought. After the publicity of the last twelve months, Sweeny had to be St Xavier's least favourite son.

'Sweeny?' the Jesuit nervously repeated. 'Mr Peter Barr Sweeny?'

'That's him. City Chamberlain Sweeny. Alderman for the Twentieth District. And mastermind behind The Tweed Ring.'

Murray recovered his composure. 'Yes, they knew each other well. The Kaufmanns sat in the pew behind the Sweenys, and Mr Sweeny also belonged to the Xavier Alumni Sodality. But what relevance does this have on Mr Kaufmann's death? As you are aware, Detective, Mr Sweeny left New York twelve months ago in unfortunate circumstances, and I fail to see any conn—'

'Please bear with me, Father. Just a couple more questions. This German-sounding priest who's gone missing on East Side—'

'Father Reikel.'

'I gather he's not been in New York long?'

'Barely three months.'

'When did he go missing?'

'Last Wednesday. When he failed to arrive back for prayers we—'

'Arrive back? From where?'

Murray's expression became cross. 'I gave all this information to the captain of the Fifteenth Precinct on Thursday morning, Detective.'

'I'm sorry, Father, but with the shortage of men because of the election, it's taken some days for it to come through to headquarters. If you would bear with me a moment longer?'

'Very well.' Murray continued to frown. 'But now that it is with your department, please do all you can. As time passes, we are becoming more and more concerned about him. This isn't at all like Father Reikel. He is the most punctilious of men and extremely attentive to his duties. I fear something terrible must have happened to him. He would never—'

'We'll do everything we can to find him,' Callaghan cut across him. 'But if we can get back to last Wednesday – from where did he fail to arrive?'

'His soup kitchen on East Side, which he started the first week he arrived from Germany. He was a most godly and caring priest.' Murray shook his head, his look inferring he feared the worst.

'Yes, Mrs Kaufmann mentioned the kitchen. Tell me, during the time he's been here at Saint Xavier's, did he ever meet Jacob Kaufmann?'

'Certainly,' the Jesuit affirmed. 'The first time at a Sodality meeting. With both being German there was an immediate affinity between them. So much so, Father Reikel became Mr Kaufmann's regular confessor.'

'Did he?' said Callaghan. 'Thank you, Father, I won't take up any more of your time.'

'And Father Reikel?'

'I'll get on to it right away. You have my word on it.'

- 17 -

'But I've met him!' Colleen exclaimed. 'In Saint Xavier's. A week ago today.'

They were sitting on opposite sides of her drawing-room hearth, as dusk closed in outside. Callaghan was momentarily lost in the pleasure of her company. With an olive green velvet skirt spread about her, the dancing flames of the fire playing shadows on her face, highlighting the copper flecks in her viridian eyes and accentuating her high cheekbones, she looked enchanting.

He forced his mind back to Reikel. 'You're sure? According to Father Murray that's the day he went missing.'

'I'm positive. He's your height. Slim. Fair hair, almost white. And the most vivid blue eyes.' Colleen hesitated. 'But there was something strange about him.'

'Strange? In what way?'

'It's difficult to explain. It was more a sort of force exuding out of him; almost elemental.' She hesitated again. 'I don't like saying this about a priest, but the only word to describe him is sinister. He made my spine go quite cold.'

Knowing Colleen wasn't given to exaggeration, Callaghan was puzzled. 'But that doesn't fit with Father Murray's description of someone who opened a soup kitchen for the poor.'

'I'm sorry, Michael,' Colleen insisted, 'that was the way he affected me. But maybe I over-reacted. Perhaps he has an antipathy for women?'

'Possibly,' Callaghan said, 'yet, he *was* Kaufmann's confessor. That, and the fact Kaufmann and Sweeny sat next to each other at church,

85

proves Mrs Kaufmann was lying. I saw it in her eyes when she said her husband never acted for The Ring.'

He gave a wry smile. 'It's always a case of being wise after the event. While I've been going around in circles serving warrants on every damned bank in New York, Kaufmann's the one I should have been looking for. When you think about it, diamonds are the perfect commodity. Easily hidden, easily convertible, and diamond exchanges in major cities across the globe. If my guess is right, he's the one who was holding The Ring's two hundred million all along.'

'Jackson!' Lowell's voice came from upstairs. 'More coffee!'

'Father.' Colleen gave an apologetic smile. 'Since yesterday he's taken to his bedroom, away from the bustle of the house, as he calls it, and surrounded by papers from his study.'

'Maybe it's to find the proof he wasn't involved?'

'Oh, I pray so,' she replied. 'And that he's at last taking a leaf out of Mother's book. She had more resilience, it was the Irish in her. She'd have told the District Attorney to go to Hell, then fought him through the courts, just like Mayor Hall.'

'So that's where you get it from,' Callaghan said. 'I'd like to have met her.'

'I wish you could have,' Colleen said, somewhat wistfully, 'You would both have got on so well. But before we digress further,' she added hastily, 'and getting back to Mr Kaufmann – who do you think decided to have him killed? And why?'

Callaghan was in no doubt. 'The order would have come from Tweed. There's a rumour circulating headquarters that someone's intending to testify against him, which would not only ensure his conviction, but have Oakey re-indicted. Assuming Kaufmann was the witness, and he'd made an immunity deal with the D.A., Tweed would have heard about it from his cronies on the force.'

'Surely not even Tweed would be desperate enough to resort to murder?' Colleen's eyebrows frowned in disbelief.

Oh, no? Callaghan thought, reviewing the facts about Boss. A fourth-generation New Yorker of Scottish descent, elected Alderman for the 7th Ward at the age of only twenty-eight, he began his career of crime selling favours to fellow businessmen: saloon licences, ferry and streetcar franchises, then moved up to building contracts and the like, practices that rapidly elevated him to Grand Sachem of Tammany Hall. By diverting city funds over the years, he now owned a huge mansion on the corner of Fifth Avenue and 43rd Street, and a magnificent steam yacht.

But would he risk losing it all by having Kaufmann murdered?

'He wouldn't think twice,' Callaghan said. 'If he's found guilty, all his assets will be sold, and the proceeds returned to the city. He'd not only be imprisoned, but also ruined. Faced with the choice between himself or Kaufmann, it would be auf weidersehen *Jacob*, thanks for your help.'

'I'm not so sure,' said Colleen, still in some doubt. 'But I think we can rule out Mayor Hall. Murder doesn't seem his style.'

Callaghan agreed. Despite all the bad publicity, Oakey was still Mayor of New York. English on his father's side, aristocratic French on his mother's and always elegantly dressed, he trained at Harvard Law School and married the daughter of one of New York's best families, the Henriques. A familiar figure at the best clubs, Oakey had survived two trials over the last twelve months, one with a hung jury, the second when all charges against him were dropped.

'You're right,' Callaghan said. 'Murder and Oakey don't go together. Besides, if he goes to a third trial, he's got the best firm of attorneys in New York. He'll keep brazening it out in court.'

'What about Connolly?' Colleen asked, wondering whether the missing City Comptroller could be involved in Kaufmann's death.

'I think we can strike him off,' Callaghan opined. 'Jennings says he's in Egypt, sightseeing down the Nile on a riverboat. It's thought he smuggled five million dollars out with him and seems perfectly content with his lot.'

'And Sweeny?'

Callaghan had already given this much thought.

'Yes and no,' he equivocated. 'We can assume he was up to his eyeballs in the scheme to convert the money into diamonds. It was probably his brainchild. But as for Kaufmann's murder, I doubt it. Since fleeing the law he's constantly on the move, and unlikely to be keeping tabs on what's happening in New York. Much as I'd like to think he was party to it, this was probably an instant decision by Boss and him alone.'

'You don't think Tweed did it himself?' Colleen hesitated.

'Well, he's certainly big enough and strong enough to snap a man's back. But I don't think he'd actually commit murder. He'd pay someone.'

Colleen pursed her lips. 'But what if the killer's not from New York? Finding him will be like looking for the proverbial needle in a haystack.'

'Not necessarily,' Callaghan prevaricated. 'I doubt Tweed had time to bring someone in from outside. But if he did, there'll be whisper of it on the streets. Most of our arrests come from tip-offs. Pillow talk in Greene Street's brothels, loose tongues in dives like Harry Hill's. Especially Harry's. Despite living in a Fifth Avenue mansion, Boss still does his drinking there, mixing with every known criminal and hooker in New York. If he wanted a killer, that's where he'd look. And Harry would know about it.'

'But will he tell you?'

'Most of the police leads come from Harry. They have a reciprocal arrangement with him. He keeps them informed, in return they approve his applications for the yearly renewal of his saloon licence.'

Colleen was silent, absorbed with her thoughts. Looking at her, Callaghan felt his heart again miss a beat.

'If Tweed is behind it, why strip the body?' she suddenly asked. 'Surely he must have realised it wouldn't take long for Kaufmann to be identified?'

Callaghan pulled himself together. 'That's been puzzling me, too,' he admitted. 'There has to be a reason, but so far I can't think of one.'

'And Father Reikel? Six days is a long time to be missing?'

'He's likely suffered the same fate as Kaufmann,' Callaghan said, sombrely.

'No, Michael!' Colleen protested. 'A priest! Surely not even Tweed could sink that low!'

'I'm sorry,' he replied, 'it's the only explanation I can come up with. Reikel was Kaufmann's confessor. Assuming Kaufmann was acting for The Ring, and he told Reikel everything about the diamonds, what if Reikel advised him to turn State's evidence? From that moment on, he'd be as much of a threat to Tweed as Kaufmann.'

'But whatever Kaufmann said during confessional would have been sacrosanct.'

'Sacrosanct! Boss wouldn't know the meaning of the word.'

Colleen looked distressed. 'I hope there's a simpler explanation. Loss of memory, perhaps?'

'Wandering the streets for a week in a priest's cassock? Highly unlikely.'

She gave a resigned sigh. 'You're probably right, nonetheless I'll pray for him. As for Tweed, if only we could *prove* he's behind Kaufmann's death, he'd be tried and convicted for murder. With nothing to lose, maybe he'd confess to the fraud charges and not only implicate Sweeny, but also reveal where in Europe he is now – if Tweed knows it, that is,' she qualified.

'It's worth a try.' Callaghan mentally tore up his resignation letter and, unable to hide his regret, he added, 'Much as I hate losing out on those Parisian evenings.'

'Paris was always a business trip,' Colleen reminded him.

But Callaghan thought he caught a similar regret to his own in the glance she gave him.

- 18 -

Briggs was leaning over *The Mary Celeste's* rail, staring disconsolately out to sea as he listened to the wind howling in through the Narrows. Beyond the channel he could see the Atlantic rollers crashing against Sandy Hook, then funnelling in, the anger partially sucked out of them as they swept across the sandbanks, finally expending themselves in the deeper waters of Lower Bay.

A steamship – Calabria, Liverpool – swept past, violently rocking the anchored *Celeste* in its wake. There were only a couple of passengers, immigrants by the look of them, leaning over the port rail and waving. Most would be on the starboard side, getting their first glimpse of New York.

He raised his hand in acknowledgement, then turned as Sarah crossed the deck and joined him. He put his arm around her shoulders. 'Where's Sophia?'

'I've tucked her up in bed for a nap.'

In silence they watched the Calabria heading across the bay, turning to starboard as she approached her berth on the Hudson.

'Benj?'

'Yes, dear?'

'Who was that man with Mr Winchester on the first day of loading?'

Not fully concentrating, Briggs asked, 'What man, Sarah?'

'The portly one with a German accent. Expensively dressed.'

'Oh, a friend of Winchester's – Jacob Kaufmann, as I remember his name. He was there out of curiosity. He'd never seen a vessel being loaded before.'

'Benj,' Sarah looked worried into her husband's eyes. 'Don't you think it was peculiar – them leaving so soon after the barrel incident? As though they attended just to ensure that particular barrel was safely loaded.' She reached for his hand. 'What if it does contain contraband, Benj? Instead of sailing, shouldn't we put financial considerations aside and inform Customs? Should it be he is involved in some felony, Mr Winchester can hardly demand repayment of his loan.'

Briggs stared out to sea, unable to meet his wife's gaze.

'Sarah, as I said before, I made too much of the matter. I've no doubts about Mr Winchester's honesty. But let us not speak of it again. Rather, we must pray for a break in the weather so we can get under way.'

'Of course,' Sarah replied.

But, looking down, she saw how tightly Benj was gripping *The Mary Celeste's* rail.

- 19 -

Fiesole

Beckx watched Sweeny's coach recede down the villa's long, dusty drive into the gathering dusk. Leaning on his stick, he limped back inside. Thanks be to Blessed Ignatius, the meeting had gone well. Also due, it had to be said, to Father Guilamo. Prevailing on Sweeny's desire to be regarded as a "Defender of the Faith", the young priest had cleverly supported Beckx' every word, adding to them whenever necessary, until all had been agreed – including an honorary papal title for Sweeny: "Knight of the Golden Spur", with his investiture in one of The Vatican's smaller chapels after Victor Emmanuel was ousted, and her rightful properties restored to Holy Church.

Beckx lowered himself into his chair, opened the ornate silver casket Sweeny had brought with him as a token of his loyalty, and gazed at the glistening diamonds brimming to the full inside.

The first stage of his plan was achieved. He could now pay those politicians already ear-marked as sellers of votes. Victor Emmanuel's evil Act was as good as vetoed. Then with God's Grace, the Father-General brooded, and the intercession of the Celestial Mary, as soon as the first vessel docked, the next phase, the removal of both satanic dictators – Bismarck as well as Victor Emmanuel – could begin.

Closing the casket, Beckx turned to Father Reikel's treatise on the situation facing Holy Church and concentrated on the passages he'd scored as most relevant – they'd discussed them in detail at their last meeting before he departed on his mission – commencing with the introductory quote from Saint Ignatius himself:

Preserve always your liberty of mind. See that you lose it not by anyone's authority, nor by any event whatsoever.

The second highlighted section related to the Bull of Canonisation of Saint Ignatius, formulated by Pope Gregory XV, in which the services rendered by the Society of Jesus to Mother Church, were clearly enumerated. One had been heavily underlined by Reikel.

The strenuous defence of the Holy See.

The treatise went on to probe the theological differences existing within Holy Church, between those who followed the teachings of the Dominican, Thomas Aquinas, and those who adhered to the views of the Franciscan, Duns Scotus. Although Jesuit theology was principally in agreement with Scotus, Reikel had nevertheless studied the doctrines of both men with eclectical discernment, and included one of Aquinas's most quoted instructions:

The morality of every action is determined by the end in view, which Reikel had précised as: The end justifies the means, then concluded his treatise with the words of the Jesuit, Francisco de Suarez, and had underlined the action that should be taken against despotic rulers:

> *The tyrant may be either a usurper, or a legitimate ruler, but whose rule has become an intolerable oppression and a menace to the Church. Because of this, he has declared war, thus allowing the just waging of a war of self-defence against him. A citizen who takes his life is acting in the name of the Church, and in the cause of its just warfare. It is therefore lawful to kill him, if the defence of the Church cannot be achieved in any other way.*

Reikel's treatise ended with this and Beckx began thinking of the second phase of his plan.

With the second vessel also soon on its way, it was time to formulate its operation.

In the time he'd known Sweeny, Guilamo Cottone had never seen him in this mood. Previously so expansive, he was sitting in the corner of the coach, bushy eyebrows knitted together, black eyes narrowed into two thin slits as he chewed an unlit cigar.

His dark mood so filled the coach it felt difficult to breathe. It was in sharp contrast to his fawning attitude of an hour ago when he'd fallen to his knees on meeting the Father-General and presented his casket of diamonds, then reverently kissed Beckx' finger-ring of office.

Father Guilamo remained silent, realising he was seeing the true nature of the man, sitting there squat and motionless, like some poisonous toad.

Sweeny suddenly snarled viciously. 'Buying votes ain't gonna be enough. And I'm speaking as someone who knows. Back in New York, I bought people's souls, but it still wasn't enough to keep me there. The Father-General's plan will only get this new Act killed off. It won't get Holy Church restored, or the Pope released. He's gonna have to come up with something bigger.'

'Which he is doing,' said Father Guilamo. 'As he explained. In great detail.'

'Sure, it's an ambitious plan,' Sweeny grated, 'but it's only got a fifty-fifty chance of success. I'm talking one hundred percent. I've already got an idea forming in my head. I'll have worked it out long before we reach Palermo. When are we meeting the Father-General again?'

'In just over five weeks. Sunday, the fifteenth of December.'

Brains rolled his cigar to the other side of his mouth. 'Five weeks. That'll give me plenty of time.'

- 20 -

Thursday, November 7, 1872. New York

'Message f'Callaghan!' Haggerty screamed, as if sheer volume might give his words impact.

Callaghan winced and looked up from his notes.

'Brennan says another stiff done in the same way as the first one's been found.'

Twenty minutes later, Callaghan was standing on the pier at the foot of Twenty-sixth Street, shivering despite his thick overcoat, collar upturned, hands in his pockets, as the *Seneca* – pride of the Harbour Police – approached the jetty, smoke pouring out of her long, black funnel.

A low, overcast sky was creeping in from the Atlantic. The buildings on the other side of the East River, all the way from Williamsburg to Long Island City, were covered by a thin blanket of mist. Away to the left, the narrow shape of Blackwells Island – home of the city's workhouse, lunatic asylum, almshouses and penitentiary – rose forlornly out of the grey waters.

Paddles in reverse, Seneca slid in sideways, bumping against the pier. Callaghan leapt on board and approached the pipe-smoking police captain leaning over the rail. 'Captain Brown?'

'And you're…' Brown asked, in a slow drawl.

'Callaghan, sir,' he replied, cautioning himself to remember Brown's rank, and showing him his detective badge. 'Detective Squad, Central Office.'

'What's your hurry, Callaghan?' Brown exhaled a stream of tobacco smoke. 'The guy's in no shape to run-away.'

'The manner of death, sir. I understand his spine was snapped?'

'By a madman, I'd say. When we picked him up he folded in two, just like a rag-doll.'

'I'm investigating a similar killing.'

Callaghan told him about Kaufmann.

'Interesting,' Brown said, chewing on his pipe stem. 'I guess you'd best take a look.'

Straightening up, he led Callaghan to an oilcloth mound in the middle of the deck and pulled back the covering. 'He's no oil painting,' he warned. 'The rats got to him before he was found.'

Callaghan looked down at the grisly sight. From chest down the body had been half eaten away, but the face, framed by blond, almost white hair, was mostly untouched. Feeling suddenly nauseated, Callaghan turned away.

'I felt the same when I first saw him,' Brown said, letting the cover drop.

Callaghan felt the deck rise and fall on the river swell. Swallowing, he asked, 'Any clothes?'

'Not a stitch.'

'Watches, rings, personal effects?'

'Only this. Under the body.' Brown dug in his pocket, handed over a heavy metal crucifix, made of jagged iron. Worn next to skin, it would cause laceration and must, Callaghan decided, have been made for hanging on a wall.

'Under the body, sir? Then he wasn't recovered from the river?'

'No. A workman found him lodged against the pilings of the new Brooklyn Bridge.'

'Was he killed there?'

'Couldn't say,' Brown drawled. 'Might also have been dumped in the river somewhere along the bank, and got carried there.'

'Downriver, sir? Or higher up?'

'Can't say. The East's got as many underlying currents as a cantankerous woman. Could have been thrown in anywhere between The Battery and Corlear's Hook.'

'Thanks for your help, sir.' Callaghan turned to go.

'One thing puzzles me,' said Brown. 'He was on his back when we found him, the rats hadn't got to that part of the body. There's no bruising at the base of his spine. A mite peculiar, don't you think, considering the way he was killed?'

Callaghan stopped in his tracks. There'd been no bruises on Kaufmann's back either.

As the cab rattled up Fifth Avenue on its way to the city morgue, Callaghan tried offering Father Murray some hope.

'There's always a chance it might not be Father Reikel.'

Murray looked at the crucifix in his hand. 'Thank you, Detective O'Callaghan, but this cross is his. I fear we must prepare for the worst.'

'With respect, Father,' said Callaghan, trying to start a conversation, 'my name's Callaghan. No "O". Blame my grandfather. He crossed to Scotland after the famine and fell for a Presbyterian, dropped the "O" to ask for her hand in marriage, and kept it like that when they came over here.'

Murray responded with a flitting smile. 'Callaghan. O'Callaghan. Your paternal roots are still Irish. Are you in the faith?'

Scenes of battle, with pieces of human bodies being blown high into the air, flashed through Callaghan's mind. He shook his head, bitterly. 'Father, if you'd been in the War and seen all the senseless suffering, you'd have lost your faith, too. I've seen men blow each other to bits, just to gain a few feet of ground.' He indicated through the window at a legless young man in a faded dark blue Northern Army uniform jacket, sitting on his haunches on a wheeled plank of wood on the sidewalk, holding out a tin cup, begging for alms, but being ignored by the passers-by. 'When I see unfortunates like him, you can keep your New Testament and its "come unto me and rest". If the Almighty exists at all, He's remained in the Old, still feeding on blood sacrifices.'

'Come, Detective O'Callaghan,' the Jesuit replied, turning his eyes away from the maimed soldier. 'The ultimate sacrifice was made nineteen hundred years ago, when Christ gave His life on the Cross for the salvation of–'

Callaghan cut across him. 'Father, can we get back to Father Reikel?'

Murray persisted. 'For the sake of your eternal soul, I would rather continue our conversation.'

Callaghan saw they were nearing the Fifth-Avenue Hotel, facing Madison Square. Six storeys of gleaming white marble, said to be the most magnificent hotel in the world, its public rooms were a popular meeting place for Wall Street brokers, while its private rooms were often used by them as a trysting-place with high-class prostitutes, pretty young things, dressed today, as always, in the latest fashions, parading outside its gilded entrance-doors, hoping to "hook" a rich client.

As Broadway's traffic merged with Fifth Avenue's in a packed sea of vehicles crawling past the square, the noise from iron-rimmed wheels and horses' hooves on cobbles, drivers shouting and honking horns, was ear-shattering, precluding further conversation.

A bulletin-wagon drew up alongside, plastered with adverts: "Barnum's Museum", "Pear's Soap", "Brandreth's Pills" – New Yorkers' latest cure-every-known-ailment fad, brown tablets and very bitter. Their cab pulled away into East 26th Street. The noise and traffic lessened. Callaghan spoke first, before Murray could resume. 'We're nearing the morgue, Father. I'd like to talk about Father Reikel. Assuming he is the victim, you said he'd been in New York three months?'

'Almost,' the Jesuit reluctantly gave in. 'He came here to escape the anti-Christian persecution currently sweeping across Europe.'

'Anti-Christian?' Callaghan responded. 'I thought it was only anti-Rome?'

'That in itself is proof we are dealing with Antichrist,' Murray remonstrated, the colour rising in his pale cheeks. 'It is Holy Church, not some apostate breakaway, that was ordained of God to be the Church Militant, and carry His message to the four-corners of the globe. *We* are Christ's army, the sole Defenders of His faith. This is why Lucifer never ceases to attack us, deploying his minions to do his evil work. Victor Emmanuel in Italy, von Bismarck in Germany. The proof is there for all to see. The Holy Father imprisoned in the Vatican. And the Society of Jesus under constant Satanic attack.'

Not strictly true, Callaghan was tempted to say. The Pope was not a prisoner in the real sense of the word. When Victor Emmanuel subjugated the Holy See, Pius refused to leave, thus allowing him to pose, in the eyes of Catholics worldwide, as being under "house arrest" by a despotic ruler. But then a Law of Guarantees passed by the Italian Assembly, promised to respect his inviolability and allowed him to remain in the Vatican, at liberty to stay in communication with the Catholic Church outside Italy by special telegraphic and postal facilities, plus an annual income of three million lire a year out of State revenues.

But *Pio Nono* had chosen to regard the Guarantee as a hostile edict imposed by a ruthless conqueror, thereby encouraging his Catholic subjects universal, to view him as "a prisoner in the Vatican", hoping to create protests from governments around the world, and so force Victor Emmanuel into restoring the Church of Rome in his new unified *Italia*. Thus far it hadn't worked. As for the Jesuits, Callaghan thought, "Satanic" was a somewhat colourful word for Murray to use, they'd been a source of controversy since their beginning, expelled from countries everywhere over the centuries. They should be used to it by now.

'Let's just agree to disagree Father,' said Callaghan, 'and get back again to Father Reikel. What can you tell me about him?'

Murray hesitated, wanting to continue defending his church, but then decided to answer. 'I'm sorry, Detective, having known him only three months, there's little I can say. At the time Rome was invaded and so flagrantly violated, he was employed by our Missionary Society in the *Piazza di Spagna*. He escaped to Berlin, and was teaching in our seminary there when Bismarck banished our Society from Germany also, and he decided to leave Europe altogether. As soon as he arrived in New York, he sought refuge in Saint Francis Xavier. Within his very first week he opened his mission on East Side. Why anyone should kill such a godly man, I simply cannot imagine.'

'Your Missionary Society?' Callaghan queried. 'Wasn't that a high office?'

'Certainly,' Murray confirmed. 'He was appointed by Father-General Beckx himself.'

Callaghan was puzzled. Researching an article for his father's newspaper on the influence of European religions on America's influx of immigrants, he'd read about the Church's Missionary Society. Or to give it its proper title, which Murray had so interestingly avoided, *Congretatio de Propaganda* – the Congregation of Propaganda. For a priest as young as Reikel to be personally recommended by the Jesuit Father-General, suggested he was being groomed for high office.

'Then why the demotion when he arrived in America?' Callaghan asked.

Father Murray gave a thin smile. 'When a Jesuit is given a position of authority, it lasts only for the duration of the appointment. There is no permanent standing within our Society. When a Jesuit priest's term of office comes to an end, even if it is by persecution, he loses all status attached to his old position. No matter how humble his new calling, he takes a vow of obedience to the one who appoints him. When

Father Reikel sought refuge at Saint Xavier, Father Hudson, after praying to the blessed Saint for guidance, made him a serving priest and Father Reikel took those vows.'

'What made him choose the United States?' Callaghan asked.

'Probably our Constitution,' Murray replied, a sudden note of pride in his voice. 'After Father Reikel's dire experiences in Italy and Germany, our American freedom of worship must have been particularly appealing.'

The Jesuit hesitated again, as though unsure whether to continue. 'Speaking personally,' he finally said, 'I'm of the opinion that Holy Church would be best served if the Holy See was moved from Rome to Washington. Europe is of the past; a Byzantium with no future other than a parallelism of the old Roman Empire. There is nothing but war, rumours of war, and revolutions ahead of it. America on the other hand, faces an exciting and challenging future. By the year two thousand, our population will be over one hundred million. It is inevitable that the seat of world power will one day be here, in the United States. This *must* be recognised both by the Church and the Holy Father. Rome's days are numbered. It is a provincial city slowly dying away in an out-of-the-way corner of a landlocked sea. If Mother Church is to continue its God-appointed task of world evangelisation, we should send request King Emmanuel to let the Holy Father leave Rome, and establish a new Vatican in Washington – *our* capital city.'

Callaghan concealed a smile. Victor Emmanuel would be only too glad to see *Pio Nono* leave. What's more, of all Catholic Orders, Jesuits were bound by a vow of obedience to their Father-General and to the Pope. Yet here was Murray betraying himself to be a true American at heart.

'Do other American Catholics take this view?' Callaghan asked.

'Almost all,' Murray replied.

'Would the Pope consider it?'

'No,' the Jesuit said emphatically. 'On this matter, the Holy Father's position is ultramontane. He sees Rome and only Rome as the chosen hub of Holy Church's authority, claiming its tradition and history as proof of its divine election, declaring he will remain in the Vatican until the See of Saint Peter has been fully restored to Mother Church.'

The cab was approaching the morgue, a gloomy-looking building behind Bellevue Hospital.

'Then the Pope must be right,' Callaghan said. 'Wasn't it only two years ago he said he was infallible?'

- 21-

Callaghan got down from the cab and waited for Murray to follow. A biting wind from the East River, the sight of its swirling grey waters flowing past at the end of the street, made him huddle into his overcoat. Winter wasn't far off.

The Jesuit priest descended from the cab, clutched up the hem of his cassock, and followed Callaghan into the morgue's lobby and through to the "Exhibition Hall".

Roughly twenty feet square, it was a depressing room, with a cold brick floor and damp mouldy walls, divided by a partition with a long window behind which were five marble slabs, tilted to display the bodies.

Today, there were four on view: three men and a young woman, all naked, apart from strips of oilcloth covering their genitals. To delay decomposition, they were being sprayed with cold water from hydrants suspended over each slab. Wall-hooks held their clothes and personal items. Bodies not identified in five days were taken to Hart's Island and dumped in a lime-pit; but clothing and effects were stored for six months to be compared against future "Missing Persons" reports, then they too were destroyed.

The rat eaten body from the East River was laid out on the fifth slab, covered up to the neck. Spray from a hydrant was bouncing off the tarpaulin, creating a misty curtain, but still allowing a clear view of the face and blond hair.

Father Murray took one look, crossed himself and knelt on the cold brick floor to pray.

Callaghan withdrew and went outside to wait.

It was five minutes before Murray appeared, his face deathly pale.

'Back to Saint Xavier's?' Callaghan asked.

The Jesuit shook his head. 'The Willett Street Mission. Father Reikel's helpers must be given the sad news.'

'Sure,' said Callaghan, his thoughts racing ahead with his own plans. First, Harry Hill's. Then the Astor. Kaufmann's office. And finally, *The New York Times*.

The cab rumbled down Bellevue, then along First Avenue, Murray staring out of the window. Suddenly, the Jesuit looked in. 'What kind of person could have committed these heinous crimes, Detective?' he confronted Callaghan. 'Mr Kaufmann? And now Father Reikel?'

'Reikel was killed before Kaufmann,' Callaghan pointed out. 'At a guess, a couple of days earlier. As to who killed them, I've an idea. But at the moment, it's just a theory.'

Murray shuddered. 'Only someone deranged could break someone's back in two.'

The cab halted outside a tumbledown, clapboard house. Placing his hand on the cab door handle, the Jesuit added. 'Whoever this killer is, I pray for Father Reikel's sake that you find him and make the punishment fit the crime. Just look at the result of his labour.'

Callaghan watched a long line of down-and-outs, male and female, slowly filing through the door of the house to claim their bowls of soup. A group of ragged children were shrieking with laughter over a game of baseball in the barely grassed front garden, using a broken piece of branch from a dead tree as a bat, and a ball made from bits of material tied together with string.

'It was in obedience to Our Lord's command, "Suffer little children to come unto me and forbid them not",' Father Murray said, 'that Father Reikel opened his heart to the neglected of East Side, showing them God's love in a practical way, providing them with food–'

'If God's so loving, Father,' Callaghan cut across him, 'He'd ensure they never went hungry in the first place.' He pulled a dollar from his pocket. 'Here, buy them some food from me.'

Ignoring the coin, the American priest opened the door. 'Your bitterness has become a self-erected barrier, Detective. While it remains, you will never know God. May He have mercy on your soul and bring you into His fellowship.' He made the sign of the Cross. 'I will remember you in my prayers.' The Jesuit descended from the cab and walked up the path exchanging brief words with the needy, and disappeared inside the house.

Callaghan re-pocketed the dollar. 'Harry Hill's,' he called up to the driver.

Callaghan climbed the wooden steps to the veranda of Harry Hill's two-storey, timber-framed dive. Paying his twenty-cents' admittance fee at the blue-lanterned door – the red-lamped was for women, who got in free – he entered the raucous, smoky atmosphere of the large bar.

With its rough counter stretching the length of the room, Harry's was second home to pimps, prostitutes, drug-dealers, pick-pockets, counterfeiters, every kind of New York criminal. Callaghan recognised many faces: "Dutch" Heinrich, "Sheeny" Mike, "Big Nose" Bunker, "Dublin" George, all well-known thieves. Among the prostitutes was "Gallus" Mag, armed as always with pistol and club, and Sadie "the Goat", and "Hell-Cat" Maggie, teeth filed to sharp fangs and pointed thimbles on her fingers to dissuade clients from trying to get away without paying.

Harry was standing behind the bar. Stocky, muscular, of indeterminable age with a squashed nose, he looked every inch the ex-prize-fighter he was. Callaghan pushed his way through the crush.

'Harry! A word?'

Pouring from a bottle into a glass, Harry looked up, his thick moustache almost concealing his answering grimace. Dropping the empty bottle to the sawdust floor, he sauntered over, wiping his hands on a grimy apron. Trading information for his tavern licence was a reluctant necessity for Harry and his manner was never too friendly.

'Hope it won't takes long, Callaghan. We's busy.'

'A couple of seconds, Harry. Tweed been in lately?'

'Nah,' Harry replied, dismissively. 'Ain't seen him for months.'

Dead-end number one, thought Callaghan. One thing about Harry, his information could be relied on, one hundred percent.

'That it?' Harry queried.

'That's it,' Callaghan confirmed.

Reaching under the counter, Harry brought out a glass and a bottle of whiskey. 'Your usual?'

'No thanks, Harry. The case I'm on needs a clear head.'

'Wonders will never cease,' said Harry.

Positioned between Barclay and Vesey, the Astor House was an impressive blue-granite, five-storied hotel with an imposing four-column entrance, and eighteen top-class shops occupying the ground floor.

Callaghan entered the crowded lobby and approached the front desk. The male clerk, a man in his mid-thirties, dark-suited, spectacles and receding hairline, greeted him politely.

'May I help you, sir?'

Callaghan showed his badge. The clerk's response was immediate, 'Follow me.' He hurried Callaghan into a windowless office behind the desk and shut the door.

'I'm enquiring about a Jacob Kaufmann,' Callaghan stated. 'He checked in here a week ago today, Thursday, November first. I'd like to see his baggage.'

'Mr Kaufmann checked out Monday evening, a day early,' the clerk replied. 'I was on duty at the time. There was a gentleman with him.'

'Can you describe the man?'

'He was about your age and height. Black suit, fair hair, almost white. And the most piercing blue eyes,' he added. 'Seemed to look right through you.'

Thanking the clerk, Callaghan made for the exit door, thinking that the details fitted Colleen's description of Father Reikel – except that the Jesuit priest had been killed days before Kaufmann. And positively identified by Father Murray.

- 22 -

Captain Briggs and First Mate Richardson stood on the bow of *The Mary Celeste*, facing into the Atlantic wind.

'Well?' Briggs asked. 'What do you think?'

'It's dropped some,' Richardson conceded. 'But not enough.'

Briggs agreed, albeit reluctantly. Morehouse's message was specific: Leave New York as instructed. And although Briggs was still unhappy about lying to Sarah that the letter was from Winchester, what else could he have done? Even more, from the urgent tone of David's words, the sooner they were out to sea, the better.

'What about this man Martens, Albert?' he queried, remembering another worry. 'Is he shaping up?'

'Some,' Richardson replied. 'I still don't think he's sailed before, but he's resilient enough. The problem is his not speaking English. There's also his attitude. I'm not keen on that, either.'

'You don't think we should replace him?' Briggs suggested. 'Being stuck here off Staten gives us the opportunity.'

'No,' Richardson dismissed the idea. 'A couple of days at sea with him and I'll soon sort him out.'

Kaufmann's office block was not what Callaghan expected. Unlike the bustle of most commercial blocks – three, four, sometimes five floors of offices of male clerks scratching away at account books – this was silent, the only noise being the muffled sound of traffic from outside.

The office was on the second floor, with just the name "J Kaufmann" in gold lettering on the door. It would take a day to get a search warrant, so he opened it with his picklock.

The room was carpeted dark green, with rosewood panelling and furnishings. The only window was draped with curtains matching the thick carpet. Hanging on the walls were three oil paintings in heavy gold frames, depicting hunting scenes: a fox hunt, a stag at bay, and a boar chase.

On the large desk near the window was a large, leather valise. It was unlocked. Callaghan opened it, revealing no more than crumpled shirts, two stained, starched collars, a night-gown, shaving tackle, discarded longjohns and vest, but it proved that after leaving the Astor, Kaufmann had called here first – and almost certainly with his killer, the man described by the hotel clerk.

Standing in the corner of the room was a large safe, Callaghan saw at a glance it would take more than his picklock to open it, and crossed to a large cupboard with a flimsier lock.

Its five shelves were divided alphabetically, each containing a number of files fastened with black ribbon. Callaghan searched the bottom shelf but neither the "S" or the "T" slots held any files for Sweeny or Tweed.

Returning to the desk, he opened its shallow top left drawer. It contained only stationery. The two drawers below were locked. He picked them open. In the first drawer was a cashbook, written up to Saturday, November 2, two days before Kaufmann was murdered. The deep bottom drawer held three ledgers: one indexed A-J, the next K-R, the third S-XYZ. Quickly flicking through them and the cash book, too, Callaghan found nothing in the names of Connolly, Hall, Sweeny or Tweed.

Moving to the deep right hand drawer, he picked it open and saw Kaufmann's diaries. Now these, he thought, could be more promising. There were five, with the current one on top, and last year's underneath it, and so on. Selecting the 1872 diary, he flicked straight to Monday 4th, the day Kaufmann was murdered. It was blank, but the facing page, Tuesday, 5th, had two elliptic entries, one with a crossed-out letter V, the other with the letters MC. Noting that the latter were his own initials, too, Callaghan flicked back through the pages.

Sunday, Saturday, Friday were also blank. But then on Thursday, October 31, both sets of initials were repeated, again with the V crossed out. There were two entries for Tuesday, October 29, this time with full names in copperplate handwriting: Harold Gould. Kenneth Maddocks.

Flicking back to January 1, Callaghan found at least one entry for every day but Sunday, all giving the full names of each client, and personal memoranda, such as "Wedding Anniversary", "Gerda's Birthday", interspersed among them. But there were no more entries with initials only.

Going back to the cupboard, Callaghan began checking through the files, starting with Gould and Maddocks. All seemed to be legitimate clients, but he found no files with a surname beginning V, and though there were four Cs and three Ms, none had the initials together.

Returning to the desk, he thumbed back through the 1871 diary's pages. December. November. Again, full names in sloping handwriting. October 31, nothing of interest. October 30, 29, 28, 27, 26, 25…and stopped on the 24th as he saw the initials: PBS.

Staring at them he felt almost triumphant. The proof he was looking for. Peter Barr Sweeny.

Even more, the date was significant. It was on the 24th when criminal proceedings were instigated against The Tweed Ring. It was also the day Sweeny skipped the country.

Quickly turning back the pages, Callaghan saw that PBS recurred on the last Friday of every previous month. There were no initials for Tweed, Hall or Connolly, but this wasn't surprising as Sweeny was the architect of The Ring's many schemes. Even more, Callaghan deliberated, with Sweeny being the only client that Kaufmann had entered as initials, it followed that the two most recent entries – V and MC – were also to do with The Ring.

Reopening the 1872 diary to Tuesday, November 5th, Callaghan again puzzled over the initials MC and the crossed out V, then turned to the next page: Wednesday, 6th.

The memo leapt up at him: "Wire PBS".

Callaghan smiled, hardly able to believe his luck. Sweeny was still involved, all the way from Europe. The day after Kaufmann's meeting with MC – MC on his own, being that V was deleted – the diamond merchant had planned to wire Sweeny…

Except he'd been murdered two days before, on the 4th.

Then maybe MC were the initials of the man who left the Astor Hotel that same evening with Kaufmann? Callaghan brooded. If so, he also had his description and gave him something to start from. As to the connection, maybe he – and V, too – were both agents used by Kaufmann to buy diamonds for The Ring. If so, then Tuesday's meeting might have been set up for MC to deliver another consignment?

Except, had Boss paid him to dispose *of Kaufmann instead?*

Continuing this line of thought, what if Brains – as seemed likely from the "wire PBS" memo – was also party to the decision? That would make him an accessory to murder.

He returned to the diary. If only he could find some hard evidence to place Tweed in the frame, maybe Boss would talk and implicate the conniving shyster?

Flicking through its pages, November 7, 8, 9, 10, 11, he turned to Tuesday, the 12[th,] and saw, in pencil, the initials: DG. The same pencilled initials were also entered for Friday, the 15th, then on Saturday was further proof of Sweeny's involvement: "Wire PBS", again written in pencil.

Pondering why these last entries were not in ink, Callaghan came to the conclusion that as Kaufmann did not seem the kind of man to do anything without reason, the ink entries must be for confirmed appointments and matters, and pencil for provisional, not yet agreed.

That being so, Callaghan promised himself, then should DG walk into this office on Tuesday – unaware of what had happened to Kaufmann – he'll find me waiting. Just ten minutes alone with him and he'll be babbling who MC is.

Ignoring the crossed-out Vs, he copied the initialled entries on to a sheet of paper:

Thursday, October 31, MC – ink

Tuesday, November 5, MC – ink

Wednesday, November 6, Telegraph PBS – ink

Tuesday, November 12, DG – pencil

Friday, November 15, DG – pencil

Saturday, November 16, Telegraph PBS – pencil

Folding the note and putting it in his pocket, he left the building and made for *The Times* on the corner of Park Row and Spruce Street – stopping first at a seaman's restaurant where, on a high from his success at Kaufmann's office, he savored a bowl of bouillabaisse.

As Callaghan approached Jennings' office, he could hear raised voices from the newsroom next door and the distant clanking of the presses. He could almost smell the print. Shrugging off a sharp pang of nostalgia, he knocked and entered.

Louis was writing, his desk and floor covered, as always, in scribbled papers and notes.

'Michael!' The Englishman rose, extending his hand. 'I was intending to call on you at your home tomorrow, you've saved me the journey. Delighted to see you, old chap. Have you found out anything more? With Tweed's trial in the offing, I'd like to present the District Attorney with as much ammo as I can muster.'

'Possibly, Louis, but first I'd like to study your files on The Ring?'

'But of course.' Jennings gestured to the only other chair. 'Brush off the papers and sit. What are you looking for?'

'Further proof that I could be on to something. If I can back up what I've found so far, it will not only ensure Boss's conviction, but Sweeny's as well.'

'You're beginning to intrigue me.' Jennings stroked his goatee. 'Care to expand?'

'I'd rather be certain first, Louis, if that's okay with you?' Callaghan replied, not wanting to raise Jenning's hopes until he'd followed Kaufmann's clues through. 'I'll put all my findings in a sealed envelope addressed to you and leave it with Sam Phelps, my attorney – Ben Phelps' brother, from the D.A's office. Should something happen to me, Sam's office is on Nassau.'

'It all sounds ominous, but right-ho, if that's the way you prefer it.' Jennings reached for his silver-knobbed walking stick and English bowler hat. 'Actually, I'm due at a meeting, so you may have the use of my desk. That's on condition…' he added, pausing at the door.

Callaghan grinned. 'The exclusive belongs to *The Times?*'

'Precisely,' Jennings said as he exited.

It took Callaghan a couple of hours to check The Ring's files, but nowhere in all the mass of papers did he find anyone with the initials V, MC, or DG.

Making a note of Sweeny's Montmartre postal address, he decided to call it a day.

- 23 -

'So,' Colleen said, 'we now know for a fact that Sweeny is still tangled up in it all.'

Tonight she was wearing a russet-brown frock with autumnal yellow lace, the shades of a New England fall, complementing her auburn hair and viridian green eyes. I'm going to find it difficult concentrating, Callaghan thought.

'Only in converting The Ring's spoils into diamonds,' he forced his mind back to what he was here for. 'But not enough to link him to the killings.'

'It's enough for me,' Colleen said. 'He and Tweed would have agreed a code for wiring messages to each other, but getting rid of Kaufmann was likely decided from the beginning, as soon as he'd completed his part of the transactions.'

'Kaufmann maybe,' Callaghan conceded. 'Sweeny would see his own mother rot in Hell if he thought he could gain from it. But not Reikel. The Catholic side of him would never sanction the killing of a priest. He also knows the confessional is sacrosanct, and that Reikel would never reveal what Kaufmann told him. Regarding his death, our suspect is Tweed, and Tweed alone.'

'You're probably right.' Colleen gave a sudden shudder. 'I know Father Reikel was no holier in God's eyes than any of us, but it makes my blood run cold to think of someone killing a priest.' She shivered again. 'It's obviously the same brute who committed both crimes. Do you still think it's the man who accompanied Kaufmann from the Astor?'

'Almost certainly. Being in ink, the final entry for MC on Tuesday, fifth November, suggests that Kaufmann thought it was to be the guy's last transaction. Except Tweed was one step ahead. MC had probably made that delivery the previous Thursday and it was now, "Thanks Jacob, but it's kaput time". Acting on Boss's instruction, MC met him at the Astor the evening of Monday the fourth, took him back to the office on the pretence of handing over the diamonds a day early–'

'But how did Kaufmann's body end up on South Street?'

'Forced him there at knife or gun point, then killed him, but before he could dump the body in the East River he was disturbed, and had to leave it in the alley–'

'Yet he still stripped his body first…' Colleen cut across him as a thought struck her. She brooded on it. 'It was an odd thing for him to do. What if it was to do with your first theory, to delay identification – not with Kaufmann himself, but rather because he was a *diamond* merchant?'

Callaghan sat up. 'You mean…'

'To buy time to get them out of New York?'

'Of course. It has nothing to do with Kaufmann as an individual. It's the stones.'

'And probably means smuggled out by–'

'Ship!' Callaghan delved into his pocket for the note he'd made from Kaufmann's diary. 'Miss Lowell,' he handed it to her, 'take a bow. MC are more likely a vessel's initials rather than the killer's–' He suddenly recalled the brig sailing down the East River the morning Kaufmann's body was found, and how he'd focused on the name on her prow: *Mary Celeste*. MC.

'In fact,' he continued, his excitement rising, 'I may have seen her making for Upper Bay the day of Kaufmann's murder. Her name's *Mary Celeste*. Her destination was in *The Times*. She's bound for Genoa.'

Colleen studied the note. 'And with Sweeny in Europe, that ties in with the "Telegraph PBS" memos. But what's the significance of the previous date, Thursday, the thirty-first?'

'Five days earlier? Probably the day she was loaded.'

'In which case,' Colleen looked up at him, her eyes all eager, 'DG's pencilled entries could mean that Kaufmann never got the chance to ink in the dates after they were confirmed. If so, she's not due to be loaded for another five days, Michael. That gives us plenty of time.'

'The Shipmasters Association, crack of dawn tomorrow,' Callaghan promised. 'They'll have her name and details on file.'

'What will you do if you find her?'

'Impound her and hope to find the diamonds. Then confront Tweed with the evidence and try to get him to confess and involve Sweeny, and also sign an affidavit clearing your father. But if he won't, Oakey will. Especially if I promise to exclude his name from my report on the two murders. Rather than have his neck stretched, he'll co-operate for sure.'

'Let's just pray it works out that way,' Colleen clutched his arm, then swiftly let go, a faint blush fusing her cheeks, and quickly looked back at his notes. 'I wonder why Kaufmann crossed out the V,' she queried, avoiding his eyes, 'especially as she was due to sail the same day as *The Mary Celeste*?'

'The Shipmasters will tell me,' said Callaghan, pretending he hadn't noticed her gesture, or her reaction. 'Unless *The Times* has something on her? Do you keep old editions?'

'For a week or so.' She was composed again. 'Father stopped reading it, but previous copies could still be in his study.'

Callaghan indicated to the communicating door. 'Would he mind?'

'Not at all. Besides, he's gone to see Mr Phelps, taking a file crammed with papers with him, promising to tell me what he's up to when he returns.'

'The start of his fight-back, perhaps?'

'Oh, I hope so.' She searched Callaghan's face for confirmation her fears were unfounded. 'I know I've been wanting him to show more fortitude, but with him knowing all he does about The Ring, and bound to be called as a witness when Tweed comes to trial...' her voice tailed off.

'Your father won't take any needless risks,' Callaghan reassured her as he made for the study.

'You're right, of course,' said Colleen, but still looking concerned. 'Forgive the mess,' she added as he entered the room, 'he's neglected it recently. Then yesterday, he went through it like a whirlwind, leaving it even worse.'

The study was in a shambles, files open and documents spread everywhere. In the corner was a pile of unopened *Times*. Callaghan returned to the drawing room with them, gave half to Colleen and dropped back into his chair. Turning to the "Marine Intelligence" pages, they started checking through the long list of vessels using New York port.

'It's certainly stormy out on the Atlantic,' Colleen remarked. 'Just listen to these arrivals: Steamship Minia, Cardiff, strong gales; Italian bark Magdalena, storm carried away foremast head and foretopmast with yards and sails.'

'Same here,' said Callaghan. 'Dutch steamship Rotterdam, strong westerly gales; brig George Latimer, strong gales, lost sails. I hope Briggs' wife and little daughter are okay.'

Colleen looked up. 'Wife and daughter?'

'The *Celeste's* captain's. I assume that's who they were. They were on deck. The mother was holding the child in her arms – a pretty little thing, no more than two – getting her to wave goodbye to New York, probably to distract her from heading out to sea.'

'Poor mite,' Colleen murmured, pausing a moment to imagine the child, then returned to her newspapers. Thumbing through them, she showed Callaghan a page from one of her editions.

'Here's the entry you saw with *The Mary Celeste's* destination as Genoa. And the name of her captain: Briggs. But there's nothing about any DG.'

'Nor here.' Callaghan discarded his copies. 'I'll check it out tomorrow. But Genoa, the *Mary Celeste's* destination, is puzzling me.'

'How?'

'Brains' still using the Montmartre address, which suggests he's somewhere in France rather than Italy. Why hasn't he chosen a French port? Brest?' Or Rochefort? Or Marseilles?'

'Maybe he's making doubly sure of covering his tracks,' Colleen suggested.

'I guess it's the only explanation. It also suggests another reason for Tweed wanting to have Kaufmann eliminated.'

She waited for him to expand.

'He's intending to skip New York before the trial and join up with Sweeny.'

'Yes,' an urgent note entered Colleen's voice, 'that makes sense. Then we must stop him. Tell Mulberry Street.'

'No way.' Callaghan replied. 'Tweed would know about it within the hour. I'll ask Louis to post a couple of his newsmen on him instead. I've promised him the exclusive.'

He looked at the mantelpiece clock. 'But talking about Mulberry Street, this is all getting bigger than just you and me. I'm going to have to tell someone what we've found out so far, and the only person I trust other than Louis is Commissioner Smith.' Callaghan stood up. 'He's usually at his desk until eight. I'll get back to headquarters and write it up, and entrust the file to him, just in case. With all that's going on, you never know what might happen next.'

Leghorn, Italy

Sweeny and Father Guilamo were sitting on the verandah connecting their lavish suite of rooms in The Victoria and Washington, the port's finest hotel. The setting sun was casting its last rays over the Porto Vecchio, highlighting the reds, blues, greens and yellows of fishing-boats tied up alongside the quays. Beyond its walls, boats with deeper draughts, ferries and ocean-going steam- ships lay at anchor in the Porto Nuovo, inside the protection of its semicircular mole.

The sky was clear, not a cloud in sight; the evening meal had been excellent, his cigar was superb and Brains was at peace with the world. Exhaling a cloud of smoke with a contented sigh, he commented. 'The stones will be well on their way now. What about your uncle's steam yacht?'

'The Santa Maria docked two hours ago,' Guilamo confirmed. 'We should arrive in Palermo around midnight, Tuesday. My uncle's coach will be waiting on the quayside, you will be in his Monreale villa by one in the morning. Monreale is also the seat of the Bishop,' the Jesuit priest added. 'Should you wish to attend church during your stay, you have only to say.'

Sweeny looked at the Sicilian with narrowed eyes. 'I thought you said Victor Emmanuel had closed all the churches?'

'On the mainland,' Guilamo gave a thin smile. 'In Sicily we organise things differently. As you yourself will discover, Signor Sweeny, when you arrive there.'

- 24 -

Returning downstairs from Commissioner Smith's room, Callaghan entered the Detective Room, crossed to his desk to pick up his overcoat, and heard Haggerty's familiar voice behind him.

'The First wants a tec!'

Now under Smith's personal order to concentrate only on Boss Tweed and the two murders, and report solely to him, Callaghan ignored the pimply youth.

'Who wants it?' Haggerty yelled, frustrated at being ignored by everyone in the room. 'Fatal stabbing. On Nassau.'

Callaghan felt his blood go cold. Please no, he prayed.

He turned around. 'I'll take it.'

The patrolman shone his lantern on Edward Lowell's body.

Callaghan looked down at Colleen's father sprawled face down in an alley. Maybe it was an illusion of the dim light, but in death his bulky frame looked half its size, blood clotting his topcoat from the knife wound in his back. The cut in the black cloth told that the blade had been thin. Inserted between Lowell's shoulder blades into his heart, death would have been instantaneous.

Detaching himself momentarily from the personal implication of the killing, and the fact he'd soon have to break the terrible news to Colleen, Callaghan summarised the facts as he saw them.

There were two suppositions as to how Lowell had come to be killed.

But only one motive.

That despite planning to skip New York, Tweed was leaving nothing to chance.

A systematic elimination of key witnesses before his trial.

First, Reikel – as Kaufmann's confessor.

Then Kaufmann himself.

And now Colleen's father.

As for the two suppositions, one was that the killing was premeditated. That Tweed had had Lowell's house watched. The first time he'd left it, he'd been followed. And silenced.

As for the other supposition…

'Cover his face,' Callaghan told the patrolman, then pushed through the inevitable crowd of curiosity seekers and back down the alley into Nassau and looked at the law office across the street.

The second supposition was that the killing was opportunistic. Callaghan read the name on the burnished brass plate outside the law firm's door. Nelson Waterbury. Grand Sachem of Tammany Hall before Tweed. The man chosen by Boss to be his defence attorney at his pending trial.

Unlike those of other firms lining Nassau Street, all with curious faces in their windows, Waterbury's office had none. As if Lowell's death, occurring so near, had no significance for them. But hours earlier maybe Lowell in life had? Hours earlier, maybe someone there had seen him go into Sam Phelps' office opposite, with a thick file under his arm. Recognising him, and knowing the threat he posed as a witness at Tweed's trial, maybe that same someone had let Boss know. Two hours would have been more than enough time for Tweed to arrange to have Lowell silenced. Maybe by the same killer who'd got rid of Kaufmann and Reikel? But this time, with no need to hide Lowell's identity, a swift knife thrust and a quick getaway had been decided upon.

But whichever supposition was the right one, how was he going to tell Colleen, Callaghan thought, his mind going to her waiting unknowing in Greenwich and realising how hard a blow her father's death would be to her, and how heartbroken she would be.

Seeing the black morgue wagon coming down the street, he entered Sam Phelps' office.

Colleen looked up at him, her eyes pleading to have misunderstood, then she sagged against him. Lifting her up in his arms, Callaghan carried her to a sofa near the fire and sat beside her holding her hand. Mute with shock, she stared into the flames, then she began to tremble.

Rising, he poured a brandy and returned to her side. 'Drink this.' She remained unmoving. He held the glass to her lips. Oblivious, she took a sip, and coughed as the spirit burnt her throat.

She turned to him, tears welling in her eyes and grabbed his arm. 'How did he die?' Her hold tightened. 'Did he suffer? Was it–' She was unable to finish her question, but Callaghan realised what she was asking.

'No, it wasn't the same as Reikel and Kaufmann. He was…he was stabbed in the back. It would have been instantaneous.'

Colleen absorbed this for but a moment, then her grief suddenly erupted, as if his words had broken through the barrier of her shock. He held her tight as her sobs racked her body and her slim shoulders shuddered in his arms. Then he felt her body stiffen. She pulled away and looked up at him. Her face was pale and drawn and wet with tears.

'Did Father get to Mr Phelps? Or was he killed before reaching there?'

'No, he got there. He was fighting back, as you thought, and volunteered to be a prosecution witness at Tweed's trial, and given Sam a dossier of evidence for his brother Ben to add to his case.'

He didn't say that the papers, though helpful, were not of real import. Better for her to know, despite having to live with its outcome, that her father had finally decided to make a stand.

'Then I will try to take comfort from knowing that when it mattered, he did what was right.'

She went silent, then, 'Was it the same killer, do you think?'

'The method was different but the attack again came from behind. Except that early evening in Nassau would have been a greater risk than South Street after dark. And with no reason to remove any identifying clothing, whoever it was would have wanted to get away as fast as he could.'

Colleen suddenly flared. 'It wasn't just Tweed who ordered this. It was Sweeny, too. Going back to when he first involved Father in his evil schemes.'

'I know just how you feel,' Callaghan said, remembering the day his father died in his arms.

She placed her hand on his arm. 'And I now understand why you reacted as you did. It's Sweeny. He destroys everyone he comes near...' tears welled in her eyes. She fought them away, composed herself, and continued. 'Michael, I'm sensible enough to know that unless the real killer is caught, Tweed will never stand trial for Father's death, but as for Sweeny, let's make a vow.' Though her eyes were still moist, her grip on his arm tightened. 'That we won't rest until we've found him. And not only found him, but proven he was involved in the deaths of both Father Reikel and Kaufmann. *Yes,*' she insisted as Callaghan looked to protest, 'Father Reikel, too. If he stands to profit by it, Sweeny is evil enough to order the killing of a priest. We must find the evidence to get him extradited. And if they hang him, he deserves it. Not just for their murders but by his involvement, my father's too.'

Her hold was now so tight, it was hurting. 'Promise me, Michael.'

'I promise.'

Removing her hand, Colleen stared long into the fire, then looked at him with forlorn entreaty.

'Michael?'

'Yes?'

'Stay with me tonight?'

'Of course. I'll make up a bed on the settee.'

'No, with me. I need to feel your arms around me, holding me tight.'

- 25 -

Briggs entered the cabin as Sarah was the tucking the bed blankets around Sophia. He waited as Sarah stroked the little girl's head, crooning softly to soothe her back to sleep. Moments passed before she turned to him. 'She's been restless,' she whispered. 'She woke up asking for Arthur and Grandma Briggs and Grandma Cobb.'

'It's understandable, cooped up in this cabin,' Briggs said in a low voice. 'She'll be better when we get under way.'

'But when, Benj? Poor baby, maybe we should have left her at home with my mother. Arthur could have called in and played with her after school. This wait is frustrating, even for me.'

'Hopefully daybreak. The wind is beginning to lessen.' Briggs began undressing for bed.

'In that case,' Sarah said, somewhat cheered, 'I'll write a parting letter to Mother Briggs, and give it to the Sandy Hook pilot for posting.' She crossed to the writing bureau, sat down, picked up a lead pencil and, by the light of the cabin's overhanging oil lamp, began to write:

Brig Mary Celeste
Off Staten Island
Nov 7th, 1872

Dear Mother Briggs,

Probably you will be surprised to receive a letter with this date, but instead of proceeding out to sea when we came out on Tuesday morning, we anchored about a mile or so from the city as it was a strong headwind and B said it looked so thick and nasty ahead we shouldn't gain much if we were beating and banging about.

She paused, thinking ahead to the dawn, hoping Benjamin was right:

Accordingly we took fresh departure this morning with wind light and favourable, so we hope to get outside without being obliged to anchor once more.

Again she paused. Benjamin's brother, Oliver, who was also captain of a brig, had been due to arrive back in New York before they sailed, and Mother Briggs had told Benj to make every effort to see him. Better say something about him:

Have kept a sharp lookout for Oliver, but so far have seen nothing of him. It was rather trying to lie in sight of the city for so long and think that most likely we had letters waiting for us there, and be unable to get them. However, we hope no great change has occurred since we did hear and shall look for a goodly supply when we reach Genoa.

Sophia thinks the figure 3 and the letter G on her blocks is the same thing, so I saw her whispering to herself yesterday with the 3 block in her hand – Gam-gam-gamma.

Wondering what next to say, she realised Mother Briggs would be concerned to hear about the new crew:

Benj thinks we have a pretty peaceable set this time all around if they continue as they have begun. Can't tell yet how smart they are.

Sarah suspended her pencil, thinking how to conclude the letter.

In the galley, Edward Head entered his thoughts for the day in his diary:

Thursday, 7 November 1 am. At last it seems the waiting is over. The First Mate reckons the wind is dropping and come morning we should be on our way. By this time tomorrow I shall have taken leave of you, my dearest Emma. I trust the voyage will be uneventful, and that before March is out I will be holding you in my arms again.

If the German crew is anything to go by this is assured. They seem a capable lot, with the possible exception of Martens, that is. I heard First Mate Richardson tell Second Mate Gilling he doubts that Martens has been to sea before, as he seems to know little about sailing

*terms, but I think the First Mate might be judging him too hasty,
being that Martens can only speak German.*

The Church of Saint Francis Xavier

In the reflected light from the candles lighting up the body of the
church, Father Murray entered the confessional, closed the curtain,
knelt down, crossed his breast and addressed the meshed grille.

'Pray, Father, bless me, for I have sinned.'

There came the answering blessing: 'The Lord be in thy heart and on
thy lips, that thou mayest truly and humbly confess thy sins, in the
Name of The Father, and of The Son, and of The Holy Ghost.'

Dutifully reciting the first part of the Confiteor, Murray proceeded
to make his confession.

'I have made a false statement, Father. My dilemma was that it was
in obedience to a supreme order from our Father-General. I also told
an untruth when I said I was not of the Holy Father's persuasion that
Rome, and only Rome, is the holy city chosen of God.'

- 26 -

Friday, November 8, 1872

Callaghan's cab entered Wall Street some hours later than "the crack of dawn" he'd yesterday promised Colleen, remembering how – with the drawing-room fire built up to last the night – she'd clung to him for comfort on the sofa, until eventually falling asleep in his arms. And on awaking early this morning, she still wanted his strength to support her until "Aunt Siobhan", her mother's sister, arrived to help her through the long day ahead of her, and arranging her father's funeral. And as he left the house, 'Be back as soon as you can, please, Michael?' she aked him.

Though the circumstances were so distressing, he brooded, they seemed to be bringing them closer together. Maybe there was hope for them yet?

The cab stopped outside 47 Wall Street. Callaghan entered the building and climbed the stairs. Occupying the floor above the offices of the Atlantic Mutual Insurance, the American Shipmasters Association was formed twelve years ago by John Divine Jones, the Atlantic Mutual's President, to collate information on ships sailing in and out of American ports, especially New York.

He approached the counter. A middle-aged clerk looked up at him over horn-rimmed glasses. 'Can I help you?' he asked in a clipped voice.

Callaghan showed the man his badge. 'Callaghan, Detective Squad. I'm after the names of three vessels? It's to do with a murder investigation. I have their initials. They've recently left, or about to leave, New York, bound for Europe.'

'Pleased to assist the police,' the clerk replied. Taking Callaghan's notations he disappeared into the next room, returning shortly with three files and opened the top folder. 'Your V stands for *Venango*. She was a brigantine—'

'Was?' Callaghan cut in, making notes.

'Owned by the Venango Oil Works, Weehawken. She was destroyed by fire—'

'When?'

'October twenty-seventh.' The man quickly calculated. 'A Sunday. Thirteen days ago.'

'Accidental?'

The clerk referred to a document. 'It's in dispute. The company's claiming smouldering pipe tobacco as the cause. But the insurers aren't satisfied and their investigators are looking into it.'

'Where was she bound?'

'Originally for Marseilles, France, but her orders were changed to Palermo, Sicily, calling into Gibraltar first.'

'Why call into Gibraltar if she was bound for Palermo?'

'A precaution. Orders often get changed, and when they do, the New York agents wire new instructions to agents in Gibraltar, who pass them on to the captains. Most vessels call in there to check, before continuing on.'

'Is there any mention of Genoa, Italy, on her file?'

The clerk checked. 'No.'

'What was her cargo?'

'One thousand, seven hundred and thirty-five barrels of petroleum,' he looked up at Callaghan, 'which has since been awarded to the brigantine *Dei Gratia* – your second initials.'

Putting the *Venango*'s folder to one side, the man opened the next one.

'The *Gratia* is a British registered brig, jointly owned by Messrs Heney and Parker, Shipping Agents, 25 Coenties Slip, South Street, and her captain David Morehouse, from Sandy Cove, Bear Island, Nova Scotia. She was originally moored at Erie Basin, preparing to sail for Curaçao, but the owners relinquished the run and two days ago sailed her down to the Venango Yard to be loaded. I guess her new contract is more profitable,' he peered owlishly at Callaghan through his spectacles and returned to the folder. 'Her ship's brokers are Funch Edye, of Beaver Street, but no crew details have yet been registered.'

Callaghan halted him from closing the file. 'The cargo's destination? Has it been changed from Palermo to Genoa?'

'There's no mention of either Palermo or Genoa here. The information we have is that the *Dei Gratia* is instructed to sail only to Gibraltar and await further orders there.'

'Are you sure?' Callaghan queried. 'Carrying a specific cargo?'

The bespectacled clerk held out a document for Callaghan to read. 'That proof enough.'

'Fine.'

The man replaced the document, put the *Dei Gratia's* file aside and opened the third file.

'MC stands for *Mary Celeste*, a brig registered in a joint venture by four men. James Henry Winchester, Shipping Agent, 52 South Street, has a half interest. Her captain, Benjamin Spooner Briggs, Marion, Massachusetts, has a third. Daniel Simpson and Sylvester Goodwin, of the same address as Winchester – presumably his partners – have a twelfth share each. The vessel left Pier Fifty on the East River on Tuesday, carrying one thousand, seven hundred barrels of alcohol, shipped by the New York branch of Meissner Ackermann, Hamburg, Germany.' The clerk looked up again. 'In this case, the *Celeste's* port of destination is Genoa.'

'Is she instructed to call into Gibraltar first, same as the *Dei Gratia*?' Callaghan asked.

The clerk checked the papers. 'Not any more. Originally bound for Marseilles, she was to call into Gibraltar first, the same as the *Venango*. But her orders were then changed to Palermo and have yet again been changed. Very unusual,' the man said. 'She's now bound for–'

'Genoa,' Callaghan brooded, 'but no longer stopping at Gibraltar…'

'Not necessarily,' the clerk cut into his thoughts, 'her captain could be under oral orders to call there. It's not always written in black and white. However,' he stressed, 'after unloading in Genoa, she *is still* bound for Palermo…' he referred to a document, 'to pick up a return cargo of fruit for New York. From a Sicilian firm named Cottone.'

Callaghan added all this to his notes.

'Would you like the *Celeste's* complement?' the man asked, now clearly taken to his role in the investigation.

'Fire away.'

'There's the captain's wife, Sarah, a two year old daughter, Sophia, and a crew of seven.' The clerk read out the crew's details, names, ages, brief physical descriptions of the two mates and four-man crew and cook. As Callaghan listed the names he saw a new factor had entered the case: A German one. Kaufmann, Reikel, Meissner Ackerman, Funch of Funch Edye sounded German, and now the four seamen: Volkert and Boz Lorenzen, Gotlieb Goodschaad and Arian Martens.

'An all German crew?' he queried. 'Isn't that unusual for an American ship?'

'Yes, it is strange,' the clerk agreed. 'But if you want a closer look, the *Celeste's* still anchored in the Bay, off Staten Island. The storms raging out in the Atlantic prevented her from sailing.'

As the Staten Island ferry tied up in New Brighton harbour, Callaghan saw a tall, scrawny postman waiting on the dock, a half-empty sack over his shoulder.

'Not much mail today, captain,' he called up as the gangplank was lowered. 'Just one from the pilot boat. Some crazy coot of a brig sailed out early this morning, without waiting for the wind to drop.' Callaghan waited for him to come on board and flashed his police badge at him. 'What was the brig's name?'

'How in tarnation should I know?' the mailman replied, truculently.

Callaghan grabbed the sack.

'Hey! No one interferes with the US mail. Not even the police. Not without a warrant.'

'Can you swim?' Callaghan asked.

'What kind of question is that?'

'You'll find out in ten seconds if you don't let go the sack.'

Seeing the look in Callaghan's eye, the mailman slipped the bag-strap off his shoulder.

Among the letters was one written in a delicate female hand, addressed to:

Mrs Sophia Briggs,
Rose Cottage,
Sippican,
Marion, Massachusetts

Callaghan hesitated, uncertain what to do. It was clearly personal, from Sarah Briggs to a relative-in-law. But what if it held a clue? Undecided whether he should open it, he placed it in his pocket. 'I'll make sure it gets posted,' he said, returning the sack.

The mailman didn't argue, but hurried away.

Crossing the deck to the opposite rail, Callaghan stared at the angry, grey horizon.

So, *The Mary Celeste* had sailed.

That just left the *Dei Gratia*.

- 27 -

The name painted on the tall, wooden double-gates read: VENANGO OIL WORKS. Ignoring the NO TRESPASSING sign below it, Callaghan pushed one of the gates slightly open and squeezed through the tight gap. A long wooden storeshed stretched toward the Hudson River. New York's ever growing skyline was emblazoned along its opposite bank.

His eyes followed a wagon-rutted track extending alongside the shed, strewn with empty casks and rusting iron. From the rear of the shed, a plankway built on poles extended over wasteland to the water's edge, where it branched into two wooden jetties reaching out into the river. The nearest pier had been reduced to burnt pilings and hanging black timbers. Alongside it, the scorched roof of a vessel's deckhouse showed above the Hudson's surface. Tied to the next pier was a brig with sails furled, moving up and down on the flow of the river.

Callaghan headed up the track. A shed window opened. 'Looking for someone?' a voice called out.

'Captain Morehouse, *Dei Gratia*,' Callaghan replied easily. The window closed.

Callaghan ploughed on, mud sticking to his shoes. Sounds of activity came from inside the shed, but on this bitter grey day no one was venturing out. Reaching the end of the storeshed, he headed down the gangway to the jetty, his footsteps echoing hollow on the planks, and to the brig. Painted in gold letters on her bow was: *Dei Gratia*.

He climbed on to her deck, crossed to the deckhouse and rapped on the closed hatchway.

'Anyone on board?'

A moment passed before the hatch opened, revealing the bearded face of a man in his middle thirties, with a sailor's weather-tanned complexion and piercing blue eyes.

'Captain Morehouse?' Callaghan queried.

'That's me,' the man replied, in a deep Nova Scotia drawl.

Callaghan showed his badge. 'Callaghan. New York Police. Detective Squad.'

'What do you want?' Morehouse grated, immediately aggressive.

'I'd prefer talking inside.'

Morehouse hesitated and turned away down the companionway. Ducking his head, Callaghan followed him and across the saloon into the captain's cabin.

It was about fourteen feet by ten in size, a separate WC in the corner creating a recess for a double bed. A writing bureau and armchair stood in a corner, a faded rug on the planked floor. Two paintings of brigantines in full sail hung on a wall.

Morehouse crossed to the bureau, flipped over what appeared to be a half written letter and turned to face Callaghan. 'And what can I do for you, Detective?' he asked a shade too briskly.

Detecting Morehouse's tenseness, Callaghan affected an authorative approach. 'It's about a brig, *Mary Celeste*,' he stated, watching the captain's face. There was now no doubting his tension. Dropping into his chair and clenching its arms, he clearly forcing himself to hold Callaghan's gaze as the latter continued. 'Her captain, Benjamin Briggs, left Pier Fifty, East River, before we could search her, headed for Genoa. We suspect she's carrying contraband. We've informed the Genoa police, and if we're proved right, he'll be brought back to New York and charged. We also have reason to believe you are involved, Captain,' Callaghan pressed on. 'I'm instructed to attend your loading and check your cargo. Should contraband be found you will be charged, along with Briggs.'

Morehouse blanched, but still didn't speak.

'There's also the question,' Callaghan piled it on, 'of Briggs and yourself being implicated in the murders of—'

'Murder!' Morehouse half-rose to his feet, only to collapse back into the chair. 'Murder!' he repeated, in shocked disbelief. 'I'm not involved in any murder!'

Callaghan produced morgue photographs of Kaufmann and Reikel, and tossed them on to Morehouse's lap. 'Two of the victims, Captain. There's since been a third.'

Morehouse stared at the two bodies lying naked on the tilted slabs and glared up at Callaghan. 'What the hell's going on? You can't involve me in the deaths of two men I've never—'

'Who discovered what you and Briggs are up to,' Callaghan pressurised. 'Both viciously and cold-bloodedly murdered to ensure their silence. Makes no difference which of you did it, you're equally guilty under the law and the DA will demand the death sentence. All we need to prove our case is the contraband. And a tip-off from a reliable source leads us to believe it's hidden in both your cargoes.'

Morehouse half-opened his mouth to protest, but Callaghan wasn't finished.

'My captain's convinced of your guilt, yours and Briggs...' He deliberately mellowed his tone. 'Personally, I don't think either of you has anything to do with their killings.' He paused to let this sink in. 'So if you want me to help you, your best chance is to tell me all you know.'

Morehouse buried his face in his hands. A long silence ensued before he looked up, despairing. 'Yes! Okay! I'll tell you.' His voice tailed off. Callaghan waited.

'On one condition.'

'Name it.'

'Your promise that my wife and children will be protected?'

'Protected?' This was unexpected. Yet, from the run of things, maybe it wasn't. 'From who?' Callaghan demanded, realising it had to be from Tweed.

'Is it agreed?' Morehouse persisted.

'You've my word on it.' Going along with the man, Callaghan sat on the bed and took out his notebook 'Your wife's name? I have her address from the Shipmasters.'

'Desiah. She was to have sailed with me,' Morehouse rushed his words, 'then this nightmare began. I was writing to her,' he indicated to the bureau, 'telling her to take the children to visit her cousin in British Columbia while I'm gone, hoping they'll be safe there.' He looked up, pleading, at Callaghan. 'But maybe there's no need, not now you've promised to—'

'I'll wire the Canadian Police as soon as I get back to headquarters,' Callaghan promised. 'But what sort of threat? And from who?'

Morehouse drew a deep breath. 'Okay, okay, I'll tell you. Right from when it all started.'

'Fire away,' Callaghan said, pencil suspended over his notebook.

Morehouse took a moment to gather his thoughts then continued, clearly relieved to unload it all on to Callaghan.

'You're right in assuming Ben and I know one another. We often sail the same routes and meet in various ports. Over the years we've become good friends, and so…' he drew another breath, '…when we found we were both in New York – Ben at Hunter's Point where the *Celeste* was undergoing a refit, me at Erie Basin getting ready to load for Curaçao – we arranged to meet for a meal at the Astor House.'

Morehouse calculated back. 'That was Monday, October twenty-eighth. Ben told me he was bound for Genoa and then Palermo, to pick up a return cargo for New York. The *Celeste* was moving down to Pier Fifty in two days to start loading, and Sarah – Ben's wife – and little Sophia, were joining him. When I told him how lucky he was –

sailing to Genoa rather than Curaçao like me, where there's nothing to do – Ben said if I could get out of my contract he might be able to help me.' He buried his face in his hands again. 'Some help it's turned out to be!'

Callaghan waited for him to gather himself.

Morehouse looked up. 'Only that morning he heard Winchester, his agent, talk to his clerk about finding a replacement for the Venango. That's her,' he indicated through his cabin window, 'burnt to a crisp. It seemed that her cargo, originally bound for Marseilles, had been reordered to Genoa, and there was some urgency–'

'Genoa?' Callaghan interrupted. 'You're sure about that? I was told there's no mention of Genoa on her file, only that she was to sail to Gibraltar and wait there for further orders?'

'That's what Ben heard them say,' Morehouse insisted. 'But you're right about Gib. I'm *also* ordered to sail there to await instructions. But if Ben heard them right and the cargo is destined for Genoa, I don't see the purpose of it.'

'What about Briggs? Is he also calling into Gibraltar?'

'He made no mention of it. But funnily enough, he did hear them say that, after Genoa, the Venango's replacement vessel – that's me, now – is also to sail to Palermo, just like the *Celeste*, to pick up a return cargo of fruit from the same company, called Cottone. Ben remembered the name because it sounded like cotton.'

Quickly churning this information over in his head, Callaghan decided that Genoa was both vessels' real destination – he'd puzzle later over why Morehouse was being ordered to first call at Gibraltar for confirmation of his orders – and Palermo was nothing more than to provide both vessels with cargoes back to New York, and so add authenticity to their voyages. It was the only explanation to make any sense. He returned his attention to Morehouse.

'Getting back to what Briggs overheard,' he prompted.

Morehouse was only too anxious to continue.

'Like I said, Winchester was wanting another brig to take-over the Venango's cargo, so Ben suggested to me I should apply, and after meeting up in Genoa we could both sail side by side to Palermo then back home. I mentioned it next day to my partners, Heney and Parker, and being that the Curaçao run was not the most profitable, they agreed, and I left them to arrange it. Two days later, I got my orders to sail the *Gratia* down to Weehawken for loading, and here I am.'

He took another deep breath. 'I wrote to Desiah telling her the good news, then sent Ben a note inviting him and Sarah to join me in another meal at the Astor House – on Monday last, that being their final evening in New York.'

Morehouse drummed his fingers on the chair arm, getting more uptight. 'Anyway, when I got there Ben said Sarah couldn't come, Sophia wasn't well, but he seemed jumpy and I guessed that was not the real reason.'

He raked his hands through his hair. 'Sure enough, soon as we'd ordered, he asked my advice over an incident that occurred on the first day of loading the *Celeste*. In fact, two things happened. First, Winchester went out of his way to tell one of the German crew to take more care of a barrel he was handling. It was the first barrel loaded, and though there's nothing peculiar in that, it was Winchester repeating the instruction that Ben later remembered. There was also a stranger with him, a rich looking man, German accent, name of...' Morehouse frowned, trying to remember.

'Jacob Kaufmann,' said Callaghan.

'Kaufmann! That was it!' Morehouse narrowed his eyes. 'But how did you–'

'That's him,' Callaghan indicated the morgue photographs, 'the fat one lying dead on a slab. The other's a Jesuit priest. For you to know what you're mixed up in.'

'Mixed up in! I've told you, I'm not mixed up in anything. I don't have a damn clue what's going on. Not a sodding clue.'

'To be honest, captain, I'm a little confused myself. So, let's get back to your story.'

'What! With you accusing me of…No, more than that, you've already decided I'm guilty!'

'Let's leave that for the moment. You said Winchester repeated his instruction?'

'That's all very well for you!' Morehouse checked his outburst. 'Okay, okay,' he gritted, regathered his thoughts and continued. 'Ben said it was as if Winchester was drawing the seaman's attention to that particular barrel. At first he dismissed it, but when loading was completed and the count was seventeen hundred and one, one more than on the Bill of Lading–'

'You're sure of that?' Callaghan cut across him. 'The *Celeste's* carrying an extra barrel?'

'Not just the *Celeste*.' Morehouse blurted. 'I'm getting an extra barrel as well.'

Callaghan looked sharply at him. 'How do you know that?'

'It'd be easier to explain if you didn't keep interrupting.'

'My apologies,' said Callaghan sarcastically. 'Carry on.'

'I will,' the Nova Scotian growled. 'In my own words. And in my own time.'

Clearing his throat, he continued. 'Ben went straight to Winchester and confronted him about the barrel. Winchester said it was human error by the shippers. Ben told him he wasn't satisfied. Winchester replied he was making a fuss over nothing. So, Ben had no choice but to leave – but in a quandary as to what he should do.'

'And it was on this that Briggs sought your advice?'

'Yes. Ben was minded to report it to the port authorities, but I eventually convinced him it wasn't uncommon for such a mistake to be made. If he told Customs his suspicions, they might open every barrel and his entire cargo would be ruined. Could he afford such a risk, I asked him, especially if he was wrong? As a new partner in the *Celeste*, his over-riding interest surely lay in getting the cargo to Genoa on time…'

Morehouse shook his head, obviously ruing his words.

'To which he agreed?' Callaghan prompted.

'Only partially. Ben's a stubborn man. He eventually agreed to sail, but as soon as he reaches Genoa and gets the Bill of Lading signed for him to be paid, he's going to report it to Customs there and leave it to them to take whatever action they decide. Then, after we meet up in Genoa, we'll sail to Palermo together – unless,' Morehouse added in a grim voice, 'when I reach Genoa, I find he's deep in it with the authorities there over the contents of the barrel'

Morehouse paused. 'But now comes the weird part,' he said, rubbing his throat like it was paining him. 'As I was making my way back to the Hoboken ferry, I was waylaid–'

'Waylaid?' Callghan interjected.

'Yes, *waylaid*. I didn't see the man's face – only that he spoke with a foreign accent–'

'Accent? What kind of accent?'

'I'm not sure. If I had to guess…German.'

Callaghan's mind swirled. The German factor again. What the hell did it all mean?

'He came up behind me and put a knife to my throat–'

'*Knife?*' Callaghan shot the question at him. 'What kind of knife?'

'Impossible to tell in the dark.'

'The blade then?'

'If I had to guess, long, thin. And blasted sharp.' Morehouse rubbed his neck again, as if he could feel the knifepoint.

The same as used on Lowell, Callaghan brooded. If it was the same man who'd also disposed of Kaufmann and Reikel, then Tweed had found himself a most ruthless killer.

Morehouse cut across his thoughts.

'He forced me to tell him everything Ben had said. I told him most of it, but left out that Ben is going to tell the Genoese authorities. I was certain he was going to kill me–' Morehouse looked with horror at the morgue photographs. 'Was it the same man did this?'

'Odds on.'

'Hell's bells! You mean if I hadn't said I was the *Gratia*'s *captain,* I would have joined those poor bastards?'

'More than likely. But as you didn't, what happened next?'

'You're an unfeeling sonofabitch,' Morehouse glowered. 'I'd like to have you as one of my crew. Work the spleen out of you.'

'I'm an old hand, Captain,' said Callaghan. 'So again, what happened next?'

Still glowering, Morehouse resumed. 'After warning me that if I told anyone about Ben's suspicions about the extra barrel, or the one coming on board the *Gratia*–'

'You're certain of that?' Callaghan cut in. 'About you also getting an extra barrel?'

'Though I'd a knife to my throat, I've got good ears,' Morehouse snapped back. 'But getting back to his warning, he said if I blabbed, Desiah and my kids would be killed. Then he disappeared down some dark alley, leaving me there paralysed, wondering what the hell to do. Ben was right. Something was going on. And it was obviously big. My first thought was for Desiah and the children. Then I realised the biggest threat was Ben himself. He was sailing early next morning, determined to tell the Genoa port authorities about his extra barrel. Somehow I had to stop him, but couldn't go to him myself in case I was being watched, so I skedaddled back here, wrote him a note, and got young Willard, my steward, to deliver it, telling Ben I had information about his extra barrel which, for his sake, and the lives of Desiah, and Ned's and Harriet's – and maybe Sarah's and Sophia's, too – we had to discuss before he reached Genoa. But,' he stressed,' ignoring Callaghan's attempt to cut in again, 'I warned him all their lives would be forfeit if he failed to sail, and begged him to make slow passage for the *Gratia* to catch the *Celeste* up and rendezvous with me at a point six hundred miles off the coast of Spain, for me to–'

'Is that possible?' Callaghan now intruded. 'For two small brigs to meet at an agreed point in the middle of an ocean?'

'Sure,' Morehouse grated. 'The only problem's these gales we're having. If they continue, I told him to sail on to Gib and wait for me there instead.'

'Will he?'

'He'd better,' Morehouse threatened.

'What do you intend doing when you meet him?'

'Tell him everything that's happened, then for us to sail together to Genoa, unload our cargoes as instructed, then head for Palermo and back home to New York as fast as the wind will carry us. It's our only choice.'

'Do you think he'll agree?'

'Like I said, he'd better. Else I'll have no wife or kids.'

Callaghan glanced down at the notes he'd made at the Shipmasters. 'Can I use your desk?'

'Help yourself. There's some checks I need to make down in the hold.'

Already writing at the desk, Callaghan hardly noticed him go.

	Mary Celeste	Venango Dei Gratia
Original destination	Marseilles	Marseilles
First alteration	Palermo	Palermo

Calling at Gibraltar	Yes	Yes
Second alteration	Genoa	Genoa (overheard)
Extra barrel	Yes	Yes
Also bound for Palermo	Yes	Yes (overheard)
Calling at Gibraltar	?	Yes (for orders)

So, where do I go from here? Callaghan pondered, studying the data. Once the brigs reached Genoa, their extra barrels would be diverted from the cargoes during unloading, and taken to wherever Sweeny had arranged.

Sweeny. Not Tweed.

Being in Europe, it was Brains who was coming more and more into the reckoning. Here in New York, while Boss was seemingly involved in the three murders – and now the threat to Desiah Morehouse and children – far across the Atlantic in Genoa, Sweeny would be arranging the sale of the diamonds – piecemeal, at a guess, to avoid flooding the market and lowering their price.

Which meant that everything here in New York had come to a dead end. Despite his German accent and distinctive fair hair, the odds of catching Boss's hired killer amongst the countless criminals on East Side, were little more than zero.

As for the *Gratia*'s cargo, even if it was searched here and the diamonds found, everyone in New York connected with the brig was certain to plead ignorance. Certainly there was no hope of Tweed confessing, not without any hard evidence against him.

Which meant that the spotlight had now switched across the ocean to Genoa.

And on to Sweeny.

Morehouse re-entered the cabin.

'Loading starts Tuesday?' Callaghan questioned.

'Daybreak.'

'Then you've got your wish, Captain. I'm sailing with you as one of your crew.'

- 28 -

'Is there no other way?' Colleen looked at Callaghan with concern. Wearing grey mourning, she was sitting near the roaring fire for warmth, her face pale but outwardly composed, despite the grief she must be feeling inside.

'No,' he replied. 'It's not just because Sweeny's in Genoa, but even if diamonds were found on the *Dei Gratia*, there's nothing more I can do here. The little evidence we have – the Saint Xavier's connection, and the "wire PBS" memos in Kaufmann's diary – it's all circumstantial. To prove Sweeny's guilt I have to catch him red-handed–'

'And have him brought back to face a judge and jury,' she cut across him, a catch in her voice. 'Although he was thousands of miles away, he's as culpable for Father's death as Tweed.'

'Sure he is.' He gave her a moment to recover. 'I asked Morehouse where *The Mary Celeste's* Pier Fifty was. It's under the new Brooklyn Bridge, next to where Reikel's body was found.'

'That suggests he was on his way there to see Briggs.' Colleen said. 'But he clearly didn't get there, or Briggs would have told Morehouse?'

'That's my conclusion, too,' Callaghan agreed.

Colleen pondered this. 'So what did Father Reikel want with Briggs?'

'Guessing, to let him know about the diamonds hidden in his cargo. Kaufmann must have told told Reikel about them – when he turned to him for guidance,' he quickly stressed, seeing Colleen look askance at him, 'not during confessional. Still guessing, Reikel first persuaded

146

Kaufmann to go to the police, then went to Pier Fifty to induce Briggs to do the same and support Kaufmann's testimony. Briggs would have had all to gain by doing so. Ten percent of a hundred million dollars as reward would have set him up for life. Except, Boss's killer got to Reikel first.'

Accepting his theory, Colleen gazed into the fire. A silence descended on the room. She broke it, still looking at the flames. 'Father Hudson is conducting the funeral service, but he then has a meeting he can't break and Father Flynn will attend the burial.' She looked up. 'Kaufmann was buried today, but should you be interested, Father Murray is performing the rites for Father Reikel.'

Callaghan just nodded.

She straightened up. 'Let's change the subject, Monday will be here soon enough. What do you plan doing after meeting up with the *Celeste*?'

Realising she needed to talk, to engage her mind, and for a moment at least, banish sorrowful thoughts, Callaghan explained.

'Get both captains to follow their instructions. Briggs to sail the *Celeste* on to Genoa. And Morehouse and the *Gratia* to wait in Gibraltar for further orders.'

'But I thought the plan was to sail together?'

'That's Morehouse's idea. But having the *Dei Gratia* sail only as far as Gibraltar is clearly Sweeny's safeguard in case something goes wrong in Genoa with the unloading of the *Celeste's* cargo. According to Morehouse, sailing time from Gibraltar to there is about ten days. The *Gratia* is leaving New York eleven days after the *Celeste*, calculated to arrive in Gibraltar about the same date the *Celeste* will be unloading in Genoa. That way, should anything go wrong there – like a check of the *Celeste's* cargo because of her extra barrel, resulting in the diamonds being found – Sweeny can wire Gibraltar and instruct Morehouse to sail the *Dei Gratia* to another port instead, maybe back to his first choice, Marseilles. So, when we do meet up with Briggs, my priority is to persuade him to go on ahead—'

'But if nothing goes wrong in Genoa, then as soon as Morehouse gets his orders from Sweeny, the *Dei Gratia* will follow on?'

'Exactly.'

'Then what?'

'I'll follow the *Gratia*'s cargo to the warehouse. Or more exact, the last wagon load. It's odds on the extra barrel will be the first to be loaded into the hold, just like the *Celeste's*.' Forcing his tone to sound positive, despite realising things could go badly wrong – especially with this present spate of Atlantic storms – Callaghan concluded, 'Then, whoever turns up to collect the barrel will hopefully lead me straight to Sweeny.'

'But will he chance compromising himself by having the diamonds taken directly to him?'

'An odds-on certainty. Brains wouldn't risk the barrel being opened up with him not being there. And with four thousand miles between him and New York, he won't be feeling at risk.'

'You're right,' Colleen agreed. 'But there are still some unanswered questions.'

'Such as?'

'The many changes of orders. Marseilles is obvious enough, knowing Sweeny was in France. As is Genoa, assuming we're right in him being on the move again. But why Palermo, then cancel the instructions – yet still make it the second port of call?'

'Maybe Palermo was first chosen because it's easier to smuggle things into?'

'So why change the orders to Genoa?'

'Because Palermo doesn't have a Diamond Exchange,' Callaghan suggested, 'and Genoa does? But Sweeny didn't find out about it until a few weeks ago.'

'Perhaps...' she only half accepted his hypothesis. 'So again, why still sail to Palermo? This explanation of both vessels going there to pick up return cargoes just doesn't ring true, not even to add credibility to their voyages. I'm sure they could have found cargoes in Genoa.'

'I would have thought so.'

'And why is Sweeny hiding the diamonds in other people's cargoes, when he could easily arrange his own?'

'Maybe both vessels *are* Sweeny's. And the firms registered as their owners are no more than his paid nominees.'

Colleen pondered his reply. 'Okay, I'll go along with that. Except, none of this explains the German factor. Kaufmann, Meissner Ackermann, Funch, the seamen on board the *Celeste*. As for the man who waylaid Morehouse and killed Father, too,' her eyes filled up, 'what possible method could he have used, leaving no bruising on Father Reikel's and Kaufmann's bodies?'

'Yes, I admit, that's a myst—'

'And what about Desiah Morehouse and her children?' Colleen added another concern. 'Is his threat against them real? Or just a bluff?'

'I have to assume it's genuine,' Callaghan said. 'In which case, until the Canadian police reply and I know for sure they're safe, I can't confront Sweeny – not without risking their lives.'

'And Tweed?'

'Louis' employing Pinkertons to watch him.'

Colleen nodded, satisfied with the last answers. 'So,' she said, 'you think there's nothing more you can achieve in New York?'

'No, it all seems to have moved to Genoa.'

'Then I'm coming with you. Just as we agreed.'

Momentarily robbed of speech, Callaghan swiftly gathered his defences and met her head on. 'Coming with me! You're most certainly not—'

'I most certainly am,' she echoed, voice steeled with determination. 'I'm too involved to back out now. My father. Your parents. Our marriage. The newspaper. I want to be there when Sweeny is finally arrested.'

Recognising her beguiling brand of resolve, telling him he had no hope of winning, he still made one final objection.

'But the *Dei Gratia* doesn't carry passen–'

'I'll take a steamer.' Getting a copy of *The Times* from a mahogany Canterbury by her side, 'Aunt Siobhan brought it with her earlier today,' she explained, and searched it.

'I'm in luck,' she exclaimed. 'A British steamship, *Asia*, leaves for Gibraltar next week.' She looked up. 'By coincidence, on the same day as you.'

She referred back to *The Times*. 'Let's see…She took three weeks to cross. Assuming she makes the same speed back, and the *Gratia* will take…' She looked questioningly at him.

'About thirty days. But, to repeat–'

'Thirty days. I should be in Gibraltar long before you. I'll check into a hotel until you arrive, then as soon as the *Gratia* receives her orders to continue on to Genoa,' she raced on as she made her plans, 'I can take a train there. That should take no more than two days, while the *Dei Gratia* will take what…ten days, did you say?'

'About that,' Callaghan said, conceding defeat.

'That will give me ample time to discover where Sweeny is staying, and–'

'Okay! You're coming. But only on condition you keep low, and also forget the "discovering where Sweeny's staying" bit. Stay away from him until I get to Genoa. Promise?'

'But–'

'Well away. Promise?'

'Promise.' Colleen's reply was half-hearted.

'You swear?' Callaghan insisted.

She hesitated, then reluctantly agreed. 'Yes, okay, I swear.'

Satisfied, Callaghan relaxed. 'There's still one thing. The *"wire PBS"* memos in Kaufmann's diary. He was killed before sending the first one.'

'But surely Tweed will have sent it?'

'I don't think so. The diary was still locked in Kaufmann's desk. If Boss had known about its incriminating entries, he'd have had the killer break into the drawer and take it.'

'So what do you intend doing?'

'Send it myself, adding Kaufmann's name.'

'But you don't know where Sweeny is. There's another thirty to forty days before he has to be in Genoa.'

'I'll send it to the Montmartre address. His go-between will forward it on.'

'But how will you word it?'

'Keep it simple, confirming the first vessel has sailed and the second's ready to leave – but omitting their names in case he doesn't yet know them. Always wise to keep something in reserve. And to prevent him wiring back, I'll say Kaufmann's skipping New York himself on the second ship, and he'll wire their details to Sweeny's Genoa hotel as soon as he reaches Gibraltar.'

'But to which hotel?' Colleen still sounded uncertain.

'With Sweeny? Genoa's finest, naturally. I'll get it from a Baedeker.'

'Think twice, please, Michael!' Colleen's concern was evinced in her voice. 'What if Tweed has sent the wire, and added that Kaufmann's been taken care of?'

'I'll just have to risk it. Because if he hasn't, and I don't either, then Sweeny's going to get twitchy. He'll wire Tweed, who'll wire him back while we're out there on the Atlantic, unaware of what's happening, and all chance of our catching him will be destroyed.'

'There could be trouble waiting for us if Tweed has already sent it,' Colleen persisted.

'With stakes this high, Colleen, it's a chance I'm willing to take.' Reaching into his pocket for his notepad, his hand closed on Sarah Briggs' letter. He showed it to Colleen. 'Sarah Briggs' last message home before sailing.' He inserted his thumb under the flap.

'You surely don't intend opening it?' Colleen protested.

'I've no choice. It may hold some clue.'

'A personal letter?'

'You never know,' Callaghan said, opening it and skimming the words...how the weather had forced them to anchor "a mile or so from the city"...of Sarah looking forward to "a goodly supply" of letters in Genoa...Briggs' assessment of his crew as "a pretty peaceable set this time, all around"...and finally, Sarah Briggs' chatty conclusion:

I should like to be present at Mr Kingsbury's ordination next week. Hope the people will be united in him and wish we might hear of Mrs K's improved health on arrival. Tell Arthur I make great dependence on the letter I shall get from him and will try to remember anything that happens on the voyage, which he will be pleased to hear.

We had some baked apples (sour) the other night about the size of a new-born infant's head. They tasted extremely well.

Please give our love to Mother and the girls, Aunt Hannah, Arthur and other friends, reserving a share for yourself. As I have nothing more to say I will follow A Ward's advice and say it at once.

Farewell, Yours aff'ly, SARAH

Now feeling sorry he'd invaded Sarah Briggs' privacy, Callaghan handed it to Colleen.

She hesitated over taking it, but curiosity won. She, too, only scanned it, and handed it back. 'She sounds a nice woman, and really must love her husband, risking these Atlantic storms in a tiny brig, just to be with him. They'll be tossed about like a cork.'

'You'll soon be braving the same storms yourself,' Callaghan pointed out.

'Yes, but on a large ship, not a brig. And in case you're making comparisons – with Father having been so brutally killed, I feel too numb to think of much else beyond that.'

'Sure,' said Callaghan, feeling a little disheartened by her reply.

A silence descended between them. Colleen broke it.

'Would you still keep me company, Michael, until after the funeral? Aunt Siobhan can't stay overnight, she has her own home to get back to. I don't want to be here on my own.'

'Of course.' Callaghan's spirits immediately lifted. 'The *Gratia*'s not loading until Tuesday.'

'Thank you. I'll get Mary to prepare you a room.'

- 29 -

Monday, November 11

The cemetery was cold and bleak. Dark grey clouds hung low in the sky, threatening rain, and a bitter wind whistled through the bare branches of the trees, swirling fallen leaves between the gloomy tombstones.

Veiled in black, the mourners restricted to Aunt Siobhan, Sam Phelps, Jackson the butler and Mary, Colleen's nanny from when she was born, and who had stayed as part of the household, Colleen held Callaghan's arm for support as Father Flynn prayed the paternoster, sprinkling her father's coffin with holy water, and finally concluded with: 'Dei requiescant in pace' – "May he rest in peace."

'Amen,' the mourners responded.

Father Flynn bowed his head for the final orison, the prayer for the living: 'O Lord, we beseech Thee that whilst we lament the departure of Thy servant, we may remember that we are most certainly to follow him. Give us grace to prepare for that last hour by a good and holy life, that we may not be taken unprepared by sudden death, but may be ever on the watch…'

I hope he's not being precipitate, Callaghan thought wryly, as they turned away from the graveside and headed back to the three waiting carriages.

As Callaghan helped Colleen into theirs, a hearse pulled up with Father Reikel's simple pine coffin. The pallbearers raised it onto their shoulders to enter the cemetery as Father Murray and four young choirboys positioned themselves to walk in front of it.

Callaghan headed for the priest to offer sympathy, but Murray turned away and started the walk to the graveside, intoning: 'In paradisum deducant te angeli.' "May the angels lead thee into paradise. May the martyrs receive thee at thy coming..."

Returning to the carriage and sitting beside Colleen, 'That was strange,' Callaghan said, tucking her arm under his.

'What was?' she asked, continuing to look towards her father's grave.

'Father Murray. He deliberately ignored me.'

Colleen turned to him, her eyes wide with astonishment. 'After you telling me about your religious debate with him the other day, I'm hardly surprised.'

Fiesole

Father-General Beckx was sitting at his desk, thinking about Father Reikel.

Assuming he'd been at sea for about a week now, he and the first $100 million should be in Genoa well before Christmas. A most propitious sign of God's blessing upon it, and the holy purpose for which it was intended.

Meanwhile, Beckx had not been idle. A Genoese diamond merchant – Jesuit schooled, a true believer – was waiting in readiness. As soon as the cargo arrived and the barrel delivered to the palazzo chosen by Father Reikel, as many of the diamonds as were necessary would be valued individually and exchanged for further votes to ensure the Act would be overwhelmingly defeated and never again be brought before the Assembly.

Time was of the essence and this was God's timing.

The Act was being introduced by the Minister of Justice on Wednesday, November 20, in exactly nine days time, but it would be another month before it was voted on.

Close, with only days to spare, but enough.

It was all a matter of strategy. The path set out by Blessed Saint Ignatius in his formulary, Spiritual Exercises, for the Society to follow until the end of time, when the militant Lord would come again to gather up His true disciples for the Wedding Feast of The Redeemed.

Meanwhile, Father Reikel had already ensured himself his heavenly reward.

- 30 -

Saturday, November 16, 1872

Callaghan was standing on the prow of the *Dei Gratia* watching New York slip by on the port side, and searching the names on the sterns of steamships moored to their Hudson River berths.

Pier Forty-three, Colleen had said, close to Canal Street. They must be nearing it.

Training his telescope on the ships, he swept them from one stern to the next, red, grey, blue, pausing as he fixed on the name *Asia*, painted in large black letters on rounded white metal.

Angling the eyeglass upwards, he saw her standing at the rails, dressed in chestnut-brown travelling clothes, trimmed with fur.

He focused in on her face, taking in every familiar feature. Then as the *Gratia* reached the *Asia*, he lowered the telescope and waved. She saw him and waved back. Walking along the port rail, he kept her in sight. The gap between them widened and he was forced to use the telescope again. As he refocused it, a black cloud passed overhead casting a shadow over the *Dei Gratia* and the *Asia*, and then the stern of another berthed ship obliterated her from view.

Still in the cloud's dark shadow, Callaghan prayed it was not a bad omen of things to come.

Palermo, Sicily

'What in the hell's the Kraut playing at?' Sweeny snarled.

Hurling his cigar into bushes below the terrace of Salvatore Cottone's luxurious villa, high on the slopes above the suburb of

Monreale, he stared disbelievingly at the wire, relayed on to him from Paris.

'What is it?' the ever attendant Father Guilamo questioned.

'Kaufmann.' Brains glowered. 'The goddamn fool's gone blasted crazy. And I sure as hell ain't apologising for my language. I'm justified!'

But seconds ago he'd been relaxing, enjoying the warmth of Sicily's winter sun as he looked down on the bay and the surrounding city of Palermo, and congratulating himself on how well his meetings with Don Salvatore had gone in the last five days. His plans accepted without question.

And then Kaufmann's telegraph, sent to Paris and relayed on to him, had been handed to him by Nino, one of Cottone's two most trusted and loyal mafiosi. An infernal message out of the blue!

Brains stood to his feet and began pacing the terrace.

'Exactly what has he done?' the young Jesuit priest asked.

'He's damned well gone and changed my instructions, that's what,' Sweeny fumed. 'Not only has he got the vessels sailing on different dates, he's also gone and skipped New York on the second one without including their names. And instead of both calling into Gibraltar to await my orders, only Kaufmann's ship is stopping, and then solely for that dumb, stupid sauerkraut to send me details by wire – to some poxing hotel in Genoa I never heard of…'

Sweeny's face was livid with rage. 'Genoa! What d'hell do I want in Genoa? I've never been there and wasn't planning on going there either. What in God's name's got into the raving imbecile? Unless I wired new orders to Gibraltar, both barrels were supposed to end up here in Palermo, not stinking Genoa!'

Taking the crumpled telegraph from Sweeny's clenched fist, Father Guilamo smoothed it out and scanned the message. 'Briefly worded,' he agreed, 'but there's no doubting its meaning. Wire the New York shipping agents for an explanation.'

'I don't know them,' Sweeny snarled. 'I left all that to Kaufmann.'

Guilamo pondered a moment then offered another solution. 'Wire a friend there to trace the names of both vessels. Mr Tweed? Or Mr Hall?'

'Them!' Sweeny voice was scathing. 'There's no ways theys involved in all this.' He visibly brought himself under control. 'What's more, there's no point. The halfwit's not given the dates of sailing. Nor whether he's using sloops, barks or brigs. In any one week, scores of them leave New York. And other than the Father-General's emissary, Father Reikel, that lunatic Kaufmann's the only one in New York who knows I'm headed here. And I don't want anyone else finding out, in case they blab to the police – or worse, *The Times*. You can't trust anybody these days.'

'Then what do you intend?' Father Guilamo queried. 'Our next meeting with Father-General Beckx is four weeks tomorrow.'

'Kaufmann's left us no choice,' Sweeny grated. 'We've gotta postpone it, get to Genoa, and register into this de Genes hotel to wait his wire. But I tell you this, Father,' Brains gave the Jesuit priest a dark look, 'and I don't mind saying it. When he does arrive, then as sure as Hell is hot, I'm gonna make the goddamn Kraut pay for this. Maybe borrow Nino from your uncle. He reckons he's the best ever with a stiletto. He can dig the wax out of Kaufmann's ears and dig deep, real deep, see if that'll help him listen better in future. Meanwhile, let's pray the Blessed Virgin keeps his ship from sinking, because he's the only one who knows the name of the first one to arrive. And I don't want anyone else opening its barrel and getting their hands on my diamonds.'

The Church of St. Francis Xavier, New York

Father Murray entered the confessional and knelt, burdened with guilt.

'Pray, Father, bless me, for I have sinned.'

'The Lord be in thy heart and on thy lips,' came the voice from the other side of the grille, 'that thou mayest truly and humbly confess thy sins. In the name of the Father, and the Son, and of the Holy Ghost.'

Father Murray closed his eyes and prayed for divine strength.

'I last made confession four days ago. But I was weak and admitted only two of my sins. I now want to confess about Father Reikel and Jacob Kaufmann.

'I know who is behind these killings, and why…'

Mid-Atlantic

December 4, 1872

- 31 -

Wednesday, December 4, 1872, Mid-Atlantic

Nineteen days out of New York. Callaghan was too tired to eat. Passing the galley, he went straight to the crew's quarters, removed his wet oilskins and flopped onto a bottom bunk.

It had been a rough voyage, with the howling gales increasing in ferocity over the last eight days, raging all day and night, and mountainous waves crashing over the *Dei Gratia*, sweeping across her deck. Many times it seemed certain she must capsize but, as if by a miracle, she had righted herself, and battled on toward the rendezvous-point with *The Mary Celeste*.

Not that there was any point in it, Callaghan brooded, despite the drop in the wind just a few hours ago, when a particularly violent gale had suddenly lessened to a squall. But it had come too late. Briggs was far too experienced a sailor to put family and crew at risk by waiting in mid-Atlantic in such storms for the *Gratia* to catch up. He would have sailed on to Gibraltar and be–

'Sail ahoy!' The voice was John Wright's, the Second Mate.

'Where to?' Callaghan heard Morehouse call out.

'Off the starboard bow!'

Callaghan rolled off his bunk, donned his oilskins, and went back on deck.

Wright, a small but compact man, was partway up the starboard rigging, looking through a spyglass and pointing out to sea. Morehouse was standing below him, training his telescope at the far horizon. "Gus" Anderson was feet away, and Russian born "Johnny" Johnson at the helm.

Following Wright's direction, Callaghan looked across the expanse of grey, rolling ocean and saw nothing. Then, as the *Dei Gratia* crested a large wave, he glimpsed a sail in the far distance.

The *Gratia* plunged into another trough, obliterating the sail from view, and rose again, the seas breaking across her deck. Callaghan narrowed his eyes but the approaching vessel was still too far away to fully take in with the naked eye.

'It's a brig,' Wright called down.

Was it the *Celeste*? Fighting the roll of the deck, Callaghan crossed to Morehouse's side.

With his 'scope fixed on the distant vessel, the captain muttered to him, strain evident in his voice, 'It's a brig, right enough.'

First Mate Deveau emerged from the Main Deckhouse and joined them. A tall, bearded man, lean, in his early thirties, he spread his feet, steadying himself on the *Gratia*'s deck, and focused his telescope.

'She's sailing erratically,' he finally proclaimed in a puzzled voice.

'I was thinking the same thing,' agreed Wright, from up the rigging. 'She's yawing and falling off, pitching in and out of the wind. And only her lower topsail and foretop-staysail are set. The others are torn to rags.'

The other two seamen, Orr and Higgins, exited the galley, wiping food from their mouths, followed by 18-year old cabin-boy, "Willie" Cleary. Standing by the foremast, they shaded their eyes with their hands and stared out to sea.

Still focused on the vessel, Morehouse declared, with a note of concern in his voice: 'She's sailing on the port tack, but her jib and foretopmast-staysail are on the starboard tack.' Lowering his 'scope, he said to Deveau. 'With that setting, in this wind, she should be heading east, toward Spain, not coming at us.'

Deveau, a man of few words, nodded in agreement. Lowering his own telescope, the two men fixed their naked eyes on the vessel as she drew nearer and ever nearer, her few untattered sails filling up, then sagging as she turned in and out of the wind.

'There's no one on deck,' Wright called down, 'not even at the wheel.'

Deveau retrained his 'scope on the vessel. 'Nor is it lashed.'

'Maybe they're all sick?' Morehouse forced himself to react normally to the situation and focused his telescope again, but Callaghan saw his hand trembling, trying to keep it steady. 'Food poisoning maybe, and they're all inside, too ill to sail her?'

'They'd still have lashed the wheel.' Deveau's tone was grim. 'No, in my opinion, Captain, she's got the look of a derelict.'

There was now no mistaking Morehouse's growing panic as he shouted up to Wright. 'John. Can you make out her name?'

The Second Mate focused his 'scope on the vessel's prow. 'Mary something or other.'

Morehouse looked silently at Callaghan, his face grey with worry.

'Mary Celeste,' Wright confirmed. 'And her boats are missing.'

'God help them,' Deveau said, his voice even grimmer. 'Something bad must have happened for the captain to launch both boats in the storms we've been having. It would've been committing suicide, especially with her wheel unlashed.'

Jerked into action by Deveau's fears, Morehouse spun about to Johnson at the helm. 'Johnny!' he yelled. 'Get as close to her as you can!' Then to Anderson. 'Gus! Fetch my trumpet.'

Anderson, a stocky fair-haired man, made his way across the slippery deck. Johnson turned the wheel and headed for the *Celeste*. Shrouded by thick spray, the *Gratia* ploughed through the heavy seas, rising then dropping as huge Atlantic rollers crashed over her bows, swamping her decks.

Anderson returned with the hailer and handed it to Morehouse.

At 300 yards, Deveau glanced anxiously at his captain. In such conditions, it would be risky getting too near, in case the unmanned vessel suddenly turned about and came straight at them.

'Brace the yards and haul!' Morehouse yelled.

Wright swarmed down the rigging and joined Callaghan, Anderson, Orr and Higgins as they all ran across the deck and pulled at the greased ropes, made even slicker by the drenching spray.

The *Gratia*'s sails finally trimmed. Callaghan turned to look at the *Celeste* as the brig slowly drifted nearer, wet deck empty and silent, her unmanned wheel turning sluggishly and aimlessly from port to starboard, then back to port as her rudder obeyed only the movement of the sea. A spar lashed across her stern davits told that the *Celeste* had carried no spare lifeboat, but a gap in her port side rails, halfway along her decks, showed that her other boat – stowed on the main hatch – had been launched from there.

Her foretopsail and upper foretopsail were mostly gone, torn from the yards by the storms. The lower foretopsail lay loose across the forrard deckhouse roof. The lower topsail jib and foretop-staysail were set, but the other sails were furled. And though the standing rigging looked to be good, most of the running rigging had been carried away.

'Her forehatch and lazarette covers are off,' Wright called down.

'Hell's bells!' Deveau swore. 'No captain in his right mind would take that risk in these high seas. They'll have swamped her decks and poured into her hold. She's lucky she's not filled and gone under.'

'The Devil take it,' Morehouse muttered, 'this nightmare keeps getting worse and worse.'

Deveau turned to him to question his captain's words, but Morehouse forestalled him and raised his hailer at the *Celeste*, now no more than a hundred yards away.

'Brig ahoy! Brig ahoy!' he yelled.

There was no reply from the *Celeste*.

Morehouse tried again. 'Brig ahoy! Brig ahoy!'

Still no answer. Just a deathly silence, broken by the eerie creaking of the *Celeste's* rigging, the dull flapping of her torn sails, and the wind whistling across her empty decks.

'What the hell's happened?' Morehouse low-voiced to Callaghan.

'God only knows,' Callaghan low-voiced back. 'Get me on board her.'

'Mr Deveau,' Morehouse turned to the First Mate, who'd seen, but not been able to hear their exchange of words, and was now looking even more perturbed. 'Lower the small boat.'

Deveau hesitated, but decided to delay his demand for answers and chose Johnson as the best oarsman on board. 'Johnny!' he shouted to him. 'Give Gus the wheel.' Then to Wright: 'Lower the small boat, John. It'll be you and me with Johnny.'

As Deveau, Wright, Callaghan, and the rest of the crew converged on the smaller lifeboat lashed across the main hatch, rather than the larger boat suspended on the stern davits, Morehouse called after the First Mate. 'Best take a fourth man, Mr Deveau. Take Lund.'

Callaghan was using an alias, "Charles Lund", in case Brains happened to read the crew list when the *Gratia* reached Genoa and saw the name "Michael Callaghan".

'Three's enough Captain,' the First Mate objected.

'That's an order, Mr Deveau.'

Deveau hesitated then gave a curt, 'Right, Captain', and returned his attention to the launching of the boat. With Willie Cleary also helping, it was swiftly untied and lowered into the water. Johnson slid down a rope into it first and took his place at the oars. Wright slid down after him. Callaghan followed, then Deveau. The First Mate sat opposite Callaghan and studied him openly, puzzled at his inclusion but still withholding his tongue.

Callaghan glanced up at Morehouse, standing at the ship's rail, suddenly looking ten years older. Callaghan nodded up to him, then saw Deveau's eyes fixed on him and looked away.

Johnson pushed an oar against the *Dei Gratia*'s side and started rowing for *The Mary Celeste*.

- 32 -

Though the storms had subsided, the sea was still rough, raising the small boat high on the crest of the rollers, then dropping it down into grey trenches that blotted both vessels from sight. But Deveau had chosen his man well. Johnson was a superb oarsman and they were soon alongside the seemingly deserted brig. He plied his oars, keeping the boat steady as Deveau, Callaghan and Wright grabbed at trailing ropes and swarmed up the wet, slippery lines, over *The Mary Celeste's* rails and on to her empty deck.

Callaghan stood there, chilled by a deathly stillness that hung over the vessel, intensified by the groaning rigging, the melancholy sighing of the wind whistling between her masts, the flapping of loose sails overhead. The silence was so oppressive it was as if there was something evil on board.

Deveau and Wright also seemed to sense it, standing still as if fearful of moving forward. The Second Mate even glanced hastily down at the lifeboat, reassuring himself that it and Johnny were still there, to row them back to the safety of their own ship.

A long moment passed as they studied the forlorn brig. The binnacle, with its compass broken, lay on the deck, torn from its cleats on the roof of the Main Deckhouse. The main hatch cover was still in place, but the forehatch and lazarette covers were off, left by the *Celeste's* crew where they lay, next to their open hatches.

Seeing them, and a sounding line lying on the deck by the main mast, prompted Deveau into action. 'Sound the pumps, John, while I lash the wheel.' Unsheathing his knife, the First Mate cut a length of loose rope lying on the deck, crossed to the helm and lashed it.

Wright fed the weighted sounding line into the pump shaft. It slackened on reaching the bottom of the hold. Wright pulled it back up and checked the length of wet cord.

'Three and a half feet,' he called across to Deveau.

'That's not much,' Deveau replied. 'Not with the seas pouring in through the hatches.'

'So it wasn't leaking that made them abandon ship,' Wright returned.

'If they all took to the boat,' Deveau specified grimly. He pointed to the loose hatch covers. 'We'd best check the hold first, John, and get them back in place. Lund, check below.'

Callagahan descended the Main Deckhouse companionway and scanned the dim saloon.

A skylight pane had been smashed in, presumably by heavy seas, and the floor was wet with a surface layer of water. An unlit paraffin lamp swung from the ceiling. A scrubbed wooden table was bare of dishes. The stove was stone cold, telling it hadn't been lit for days. But there was no sign of panic. All seemed normal – other than everyone on board having seemingly vanished into thin air.

In that same moment, Callaghan was overwhelmed with a feeling of uneasiness.

It came from beyond the closed door to the captain's cabin.

The same presentiment of evil he'd felt up on deck.

He threw the door open.

The cabin was in semi-darkness, its windows covered with strips of sail-canvas. But there was no sign of hasty flight. The captain's writing bureau was closed, with no hurried note left behind. The bed was made up. Three depressions, one a child's, showed where Briggs, Sarah, and little Sophia had once lain.

Seeing them, Callaghan's mind flashed back to the pretty faces of the little girl and her young mother waving goodbye to New York as

The Mary Celeste sailed down the East River but four weeks ago. What the hell had happened here to make Briggs, a husband and father, and seasoned mariner, decide to abandon ship, risking the lives of his loved ones to a small boat – and the wild storms that had been raging across the Atlantic for over a month now?

He forced his mind back to the cabin.

At the foot of the bed were two sea chests, with "Briggs" painted on them. A melodeon stood against a wall. Alongside it was a sewing machine and a woman's workbag. In a corner, rocking slowly to and fro to the sway of the ship, was a child's chair with a seated wax doll, her porcelain eyes staring fixed and eerily up at Callaghan, as if trying to convey something to him.

He tore his eyes away and focused on a sea-chest in the left corner of the cabin. Painted black, front to the wall, hiding the name painted on it, it drew Callaghan to it. He knelt to turn it around.

The heads door flew open and a man dressed all in black – suit, shirt, leather boots – and holding a rapier, stepped out. Before Callaghan could move, the rapier's point was at his throat.

About five foot eleven, the man's slim build and vantage, looking down on Callaghan, made him seem taller. His skin was so pale, his hair so fair, Callaghan thought he was an albino, but then he saw the frightening intensity of the man's slate-blue eyes.

Black clothes, pale skin, white hair, eyes like blue ice in midwinter, he looked the very personification of evil, the fulfilment of all Callaghan's forebodings from his first moment of standing on the *Celeste's* empty deck.

'Your vessel is the *Dei Gratia*?' His voice was little more than a whisper, the German accent unmistakable. Was this the man who had waylaid Morehouse? Kaufmann's and Reikel's killer? Colleen's father, too? But no, the *Celeste* had sailed before Lowell was killed. Nevertheless, if he was the one who had murdered the others in such an inhumane way, snapping their spines in two, he was without mercy. With the rapier's needle point pricking his skin, it banished all Callaghan's thought of trying to take him.

'Yes,' he replied to the man's question, deliberately adding a tone of fear to his voice, at the same time trying to memorise the rapier's ornate filigree hilt. The chill of the German's slate-blue eyes seemed to intensify.

'There were four in the boat. Where are the others?'

'Two mates up on deck. A seaman still at the oars.'

'On your feet. Make no sudden move.'

Callaghan slowly stood. Threatening to thrust the rapier's point deeper, the German forced him backwards through the door, across the saloon to the foot of the companionway.

'Call your First Mate down. Do not try to warn him.'

'Mr Deveau!' Callaghan shouted up the steps.

'Lund?' Deveau's voice floated back through the open hatch.

'Log book. Captain's cabin.'

'Be right down.'

Holding the rapier to his throat, the German forced Callaghan to circle around him, then back into the captain's cabin, kicked the door shut and thrust him up against the far wall.

Footsteps descended the companionway and crossed the saloon floor. The door flung open. Deveau entered the cabin. His eyes registered his shock as he took in the scene.

'What in God's name!' he exploded, only his eyes betraying his alarm.

'I have a message for your captain,' the German cut across him.

'Message! What the hell's going on here!' Deveau stepped toward them. 'I'm taking no mess—'

Callaghan felt a stab of pain as the rapier punctured his skin. It must have drawn blood because Deveau stopped dead, staring helplessly at him.

'Tell him to ignore his sailing orders,' the German instructed. 'And sail past Gibraltar, straight to Genoa. When we arrive there he is to say he found *The Mary Celeste* abandoned–'

'Like hell I will,' Deveau rasped. 'Half-crews! In this weather! You must be mad! We'd never make it–'

The German flicked the rapier from Callaghan's throat to Deveau's.

'Should he refuse,' the German's sibilant whisper intensified his threat, 'remind him of the warning I gave him in New York. His own wife and children will die, as surely as Captain Briggs' wife and child.'

Deveau's gaze flashed to the doll in the small rocking chair. His face twisted in horror.

'You mean you've killed…killed a mother and her–' he choked. 'What kind of animal are you?' He spat out the question, ignoring the rapier at his neck, repugnance in his expression and tone.

The German's face remained impassive, impervious to Deveau's condemnation. 'If he wishes to see them alive again, he must ensure I reach Genoa. If I do not – they will die.'

'Best do as he says, Mr Deveau,' Callaghan blurted, keeping up his pretence of being no more than a seaman. Wiping his throat, he stared in faked panic at the blood on his hand to impress on the First Mate the kind of man he was dealing with.

'Who the hell asked you, Lund?'

'Mr Deveau,' Callaghan's tone hardened. 'The lives of the Captain's wife and children are at stake here.'

Deveau glared back at him. Callaghan held his gaze, then flicked his eyes at the door.

Suddenly realising that the seaman he knew as "Lund", the man with whom he had sailed for three weeks, was not what he seemed to be, Deaveau brought himself under control.

'Okay,' he gritted to the German, feigning capitulation. 'I'll take your damned message.'

The German put his rapier back to Callaghan's throat. 'This man stays here.'

'Like Hell,' Deveau brushed the rapier away, yanking Callaghan towards the cabin door. 'He comes with me. You've got enough of a threat hanging over us with the Captain's wife and kids.'

Pushing Callaghan out of the cabin before the German could react, Deveau followed, closing the door. Crossing the saloon to the companionway, he clamped his hand on Callaghan's shoulder. 'What's going on, Lund?' he kept his voice low. 'Meeting the *Celeste* was no accident–'

'My name's Callaghan, not Lund,' Callaghan cut across him. 'New York Police.' Curtailing Deveau's angry reply, he continued. 'I'll explain everything once we're back on the *Gratia*. But say nothing to Wright or Johnson. If anyone asks about my neck, I had an accident.'

'Say nothing?' Deveau hissed. 'A mad foreigner with a sword! Now a blasted copper-badge–'

'Deveau!' Callaghan placed his foot on the companionway's bottom rung. 'I have to get back urgently to Captain Morehouse.'

'Okay,' the First Mate grated. 'But how d'you plan to deal with Wright, copper-badge? As Second Mate, he'll expect to be present when we report to the Captain.'

'You'll think of something.'

'Such as what, for God's sake?'

'Anything. Forget blasted protocol. Wright's the least of our worries. Put him in charge of the *Gratia* while you and I see the Captain. I'll tell you all then.'

- 33 -

Morehouse collapsed into his chair and buried his face in his hands, then looked up, his eyes filled with pain at Callaghan. 'Ben dead? Murdered? And Sarah? And little Sophia?'

His fraught tone sought denial, but at Callaghan's terse nod he forcibly recovered himself. 'The Devil take him, what about my family? Unless we do as he says, they'll be killed for sure. But half-crews! In these conditions!' He looked through his cabin window. 'It would be like signing our own death warrants!'

'Will one of you tell me what the hell's going on?' Deveau demanded.

Morehouse looked helplessly at Callaghan for guidance.

'We have to confide in Mr Deveau, Captain,' Callaghan said, wiping the cut at his throat.

Eyes still reflecting his anguish, Morehouse nodded. 'You tell him, I'm too choked.'

Minutes later, Callaghan summed up the situation. 'The Canadian police failed to find Mrs Morehouse before we sailed. Whatever happened to everyone on the *Celeste*, it's odds on he's the butcher who killed Kaufmann and Reikel. That makes the threat against the Captain's wife and children very real. And gives us no choice but do as he's telling us.'

'But where can they be?' Deveau questioned in frustration. 'D'you think–' His voice trailed off as he tried to reject the dire conclusion.

'We're hoping they're with relatives,' Morehouse spoke out with desperate hope in his voice. 'It's what she does when I'm away, she's got them across Canada. I wrote telling her to – without saying why, so as not to scare her out of her wits – but we won't know if they're safe with one of them until all have been checked out. We were intending to wire for news when we reached Gib–'

'But until we do,' said Callaghan, 'Sweeny's hired maniac holds the aces. I need it to be me.'

A silence fell over the cabin as each man brooded on his own thoughts: Morehouse distressed about his family. Deveau worrying over his men sailing two vessels with half-crews. Callaghan mystified as to what could have happened on the Celeste before she appeared over the horizon.

'If he's killed them all, then why? And how – one man against so many?' Deveau expressed the same thoughts as Callaghan. 'And if he's on the Celeste to protect the diamonds, why wasn't a man put on the Gratia as well?'

'I can't begin to think how,' Callaghan said, still brooding about it, 'but as to why the Celeste, it has to be because she was the first brig to leave. The ten days difference in sailing time was for him to reach Genoa and report to Sweeny, the same time the Gratia would be entering Gibraltar.'

'But how did he find out about the rendezvous?' the First Mate persisted. 'And why keep it? Why didn't he make for Spain or Portugal instead? They're only six hundred miles away. He could have beached the Celeste in a quiet cove, axed the barrel open, removed the diamonds and taken a train to Genoa in plenty of time for the Gratia to reach Gibraltar?'

'Because the barrel was the first to be loaded. Impossible to get at without removing the others. As for lugging a hundred million dollars of diamonds all the way to Genoa in a sack, they'd be far too heavy. But as to how he found out about the rendezvous – your guess is as good as mine.'

Deveau went silent again, considering the options. 'Then we've no choice,' he declared. 'Mrs Morehouse and the kids come before all else.'

'Damn well sure they do,' Morehouse glared up at Callaghan.

'Except, we can't sail straight to Genoa,' Callaghan said. 'We have to stop in Gibraltar first to wire headquarters and check if the Canadian police have found the captain's wife and children. Until I know they're safe, I can't take Sweeny on without risking their lives. Or his killer either, because believe me,' he grated, thinking about Sarah and little Sophia, 'I want him just as much.'

'I don't care a damn about Sweeny,' Morehouse swore. 'Desiah, Ned and Harriet are all that matter to me. Wire New York from Genoa.'

'But that won't give me enough time. In the four or five days it will take them to reply, the cargoes will be unloaded and both men will have flown—'

'That's *your* problem,' Morehouse snapped.

'No, it's our problem,' Callaghan argued back. 'Don't forget the *Gratia*'s under orders to sail only as far Gibraltar. We're not even supposed to know that Genoa's our port of destination. What would the authorities there think, finding we'd sailed past Gib, yet arrived at the right port without any orders – with a derelict whose entire complement is missing, also bound for the same port?'

'We'd be arrested within an hour of docking,' Deveau cut in.

'*We?*' Callaghan stressed. 'Meaning everyone on board?'

'The whole crew,' Deveau replied. 'Every jack one of us.'

'Including the German?'

'Him first of all,' said the First Mate, suddenly realising Callaghan was going somewhere with this, but puzzled as to where. 'As the *Celeste's* only survivor, he'd be the biggest suspect.'

'What about the cargoes? Especially when they discover both brigs hold extra barrels?'

'They'd be impounded and searched, for sure.'

'And the diamonds discovered?'

Morehouse groaned as he pictured the scenario.

'Making us all look guilty as hell,' said Deveau.

Callaghan paused for both men to realise where this would leave them all, then continued.

'But if we sail into Gibraltar as ordered, would the authorities there ask questions?'

'*Only* if that scurvy sod's not on board,' said Deveau.

'Then our answer,' Callaghan grabbed the opening, 'is to land him somewhere on the Spanish coast first. And for him to make his own way to Gibraltar—'

'And sign on the *Celeste* under another name,' said Deveau, now realising where Callaghan had been leading up to. 'We'd also be expected to claim salvage there,' he added. Despite whatever tragedy had taken place on the *Celeste*, Deveau was nevertheless aware of the financial gain to be made out of her. 'And once it's been agreed, both vessels will be free to sail on to Genoa.'

'Exactly,' said Callaghan.

'That's great, Michael,' the First Mate used Callaghan's real name for the first time. 'In fact it's our *only* answer.'

'Captain?' Callaghan turned to Morehouse, seeing fear and doubt still in his eyes, but hoping his First Mate's lead would help him to agree.

'If you want see your wife and children alive again, Captain,' Deveau prompted, backing Callaghan up. 'I'd say we've no choice.'

Morehouse deliberated, then reluctantly nodded.

'You've made the right decision, Captain,' said Callaghan. He turned to Deveau, grateful again for his intervention. 'Oliver,' he now used the Mate's first name. 'It would be more convincing if you returned to the *Celeste* and accepted his terms?'

Deveau nodded his agreement.

'But you must convey to him that Genoa spells disaster. That his only hope is for the *Gratia* to sail to Gibraltar as ordered. It all rests with you, Oliver,' Callaghan stressed. 'Make him realise that unless he agrees, he's bound to fail.'

He paused and added. 'And so will we all.'

- 34 -

An hour later – the German having impassively accepted that both vessels would have to call into Gibraltar and not sail straight to Genoa – Callaghan, Deveau and Anderson – chosen for his strength and capacity to work days without seeming to tire – dropped over the *Dei Gratia*'s side into the lifeboat with two sacks of provisions, and headed for *The Mary Celeste*.

In the hope of keeping the killer's presence on board from Anderson, Callaghan decided he and Gus would bunk in the Forrard Deckhouse crew's quarters, and Deveau in the First Mate's cabin in the Main Deckhouse, next to the German's – its windows still canvas-covered. Callaghan would do the cooking and take Deveau's meals – enough to feed two – to the Main Deckhouse. There'd be so much work to do just sailing the brig – three men doing the work of seven – it was to be prayed that Gus would be too flagged to realise there was a fourth man on board.

As they swarmed up on to the *Celeste's* empty deck, Callaghan gave a shiver knowing he was boarding a death-ship, again brooding how one man could have overpowered so many–

'Lund,' Deveau cut across his thoughts, 'secure the lifeboat to the stern rail, we'll hoist her up later. Gus, you and I'll finish pumping her dry, after which we'll light the lamps and get under way.'

Four hours later, as darkness descended, they'd set the main staysail, lower topsail and fore-topmast sail and, with Gus at the wheel, were following the *Dei Gratia*'s stern lights – her canvas reduced for them to keep up – some 100 yards ahead of them, off the port bow.

Callaghan was coiling rope by the Forrard Deckhouse when Deveau emerged from the Main Deckhouse. Crossing the deck, he muttered, 'I've something to show you,' and entered the crews' quarters. Callaghan followed him. Deveau closed the bunkhouse door, put his oil lamp on the table, removed a canvas bundle from under his seaman's jacket and placed it under the fluttering light.

'The *Celeste's* log and log-slate. They were in the First Mate's cabin.'

Callaghan opened the canvas bundle and flicked through the logbook. 'Sorry, Oliver, means nothing to me. You'll have to explain.'

Stabbing a log entry with his finger, the First Mate stressed. 'When Briggs left New York, it was the longer southern route he took, below the Azores.' He stabbed another entry 'But when we first saw the *Celeste* she was dead to rights on the shorter, northern route, above the Azores.' He fixed his eyes into Callaghan's. 'There can be only one explanation for Briggs taking the first course – to lengthen his voyage to let the *Gratia* catch up. But then, eight o'clock Sunday evening, November twenty-fourth,' he stabbed another entry, 'with the *Celeste* still south of the Azores, Briggs ordered her royal and topgallant sails taken in, and shortened sail to two jibs, upper and lower topsails, foresail, and staysail – the same setting as when we boarded her eleven days later.'

Deveau handed Callaghan the slate. 'Now read that.'

Knowing that log-slates were used to record each day's events, before transferring them later into the logbook, Callaghan studied the chalked words:

Monday, 25th

Hour	Knots	
6	8	at 5 o'clock made the island of S. Mary's bearing E.S.E
7	8	
8	8	at 8 Eastern point bore S.S.W. 6 miles distant.

'It means,' Deveau interpreted, 'that at eight the next morning, exactly twelve hours after the last log entry, the *Celeste* changed direction and was now sailing north, no longer *south* of Saint Mary's, a small island east of the Azores, and heading north-west – a course that confirms,' Deveau stressed, 'that despite the storms, Briggs was making for the rendezvous-point with the *Gratia*.'

He stabbed at words chalked beneath the entries:

Fanny, My Dear Wife, Frances N.R.

'These were the last words written by First Mate Richardson, the man on watch. He must have started drafting a letter to his wife in reply to hers – I found it in his cabin – and maybe pass the time away and write up later in his cabin, only for him to be interrupted. From this *one* entry alone,' Deveau emphasised, 'we now know the *exact* time for whatever happened on the *Celeste*. Eight o'clock, the morning of Monday, November twenty-fifth. All of *ten days* before we met up with her.'

The First Mate paused. 'We may never know what befell those on board, *but* Briggs' change of direction would seem to be the cause.'

- 35 -

Sunday, December 8

It wasn't until Sunday evening, three days after boarding the *Celeste*, that Callaghan found time to check the galley.

It had taken them this long to get the vessel into some sort of shape. On day one, the wind abated as another impending storm shifted direction, reducing the rollers to no more than a swell, enabling them to clear away the torn sails, braces and loose ropes hanging over the vessel's sides. Cold, exhausted, they'd also had to take turns at the wheel, and all in all, it had been a particularly long and tiring seventy-two hours for all three.

In between, they'd managed to take only catnaps, in alternating turns. Then a smell of alcohol from the hold reminded Deveau of the two hatches they'd found open on first boarding the vessel. Realising their covers were removed for leaking fumes to escape, he'd had the cargo and lashings checked to make sure all was safe, and rather than risk explosion, had the covers left off again.

All this and many other chores – pumping the hold dry every morning and evening, repairing the sails, replacing the rigging – had given Callaghan no time to cook them a meal, and they'd worked through without any hot food in their stomachs, eating only hard tack brought with them from the *Gratia*. But by midday Sunday, Deveau declared the *Celeste* was "well enough set to rights", and the vital order of the day – while he slept before taking the watch after Anderson – was for Callaghan to make a "hot broth to warm our bones".

Leaving Gus at the helm, Callaghan crossed the deck to the galley, where cooking utensils, potatoes, onions, vegetables, were strewn over the sodden floor, along with spilt sacks of rice and flour, caused by the battering *The Mary Celeste* must have taken over the ten days the German had manned her alone, waiting for the *Gratia* to catch up. Even the stove was knocked out of place.

It took over an hour to get it all back in shape. Lighting the stove and putting a large pan of water on it, he checked for some usable provisions while waiting for it to heat up. There was a good stock of tea, coffee, pork and salt-beef wrapped in muslin, biscuits, apples, cranberries. And on the top shelf, as if pushed into the furthermost corner, was a sealed tin. Callaghan prised the lid off and saw it contained a bottle of ink, a pen, and a book. Sitting with it on his bunk, he read the grandly styled cover and smiled sadly to himself. Poor Head had obviously had literary pretensions.

The Diary of Edward Head
145 Newell Street, Greenpoint, Brooklyn.
Steward on-board the brigantine 'Mary Celeste'
Voyage across the Atlantic

He opened the diary, saw Head's dedication to "Emma", flicked past his pages on leaving New York, and fixed on the crew's puzzlement as to why, on heading out to sea, Captain Briggs had chosen the longer, southern route below the Azores, not the shorter, northern lane.

He now read every word: The numerous pages describing the terrible weather, the many times it seemed all was lost; Mrs Briggs and Sophia staying in the Main Deckhouse rather than venture out on deck; the removal of the forehatch and lazarette covers to allow a build-up of alcohol fumes in the hold to escape, and saw he'd come to Sunday, 24th November...

The date of the Celeste's last recorded log entry...

And that Head's diary continued after this date – *way past it...*

He flicked through the pages – to Wednesday, December 4th.

The day the *Dei Gratia* met the vessel, with only the German on board!

Sitting there, still in his oilskins, Callaghan's heart quickened as he realised that Head's diary likely held the answer to what had happened on board *The Mary Celeste*.

He turned back to Sunday, November the 24th.

Now realising that Head had probably written up the diary alone in his galley after ending his day's duties with no one else on the *Celeste* aware of its existence – and after the 24th, must have hidden it from the albino killer in the hope someone would find it – Callaghan devoured the entries:

> *Sunday, 24 November, 1am. As from tomorrow, Captain Briggs has ordered a change of course. We cannot understand why, Gilling says it will take us north of Saint Mary Island, and towards a dangerous shoal known as the Dollobarat, on which the sea breaks with great violence in stormy conditions such as we are experiencing, but whose rocks are hidden under the surface when the sea is calm. Gilling says that with a shifting wind, which is not unusual in these waters, our position might become perilous. We are all concerned as to why the Captain is sailing north of the island, instead of staying on the southward route. Gilling says he will ask Richardson to ask Captain Briggs.*

> *Monday, 25 November, 1am. The answer is known, and it is like one reads in a mystery book.*

> *When Gilling asked Richardson, it seems Captain Briggs had already spoken to the First Mate, so he was able to tell Gilling in confidence, but naturally Gilling told us to allay our fears. It appears that before sailing, the Captain received a message from a good friend, who is also Captain of a brig sailing from New York to Genoa which left ten days after us, asking Captain Briggs to meet him in the Atlantic, at a point, Latitude 38' North, Longitude 17' West. It seems he has something he wants to discuss with the Captain before we reach Genoa. We have all been trying to guess what it can be, but our opinions were so varied and far-fetched, we gave up and returned to our duties.*

Callaghan turned over the page.

Tuesday, 26 November, 1am. If anyone finds this book, please hand it to the authorities…

Callaghan paused and calculated. Written *seventeen* hours *after* First Mate Richardson broke off chalking the draft log-slate letter to his wife. He swiftly read on:

I pray it will bring these evil men to justice. Captain Briggs, Richardson and Gilling, have all been killed, leaving Mrs Briggs, Sophia and myself to the mercy — of which they have none — of the four Germans. At eight this morning, only minutes after Martens took him his breakfast, Captain Briggs, who yesterday was complaining of an upset stomach, was taken violently ill. His screams could be heard from every part of the ship and by the time we got to his cabin he was dead. The sight that met our eyes is almost too terrible to describe. He was lying twisted on the floor, spine broken, body bent backward the wrong way like a snapped stick. Mrs Briggs was near to collapse but confirmed no one was near him at the time. It was like he was having a violent fit, she said, and we were all left puzzled as to what could have caused such an awful death.

Callaghan stopped reading, realising that Briggs had died the same way as Kaufmann and Father Reikel. What's more, in Briggs' case it happened straight after the German, Arian Martens, took him his breakfast. The seaman that Head, at the start of his diary, had expressed an unease about, and was presumably the one now occupying Briggs' cabin, armed with a rapier.

Brooding on the scenario, Callaghan realised he must have given Briggs a poison mixed in his breakfast. There no other explanation. But what could it have been? A substance so lethal it caused such frenzied convulsions as to snap Briggs' spine in two — like "a snapped stick", as Head described it — yet without the bitter taste associated with any known poison, or Briggs would have spat the food out?

Did the diary offer any clue:

We all gathered in the saloon to discuss what best to do. Richardson, Gilling and myself were for turning back to the Azores and handing over Captain Briggs body to the authorities there. But Martens – who now disclosed he can speak English after all – and the other three Germans wanted him buried at sea, and for us to continue on to Genoa and report Briggs death when we got there. Richardson and Gilling wouldn't agree and ordered the boat to come about. Martens refused, and the three went to the First Mate's cabin to discuss the matter further. Moments later, screams came from there and I rushed to it. Martens was standing over Richardson's and Gilling's bodies with a bloodied sword in his hand and their throats sliced open. Then Mrs Briggs ran in from her cabin and fainted at seeing them. Then the other three Germans arrived.

So, the albino killer *was* Arian Martens. Nor was he a common East Side thug. His methods were those of a practised killer, cold, ruthless, without mercy.

Callaghan returned to Head's diary:

Martens took control. He ordered the Germans to carry Mrs Briggs to her cabin, and locked in. I was made to scrub Richardson's cabin clean of blood, then told to return to my galley duties and remain there, or forfeit my life. Captain Briggs', Richardson's and Gilling's bodies were thrown overboard. And as much as I can tell from the set of her sails, the Celeste is continuing towards the meeting with the other brig, though why I cannot guess. Her Captain is said to be a friend of Briggs and will be suspicious when he finds the Captain and First and Second Mates are missing. And it is certain that Martens cannot meet the other brig with Mrs Briggs and myself on board to tell of the terrible things we have witnessed.

I only pray to Almighty God that they will be merciful to little Sophia and let her live.

Callaghan felt the old bitterness rise up inside him. Poor Head's prayers had been in vain, proving there was no one up there listening. But if he was so convinced there was no God, why did he feel so bitter?

He closed his eyes, forcing himself to concentrate on Briggs' murder.

He was killed after the crew were told by Gilling about the rendezvous. Realising it was with Morehouse, Martens had not only wanted to prevent it, but continue the *Celeste's* course to Genoa.

He must have used poison on Briggs – again there was no other explanation – hoping Richardson and Gilling would accept the death as a natural, if somewhat violent one, agree to bury the body at sea and sail on. But both Mates had insisted on making for the Azores. A post-mortem would have revealed the deadly substance. So Martens had killed them, too.

And what had happened to Sarah and Sophia? Head, too? And the other three Germans, seeing they were no longer on board? Did the diary say?

> *Wednesday, 27 November, 1 am. Martens luffing the Celeste, making time for the other brig to catch up.*
>
> *Thursday, 28 November, 1 am. Sails torn by gale winds. Crew too busy and tired to change setting. High seas smashed binnacle and ship's compass. Martens using Richardson's compass.*
>
> *Friday, 29 November, 1 am. Atmosphere very tense.*
>
> *Saturday, 30 November, 1 am. Goodschaad has told me that he and the Lorenzen brothers are planning to overpower Martens. It seems they got involved in all this when a stranger, another German like themselves, and very rich, judging by his clothes, approached them in New York and offered them a large sum of money to enlist on board the Celeste. He told them the cargo was needed by Germany – the Fatherland, as Goodschaad calls it – to ensure its new position of power in Europe, and that another German, who turned out to be Martens, would be joining them in their lodging-house the next day. He had been chosen to protect the cargo, and needed fellow countrymen on board, for him to converse with and instruct them, without any of us knowing what they were saying. But the Germans had not bargained on Captain Briggs and the two Mates being killed. Gilling was a friend with who they often worked, and he only signed up because they had. They now realise Martens must kill myself and Mrs Briggs before meeting up with the other brig, and so are planning to take over the*

Celeste, sail for the nearest port and give themselves up. Goodschaad asked me to promise I will testify they had nothing to do with Briggs' and the Mates killings. To ensure the lives of Mrs Briggs and Sophia, and mine too, will be saved if they succeed, I agreed. But whether they are innocent as they say, I will let the court decide.

The man who enlisted Goodschaad and the Lorenzens in New York, Callaghan realized, must have been Jacob Kaufmann. Who had paid for his involvement with his life.

Nevertheless, it was the German factor again.

But how could two barrels of diamonds, even if they were worth $200,000,000, affect a country as powerful as Germany. The dominant military power in Europe, the Second Reich had recently invaded France, forcing her government to pay a huge ransom of 5,000,000,000 francs to secure its Army's withdrawal, and also cede the rich provinces of Alsace Lorraine.

$200,000,000 was a vast amount in any country's currency, but it was paltry compared with Germany's immense wealth. Yet, the connection to the diamonds could not be denied. As Colleen had observed, it was more than just a coincidence. And now confirmed by Head's diary.

And how was Sweeny involved in it all? He read on.

Sunday, 1 December. Goodschaad says they intend taking the ship over at first light. I pray they will succeed.

Monday, 2 December. The attempt failed. I saw it through the galley window. Martens was at the ship's rail scanning the seas with his telescope. He must have sensed them creep up behind him, and as Goodschaad swung his axe at him, he side-stepped, slicing Goodschaad's arm open with his sword and the axe embedded in the ships rail. Before Goodschaad could move, Martens put his sword to his throat and forced the others to surrender. He then sent for Mrs Briggs and Sophia and held the sword to Sophia while the Germans launched the longboat, then ordered them all in, Mrs Briggs and little Sophia too, and set them adrift. And then — horror of horrors — he turned the Celeste around and aimed straight for them. I did not see the collision but heard the rending sound as he cut through the boat, and the terrible sounds of their screams. May God have mercy on their souls.

Callaghan closed his eyes, but this only made the dreadful scene more vivid. Devastated by the terrible visions flooding his mind, angry with God for not intervening to save mother and child, and swearing vengeance against Martens for his evil action, Callaghan reopened his eyes and read Head's last words.

Tuesday, 3 December. We must be at the meeting-point. Martens is sailing the Celeste in big circles and sweeping the horizon with his telescope. My final prayer, as I await my end, is that someone will find this diary and use its pages to bring this evil killer to justice.

I commend my soul into God's keeping. Amen.

Realising now that the mess in the galley had been caused by poor Head's desperate fight to survive, Callaghan sat a while in respectful silence, then stowed the diary in his sea-bag, knowing it would be fatal to let Oliver read it. In a red haze, he would forget Desiah Morehouse and tear Martens limb from limb.

Looking around the galley for something to occupy his mind, Callaghan saw the water was bubbling in the pan on the stove. Tossing potatoes, onions, vegetables and salted meat into it, he went out on deck.

Dusk was descending, the *Dei Gratia's* lights looked to be some 300 yards ahead, off the port bow, and another ominous cloud formation was looming up on the dark horizon.

Peering at the *Celeste's* bows as the vessel crested a wave, he saw marks on both sides, confirming Head's account of Martens ploughing through the lifeboat – and Sarah and Sophia being hurled into the cold merciless sea. Looking up at the sky, he swore to the God he didn't believe in: 'If You don't make him pay, I will.'

What was more, with Martens being German, it was now pointing to him having been sent over from Europe by Sweeny, rather than hired in New York by Boss. Following this thought, it also pointed to Sweeny having double-crossed Tweed, and he was smuggling the entire 200 million dollars worth of diamonds to Genoa for his own greed.

Typical Sweeny. Machiavellian. Evil. But no one could go unpunished forever. Both he and Martens would have their day of retribution.

Turning away, he crossed over to a tired-looking Anderson. 'I'll take over, Gus. There's hot stew brewing on the stove.' Grunting his thanks, Anderson headed for the galley.

Callaghan gripped the wheel, braced his legs against the ship's pitching and glanced at the Captain's cabin, hating the man inside. Seeing a tear in the canvas covering the window, he lashed the wheel, knelt and peered in.

The room was dimly lit by a lamp swinging from the ceiling, but the scene that met his eye was unexpected. Wearing a black robe tied at the waist with a red sash, the albino-haired Martens was kneeling before his rapier, embedded in the wooden floor, head bowed as if in vigil.

Callaghan stared, mystified. What in the hell did this tableau mean? Narrowing his gaze, he again studied the sword's ornate hilt, trying to commit its design to memory, then started as a hand clasped his shoulder.

'Thought you were up to something,' Deveau whispered, kneeling beside him. 'I could tell by the ship's movement you'd lashed the wheel. What's to see?'

Callaghan moved to one side for the First Mate to look into the cabin.

'Looks like a damned Knight Templar at prayer, night before battle.' Deveau grated. 'Except he's wearing black, not white, like he's from Hell itself. Any inkling what it's all about?'

Callaghan shook his head while at the same time brooding as to what manner of killer had Sweeny hired? It was like something out of mediaeval times, a throwback to the Dark Ages–

Deveau glanced up and leapt to his feet, his face filled with sudden alarm.

'Michael!' he exclaimed, pointing out to sea.

Callaghan turned. A rogue wave was bearing down on them. In the darkening gloom, the black wall of water looked taller than the Celeste's masts.

Deveau dived for the wheel, unlashed it and spun it, bringing the bows about to meet the wave head-on. Callaghan clutched the stern rail, holding on for dear life. Both men waited.

The huge roller came nearer and nearer, lifting the *Celeste* up its first swell and tilting her almost vertical up a sheer slope of water. Its towering crest loomed over the vessel, sucking her into its grey vortex, curled over her and crashed down, cascading across the *Celeste's* deck. For one terrible moment, Callaghan was certain they would turn completely over, but somehow the *Celeste* broke through, stood still as if suspended on the other side of the roller, hanging over a grey abyss, then plunged down, hitting the bottom of the trough with a judder.

Tossed about like a cork, the seas crashed over her, then her bows righted and she ploughed on, heading into an angry ocean, the harbinger of yet another storm coming in off the horizon.

Callaghan looked for the *Gratia*. She was nowhere in sight. Not even her stern lights.

Had the rogue wave capsized her?

- 36 -

Colleen threw a tartan scarf over her fur-lined travel coat. After days cooped-up inside the *Asia*, she ventured out on deck, preferring the open promenade to the tobacco-stale air of the saloon.

The winds were still blowing strong, lifting her hair from her shoulders and sending her tresses streaming behind her. But this only emboldened her to cross to the ship's rail and hold on tight, exhilarated by the waves breaking against the vessel, and spattering her in their salty spray.

Never before had she experienced such storms, especially the last three days. Roaring gales lashing the seas into a frenzy, creating rollers that completely dwarfed the steamer, lifting her so high, she'd seemed at times suspended in space, only to drop her deep into grey watery valleys with overhanging cliffs on either side, until it seemed the ship could take no more. Even hardened passengers who'd been at the gaming tables within hours of leaving New York, had fallen to their knees in terror, invoking God to come to their aid. Now, with a sudden lull in the weather, God was forgotten and they were back playing roulette, trusting in the wheel of Fortune instead.

Dark clouds rolled low overhead, portents of still more storms in the offing.

Looking up at the skies, Colleen prayed for Michael to be safe. Sarah and Sophia, too. If a solid steamship like the *Asia* had come close to foundering, Heaven only knew what it must be like out there, on small sailing brigs like the *Dei Gratia* and *The Mary Celeste* – at the mercy of the elements and with only minimum crews to man them. One slip, a sudden high wave...

The very thought of losing Michael forever was enough to make her confront the truth in her heart. Whatever had happened in the past, she loved him still. And Michael loved her, she'd seen it in his eyes. What good was all her caution? Life was too short, too uncertain. The sudden and vicious loss of her father was proof of that. She'd almost lost Michael twice now. But life was offering them another chance. Why hold back on the opportunity to make-up, to talk, to whisper, to touch, to kiss, to love... To do so, it might be lost forever. Yesterday was over. But with God's providence they would, in the coming weeks, come through whatever lay ahead of them, and the rest of their lives lay before them.

Remembering back to their first four years together, the strength of his familiar arms around her, the easy fit of their bodies, perfectly complementing each other, Colleen decided that when – when, because from now on no storm of life could keep her from him – when Michael arrived in Gibraltar, her hotel suite was his to share.

No more accusations, no more recriminations.

It was time to start making up for the wasted years.

- 37 -

Thursday, December 12, 1872

Deveau pointed to twin-peaks rising out of the sea on the rain-lashed horizon.

'The pillars of Hercules,' he yelled, to make himself heard above the wind. 'The Rock of Gibraltar to port. Mount Cueta to starboard.' Callaghan was too exhausted to reply. During the last three days of continuous storms, everyone – Sweeny, Martens, Desiah Morehouse, her children, even Sarah and little Sophia – all but Colleen had been banished from his mind.

There'd been no more rogue waves, nevertheless the fight had often seemed lost, with howling winds whipping up seas high enough to swamp the *Celeste*, leaving them soaked through and chill to the bone, no time for sleep, hungry, forced to eat hard tack again, no more hot stew.

Yet in spite of the elements, they found the *Dei Gratia* and kept up with her – "a supreme feat of seamanship," Deveau called it, complimenting Callaghan and Gus – until a new gale-force wind had yesterday separated the two vessels. Even now, as the Spanish and Moroccan shore-lines, and faraway mountain ranges, slipped by on either side of the straits with Gus at the helm, the weather was still rough.

Lashed by driving rain, rivulets of water streamed off Deveau's sou'wester down his face, soaking his beard, further drenching his wet oilskins. 'Ideal!' He again yelled, holding on to the *Celeste's* rigging as the vessel gave a violent pitch, then righted herself.

'Perfect!' Callaghan shouted back in sarcasm.

'For dropping Martens off,' the First Mate hollered. 'With this wind…' The driving spray was forcing him to speak in snatches, 'and only three of us…no questions will be asked if we sail past Gib…and into the Med for shelter.'

Crossing the deck and taking over the wheel, Deveau let the *Celeste* run before the wind.

Riding the in-flowing Atlantic current, he held her on a straight course, passing between the Rock of Gibraltar towering above them off their port side, and entered the Mediterranean. As they rounded the Point, keeping close to the Spanish coast, the wind abated and the waters became easier. The sky began to clear, and after four weeks of storms since leaving New York, the sun broke through the clouds, sending shafts of golden light down on the grey waters, creating large patches of transparent green crowned with small waves flecked with masses of snow-white foam.

Callaghan breathed in the air. My, but it felt good.

They sailed on, searching for calmer waters in which to drop anchor, past small fishing villages with gaily painted boats beached high up on the sands, and beyond them, parched hills devoid of vegetation. Then they saw the mouth of a large river in the distance, bounded on both sides by deserted stretches of white strand.

'Get ready to lower the sails,' Deveau instructed. 'I'll take her close in so we can anchor and get some sleep for a couple of hours. You first, Gus, you look as if you need it.'

Finally lowering sails and dropping anchors within a hundred yards of Spanish soil, Callaghan leant on the rail and gave an audible sigh of relief. After 3,000 miles of angry ocean, it was great being so near land again, and to hear waves breaking on the shore, instead of being surrounded by grey mountains of water, and the howling sound of gales blowing through the rigging.

Deveau leant alongside him as Gus entered the bunkhouse and closed the door. 'Feels good?'

'That's putting it mildly.'

'So you're not planning a new career at sea?' Oliver grinned.

'Not at any price. But as great as it is, being so near land again, I'd best hide in the galley. I don't want Martens seeing me.'

'Why not?' asked Deveau. 'He's already seen you once.'

'Briefly, in semi-darkness, before I grew this beard. By the time we reach Genoa, and another ten days growth, he'll have forgotten my face.' Crossing the deck, Callaghan entered the galley and watched through the window as Martens emerged naked from the Main Deckhouse, a canvas-wrapped bundle strapped on his alabaster white shoulders, and lowered himself over the side.

Following the German's white hair to the shore, Callaghan stayed fixed on him as he brushed water from his body with his hands, unrolled the canvas, put on his black shirt and suit, and loped off across the sands carrying his boots, over a dune and from view.

Callaghan went back out on deck to Deveau.

'Pity he didn't drown,' the First Mate spat over the rail into the water.

'And where would that have left Desiah and the children?'

Deveau ignored the question. 'Whenever I was in his cabin his eyes never left me, like a snake watching me, ready to stick that damn rapier into me if I made any sort of move. And all the time, I kept thinking,' the First Mate screwed his strong hands, 'one twist of his neck that's all it would take. But then I'd remember about Desiah…'

He brooded a moment, staring into the clear water below, then re-faced Callaghan. 'But now that we're free of the goddamned psycopath, I'm going to join Gus and close my eyes for a short while. You'd best get some rest, too.'

'After first seeing whether he left any clues.'

Deveau made for the bunkhouse. Callaghan slid down the Main Deckhouse companionway, crossed the saloon and entered the captain's cabin.

Looking around, every item prompted an image of Sarah and Sophia, from the melodeon that once resounded to the young mother's playing, to the china doll still sitting on the rocking chair. How Martens could have slept surrounded by these reminders of them beggered the imagination. Only by having iced water in his veins instead of blood.

Ignoring the two "Briggs" sea chests at the foot of the bed, Callaghan pulled the third one away from the wall, and saw the name "Martens" painted on the front. Picking the clasps open, he began removing the contents and laying them out on the bed, wanting to put everything back in the chest in the same order. When Martens rejoined the *Celeste* in Gibraltar as one of her new crew on to Genoa, he must find it all just as he'd left it.

Four working shirts. Four pairs of working pants. A woollen shirt. A belt. A cotton cap. A bag containing pieces of cloth and flannel for patching. A razor strop. Light coat. Six white shirts and loose collars. Overcoat. A pair of half boots in best leather. Nothing exceptional so far. Except the boots and overcoat were of a finer quality than a seaman would be expected to own.

He next removed layers of black-bound books, thirteen, all in German, evincing Martens to be a dedicated reader. The thought of an intellectual assassin was even more chilling.

Under them was a flute, lamp, sextant inside a wooden case, two parcels fastened with cord. Making sure the knots were normal, for him to re-fasten the same way, Callaghan untied them.

The first parcel contained a bundle of papers, also in German. Understanding only the odd word, he took two sheets from the middle and put them aside.

The second parcel contained two items. One, a jar labelled Brandreth Pills, New York's latest patent pills, claimed by their maker to cure every ailment known to man, they were, so he'd been told, very bitter to taste—

Bitter! Callaghan poured a pill into his palm and examined it. This could be how Martens had given Briggs the poison? According to Head, Briggs had complained of an upset stomach.

Had Martens caused it, mixing a substance into his food? And next morning, when he took Briggs his breakfast, had given him a Brandreth as a cure for it? Except that Martens' pill was made from a deadly toxin. Briggs swallowed it, ignoring its bitterness, seconds later he was dead. The same with Kaufmann and Reikel, in both cases a pill thrust into their mouths from behind without warning and so forced to swallow it. But if so, what poison could be so lethal as to cause writhings so frenzied they could snap a man's back in two?

Callaghan placed a pill with the two sheets of papers.

The last package contained a cloth bag filled with what appeared to be flax seed. Delving into it, Callaghan felt large pods. Five in all. He removed one. It was oval, shiny and green, inch and a half or so in length with a hard surface and covered in silky hairs. Placing it with the pill and adding a handful of seed, he folded the papers around them and put them in his pocket.

Carefully replacing everything in the sea chest, he re-locked it and slid it to the door to return it to the crew's quarters. When the British authorities came on board in Gibraltar to survey the vessel before agreeing Morehouse's salvage claim, finding Marten's chest in the captain's cabin might create suspicion. And that he wanted to avoid at all cost.

Picking open the bureau, he found Morehouse's letter, asking Briggs to meet him in mid-Atlantic, pocketed that, too. Then entered First Mate Richardson's cabin next door, gathered up the *Celeste's* papers, navigation book, register, sextant, chronometer – all that the British authorities would expect Briggs to have taken with him if some sudden danger to the ship had decided him to take to the lifeboat – went back up on deck and threw them overboard.

They entered Gibraltar harbour as dawn was breaking, with the Rock casting a dark shadow over the town. As they dropped anchors, they saw a British-flagged pratique boat approaching.

Deveau focused his telescope. 'The Captain's on it, he's looking mighty upset. There's also a man in a dark suit clutching a holdall, and three British redcoats, all armed.' Lowering his glass, he turned to Callaghan. 'Something's wrong. I don't like the look of it.'

The pratique boat drew alongside. The suited official was first to board. He crossed the deck, removed a hammer and framed notice from his holdall, nailed the order to the main mast. Two red-jacketed soldiers with rifles followed him up on board. One marched to the Main Deckhouse, the other to the Forrard Deckhouse. Both about turned, boots crashing on the planks, and took-up sentry positions, blocking access to them. Morehouse clambered up, face grey and drawn.

'What's going on?' Oliver demanded.

'The damned British are placing the *Celeste* under arrest.' Morehouse looked on the verge of collapse. 'A jumped-up Admiralty solicitor named Solly sodding Flood, doesn't believe our story of how we found her abandoned. We're accused of killing everyone on board just for the salvage. The guards are to stop us removing anything, and we're all under port arrest awaiting an Inquiry to determine whether or not we're to stand trial for murder–'

'Murder!' Deveau exclaimed. 'I'm not facing trial for any murder–'

'The rapier!' Callaghan cut across him.

'What about it?' Morehouse questioned.

'Martens didn't have it with him when he swam ashore.' Callaghan cursed himself for having overlooked it when he threw the other items overboard. 'He must have hidden it somewhere in the cabin. They're bound to find it. What if it's still bloodstained?'

'It's too damned late to do anything about it now,' said Deveau.

From the top of the Rock came the resounding boom of a canon.

'What's that all about?' Callaghan asked.

'The morning gun,' Morehouse replied.

'Welcome to Europe,' Callaghan said.

'It's Friday the thirteenth,' said Deveau.

Gibraltar

December 13, 1872

- 38 -

Friday, December 13, 1872, Gibraltar

Weeping silently, Colleen stepped out onto the balcony of her Royal Hotel suite.

Callaghan followed her. Below them, Waterport Street, the port's main thoroughfare, with its mixture of European shops and Arab bazaars, was crowded with people. Pulling her handkerchief from under her cuff, Colleen dabbed her eyes and forced herself to focus her senses on the busy scene below, trying to obliterate the haunting image of a young mother and her tiny child being hurled into the cold, grey Atlantic as *The Mary Celeste* cut their small boat in two.

Turning back to Callaghan, he put his arms around her and held her tight, but the picture remained vivid in her mind. 'Oh, Michael, the evil of it. This wasn't in the heat of battle. It was cold blooded–' her voice broke off, she wrapped her arms around his waist, needing the comfort of his strong body.

Behind her, the everyday noises of Gibraltar slowly restored her composure. Wiping her eyes again, she looked up at Callaghan, and in his bearded face saw the strain of all he'd come through, mental as well as physical, the exhaustion from bringing the *Celeste* into Gibraltar, deeply etched in his eyes.

'You look worn out, nor will you have eaten properly in weeks.' She lead him back inside to an arm chair by a roaring fire. 'I'll order you breakfast, then you can sleep for a couple of hours.'

'Breakfast sounds good. I assume it will be an English one? Bacon, eggs, sausages, fried bread, the whole caboodle?'

Colleen smiled, the old feeling of tenderness for him welling up inside her. 'Of course.'

'That would certainly hit the spot. But if you don't mind, I'll catch up on the sleep part later. My mind's too full for rest.'

She pulled a bell cord for room service and sat facing him. 'You said his name is Martens? Arian Martens?'

Callaghan nodded.

'Then there's no doubting he's German. But he clearly can't be the one who killed my father. It must have been Tweed who–' Her voice broke again.

'I'll wire Commissioner Smith. Ask him to put Fred Dain on it. He's a rare commodity. An honest gumshoe, and keen. Like a Jack Russell with a bone he won't give it up until he's found proof of Boss's guilt.'

'Thank you, Michael,' but the smile she gave him reflected pain. Lapsing into a momentary recollection of her father, she broke it and returned to Martens. 'How on earth did Sweeny find so vile a man?'

'Your guess is as good as mine. Neither *The Times* or Mulberry Street have any record of Sweeny ever being to Germany, just that his escape route took him to Ireland, then on to France. Maybe he hired him in Paris? The one thing certain is that he's a professional killer. Three by poison, if my guess is right. Two by the sword. Five cold-bloodedly drowned. As for poor Head, we'll probably never know how he died.'

'Bestial!' Colleen's tone was filled with repugnance. 'But Sweeny must have known what kind of vicious sadist he was hiring. Which makes him equally contemptible. And guilty under the law.'

'I'll make sure they both pay,' Callaghan grimly reassured her.

She leant forward and held both his hands. 'Except there's this Inquiry now hanging over you. Wouldn't it best to confide everything to the British authorities? Including your identity? And give them Head's diary, for them to read what really happened?'

'Not with this Flood character seemingly in charge,' Callaghan replied ruefully. 'Especially from what David Morehouse says about the man.'

'But if he's an advocate, surely his concern is to bring the right people to account?'

'You'd think so, but it seems he's more interested in self publicity than justice. He's already leaking *his* version of it to American and English newspapers, with headlines like: "The Enigma of the Celestial Ghost Ship" already hitting the streets, and envisioning his name plastered across their front pages as the man who solved the mystery.'

'Which means that Sweeny might also read about it.'

'Not yet. But if the Hotel de Genes provides English newspapers for its guests, he could in a few days time. So, just like Flood, the last thing we want published at this moment is the truth. Can you imagine the captions? "Brains Sweeny's two hundred million dollar loot found on board two New York brigs, an entire complement murdered." No, what I want, Colleen, is a swift salvage resolution then on to Genoa.' His voice hardened. 'I want them both, Sweeny **and** Martens, and I'm not losing either of them.'

They were interrupted by a tap on the door. A waiter entered, took Colleen's breakfast order and exited. 'And a large pot of coffee,' Callaghan called after him, stifling a yawn.

'What's your next step?' Colleen asked.

'Find the best attorney in Gibraltar.'

'Mr Sprague, our American Consul here, would advise you. Also, relations between Britain and us are pretty good at the moment. Perhaps Sprague could speak to Flood on your behalf,' she added, 'persuade him his case is purely theoretical, and that if Captain Morehouse is willing to forego his salvage claim, it would be in the interests of both countries if the matter was dropped?

'It's worth a try,' Callaghan nodded. 'I'll discuss it with Morehouse and Oliver.'

Colleen was suddenly reminded of another step in Michael's original plan.

'What about Kaufmann's second telegraph to Sweeny?'

He thought about it a moment. 'There's no need for me to send it now,' he finally decided. 'Sweeny's bound to have arranged for Martens to wire him before the *Celeste* set sail from New York, confirming that Kaufmann's been disposed of. So, when my first wire – to the Montmartre address – was forwarded on to him, he'll have assumed Kaufmann sent it before he was killed and won't be expecting a second one.'

Colleen nodded, accepting Callaghan's logic, and moved on to another problem. 'What about Martens, when he arrives in Gibraltar and finds the *Celeste* under arrest, and the *Gratia* facing an Inquiry? What do you think he'll do?'

'Like myself and the rest of the crew, he's no choice but to hang around for the result. The question is: does he know where to wire Sweeny and keep him informed? I assume he does. If we're awarded salvage, then everything's back to normal. But, if we're put on trial, who knows? Much depends on whether the British Admiralty decide to search the *Celeste's* cargo. If they do and find the diamonds, God only knows what will happen. Flood will throw the book at us.'

Colleen subsided into silence, brewing over all this, then turned to him.

'Michael?' she hesitated. 'Since you'll be occupied with this Inquiry business over the next few days, what if I try investigating the items from the sea-chest? I know you can't introduce them into the proceedings, but it may throw light on who Martens is, and how Sweeny came to hire him. It would also give me something useful to do – instead of just sitting here worrying.'

Callaghan pondered but could see no risk in it to her. 'Yes, why not?' Withdrawing the folded papers from his longbag, he gave them to her.

'The bean, flax-seed, and Brandreth pill are inside. As for the papers themselves, where will you find someone to do the translation?'

'Hopefully, the Garrison Library. What about the rapier hilt? Can you recollect the design?'

'I think so.'

He crossed to a writing table and began drawing on a sheet of hotel stationery. The lines were hesitant at first, but became bolder as he saw the pattern taking shape. He handed the sketch to Colleen. 'That's as near as I can remember.'

'It's extremely ornate,' she observed.

'That's why I keep thinking the design stands for something, and why I'm hoping it won't be too difficult to identify.'

'I'll do my best,' Colleen promised.

There was a knock on the door. 'And now breakfast is served,' she added with a smile.

- 39 -

As he walked through Gibraltar, the newspaperman in Callaghan could not help but compare it to New York, contrasting its narrow twisting alleys against the straight, wide avenues back home; its sprawling open market-places to Fifth Avenue's contained emporia, the low, flat-roofed terracotta villas so different to New York's tall granite buildings pushing ever upward in the current architectural trend. Judging by the babel of languages and exotic apparel – dark-skinned Moors wearing gold earrings, turbaned market traders from India, long-bearded Jews in dark suits and hats – every race looked to be represented. Their individual culture maintained, they gave Gibraltar a unique cosmopolitan atmosphere that was the very antithesis of New York's "melting pot".

Off-duty soldiers in vivid red coats, strolling amongst the crowd, reminded Callaghan that Gibraltar was a British garrison town. The scene of much bloodshed over the centuries, the strategically positioned port had been conquered by many invaders, and always in the name of religion. Spain's Roman Catholic "God" had lost it to the "Allah" of the Moors, but then returned in glory 700 years later, only to be deposed by the British Empire's Protestant "God". Gibraltar's history, thought Callaghan to himself, was proof that on earth the ruthless held the power, and The Almighty – *if* He existed – was happy to let them get on with it, despite the suffering caused to the rest of mankind.

'As luck would have it, you couldn't have chosen a worse adversary than Solly Flood,' said Horatio Jones Sprague, looking at them over the top of his half-spectacles.

A distinguished looking man, dressed in a dark, waistcoated suit with gold watch and chain, the United States Consul sat behind a red leather-topped desk. On the wall behind him was a large unfurled American flag with its 37 stars and hanging gold tassels, its polished stick supported by two brackets.

'The man's seventy-one,' Sprague continued. 'Hasn't been here long and never wanted the posting. He's Irish by blood but was born in London, and hoped to spend his remaining years there, enjoying the theatres and the galleries. You can take it from me, gentlemen, Flood won't let this one go. Conjure up a motive and he'll have thought of it – piracy, murder, fraud – just as long as it gets him to the attention of the British Admiralty in London and a transfer back home. Naturally I'll do my best to try to dissuade him, but I'm afraid I can't offer much hope.'

'Then he's going to find plenty to support his case,' said Callaghan. 'As we said, there's Briggs' rapier. It's more than likely a souvenir of a past voyage, but from what you say of Flood, he's bound to make it seem like damning evidence. There are also the recent scrape marks on the bow and axe cut in the rail, both of which probably happened back in New York–'

'Lund…' Horatio Sprague interrupted. 'You seem to have made yourself the spokesman for all this. I find it somewhat surprising, especially from a seaman. I would have thought that Captain Morehouse – or Mr Deveau – could do their own explaining?'

David and Oliver fidgeted in their chairs but stayed silent. Callaghan hesitated then decided to tell the Consul the truth – or at least, a necessary part of it.

'My name's Callaghan, sir, not Lund. Michael Callaghan, New York Police, Detective Bureau. I'm investigating two murders that took place in New York.' Seeing Sprague frown, Callaghan dug into his pocket. 'My warrant card and badge. Should you need further proof, a wire to Police Commissioner Smith, at Mulberry Street, will confirm my identity; I'm acting under his authority. I sailed on board the *Gratia* with Captain Morehouse's permission–'

Sprague cut across him again, his face stern. "This all sounds most unorthodox. I rather think that a full explanation is in order...'

Having described Kaufmann's and Reikel's deaths, Callaghan explained that both seemed to point to Sweeny being behind them. His Commissioner's reason for this assumption, Callaghan belied, was that a man fitting the killer's description had waylaid Captain Morehouse in New York, and by threatening the lives of his wife and children was forcing him to deliver a sealed letter to Genoa's Hotel De Genes, where – according to information – Sweeny was thought to be hiding. Admittedly, the evidence was circumstantial, Callaghan concluded, nevertheless, it was why he was on the *Dei Gratia*.

'Except that finding the *Celeste* abandoned couldn't have come at a worse time. Especially as Sweeny knows my real name – and I must continue to use my alias when we finally reach Genoa.'

Sprague drummed his fingers on the desktop as he looked from Callaghan to the badge and warrant-card, then back at Callaghan.

'All right, Callaghan,' he said. 'This is crazy logic, but your story's too damned unbelievable for it not to be true, though I intend wiring New York for confirmation.'

'Of course, sir. But please mark it confidential for General Smith. And leave Sweeny's name out of the message, in case it gets read by Captain Irving of the Detective Bureau. He's suspected of being a Ring man, and could maybe try to warn Sweeny I'm on the way.'

Morehouse interjected. 'And could you ask for confirmation that Desiah and my children are being protected by the Canadian Police – if you would, sir?' he added.

'I surely will,' Horatio Sprague confirmed, jotting it all down, then looking back at them. 'In the meantime, having been given all the facts, I'll redouble my efforts to try to get Flood to drop the case against you all.' He turned to Callaghan. 'Don't you think it advisable for you to also take him into your confidence, Callaghan? Should I fail to persuade him, then once you, and Captain Morehouse and Mr Deveau have taken the stand and withheld evidence – especially you, Callaghan, swearing on oath under a false name – it will only make matters worse for you all.'

'From what I hear of this Solly Flood, sir,' Callaghan replied, 'telling him I'm investigating two vicious murders would be extra grist to the mill for him.'

'True,' Sprague brooded. He turned to Morehouse. How do you feel about all this, Captain?'

'I just want my wife and children safe, sir.'

'Mr Deveau?'

'I'm with Michael and the Captain one hundred percent, sir,' Oliver stated.

'In that case, gentlemen,' Sprague reached for a telegraph pad, 'we'd better start sending some urgent wires.' He licked the point of his pencil. 'The first priority is obviously to establish Mrs Morehouse's safety. So this one is to…' He looked up at Callaghan.

'Police Commissioner, General William Smith, sir. Headquarters, Mulberry Street.'

Sprague repeated the name and address aloud as he wrote them down, and continued to do so with the message, 'Callaghan here. Confirm investigating Kaufmann Reikel deaths. Also Canadian Police protecting Mrs Morehouse. Urgent. Sprague, American Consul, Gibraltar.'

He looked up. 'That sufficient, Callaghan?'

'Exactly right, sir.'

Sprague gave a slight cough of someone pleased with himself. 'Then I suggest our next priority should be to try to undermine Flood and get *The Mary Celeste* released from custody?'

'If you could manage that, sir,' Callaghan replied. 'It would be an answer to prayer.'

'Right,' Sprague responded briskly and returned to his pad. 'So, this will be to the Board of Underwriters in New York saying – how can I best word it?' He again repeated the words as he wrote: 'Brig *Mary Celeste* here derelict. Urgent send power of attorney to claim her from British Admiralty Court.'

He again glanced up at Callaghan. 'How's that?'

'Fine, sir. Let's hope it works.'

'We can but try, Callaghan. We can but try.'

Despite the gravity of the situation, Callaghan smiled inwardly at the Consul's use of the plural pronoun, clearly identifying himself as being in this with them as he continued. Now fully into his new role as an intriguer, Sprague pursed his lips. 'Next, I suggest we should also send one to my colleague, Oswald Spencer in Genoa. Before the *Celeste* can be released from British custody,' he explained, 'we will require copies of her documentation.'

Raising quizzical eyebrows at Callaghan as if seeking his approval, he nevertheless assumed his agreement and put pencil to paper. 'I'll use similar wording. American brig *Mary Celeste* here derelict. Urgent send copy bill of lading to claim her from British Admiralty Court.'

'Sir?' Callaghan intervened. 'Would you also ask Mr Spencer to find out whether Sweeny's in Genoa yet?'

'Of course,' Sprague tut-tutted. 'I should have thought of that.'

Looking down again, he added the words: 'Confirm Peter Sweeny staying at Hotel de Genes.' His raised gaze included all three. 'No need to add who he is. Like me, Spencer will know all about the man. And in case he's not there, I'll check with our Embassy in Paris, where he was last seen. It's possible they might know his current whereabouts.'

'That makes good sense, sir,' Callaghan agreed.

Sprague wrote the message. 'Ambassador Washbourne, US Embassy, Paris. Urgent confirm present location Peter Sweeny.'

The consul stood up, the three of them also stood. 'They'll be sent today,' he said. 'Spencer will dispatch the papers by rail to Algeciras – that's our nearest station, just across our border with Spain – and I'll arrange for someone to meet the train. And also let you know as soon as I receive replies to any of my wires. Especially any news about your wife and children, Captain Morehouse. Meanwhile, keep your chin up.'

'I'll do my best, sir.' Morehouse replied, grasping the Consul's proffered hand.

'And you, Mr Deveau.'

'Thank you, sir.' Deveau responded.

'If there's anything more I can do for you, Callaghan, don't hesitate to ask. In the meantime I'll arrange a meeting with Flood, but...' Sprague pulled a reluctant face, 'I'm afraid I don't hold out much hope.'

'Then nor will I, sir,' said Callaghan. 'In that case, can you recommend a top attorney?'

'Henry Pisani. Galliano Bank Chambers, Cannon Lane. He's not up to New York standards, but he's the best Gibraltar has to offer.'

He escorted them to the door and held it open for them. 'The best of luck to all three of you, gentlemen. With Solly Flood as your adversary you're going to need it.'

- 40 -

The pharmacy had small square panes in a bowed window-frame, and the name W F ROBERTS CHEMIST in faded gold letters over the door.

The brass doorbell jangled as Colleen entered. She crossed the stone-flagged floor to the counter. The dispensary's open door revealed a tall thin man pounding a substance with a pestle. 'Be right with you, madam,' he said, wiping his hands on his powder stained, once-white overall, soiling it even more with yellow residue, and approached her.

'Mr Roberts?' Colleen questioned.

'How may I help you, madam?' he peered at her over the top of his half moon spectacles.

'I'm an American, touring the Mediterranean and staying at the Royal Hotel.' Opening her carryall, she withdrew a hotel envelope. 'I've purchased an old Moorish chest to ship back home and found these in a secret drawer,' she opened the envelope for Mr W F Roberts to peer inside. 'I'm concerned they might be dangerous and wondered if you would identify them for me?'

'Why not just let me dispose of them,' he suggested, with a long face.

'Curiosity,' Colleen smiled back at him. 'My name's Callaghan, Mrs Colleen Callaghan. I'm a writer. I thought they might reveal something about what the Moors used to get up to, and maybe provide an interesting storyline? Of course, I shall pay you for your time.'

Mr W F Roberts sighed. 'Very well, Mrs Callaghan.'

Accepting the envelope, he emptied the three items on to the counter. 'The seed looks like flax seed, but I'll check it. And the bean should be easy to identify from my books of reference. But the pill will be more of a problem. I'll have to subject it to analysis.'

'How long will that take?" Colleen asked, affecting polite curiosity. 'I'm leaving in a few days' time.'

'Late tomorrow. Say, six o'clock.'

'Thank you, Mr Roberts. I'll be back at that time.'

The brass doorbell jangled again as she exited.

Colleen approached the uniformed commissionaire at the Garrison Library on Gunners Parade.

'Madam?' His upright stance told he was an old soldier.

'I'm hoping you have someone here who can help me,' she said. 'I have some papers I'd like translated. They're in German.'

'You'll want Mr Joseph Turner, madam. He was the librarian, retired now, but still spends most days, apart from Sundays, in the Members' Room. Whom shall I say wishes to see him?'

'Mrs Colleen Callaghan. From New York.'

'If you'll wait here just a moment, madam.' Turning smartly, the old soldier marched off down the corridor and was back in less than two minutes.

'Mr Turner says he will be delighted to see you, Mrs Callaghan. If you will follow me.'

Leading the way past the Reference Room into the wood-panelled stillness of the Members Room, he pointed to a white-haired, white-bearded, elderly gentleman who, apart from a dark suit and pince-nez, looked like Santa Claus sitting ensconced in a deep leather armchair by a large fire.

Colleen crossed to his side. 'Mr Turner?'

Beaming at her, the librarian struggled out of his chair. 'Mrs Callaghan,' he returned, sotto voce to accord with his surroundings and offered her his hand. Colleen took it. 'Won't you sit down?' He indicated another armchair alongside his, waited for her to sit, then settled back into his relaxed position. 'I understand you've some German documents you would like me to translate for you?' he questioned.

'If you are able to tell me the subject matter, that might be enough.' Colleen took the papers out of her bag. 'I'm extremely grateful and will recompense you for your time.'

'Gracious me,' the old gentleman chuckled. 'I will not require a fee.' Producing a spotless handkerchief, he polished his pince-nez, re-clipped it to his nose, studied each paper carefully and peered at her.

'May I enquire what is your interest in them, Mrs Callaghan?'

'They were my late father's,' she replied. 'I found them amongst his papers just before I set sail for Europe. Rather than leave them behind, I brought them with me in case they were of value.'

'I'm afraid not,' Mr Turner shook his head. 'At least not of any monetary value. But they may be of historical interest. Your father wasn't, by any chance, a chronicler?'

Colleen seized the opening. 'Yes, he was. That's very perceptive of you, Mr Turner.'

The elderly gentleman gave a smile of inward pleasure. 'Not really. These papers would seem to be extracts from a project he may have been researching. By any chance, do you know whether he was he interested in secret societies?'

'Yes, he was,' she quickly replied. 'As it happens, he was writing a book on them. I also found a drawing similar to this amongst his notes.' She produced Michael's sketch of the rapier-hilt from her bag. 'The original was falling to pieces, so I made this copy last night in my hotel room.'

Mr Turner gazed at the sketch then handed it back. 'Yes, its design certainly suggests it was used for ceremonial, rather than practical purposes, and probably belonged to some covert sect. All of which implies, Mrs Callaghan, your father was researching the already proven connection between such organisations, and the sect mentioned in these documents…' he tapped the papers and stressed, 'The Assassins.'

'The Assassins!' Colleen exclaimed. 'What a dreadful name!'

'No more dreadful than the reality of their evil deeds, I can assure you, Mrs Callaghan.'

'Mr Turner,' Colleen hoped she was on to a vital lead, 'I don't want to impose, but would you have time to tell me something about them?' She extracted a note book and pencil from her bag. 'I hope you won't mind me making notes but I'd like to finish my father's book, if only in memory of his name.'

'An admirable thought,' the old gentleman approved. 'And being in the twilight of my years, I have all the time in the world to tell you what I know, albeit meager.'

Settling deeper into his chair, Mr Turner cleared his throat and began. 'To start at their beginning, the Assassins were an Islamic cult of fanatical killers who existed between the eleventh and thirteenth centuries. And although the original sect has long passed into history, their methods of recruitment, indoctrination and organisation, have provided what can best be described as a blueprint for other secret societies – not just Islamic but, sad to say, European as well – right up to our present time.'

'Methods, Mr Turner?' Colleen seized on the word. 'Could you elaborate?'

'I would be only too pleased,' the old man replied. 'Initially, the Assassins were formed as a fundamentalist Shi'ite sect–'

'You mean, religious?' Colleen almost protested, knowing how Michael would react.

'Zealously so,' the elderly librarian nodded. 'To such an extreme they regarded the murder of their enemies as a sacred duty – of the same level as a jihad, the word used by Muslims for a holy war against unbelievers, or infidels as they call them.'

Colleen leant forward to listen as Mr Turner continued.

'To understand why, one has to go way back to the cause of their formation, to the death of the prophet Mohammed in AD six hundred and thirty-two. Following this, Islam underwent a struggle over who should succeed him. The orthodox Muslims, the Sunnis, believed their rightful leader should be the elected Caliph of Baghdad, whereas the Shias, the fundamentalist Muslims, were vehement that the "Appointed One" – as they call him – should be chosen from among their priest-kings, their Imams, who they believed – and still do, to this present day – to be directly descended from Mohammed, through his daughter, Fatima, and his son-in-law, Ali.'

The old gentleman paused. 'I hope this isn't too boring for you, Mrs Callaghan?'

'On the contrary,' Colleen smiled at him. 'This is all new to me. I'm finding it fascinating.'

Looking pleased by her response, Mr Turner cleared his throat and continued.

'To cut a long story short, the Sunnis won. But some four centuries later, around the year ten-ninety, when the incumbent Caliph of Baghdad died, a Shi'ite sect calling themselves the Nizari Ismailis, decided their claim could be best enforced through a reign of assassination and terror. To achieve this they set up what can best be described as a mujahidin training-camp – an Arabic word, derived from a person who fights a jihad – situated it in an isolated castle called Alamut – meaning Eagle's Nest – high up in the mountains, south of the Caspian Sea…Are you sure this isn't too tedious for you, Mrs Callaghan?'

'Please, Mr Turner.'

The old man cleared his throat again. 'Their strength lay in the structure of their organisation. Their founder, a fanatic named Hasan-i-Sabbah, was their first Grand Master. Then came the missionaries, known as Da'is, followed by their disciples, the Rafiqs, and finally, the Fida'is, the devotees and actual assassins, trained experts in sword-play, and the use of drugs–'

'Drugs?' Colleen cut in, scenting another lead, 'and swords?'

'Very much so,' Joseph Turner replied. 'The name Assassins is derived from their word hasisi – meaning "hashish-eater" – based on their taking the drug to give them courage before being setting out on their murderous missions. In fact their knowledge of drugs – and not just hashish – was remarkable, not only as a means of assassination, but also to control the minds of the Fida'is to believe that dying for their cause was a sacred duty.'

The ex-librarian took a sip of water from a glass on a table beside him. 'To elaborate. First, the Fida'i would be given a drug to make him experience the terrors of Hell, and when he'd recovered, given another narcotic to induce a vision of Heaven – rather,' he added, 'like the Jesuits.'

'The Jesuits?' Colleen exclaimed, feeling the old-timer was making too strong a comparison, comparing heathens with an order of her own Catholic faith.

'Very much so,' Mr Turner insisted, 'except the Jesuits use the power of the imagination, rather than drugs.'

Seeing Colleen about to protest again, 'But forgive me,' he smiled from the depths of his chair, 'I'm digressing. An old man's weakness.' And before she could do so, he continued.

'During this second dream, the Fida'i would be taken to Alamut, then to a hidden valley guarded by the castle, specially created to be the most beautiful, fruitful garden ever seen. Marco Polo, who visited it after the Mongols destroyed the Assassins, said it rivalled our conception of the Biblical Garden of Eden. The Fida'i would wake up there, in a state of semi-consciousness, believing himself to be in Assama – Paradise – and see Hasan, the Grand Master – or Ayatollah, another name for him – standing before him clothed in white, pretending to be Allah, and telling him he had been specially chosen for a holy mission to kill Sunni leaders, the more the merrier – but should he be killed in his quest, he would spend his eternal life there, in Assama – with seventy beautiful maidens all exclusively his, to tend to his every need – rather than the Hell of his first drug created vision. The Fida'i would then be drugged again and taken back to the castle, where he'd wake up believing he'd seen Allah and, with his courage bolstered by more hashish, would set out on his holy mission, determined to earn martyrdom and so earn himself life eternal in some Islamic garden of Paradise.'

Colleen shook her head. 'Hearing all this makes me sympathise with Michael. When it comes to the Day of Judgement, even religion itself is going to have much to answer for.'

'Michael?' Joseph Turner queried.

'My husband. He was a cavalry officer during our civil war. The sights he saw turned him away from God.'

'But one cannot blame religion for the acts of warfare. Or for the acts of individuals.'

'According to Michael, it's the cause of most of our troubles.'

'And what about yourself, Mrs Callaghan?'

'I'm a Catholic, but there are times when my faith is sorely shaken.'

'But surely it is how each of us responds to religion that ultimately matters,' Mr Turner persevered. 'Otherwise God would have made us all His puppets. But in His infinite wisdom He gave us free will, to choose our own destinies.'

The old man peered at her over the top of his pince-nez. 'Suggest to your husband that he might consider the matter prayerfully – and he could find himself agreeing.'

'I'll try,' Colleen responded, 'but I don't hold out much hope.'

Joseph Turner gave her an understanding smile then touched the papers. 'Well, whatever the outcome, Mrs Callaghan, there is more, should you care to hear it.'

- 41 -

Henry Pisani's first-floor office above the Galliano Bank was the untidiest Callaghan had ever seen. Worse even than Louis Jennings' at The New York Times. Bookcases overflowing with battered law books; cupboards crammed so full of splitting document-cases the doors would not close; and a plethora of loose files scattered over the floor. Pisani's desk was no better, littered with papers and documents, yet the slim, olive-skinned, dark-haired man sitting behind it, had the confident air of one who knew where everything was.

'I shall be happy to represent you, gentlemen,' he agreed, from his chair behind the desk. In his thirties, the son of a penniless Italian count who had married the daughter of a wealthy British army major stationed in Gibraltar, Henry Peter Pisani was sent to England at the age of seven to be educated at a preparatory school, then Harrow, finally graduating with a law degree from Oxford University and returning home to set up his own law practice.

'My fee for salvage claims is ten percent. But I must warn you, our task will not be an easy one. From what I hear, Captain, Mr Flood seems to regard you as a modern day Blackbeard, and your crew as the most unprincipled villains.

'Please don't misunderstand me,' he raised his hand to prevent Morehouse from protesting. 'This is not my view. I am merely emphasising how determined he apparently is to see you all brought to trial. And because such stories are circulating, I must ask each of you for confirmation that there is absolutely no truth whatsoever in what he is claiming. I trust you will forgive my having to ask such a question, but before we start preparing for the Inquiry, you will appreciate I do so only in your best interests.'

Henry Pisani sat back, waiting expectantly for their response.

Seeing David and Oliver tensing, Callaghan replied. 'There's no truth in any of it, Mr Pisani."

Their given reason for Callaghan and Deveau being present at this meeting, was that Michael had been chosen to speak for the crew, whilst Oliver was representing himself and John Wright.

'Captain Morehouse?'

'It's all fabrication,' David growled.

'Mr Deveau?'

'Lies, Mr Pisani.'

'Excellent!' exclaimed the lawyer, magically producing pen and paper from the chaos of the desktop. 'Now, take me through the events, step by step, starting from the moment the *Dei Gratia* first sighted *The Mary Celeste*. Captain Morehouse?'

- 42 -

'I'd forgotten roast beef tasted that good,' said Callaghan, surveying the empty plate. 'And of all the treats, Yorkshire pudding.'

'I noticed you seemed to be enjoying it,' said Colleen. 'Coffee?'

'I'll ring.'

He got to his feet, tugged the bell-cord, and pulled back Colleen's dining chair for her as she arose out of it. They crossed to two armchairs facing the welcoming fire and sat down.

'So, you're seeing Mr Turner again tomorrow?'

'Ten o'clock. I'd love you to meet him. He's a dear.'

'Maybe next week. Except, now we know there's nothing significant about the papers, I don't think there's need to delve any deeper. The chemist's analysis is far more important.'

'I don't agree, Michael,' Colleen protested. 'I still have the feeling we're missing something. I can't help thinking there's more to the documents than Martens being interested in the history of the Assassins. Don't forget the other books inside his sea chest. That's not what you'd expect of a cold-blooded killer.'

'And because he's some kind of psychopathic bookworm, you think the answer lies in them?'

'As could identifying the rapier. Should it belong to a secret society, as Mr Turner thinks, it might also tell us more about our esoteric killer. What he stands for, what his aims are. And may also provide some clue as to how he and Sweeny met–'

Callaghan smiled to soften the harshness of his words. 'I don't want to pour cold water on your theorising, but don't you think you're getting somewhat carried away with all this?'

'In what way?'

'The Assassins, and all the others they spawned, were fanatics dedicated to some religio-political purpose. Martens is Brains' hired assassin. And no matter how catholic Sweeny acts, his only interest in religion is nothing more than an insurance policy in case it turns out there is some sort of life after death. As for politics, we know what motivates him there. Money and power. But Brains getting involved in European politics – why should he? Especially when he's expecting delivery of two barrels containing diamonds worth over two hundred million? Even Sweeny can retire comfortably and happily on that kind of lucre.'

'Comfortably, yes,' Colleen agreed. 'But happily? No. The only time he's happy is when he's doubling or trebling what he's got. As for my getting carried away, there are a number of questions still needing to be answered – Palermo, for example. One ship bound there could be routine. But both must surely be more than a coincidence?'

'Maybe,' said Callaghan, noncommittally. 'It will all be revealed in the end. Still, if you feel so strongly about Martens' interest in the Assassins, how about getting back to them? You'd just started on how they evolved into professional killers for hire, when dinner was served.'

Colleen opened her eyes wide in mock surprise. 'Are you sure you want to hear it? With it being so superfluous and all?'

'But of course,' Callaghan replied, in the same vein. 'What else is there to do behind the closed doors of a beautiful woman's luxury hotel suite, on a cold winter's night?'

Colleen held his gaze. 'Other than continuing my story, I can't imagine.' Suddenly blushing, she returned to where she'd left off in her notes. 'Did I reach the Knights Templar modelling themselves on the Assassins, not only their tiers of organisation, but to the wearing of white tunics like the Rafiqs, the disciples?'

'You did.'

She glanced back at the page. 'Right. Well, some seventy or so years after the Assassins were first formed, the Syrian Islamics broke away from the Persians. Led by their Grand Master, Rashid Ad-Din Sinan, they decided that rather than remain religio-killers, they would sell their services for gold. Saladin, or the Crusaders, it made no difference to them, provided the price was right. One of their first victims was a Conrad of Montserrat, King of Jerusalem and Prince of Tyre. From this, news of these killers for hire spread to the courts of Europe, and as a result they were summoned first to Sicily, then the various states of Italy, followed by France, Spain and Germany. Even some Kings of England are said to have used them to dispose of their enemies. In fact, it's through this sect that the word assassin has become part of our language.'

Colleen looked up from her notes and stressed her next words.

'And though both the Syrian and Persian Assassins were eventually wiped out by the Mongols, similar secret sects had by then sprung up in most European countries. In cases like the Knights Templar their garb was usually white. But any sect created for political or religious assassination, followed the custom of the original Fida'is, wearing black robes with red sashes for the initiation ceremonies, and also their methods of killing with the sword, or failing that, poison…

'Black robes…red sashes…swords…poison,' she emphasised. 'Just like Martens.'

'Except it brings us back to where we started – Sweeny involving himself in European politics. Again, why bother, when he's got two hundred thousand times more than enough as it is?'

'I don't know, Michael,' Colleen confessed. 'But,' she accented, determined not to be daunted, 'if Mr Turner can identify the rapier, maybe it will lead us to the answers. Which reminds me,' she added. 'When Mr Turner was telling me about the religious motive behind the formation of the Assassins, I suddenly thought about the names of both vessels. *Mary Celeste*: Celestial Mary, *Dei Gratia*: God's Grace, and realised both are religious. Like the Palermo riddle, one vessel I could accept. But for both to have religious names seems again to be more than a coincidence.'

A nearby church clock struck ten.

'Maybe.' Callaghan yawned with sudden tiredness. 'Do you mind if we discuss it tomorrow? The last eleven days have suddenly caught up with me, and I'm dead on my feet.'

'You'll never make it to the harbour, Michael,' she seized on on his words, 'let alone the *Dei Gratia*. I think you should stay here the night.'

There was a knock on the door.

'The coffee. That's decided it, Michael. Get into bed and I'll bring it to you.'

Callaghan needed no second invitation.

Colleen opened the door for the waiter to enter, place the tray on a side table and leave. She poured the coffee and took Michael's cup to the bedroom. He was stretched out in the king-sized bed, already asleep. His bare shoulders suggested he was naked. She smiled, her heart soaring at seeing him there.

Kissing him gently, she changed into her silk nightdress and got in beside him.

- 43 -

Colleen was already awake when the morning cannon sent its resounding boom echoing through Gibraltar's narrow alleys. Feeling the chill of winter in the air, she burrowed closer to Michael under the blankets. The dawn light seeping in between the slightly parted curtains enabled her to see his face sleeping beside her.

He stirred slightly at the sound of the gun and moved nearer to her. Feeling the heat of his body radiating towards her, Colleen remembered their cold winter mornings in New York, and the way she'd cosy up to him for warmth as he held her tight in a snug cocoon. They would slowly kiss. And then they would–

His arm went over her. She saw he still was asleep and relaxed against him. Through her silk nightdress she could feel his lean, hard body. Slowly waking up, he drew her closer to him, one leg parted her thighs, his eyelids fluttered open. There was a look of dazed puzzlement on his face as he tried to make out where he was.

His eyes fully opened. The room was too dusky for her to make out their blueness, but they looked into hers for a long moment, then he smiled. 'Good morning, Miss Lowell.'

'Good morning, Mr Callaghan.' she responded.

His lips brushed hers in a gentle yet searching kiss. She returned it, both re-exploring the half-forgotten, yet still remembered fullness of each other's mouths. He drew her closer to him, his hand caressed her back. The pressure of his lips increased. Through her nightdress she felt his body responding. Succumbing to his caress she became possessed by a yearning, long kept under subjugation, a luxuriating sensual feeling that began deep in the pit of her stomach and spread through her entire body. She pressed herself against him. The kiss became more searching as their desire for each other increased.

And overwhelmed them.

She was late getting to the library, but found Turner in the chilly Reference Room, wearing an overcoat, absorbed in a thick, heavy book on the table before him. As she reached him, he looked up, smiling with satisfaction.

'I think I've found what you're searching for, Mrs Callaghan. Do you have your sketch of the rapier with you?'

Colleen produced it from her bag. The ex librarian studied it only briefly. 'Yes, I thought so,' he said, turning the book around for her to see the page.

The book title was in block print at the top of the page:

SECRET SOCIETIES OVER THE AGES

Immediately below it was a chapter heading:

The Black Knights

Halfway down the ensuing text was a detailed drawing of the filigree hilt of a rapier. Though Michael's drawing lacked some of the finer details, there was no doubting they were the same.

'I came in early, anxious to make a start,' Mr Turner said, looking more like Santa Claus than ever, eyes twinkling, his face shining with the pleasure of his success, 'and decided to concentrate on German societies because of the papers you asked me to translate.'

'Thank you, Mr Turner.' Colleen was so thrilled she had to restrain herself from hugging the old man.

'There is quite a bit about them, but if you'd like me to, I can give you a brief summary,' he offered.

'Please, Mr Turner, then I can research the pertinent leads – for my father's book,' she quickly added, withdrawing her notebook and pencil.

'Only too pleased to be of help,' the elderly librarian's face lit up even more. Putting his hand to his mouth, he gave his customary preliminary cough and began.

'There's no doubt that this particular German sect owed their origins to The Assassins. "The Black Knights" was the name they first chose – but now call themselves Totenbund, which means Death League. They're a particularly noxious branch of a German revolutionary movement known as Tugendbund. It's not known when the Totenbund were first formed, but they certainly existed as far back as mediaeval times, maybe further. Being political assassins available for hire, they're known to be ruthless and have their own particular initiation ceremony in which a new member kneels before a table with seven lighted candles, and seven swords laid crosswise, then swears the following oath of fidelity, and I quote…'

Mr Turner peered through his pince-nez at the book, '…If I become unfaithful to my oath, my brethren shall be justified to use these swords against me.'

The ex-librarian looked up at Colleen to stress his next words. 'The new member is then presented with a rapier, a replica of your drawing, *Mrs Callaghan,* and a black robe and red sash.'

Rapier. Black robe. Red sash, Colleen thought. Michael Callaghan, are you going to have to eat your words.

'The book gives many examples of their ruthlessness,' the old man continued, 'but let me quote you one,' he again referred to the book, 'authenticated by a letter from a Doctor Breidenstein, a leading member of the Tugendbund, to Mazzini in November, 1835–'

'Mazzini?' Colleen interjected.

Joseph Turner looked up.

'I'm sorry,' she apologised, 'the name prompted a question in my mind. But it will keep until later. Please continue.'

'Are you sure?'

'Positive.'

'Then the letter was to inform Mazzini that a man living in the Sihl Valley, near Zurich, a Tugendbund member named Louis Lessing, was selling their secrets to the German government, and had therefore been sentenced to be executed by the Totenbund – the Black Knights.'

Turner closed the book. 'Lessing's body was found staked to the ground, stabbed forty-nine times – seven times seven,' he emphasised, and explained the relevance. 'Seven, as you will know, being religious, is regarded as the mystical number, and thus zealously popular with secret societies, its multiplication as a square root especially so.'

'There's a great deal of emphasis on swords,' Colleen observed. 'Does the book say whether the Totenbund also use drugs or poison?'

'No,' Mr Turner shook his head. 'Modern revolutionaries tend to regard themselves more as front-line soldiers, preferring swords, daggers, or pistols, rather than mediaeval, Lucrezia Borgia-type methods.'

'So, drugs remain more associated with the Assassins?'

'Very much so.'

'But as far as you know, would any Black Knight be restricted from copying their methods?'

'I'm no expert on secret societies, Mrs Callaghan. But provided he achieved the end aim, I see no reason why one should not ape them if he so desired.'

'I see,' Colleen assimilated this for a moment, then changed her line of questioning.

'Mr Turner, a moment ago you mentioned Mazzini. I assume you were referring to Giuseppe Mazzini, the Italian revolutionary?'

The ex-librarian nodded. 'The most untiring political agitator in European history.'

'Wasn't he born in Genoa?'

'Born there. Studied there. And died only nine months ago. During his lifetime the whole Italian peninsula became a veritable hotbed of conspiracy and revolt. The Palermo uprising of 1848 was Mazzini inspired. As was Mantua in '52. Milan, '53. Genoa, '57.' The elderly librarian recited the dates from memory, without hesitation. 'Since his death, it's rumoured his leadership of the Carbonari has been taken over by someone even more militant. And there are more than a few whispers of an intended uprising against Victor Emmanuel's rule, with the threat of blood running on the streets, etcetera, etcetera.'

'Carbonari? I assume they're also revolutionaries?'

'A rabid Italian underground movement, in league with the Tugendbund, Mrs Callaghan, in the common interest of ridding themselves of the so-called shackles of their existing governments. Between them, they've attracted every fanatic, every idealist in Europe; men for whom no project is too fantastic, no vision too unrealistic.'

Lowering his voice as if letting Colleen into a great secret, Mr Turner elaborated. 'Ever since Victor Emmanuel's and von Bismarck's attacks on the Catholic Church, they are said to have attracted many men of power and influence. Including Freemasons.'

'Freemasons?' Colleen queried. 'I thought Freemasonry was non-political?'

'In your country, maybe,' the old man replied, 'but in Europe it most certainly isn't.'

He hesitated as if unsure whether to continue then decided to, still in a low voice. 'Take as an example the Grand Orients of the Continent, a branch of the Freemasons which is so political that both the Carbonari and the Tugendbund hide behind it, meeting in Freemasonry owned buildings. And there's nothing either Victor

Emmanuel or von Bismarck can do to prevent them, so powerful is Masonic influence on this side of the Atlantic.'

'Goodness!' Colleen exclaimed. 'What sort of men are we talking about?'

'Magistrates, lawyers, bankers, army officers, and more recently, in both Germany and Italy, even prelates and priests.'

'Priests!' Colleen expressed her surprise. 'Joining up with revolutionaries?'

'I'm afraid there's nothing unusual in this, Mrs Callaghan. The Jesuits have been doing it for centuries. And now, with the Church of Rome under sustained attack, and the Pope a prisoner in the Vatican, clerics from other orders also see revolution as the only way to restore the Church to its former position of power. In addition to the Carbonari and Tugenbund rumours, there is also much talk of Popish-inspired plots to assassinate both Victor Emmanuel and von Bismarck. Even to them working hand in hand to achieve their common aim. Some say this is nothing but evil gossip, but when the Pope himself seems to be openly inciting violence, it is hardly to be wondered that others give it credence. Take his recent speech to a consistory of Cardinals in the Vatican, quoted verbatim in yesterday's *Gibraltar Guardian.* There's one on the table over there, should you care to read it.'

Crossing to the table, Colleen read the *Guardian's* headline, splashed across the front page:

THE POPE ATTACKS
KING VICTOR EMMANUEL AND COUNT BISMARCK

'Take time to read the whole article,' Mr Turner invited. 'In my opinion it is nothing less than a papal call for the faithful to rise up and take up arms in defence of his Catholic Church.'

- 44 -

By the time Callaghan got to Pisani's office, Wright, Anderson and Johnson, were waiting on the landing.

'You're late, Lund,' said the Second Mate. 'The captain and Mr Deveau are already inside. Where did you get to last night?'

'Captain's permission, Mr Wright. I met an old friend. Where are Jimmy, Jorjo and Willie?'

'Mr Pisani sent word that he needs only the testimonies of the men directly involved.'

'Then I'd best go straight in.'

Anderson clapped Callaghan on the shoulder. 'Protect our interests, Charlie.'

'Don't worry, Gus. I will.'

Callaghan knocked on Pisani's door and entered the room. Morehouse and Deveau, sitting stiffly in front of Pisani's desk, looked relieved to see him.

'Sorry to be late, Mr Pisani, Captain Morehouse,' Callaghan apologised.

'No matter, Lund, you're here now,' Morehouse replied, maintaining their pretence.

Pisani indicated the empty chair next to Deveau, waited for Callaghan to sit, then began.

'First, gentlemen, I have bad but not unexpected news from Mr Sprague. He met Flood last evening and failed to persuade him to cancel the Inquiry. The date is next Wednesday. The judge will be Sir James Cochrane. He's a fair but stern man. Nevertheless, apart from being careful how you answer Flood's questions, which I warn you will be subtly, or even craftily worded, Sir James is the one you must satisfy.' Pisani reached for a pencil. 'So, with only three days in which to prepare my case, if I could begin with you, Captain Morehouse?'

'No!' Morehouse exclaimed.

Pisani looked startled. 'I'm sorry, Captain?'

'I can't face him!'

'Can't face him?' Pisani looked puzzled, then his face cleared. 'You mean Flood? Please don't concern yourself about him. Come Wednesday, I will have briefed you well enough to be able to—'

'No!' Morehouse flared, cutting across Pisani. 'I'm not taking the stand.'

'Not taking the stand?' Pisani repeated Morehouse's words. 'Captain, do you realise how this will be interpreted? Especially as you are the main one claiming salvage. It will be tantamount to confessing your own guilt!'

'I'll have to take that chance.' Morehouse gritted.

Pisani regarded his client with bewilderment. 'Would you care to elaborate why?'

'No!' Springing to his feet, knocking over his chair, Morehouse stalked out of the room.

'Mr Deveau,' Pisani appealed to the First Mate, who was himself looking thunderstruck, 'can you explain your Captain's outburst? Which seems to border on the eccentric, if not suicidal?'

'I'm sorry, Mr Pisani,' the flabbergasted Oliver replied. 'It must be the strain he's been under – bringing both vessels in to port with half-crews. And now the added worry of financial penalties should he fail to get his cargo to Genoa on time. They could cripple him.'

'Then all the more reason for him to give evidence, surely,' Pisani argued. 'Forgive me for repeating it, but there is grave danger this could escalate into a full trial and, if found guilty, the death penalty will be requested for you all. You cannot leave anything to chance.

Should your captain persist in his refusal, it is certain that Mr Flood will make great capital of it.'

'Leave him to me, Mr Pisani,' said Oliver, recovering. 'I'll try persuading him.'

'I only pray for you all that you succeed, Mr Deveau. But first,' the lawyer held his pencil poised over a sheet of paper, 'I will take yours and Lund's statements, then allow you to find him while I interview the other three members of your crew.'

Morehouse was waiting for them in the street below.

'I'm sorry,' he said, his eyes filled with anguish. 'But the moment Mr Pisani started asking questions, I realised there's no way I can take the stand.'

'But you're only going to make things look worse,' Callaghan argued. 'Where will that leave Desiah and the children if the Inquiry goes against us and we're put on trial?'

'At least with a fifty-fifty chance,' Morehouse growled. 'But if Flood made me contradict myself, as he'd be bound to do, the odds would be nil. I'm fine behind a ship's wheel, but when it comes to speaking, I get tongue-tied. And my worry over Desiah and the kids would make me worse. I'd have to be one hundred percent sure she was safe before I could take the oath.'

Massaging his furrowed brow, he screwed his eyes closed and opened them. 'Okay, so here's where I stand. If we hear by Wednesday that all three are safe, I'll testify. But if we don't, you'll have to face the Inquiry without me.'

'Then let's just hope we get that reply,' said Callaghan.

- 45 -

Mr W F Roberts looked troubled across the counter at Colleen.

'The seed was just flax, Mrs Callaghan – but the pill is pure strychnine.'

'Merciful heavens!' Colleen clapped her hands to her face in horror.

The chemist's heavy jowls seemed to lengthen. 'What's more, I'd say it was only recently manufactured, and not too long hidden in the Moorish chest you purchased.' He looked grim. 'It is extremely fortunate it did not fall into the wrong hands.'

'Gracious! I'm glad I brought it to you.'

'So am I, Mrs Callaghan,' Mr Roberts replied. 'Otherwise it could so easily have resulted in tragedy.'

Colleen recovered from her shock. 'This isn't morbid curiosity, but as a writer, is death by strychnine violent?'

'Not necessarily,' the chemist seemed reluctant to discuss the subject, 'Not if caused by a strychnos plant of the order Loganiaceae – such as the South American varieties strychnos gubleri and strychnos castelnaei. In such cases death occurs through respiratory paralysis.'

He hesitated, then decided to continue. 'But an alkaloid strychnine taken from a convulsant plant – like the seed of the strychnos nux vomica or the strychnos multiflora, found in the East Indies and the Malay Archipelago – or from the bean you gave me to identify – there's a drawing of it in my reference book–'

'Was that from a convulsant plant?' Colleen cut across him.

'Most definitely. Found only in the Philippines.'

'Mr Roberts,' Colleen continued to play her role, 'this could be a basis for a plot for a novel. Exactly how would you describe a convulsant plant's effect?'

'Most horrific. The pill you found had enough strychnine to kill ten men. Anyone hapless enough to have taken it would have experienced such extreme tetanic convulsions that the spine would almost certainly be snapped in two. It's botanical name is—'

'Heavens above!' Colleen exclaimed. The method of killing confirmed, she wanted to get back to her hotel suite and focus on a wild theory in her mind – prompted by reading the Gibraltar Guardian article. 'Thank you, Mr Roberts. May I leave it to you to dispose of both the pill and the bean?' She turned away from the counter and made for the door.

'Most assuredly,' he replied. 'Mrs Callaghan!' he called out to her as the doorbell jangled, wanting to finish what he was about to say when she interrupted him.

But she didn't hear him.

Mr Roberts watched her pass the window, wondering whether, as a writer, she might have been intrigued by the name of the bean: strychnos ignatii, discovered by Jesuit missionaries in the Philippines, hence its more common name:

The Bean of Saint Ignatius.

- 46 -

'Have I got things to tell you!' Colleen exclaimed as Michael opened the door to her.

He held her close. 'And I've got something to tell you. I've missed you.'

She returned his hug, 'Me, too.' Pulling free, she looked up into his face, unable to control her excitement, yet her green eyes were serious. 'I think I've found the motive for Kaufmann, Reikel and Briggs being killed,' she said, enjoying his look of surprise, then adding, wanting to impress him even more. 'And the method. And the significance of the rapier hilt.'

'My, you have been busy,' Callaghan said with a smile. 'I think we'd best sit down, so you can bring me up to date.'

He led her to their chairs by the lit hearth and sat facing her.

'Okay, so what comes first?'

'The rapier hilt, I think.' Colleen decided. 'It all evolves from that.'

'Then fire away.'

'It belongs to a secret society of political assassins who are not only German but also, just like Martens, wear black robes and red sashes,' she rushed her words, anxious to share it all with him. 'And I think I've worked out the connection between them and Uncle Peter. If I'm correct, it explains how and why he and Martens met. And what we're up against.'

Callaghan listened in silence as Colleen recounted her conversation with Joseph Turner.

'Black Knights? German Totenbund?' he queried when she'd finished, not wholly convinced.

'Are you sure it was the same design?'

'Absolutely certain.'

'But that doesn't make sense. Why would Sweeny involve himself with a bunch of German political assassins?'

'A common purpose?'

'Such as?'

'To rid Italy and Germany of their present governments – or more exact, their dictators.'

'And why would he want to do that?'

'Because Victor Emmanuel and von Bismarck have one thing in common. They're persecuting his Church, especially the Jesuits. Sweeny's not only an ardent Catholic, he's also a fervent Jesuit. I don't know how he got to be involved but his reason is clear – to see his Church restored and the Jesuits reinstated, and the Pope released from captivity.'

Callaghan shook his head. 'I'm sorry Colleen, but I don't buy it. Brains as defender of the faith! No way! Not unless there was something in it for him.'

'Ah, but there is,' she replied with conviction. 'In fact he probably has two motives. First, a passport to Heaven endorsed by the Holy Father himself – rather like a medieval indulgence – against the day when his soul – should he have one – shuffles off his mortal coil. It also explains why he chose religious names for the vessels: Celestial Mary and God's Grace.'

'And the second motive?' Callaghan asked, intrigued.

'Even more enticing for him – financing arms to ensure the counter revolution's success. I'm not saying he's invested the full two hundred million, but big enough to make a handsome profit.'

'He'd want to be guaranteed a three hundred percent return on it,' Callaghan remarked. 'By none other than the Pope himself.' He thought carefully for a moment. 'Okay,' he relented, 'let's for the moment assume you're right, and Martens is a member of these so-called Black Knights – or Totenbund or Death League, whatever they want to call themselves. You think he was chosen by some joint Carbonari-Tugendbund revolutionary committee–'

'Meeting in a Freemasonry building in Genoa,' Colleen interjected. 'It's Mazzini territory with a history of revolution as long as your arm. That explains why the diamonds are bound there – to be sold by a diamond merchant who belongs to the movement.'

'Hold on,' Michael cautioned, 'let's not get side-tracked. Let's stick to your original thought. You believe Martens was sent to New York by Sweeny to liaise with Kaufmann, in order to–'

'No,' she leant forward in her chair. 'It was Father Reikel who was sent – with Sweeny's knowledge – to liaise with Kaufmann. Martens was his bodyguard.'

'Bodyguard!' Callaghan protested. 'Why would Reikel have been involved?'

'Because the threat to Holy Church is now so acute that, according to Mr Turner, priests, even prelates, in both Italy and Germany, are embracing the idea of a counter revolution by the score, seeing it as the only way to remove King Victor Emmanuel and Count Bismarck.'

Seeing Callaghan about to protest again, she elaborated on her theory.

'I think Father Reikel was one of them, chosen because of his ability as an administrator at the College of Propaganda. And Martens was his strong arm protector, a Totenbund assassin, picked because of his known ruthlessness.'

'No,' Callaghan objected. 'I can't buy it. What about Reikel's soup kitchen?'

'What about it?'

'Don't you think it's somewhat contradictory for him to be so concerned for the starving on the one hand, yet be involved in revolution on the other?'

'Not for Reikel. I met him. The look in his eyes made my flesh creep. He'd have seen the restoration of Holy Church as sacred a duty as feeding the five thousand.'

Catching Callaghan's smile, she defended herself. 'I'm not condemning my own faith, just the odd fanatic like Father Reikel, who for some reason almost always turns out to be a Jesuit. Maybe it's to do with their training. It's said to be so intensive it can send the more susceptible of them beyond the bounds of sanity. To the point that Jesuits once masterminded a plot to blow up a king of England and his entire House of Lords, just because he'd banished them from the country. The way Mr Turner told the story was like hearing some lurid novel. Hiding in castle priest holes, and escaping along secret passages—

'Yes. Guy Fawkes, I've read about him. But that was then, this is now.'

'Except they've not changed,' she stressed, 'even to getting rid of a Pope. And that was only a hundred years ago. Pope Clement the Eighth, according to Mr Turner. Killed by poison when he suppressed the Society, and ordered the papal troops to expel them from Rome.'

She produced a newspaper from her carryall 'But it's not just the Jesuits this time. It's the whole Church, with even Pope Pius calling for civil disobedience. But see for yourself,' she gave Callaghan the broadsheet. 'Yesterday's *Gibraltar Guardian*. For you from Mr Turner.'

Callaghan opened the newspaper saw the headline and read on:

THE POPE ATTACKS KING VICTOR EMMANUEL AND COUNT BISMARCK

The article began by reminding its readers of the events leading up to the present situation facing the Church of Rome, quoting from a speech by Francesco Crispi, a leading Italian minister, who advocated "throwing all cardinals into the Tiber" and that "Christianity must be purged of the vices of the Roman Church or else it will perish", and then by Garibaldi, the Italian freedom-fighter and friend of the late Mazzini, comparing priests to "wolves and assassins" and stating that "the Pope is not a true Christian".

As to the bulk of the article, it seemed the Vatican's worst fear – that Rome itself would be lost to Holy Church – was soon to be realised. The Italian Assembly was expected to vote in favour of a Bill to be introduced by the Minister of Justice on November 20, the main provision of which, according to an exact quote from the Bill, was:

> *The laws of 1866, 1867, 1868, 1870, relative to the suppression of religious corporations and conversion of their properties, are to be applied to the province and city of Rome. The properties of religious corporations in the city of Rome are to be converted into inalienable public rentes.*

Even before the 1866 ruling, the report stated, some 13,000 properties owned by the Church, seminaries, churches, monasteries, had been suppressed, with 25,000 seized since. Furthermore, the new Bill was for the State to take over all Mother Church's remaining properties, including the Vatican, with its real threat being to demolish the Holy See's position in the Eternal City itself.

It had prompted an angry reply from Pio Nono, made in an allocution to a consistory of twenty-two cardinals. Callaghan could imagine the scene: A consistory was the highest court in the Church of Rome, composed of the whole body of cardinals and presided over by the Pope himself – in effect a papal senate. But this consistory had clearly been an emergency meeting, because twenty-two cardinals surely represented only those who resided in the Vatican, plus maybe a persecuted few who'd fled there for refuge.

As Callaghan read the extract from the Pope's speech, he was struck by Pio's emotive phraseology, patently worded in order to create total effect in newspapers around the world:

> *The Church continues to be sorely persecuted. This persecution has for its object the destruction of the Catholic Church. It is manifested in the acts of the Italian Government, which summons the clergy to serve in the army, deprives the bishops of the faculty of teaching, and taxes the property of the Church by heavy burdens. This law presented to Parliament on the subject of religious corporations deeply wounds the rights of possession of the Universal Church, and violates the right of our Apostolic mission.*
>
> *In the face of the presentation of this law, we raise our voices before you and the entire Church, and condemn any enactment that suppresses religious families in Rome or neighbouring provinces. We consequently declare void every acquisition of their property made under any title whatsoever.*

The Holy Father was certainly laying it on thick, Callaghan thought, reading on:

> *But our grief at the injuries inflicted on the Church of Italy, is much aggravated by the cruel persecutions to which the Church is subjected in the German Empire, where not only by pitfalls, but even by open violence, it is sought to destroy her, because the persons who not only do not profess our religion, but who do not even know that religion, arrogate to themselves the power of defining the teachings and rights of the Catholic Church. These men, beside heaping calumny upon ridicule, do not blush to attribute persecution to Roman Catholics, and bring accusations against the bishops and the clergy because they will not prefer the laws and will of the State to the holy commandments of the Church.*

In this, our darkest hour, we invoke Almighty God to come to the aid of His Church, and thank Him for the activity of those of our number who do battle against the iniquity of the oppressors.

Callaghan looked up.

'Well?' Colleen questioned. 'What do you think?'

'Inflammatory, to say the least.'

'And that's an understatement.'

Callaghan was near to surrendering. 'Okay, so assuming Reikel was the one sent to New York, why did Martens kill him?'

'Because he refused to agree to the death of Kaufmann, a fellow Catholic. But, by that time, Reikel's work was over and Martens killed him, too.'

'Why use poison?'

'A rapier's not the easiest weapon to carry about the streets of a city. Then later, with Briggs, in the hope that Richardson and Gilling would think his death to be a natural one, bury the body at sea, and continue on to Genoa.'

Callaghan was silent, pondering Colleen's theories.

'All of which explains Martens' interest in the Assassins,' she prompted him. 'Especially their use of drugs. You were right about the Brandreth pill. It had enough strychnine to kill ten men, and cause such convulsions it explains the snapped spines of all three victims, Father Reikel, Kaufmann and Briggs.'

Callaghan was almost convinced. 'Okay, so it all fits – except for your reservation about both vessels sailing to Palermo being more than a coincidence.'

'Perhaps I made too much of it? Maybe Palermo is nothing more than a cover, as we first thought? To pick up return cargoes rather than return home with empty holds?'

'Okay, let's say you're right,' Callaghan conceded he could find no further holes in Colleen's reasoning. 'In which case we can assume that Martens must be in Gibraltar by now, and that he's wired Sweeny – probably in some code they've agreed on – telling him both brigs are under arrest pending an Inquiry.'

'Yes, more than likely. So what do you think Sweeny will do?'

'Guessing, the same as Consul Sprague. Forward the bills of lading to the British Admiralty Court and apply for both cargoes to be released – but to other vessels. Despite Mr Sprague's optimism, I think the *Gratia*, her crew, and the *Celeste*, will all remain confined to Gibraltar until this Inquiry's over. But its only interest is what happened to *The Mary Celeste's* captain and crew, there's nothing to stop the legal owners of the cargoes – in other words, the companies Sweeny's hiding behind – from demanding they be transferred to other ships, and allowed to continue on to Genoa, their port of destination.'

'If he does that,' Colleen observed, 'then our own plans could end right here.'

'As they can anyway,' Callaghan reminded her, 'if the Inquiry goes against us and we're put on trial for murder.'

Genoa

As Don Cottone's large steam yacht, Santa Maria, entered Genoa harbour, Sweeny stood at the rail, getting his first glimpse of the ancient city known throughout Italy as La Superba. Yet he was indifferent to the sight of its many-hued, multi-tiered beauty, ascending the encircling hills.

His mind was racing ahead to the wire from Kaufmann that should be waiting for him in the Hotel de Genes. As soon as he knew the names of both vessels and their dates of arrival in Genoa, he and Cottone could get down to the final agreement of his big new scheme. But not, of course, on paper. No incriminatory signatures.

He would have preferred Guilamo to have been with them, rather than Carlo Maranzano, Cottone's son-in-law, guiding their talks in the Jesuit priest's diplomatic way, quietly advising Sweeny if his terms were too high, and subtly guiding Cottone to meet Sweeny halfway. And above all, emphasising to them both the colossal money they would make, once every condition was agreed to, and their hugely ambitious scheme no longer just talk, but a reality.

But what the hell, "Brains" inwardly shrugged, you can't have it all ways.

Guilamo, because of his greater ability to administrate than Maranzano, had been the one chosen to remain behind in Monreale, to make arrangements for the gradual sale of the diamonds once Kaufmann's asinine bungle had been rectified–

For a brief moment, Sweeny allowed his thoughts to be sidetracked. When Kaufmann finally arrived, then as sure as Hell was hot, the stupid jerk would find himself paying for it, he again vowed to himself. And by pay, he meant pay. Long. Slow. And painful…

But getting back to main issue.

Once both barrels were safely delivered to Palermo, the diamonds would be filtered in batches to Exchanges throughout Europe and sold. $200 million. Sweeny almost salivated at the thought, keeping $150 million himself, and putting $50 million into the new partnership – "The Sweeny Ring", as he liked to think of it, he'd never taken to playing second fiddle to Tweed. After all, it was he, Peter Barr Sweeny, who'd masterminded every scheme bearing Boss Tweed's name.

Brains chomped his cigar, gloating as he thought of the immensity of the plan, and – quoting Guilamo – "the huge scale of the rewards".

Especially all the lucre he planned to cream off for himself.

- 47 -

Wednesday, December 18, 1872

'All rise!' The command came from the registrar, Edward Baumgartner.

The packed courtroom stood. Over the years, many cases had been heard by Gibraltar's Vice-Admiralty Court but none, according to Pisani, had attracted so many rumours: piracy and murder on the high seas, collusion between Briggs and Morehouse to fraudulently claim salvage on the *Mary Celeste*, with Briggs and his crew being landed somewhere on the coast of Spain or the Azores, to await their share of the prize money.

Again according to Pisani, these and other such stories had been created by Solly Flood himself, to achieve maximum publicity and thus ensure the Inquiry received a full and captive audience, with the spotlight very much on himself – and headlined in the international press.

If so, he'd achieved his aim, Callaghan glanced over the room behind him. Every row filled and people standing as many as six-deep at the back. Colleen was sitting three rows behind Consul Sprague, in the second row. There was no sign of Martens. Relieved his face was still protected from the German for when they would hopefully be released to continue on to Genoa, he gave Colleen a flitting nod of confirmation and refaced the Bench.

The proceedings being an Inquiry, not a full trial, he and the rest of the *Gratia's* crew were in the front row, seated in the order Pisani intended calling them to take the stand: Deveau by the aisle, then Wright, followed by himself, Gus Anderson and Johnson. Next was

Morehouse. With no reply yet from Commissioner Smith regarding Desiah and the children, he was still refusing to give evidence, despite Pisani's warnings of how this would be construed by Sir James Cochrane. Next to Morehouse was Orr, then Higgins, and finally young Cleary, his face deathly pale and his hands visibly trembling.

Pisani was on the other side of the barrier, his papers spread across a table, with Solly Flood at a second table. Their first glimpse of their seventy-one year old antagonist had been only a few minutes earlier, when the Queen's Proctor entered the room. Narrow of face and thin lipped with darting eyes, he resembled a weasel wearing a grey wig, Callaghan thought.

The door behind the Bench opened, Sir James Cochrane entered. A tall man with a lined face, he looked to be in his mid-sixties. Everyone in the courtroom stood up.

'Before the worshipful Sir James Cochrane,' proclaimed Mr Baumgartner. 'Judge and Commissary of the Vice-Admiralty Court of Gibraltar, this day, Wednesday, the eighteenth of December, in the year eighteen hundred and seventy-two, this being the day to take evidence of First Mate Oliver Deveau and Second Mate John Wright, of the brigantine *Dei Gratia*, and three of her crew, Charles Lund, Augustus Anderson, John Johnson, against the vessel called *Mary Celeste* and her cargo, proceeded against as a derelict. This Court is now in session. Be seated.'

The courtroom sat down again with a muted hum of anticipation. The registrar continued.

'The Queen, in Her Office of Admiralty, is represented by Frederick Solly Flood, Esquire, Advocate and Proctor for the Queen in Her Office of Admiralty. Captain David Morehouse, the officers and crew of the brigantine *Dei Gratia*, claiming as salvors, are represented by Mr Henry Peter Pisani, Advocate and Proctor.' Mr Baumgartner sat down and the Inquiry began.

'Mr Pisani?' Sir James addressed the attorney.

'Your worship?' Pisani questioned.

'I see that Captain Morehouse is not to give evidence.'

Pisani's face tightened. 'No, your worship.'

'I assume you have your reasons, Mr Pisani,' Sir James commented. 'But it seems strange not to call on the *Dei Gratia*'s captain, and rely instead on the testimonies of her First and Second Mates and three of her crew. You may call your first witness.'

'Your worship,' Pisani replied, tension clearly heard in his voice at this immediate setback. 'I call Oliver Deveau.'

Oliver entered the witness stand. The registrar handed him a Bible. The First Mate placed his hand on it and swore: "The evidence I shall give will be the truth, the whole truth and nothing but the truth, so help me God.' He gave the Bible back and gripped the rail with both hands.

Pisani began with a simple question to put him at ease. 'Mr Deveau, would you tell us your occupation?'

'I am the Chief Mate of the vessel *Dei Gratia*,' Deveau blurted.

'You may take your time replying, Mr Deveau,' Pisani said in another attempt to calm him. 'Now, please tell us about your voyage?'

Deveau took a deep breath. 'We left New York on the fifteenth of November, bound for Gibraltar for orders.'

'And your Captain's name?'

'Captain Morehouse, Ship's Master.'

'When did you first sight *The Mary Celeste*?'

'On the fifth of December, sea time.'

'Would you describe the circumstances?'

'I was below at the time. The Captain called me and said there was a strange sail on the wind-ward bow, apparently in distress.'

'What time was this?'

'About three pm, sea time.'

'And what happened next?'

251

'I came on deck and saw a vessel through the glass. She appeared to be four or five miles off. The master proposed to speak to the vessel in order to render assistance, if necessary. We hauled up, hailed the vessel, but there was no answer. We lowered the boat and I and two men boarded her. The first thing I did was sound the pumps which were in good order.'

'Did you find anyone on board?'

Glancing at Callaghan, mindful of the oath he'd just sworn, Deveau declared, 'No, sir, no one,' then, under Pisani's careful prompting, he continued his evidence, telling the hushed court about finding the hatches off; three and a half feet of water in the hold; the condition of the *Celeste's* sails; the binnacle stove-in; that the crew's clothes, and those of a woman's and child's, were still on board – as if everyone had left in a panic – that there was no sign of the ship's register or any other papers, only the log book written up to the 24th November; and the log-slate for the 25th which told that on that day, the *Celeste* had made the island of Saint Mary.

This took up the morning session. During the break Callaghan stood with Wright and the crew, away from Morehouse and Deveau, and apart from Colleen. When the Inquiry resumed it was the middle of the afternoon before Pisani reached his final question.

'Mr Deveau, would you please tell the court why you erased the log-slate, not realising it would be subsequently required as evidence of *The Mary Celeste's* abandonment?'

'I had to use it for my own entries, and unintentionally rubbed it clean when I came to use it.'

'Thank you, Mr Deveau. That concludes my examination of this witness, your worship.'

Solly Flood prepared to rise.

'Mr Flood,' Sir James intervened. 'I have some questions I wish to ask Mr Deveau.'

'Certainly, your worship.' Flood sat down again with evident bad grace.

'Mr Deveau,' Sir James addressed the First Mate. 'What type of vessel is the *Celeste*?'

'The vessel is a brigantine rigged, your worship, of, I should say, over two hundred tons.'

'In your opinion, was she seaworthy?'

'The vessel, I would say, was seaworthy, and almost a new vessel.'

'Did she have a lifeboat?'

'It appeared as if she carried a boat on deck. There was a spar lashed across the stern davits, so that no boat had been there.'

'Somewhat unusual? To carry only one boat? After checking her, what did you do next?'

'I went back to my own vessel, told her state to the Captain, and proposed taking her in.'

'And as it appears we are not to hear from Captain Morehouse, what was his reply?'

Oliver's hands again tightened on the rail. 'He told me to weigh the matter well, your worship, as there would be grave risk to our lives and to our own vessel.'

'Nevertheless,' Sir James looked across the court-well at Morehouse, 'after weighing up the considerable benefit of a successful salvage claim, he allowed you to persuade him?'

'Yes, your worship. He gave me two men, the small boat, barometer, compass and watch. I took with me my own nautical instruments, and some food our steward had prepared. We went on board that afternoon, the fifth, and arrived in Gibraltar the morning of the thirteenth of December.'

'The day after the *Dei Gratia*,' Sir James stressed. 'Being so undermanned, did you not think it advisable to stay together?'

Deveau quickly glanced at Callaghan and drew on a well-rehearsed reply. 'When we got into the Straits, it came on a storm, so I dare not make the bay, but laid under Cueta, and afterwards on the Spanish coast to the East.'

Callaghan saw Flood look back at him, then make a hurried note.

'When did you next speak to your Captain?' Sir James prompted.

'When I arrived in Gibraltar, your worship, and found the *Dei Gratia* already there. I had seen her every day during the voyage, and spoke to him three or four times – until the night of the storm when our vessels lost sight of each other.'

'Thank you, Mr Deveau.' Sir James turned to the Queen's Proctor. 'Mr Flood.'

'Your worship.' Flood rose to his feet and advanced on the witness-box. Callaghan saw Deveau swallow hard.

'Mr Deveau,' Flood's tone was immediately accusing. 'Exactly when did the *Dei Gratia* leave New York?'

'On the fifteenth of November,' Deveau replied, a pitch higher than his normal voice and a sign of his tension.

'And by the oddest of coincidences,' the Queens's Proctor returned, adding incredulity to his tone, '*The Mary Celeste* also set sail from the same port. Would you happen to know the date of her departure?'

'According to the log, she left eight days before us…Or eleven.'

Flood raised his eyebrows. 'Eight?' He deliberately paused. 'Or maybe eleven?'

'More or less,' Deveau faltered.

'Mr Deveau,' the Queen's Proctor protested, 'as a First Mate you must surely know how to read a ship's log? Was it eight? Was it eleven? Or might it have been in between? Nine, perhaps? Or maybe ten?'

'I can't say,' Oliver replied, desperately trying to recall. 'I don't exactly know what number of days she left before us.'

'How very strange. I would have thought a trained seaman like yourself was capable of being more precise. However, calling on your now proven expertise as a First Mate, please tell me – what is your opinion of *The Mary Celeste's* seaworthiness?'

'I found the vessel a fair sailor,' Deveau replied, warily.

'What about the *Dei Gratia*?'

'I would call her a fair sailor also.'

'In other words, there was very little or no difference between the two vessels?'

Deveau again hesitated, unsure where the Queen's Proctor was leading him. 'I suppose,' he finally stated, 'that if both vessels were equally manned, *The Mary Celeste* would be faster than the *Dei Gratia*.'

Flood seized on the reply. 'Yet the slower *Dei Gratia* reached Gibraltar first. What's more, it did so despite it being a storm, whereas…' crossing to his table, he referred to a sheet of paper, 'the swifter *Celeste* – quoting your own words – dare not make the bay but laid under Cueta, and afterwards on the Spanish coast to the East. End of quote.'

'There were only three of us,' Deveau protested.

'And I would remind you Mr Deveau, that excluding Captain Morehouse and the ship's cook, the slower *Dei Gratia* had a crew of only four.'

The thin-lipped advocate allowed this retort to hang in the air, then theatrically hitched up his gown. 'But be that as it may, let us go back to when you first found the *Celeste*. You will agree with me, I take it, that the shipping lane between New York and Gibraltar is an extremely busy one? And that *The Mary Celeste* left New York some eight…nine…ten, or maybe even eleven days before the *Dei Gratia*? By then, she had – according to her log-slate – been abandoned for ten days. Yet no other ship on this busy shipping route seems to have seen her, until you arrived on the scene.'

The Queen's Proctor paused for effect. 'I confess, Mr Deveau, that I find this hard to believe.'

Oliver took a moment to gather himself. 'We spoke to only one other brig, bound for Boston. We saw no other vessel of any class, on our outward voyage.'

'If that is your story, Mr Deveau, then although I find it to be very strange, we must accept it as fact. In which case, let us go further back to the twenty-fifth of November, the day – according to her slate – that *The Mary Celeste* was supposedly abandoned. What was the *Dei Gratia*'s position on that same day?'

'I can't say,' Deveau objected, 'not without referring to the ship's log. Only that we were to the north of the *Celeste*, somewhere between latitudes forty and forty-two degrees.'

'But if you cannot recollect your position,' Flood narrowed his eyes in fake perplexity, 'how do you know you were to the north of the Celeste?'

'From seeing the *Celeste's* track, traced on her chart.'

'Ah, yes, from the chart which, if my memory serves me well, showed *The Mary Celeste* to be off the island of Saint Mary? Are you acquainted with the island, Mr Deveau?'

'No. I have made only one voyage from New York to Gibraltar before, and did not sight Saint Mary then.'

'You are certain?'

'I never was at Saint Mary. Never saw it.'

'But as an experienced First Mate, as we now know you to be, could you land on it?'

Deveau ignored the barb. 'I could enter Saint Mary with the help of charts, just as well as any port to which I've not previously been without reference to a chart or sailing directions.'

'I said land, Mr Deveau, by which I meant beaching a small boat on a stretch of her shore. You used enter. Do I understand you to be saying that you could sail into Saint Mary harbour without ever having entered it before?'

'I don't know what sort of harbour Saint Mary is,' Deveau countered.

'Then let us leave this point for the moment, though we will return to it.' Flood put his hand to his chin, pretending to ponder. 'When you met the *Celeste*, which direction was she headed?'

'Her head was westward when we first met her.'

'And her tack?'

'She was on a starboard tack.'

'Her wheel was presumably lashed?'

'The wheel was not lashed.'

'Indeed? How very odd. From which direction was the wind?'

'The wind was north.'

'And for me to understand the situation properly, you did say her lifeboat was gone?'

'Yes. We could see where it had been lashed across the mainhatch, although that was not the right place for it.'

'Nor the easiest place from which to launch it, especially during a storm with the wheel unlashed. How do you suppose they accomplished it, Mr Deveau?'

'There was nothing to show how the boat was launched, or signs of any tackle to launch her.'

After a full day of being questioned, Deveau's voice was suddenly sounding weary.

Flood narrowed his eyes again. 'But on finding the *Celeste's* entire complement missing – and remembering that this is a vessel you yourself stated to be so seaworthy she looked like a new ship – did you not consider that some other vessel might have found her before you?' Flood's tone was suddenly accusatory. 'And maybe killed everyone on board? When you searched her, did you look for weapons? Knives? Or maybe even swords?'

'No,' Oliver exclaimed. 'I did not see any knives.'

'Oh, come, Mr Deveau. No knives? Not even in the galley?'

'Mr Flood,' Sir James interrupted sternly. 'I think we are digressing. If you have a point to make, please do so.'

The Proctor hesitated then changed his mind. 'With your worship's permission, I would prefer to return to it at a later stage.'

'As you wish, Mr Flood,' said Sir James, again addressing his own question to the First Mate. 'Mr Deveau, do you have any explanation to offer as to why the *Celeste* was abandoned?'

With visible relief, Deveau looked away from Flood. 'My idea, your worship, is that the crew got alarmed. The sounding rod was lying alongside the pumps. They must have sounded them, found perhaps a quantity of water in them, and thinking she'd go down, abandoned her.'

'Hm,' Sir James reflected. 'Abandoned in panic.'

The darkened windows showed that dusk was fast approaching. Flood had returned to his table and was already gathering up his papers, as was Pisani.

'One last point, Mr Deveau,' asked Sir James. 'After reaching the Straits, exactly how far along the Spanish coast did you sail?'

Flood looked up and watched Deveau closely as the First Mate drew on another rehearsed reply. 'We must have run up the Spanish coast some thirty miles after leaving Cape Cueta, your worship. Maybe even forty miles.'

'A devil of a way to sail before finding calm waters,' Sir James observed. 'Especially as the *Dei Gratia* was able to make Gibraltar without any trouble. But we will leave it at that for today. I am unable to be in court tomorrow. We will therefore adjourn until Friday.'

Callaghan looked across at Solly Flood. He was so busy making notes on Deveau's reply, he seemed reluctant to stand as the court rose for Justice Cochrane to vacate the Bench.

'Michael?' Colleen murmured, nestling against him and pulling the blankets around them.

'Yes?'

'Why did Flood stop asking about the sword?'

'Where did that suddenly spring from?'

'From nowhere.'

'And here's me thinking you were dreaming back to a moment ago.'

'That was then. This is now.'

'Will a man ever understand the workings of a woman's mind?'

'Sometimes. But not often.'

'The sometimes is worth it,' Callaghan murmured.

'Mmm. But why did he?'

'I take it we're back to Flood?'

'Yes.'

'Ever see a cat play with a mouse?'

'Deliberately leaving the kill to the end?'

'Until he thinks, that we think, we've escaped his claws. Then he'll pounce, if you can imagine a scrawny bewigged Queen's Proctor pouncing.'

'Ugh. I don't like the look of him.'

'I'm not too keen on him myself.'

'I wonder what Sweeny's planning at this moment?'

'Your mind does wander.' He stroked her shoulder. 'At the most untimely moments.'

'What time are you calling again on Consul Sprague?' But her voice was a whisper now.

'You see. Point made. Later today. Why?'

'I thought an extra lie-in would do us both good.'

'I'll need persuading.'

Turning on to her back, Colleen put her arms around him and drew his lips down to hers.

'Since when?'

- 48 -

Mr Sprague gave Callaghan the first of three telegraphs to read:

```
NEW YORK, DECEMBER 18, 1872

AMERICAN CONSUL, GIBRALTAR

CALLAGHAN AUTHORISED. DESIAH MOREHOUSE STILL
UNTRACED.

GENERAL W SMITH, NY POLICE
```

'Which means David Morehouse will still refuse to take the stand,' Callaghan said, and gave a heartfelt sigh. 'Can it get any worse? And Solly Flood only too anxious to capitalise on it!'

'Yes, I was in court yesterday,' said Sprague, 'and got the distinct feeling he intends to prove you all guilty and have you face a full trial for murder.'

He handed Callaghan the other two wires. 'I've had these a couple of days, but knowing you were busy with Pisani, I held them back.'

Callaghan scanned the top one:

```
GENOA, 14 DECEMBER 1872 ·

AMERICAN CONSUL, GIBRALTAR

DOCUMENTATION SENT BY RAIL. SWEENY NOT HERE

O M SPENCER, CONSUL
```

'Not there?' Callaghan looked up at Sprague. 'Then where on earth is he?'

Sprague indicated the other wire. 'Palermo.' Callaghan read it:

```
PARIS, 14 DECEMBER 1872

AMERICAN CONSUL, GIBRALTAR

POSTAL REDIRECTIONS SUGGEST SWEENY IN PALERMO

HOFFMAN, FIRST SECRETARY
```

'Palermo!' Callaghan exclaimed. 'What the hell's he doing there?'

'This explains why both vessels are bound there,' said Colleen. 'They can unload the correct number of barrels in Genoa to agree with the bills of lading, and then continue on to Palermo with the extra barrels on board, without any—'

'That explains how, it doesn't explain why,' Callaghan cut across her, poking the fire and watching the flames leap up the chimney.

'Oh, but it does,' said Colleen. 'According to Mr Turner, Palermo has a history of revolution every bit as long and violent as Genoa's. From the Mazzini-led uprising of '48, to only six years ago when Victor Emmanuel had to send in gunboats to bombard it into submission. But despite that, it's now seemingly as ungovernable as ever, which makes it the ideal place for storing arms, as well as distributing them to both sides of the Italian peninsula.'

Callaghan wasn't convinced. 'In that case, why bother with Genoa? Why not sail straight to Palermo?'

'I'm not sure,' Colleen pondered. 'Going with our original thought, maybe the attraction of Genoa was her Diamond Exchange, but the plan was changed when Sweeny decided Palermo was a safer haven, forcing Kaufmann to add extra barrels, and alter the destinations as best he could.'

'Maybe,' Callaghan conceded reluctantly. 'But I still get the feeling there's more to it.'

'Except should Sweeny succeed in getting the cargoes transferred to other vessels before the Inquiry's over,' Colleen stressed, 'we may never get the chance of finding out.'

'It's all one hell of a mess,' Michael agreed. 'Sweeny somewhere in Palermo, God only knows exactly where. Martens gone missing and unlikely to appear unless the Inquiry finishes quickly in our favour. And Desiah Morehouse still not found.'

'Do you think Martens' accomplices are holding her?'

'No,' Callaghan shook his head. 'Coming from Europe, I doubt he made any New York connections. I think his threat's a bluff, made up on the hoof. But on the chance that he is part of some universal fraternity of assassins, we can't take the risk. However, one thing's for certain...'

Sipping her coffee, Colleen's eyes stayed fixed on his face.

'David will still refuse to give evidence until she's found. Which won't help Judge Cochrane decide in our favour. And tomorrow I'm called to the stand, which means swearing the oath under a false name, and getting deeper and deeper into the mire.'

- 49 -

Friday, December 20, 1872

Callaghan took the stand, swore the oath and waited for Pisani's first question.

The courtroom was in dusk, most of the day having been spent by Solly Flood continuing to cross-question Deveau, then Wright, whose replies had mostly repeated the First Mate's testimony.

'What is your name?' Pisani began.

'Charles Lund,' Callaghan lied, ignoring Colleen's and Sprague's worried frowns.

'And your occupation?'

'I am one of the crew of the *Dei Gratia*.'

'Would you please recount the events, from the first sighting of *The Mary Celeste*, to bringing her into Gibraltar. As concisely as possible, Mr Lund. Mr Deveau and Mr Wright have already given them in considerable detail, in reply to Mr Flood's flood of questions.'

There was a burst of laughter in court. Sir James banged his gavel and silence was restored.

'We sighted *The Mary Celeste* on the fifth of December, sea time,' Callaghan replied. 'I was not on watch, but came up from below. I was ordered to board the vessel the second time with the First Mate and Anderson. It was three o'clock when we went on board. We brought the vessel to Gibraltar, arriving on the thirteenth, and found the *Gratia* already there. We had kept sight of her until reaching the Straits, but lost her when the weather began blowing hard.'

'Thank you, Mr Lund,' said Pisani, returning to his table. 'Mr Flood.'

Solly Flood stood up and gave Callaghan a suspicious look. 'I must congratulate you, Lund. When Mr Pisani asked you to be concise I doubt even he expected such a succinct, or should I say, well-rehearsed reply.' With sarcastic emphasis, he added. 'I trust you will not mind if I ask you to elaborate a little?'

'Not at all.'

'Thank you. I am extremely grateful.'

Flood moved out from behind his table. 'Now, Mr Lund, according to the testimonies of both Mr Deveau and Mr Wright, we are being asked to believe that only three persons – First Mate Deveau, Anderson, and yourself – sailed the *Celeste* to Gibraltar. A most remarkable achievement. One might even say extraordinary. Heroic, even,' he added with irony. 'However, in your most concise of statements, you said you kept the *Dei Gratia* in sight until reaching the Straits. Exactly how many days out of Gibraltar would that have been, Mr Lund?'

'About two days.'

'Two days? You are sure of that?'

'I think so,' Callaghan deliberately hedged, realising Flood was leading up to something.

'Mr Wright stated three?'

Callaghan shrugged. 'It may have been three.'

'Two days…or perhaps three? Maybe, like Mr Deveau's memory on leaving New York, it could have been five…or even ten?'

'It was neither ten or five,' Callaghan replied calmly. 'To the best of my recollection it was two or three.'

'I see. Two.' Solly Flood gave his now familiar pause. 'Or three?'

'I'm sure it was two.'

'Sure – but not certain. Nevertheless, now within sight of land, you suddenly lost sight of her? Yet for over six hundred miles of open sea you managed to sail together side by side?'

'It was bad weather.'

'It must have been,' Flood said sarcastically. 'So bad it forced the *Celeste* to sail forty miles into the Mediterranean. Yet not so bad as to prevent the *Dei Gratia* from entering Gibraltar and registering a claim for salvage. Eh, Mr Lund?'

Flood glared at him, trying to goad him into replying, but Callaghan refused to be drawn, letting silence provide his answer.

The Queen's Proctor now reverted to his familiar line of questioning, starting with the first sighting of the *Celeste*, and continuing through to her voyage to Gibraltar, with questions about the sail-setting, the amount of damage suffered by the vessel, the depth of water in the hold and how long it took to pump her dry, clearly trying place doubt on the previous evidence of Deveau and Wright. But Callaghan persisted in giving only the briefest of answers until, with the light continuing to fade inside the courtroom, Flood gave him a final glare and returned to his table.

'Mr Pisani,' said Sir James from the Bench, 'I suggest we examine your remaining witnesses tomorrow.'

Pisani rose to his feet. 'As your worship wishes.'

'Mr Flood?' Sir James queried. 'I take it you have no objections?'

Turning to the *Dei Gratia*'s crew, the Proctor coldly studied them. Seeing the hint of a sneer on his thin lips, Callaghan prepared himself for Flood to now bring up the sword under Briggs bed.

Floood refaced the Bench. 'None, your worship.'

Sir James banged his gavel. 'Court is adjourned until tomorrow, Saturday, the twenty-first of December.'

- 50 -

Born and bred in Gibraltar, Walter Simms had worked in the offices of James Turner & Co (Gibraltar) Limited, Shipping Agents, from the age of fifteen, almost forty years now. And since the advent of the global telegraph system, he had seen Gibraltar become a busy calling-in port for commercial vessels plying the Atlantic and Mediterranean sea routes, a pick-up for new shipping orders negotiated after their last port of call. Much of Turner & Co's work came from acting as intermediaries for the shipping-agents of other countries, and Walter Simms' job was to ensure the necessary paperwork was always ready for the masters of the vessels waiting in the harbour.

Walter Simms loved his work. It put him in touch with almost every port in the western hemisphere – and many in the eastern as well – giving him the feeling of having travelled the world, despite never leaving the Rock. Today, however, was not enjoyable. A partner of Meissner Ackermann, Hamburg and New York, was making Simms uneasy and he was impatient for the meeting to be over. It wasn't so much the German's appearance – black suit contrasting with his abnormally fair hair – it was the way his mesmeric blue eyes were looking straight through Simms, sending a coldness right down to the base of his spine, and making him shiver.

'Right, Herr Meissner,' said Simms, averting his gaze from that of the albinotic partner. 'Your cargo papers as far as Gibraltar are in order. To which port is it now destined?'

'Genoa,' came the whispered reply.

Even the voice was sinister, thought Simms. He hurried on. 'The consignees are presumably yourselves, Meissner Ackermann?'

'Correct.'

'Negotiated price? In British money, if you know it?'

'Seven shillings and three pence a barrel.'

'Is the cargo to be despatched to Hamburg, or remain bonded in Genoa?'

'Bonded.'

'The name of the vessel?'

'It was the *Dei Gratia.*'

Simms looked up sharply. The news of Sir James Cochrane's extended port restriction on this vessel was common knowledge throughout Gibraltar. But Herr Meissner was continuing, 'We cannot wait for the cargo to be held up here any longer, and are arranging to have it transferred to another vessel.'

'And the name of the new vessel?' Walter Simms asked.

'It is not yet decided. I am discussing tenders.'

'Then I will leave it for you to fill in when you know,' Simms volunteered eagerly.

'When will the papers be ready?' the German asked.

Walter Simms calculated. Tomorrow was Sunday. And Herr Meissner had still not agreed an alternative vessel. 'Monday?'

'No later,' Herr Meissner intoned the words. And Simms had the distinct feeling he'd been given an ultimatum.

'Certainly not,' he promised. 'Monday morning. First thing.'

'I will collect them myself.'

'Certainly, Herr Meissner. I will ensure they are ready.'

Even if I have to get here extra early, Walter Simms thought to himself.

- 51 -

The courtroom was again crowded.

Gus Anderson was called to the stand. Pisani began in his usual manner, asking Gus to state his version of the events. Then Flood cross-questioned him, probing for contradictions between his account and earlier testimonies. Eventually the Queen's Proctor asked how long it had taken to straighten the *Celeste*, before making for Gibraltar.

'We got her under sail the same night,' Anderson replied. 'But it took two or three days before we got her right. We had to pump her out first.'

'What is your opinion of *The Mary Celeste?*' Flood asked.

'She was in a fit state to go round the world.' Gus volunteered to Callaghan's dismay.

'Indeed?' Solly Flood commented, raising his eyebrows. 'Which makes it even more difficult to believe that Captain Briggs could have voluntarily deserted her in mid-Atlantic, and ordered everyone to take to the lifeboat, especially with his wife and child on board. Thank you, Anderson. You may step down.'

Still not having made any move to sensationalise the proceedings, Flood re-took his seat.

The final witness was Russian-born "Johnny" Johnson. Knowing that he spoke only limited English, Pisani kept his prompting to a minimum and sat down.

With slow deliberation, Flood got to his feet: 'I have no questions to ask of this witness, your worship. But with your indulgence, I ask permission to meet in the privacy of your chambers.'

Sir James looked stern. 'For what purpose, Mr Flood?'

'In order, your worship...' Flood turned to again play to the court, coldly studying the *Dei Gratia*'s crew, 'to discuss new and alarming matters relating to this case.'

'Is this necessary, Mr Flood?' Sir James demanded.

'Respectfully, yes, your worship.'

'Then I trust I will concur with you, Mr Flood. Mr Pisani?'

'Yes, your worship?'

'Would you accompany us?'

The instant the door closed behind the three men, the courtroom burst into a hubbub of conversations, with spectators huddling into various groups to discuss this latest twist of events.

Morehouse leant across his seat, his face suddenly drawn and anxious. 'What the hell's he up to?' he hissed at Callaghan. Realising it had to be the rapier and aware of Wright and the others watching them, Callaghan shrugged as if ignorant of what was happening and turned to glance at Colleen. Her returned look betrayed her own fears.

The minutes ticked by, then the door suddenly opened. Mr Baumgartner called out, 'All rise.'

The three men re-emerged. Sir James with a grave face. Solly Flood looking exultant. And Pisani clearly angry. The lawyer avoided looking at them. Reaching his table, he turned and faced the Bench.

Sir James remained standing. 'Certain evidence has been brought to my notice regarding the vessel, *Mary Celeste*,' he announced, 'which make further investigations imperative. These will commence Monday. Pending the results, all parties to this claim for salvage are hereby ordered to remain under arrest in Gibraltar and are not, under any circumstances, to leave this port.'

He banged his gavel down hard. 'This court is adjourned until further notice.'

As Sir James exited, the courtroom erupted into a babel of voices. Flood turned to regard the *Gratia*'s crew, hands on hips, a triumphal, gloating smile on his face.

Stepping over the barrier, Morehouse made for Pisani, followed by Callaghan, Deveau and the rest of the crew.

'What the hell happened in there?' Morehouse demanded.

'You mean, apart from a rapier being found under Captain Briggs's bed,' Pisani answered with sarcasm, 'stained with what appears to be blood? And traces of yet more blood also being found in First Mate Richardson's cabin, despite obvious attempts to scrub it clean – all of which are to be subjected to microscopic analysis by Doctor Patron, Gibraltar's leading physician.'

He paused in an attempt to control his temper. 'There are also, it seems, unweathered scrape marks on the *Celeste's* bows, but these need give you no concern, Captain Morehouse, despite the fact that Mr Austin, the Admiralty's surveyor, regards them as consistent with slicing a small boat in two. There is also the matter of a deep axe cut in the rail – which likewise appears to be recent.'

Hitching up his gown, Pisani busied himself with his briefcase.

'What with Christmas only five days away, I won't spoil it by going any further Captain, but should you wish me to continue representing you, I suggest you call on me as soon as your festive celebrations are over. If I am to prevent you and your entire crew from being indicted for murder, the sooner the better we start preparing for the Inquiry's resumption is my advice to you.'

Pisani turned to leave. 'I should perhaps wish you all festive blessings – but maybe this is not the opportune moment.'

- 52 -

Father Shaw was facing a terrible dilemma and it was tearing his very soul apart. Through the fine-meshed grille, in a whispered tone that was making him shiver, a penitent was confessing his sins and would soon be asking for absolution. That would be his moment of decision, when the transgressor asked to be made clean in the sight of God, and his dilemma would have to be resolved.

Father Shaw had served as a priest for nearly forty years now and in that time had heard many thousands of confessions, but never anything like this. Never had his heart pounded so badly, nor had he ever been so sickened. Nothing in his sheltered life had prepared him to deal with such evil.

The seventh child of devout, Irish Catholic parents, Father Shaw had been content – especially these last ten years in Gibraltar at The Church Of The Sacred Heart of Jesus, where the cloistered atmosphere of both the cathedral and town had so suited his nature – to remain a humble priest, caring for the poor, the sick and the dying, hearing the confessions of the penitent, and granting absolution according to the power vested in him by Holy Church.

The power vested, this was the root of the terrible burden now thrust upon him. In agony of mind and spirit, Father Shaw felt his chest tightening with the burden of his responsibility, and his breathing was becoming more difficult by the second.

Scriptural authority for his power to absolve sins, granted by the risen Saviour to His Apostles and thus their successors, was in Saint John's gospel, Chapter 20, verse 23: "Whose soever sins ye remit, they are remitted unto them". But this power bestowed by the Christ to His Apostles, did not stop there, for He had gone on to instruct them:

"Whosoever sins ye retain, they are retained". Consequently, through his priestly line of succession, Father Shaw not only had the power to grant God's absolution – he also had the power to refuse it.

It was an awesome responsibility.

It all rested on whether he believed the whispered voice the other side of the grille belonged to a true penitent, confessing from supernatural sorrow for his guilt.

Father Shaw did not believe it. Hence his anguish.

The sacrament had begun in the normal way, the whispered voice requesting: 'Pray, Father, bless me, for I have sinned,' and Father Shaw repeating the blessing: 'The Lord be in thy heart and on thy lips, that thou mayest truly and humbly confess thy sins, in the name of the Father, and of the Son, and of the Holy Ghost.'

But then, to his increasing horror, this had been followed by an account of two murders in New York and the terrible way they had been perpetrated. He had clutched his stole and begun praying with all fervour: 'Almighty God, if it be possible, let this cup pass from me', echoing the words of the Christ at the Garden of Gethsemane, and with such agony of soul he could feel sweat running down his forehead. Wiping the beads with his hand, he had almost expected them to show blood, as had happened to the Blessed Son when He begged the same prayer of His Father, and God had sent an angel from Heaven to strengthen Him. But no similar angel of mercy had entered the confessional, and he was left to decide in his own strength.

And now – Father Shaw held back a cry of revulsion – the whispered voice was confessing to the murder of the captain of The Mary Celeste, the vessel brought into Gibraltar by the crew of the brigantine Dei Gratia, all of whom were under suspicion of a crime they clearly had not committed.

Almighty God, Father Shaw begged, his heart pounding faster, please grant me Thy strength and Thy insight. Fighting to control his breathing, he tried to examine the dilemma doctrinally.

Contrition fell into two categories: perfect contrition which came from the penitent's genuine love of God...and imperfect contrition, which sprang from lower motives, mainly the fear of eternal damnation. The latter, though insufficient in itself to justify reconciliation with God, was nevertheless made sacramentally efficacious by the *priestly* pronouncement of absolution.

But the whispered voice from behind the grille was seeking to create a third category: justified contrition – claiming his actions had been vital to ridding Italy of King Victor Emmanuel, and Germany of Count von Bismarck, thus restoring Holy Church back into the purposes of God, and freeing blessed Pio Nono from his enforced imprisonment in the Vatican.

Father Shaw was horrified by the penitent's reasoning. Even Judas Iscariot, the evil "son of perdition", had shown remorse for betraying the Son of God, hurling his tainted thirty pieces of silver down on the floor of the temple, and then hanging himself.

But this man was evidencing no sign of contrition – either perfect or imperfect – only cold bloodedly enumerating his actions.

The First and Second Mates.

Father Shaw shielded his face in horror.

Three German seamen.

The band around Father Shaw's chest tightened.

A woman, the wife of The Mary Celeste's captain, and their little girl.

Father Shaw was suddenly unable to breathe.

A woman and an innocent child!

Father Shaw struggled to force out the words to tell the penitent he was no longer able to hear his confession, that the question of absolution would have to be referred to the bishop, but the pain in his chest was now so acute he was unable to utter a sound.

The ship's steward forced at sword point to jump overboard into the ocean and left to drown.

273

With this, the recited list of sins was ended and the penitent was now whispering through the grille: 'For these and all my other sins which I cannot now remember, I ask pardon of God, and penance and absolution of you, my ghostly Father.'

Pardon! Father Shaw rebelled at the thought. The unknown man was nothing more than an evil cold-blooded killer and did not merit pardon. Not from himself, not from the bishop, not even from the Holy Father, the chosen Vicar of Christ on Earth, the Supreme Judge of all.

Even more, and despite his pain, Father Shaw discerned the omissions in the man's plea. No admission of being "heartily sorry", no intent to "purpose amendment in the future". Nor was the request for pardon made "humbly".

Father Shaw thought of the nine innocent men who might yet be indicted for murder. As a priest, he was under the "seal of confession" never to break his vow of silence, not even on pain of death. But was it possible that his decision not to grant absolution, might in some way negate his holy vow? The fate of the *Dei Gratia*'s crew lay in his hands.

Father Shaw knelt to pray for God's guidance and tried to spread his arms out, to adopt the position of Christ on the Cross. A flash of pain shot across his heart. Sinking back on his heels, Father Shaw clawed at the tight band encircling his chest, squeezing the breath from his lungs.

The curtain opened, revealing a man dressed all in black. His hair was so fair it was almost white. He knelt down, his pale-blue eyes staring into Father Shaw's with frightening, hypnotic intensity, and the priest realised he had been listening, not to a cold-blooded murderer, but to a psychopath...who even now was committing further profanity.

Father Shaw tried desperately to resist, but his limpless hand was lifted to the man's own breast, and then guided to make the sign of the Cross, while the albinotic killer intoned the absolution which Father Shaw had determined to refuse: "Deindi ego te absolvo a peccatis tuis, in nomine patris, et filii, et spiritus sancti. Amen."

Father Shaw opened his mouth to condemn the act. The man's hand came down over his face, choking the words, and closing his nostrils tight between thumb and first finger.

And a black veil descended over Father Shaw's eyes.

Standing with Morehouse and Deveau outside the courthouse, the low dark clouds hanging over the Rock seemed to typify their gloom as Callaghan watched the rest of the *Dei Gratia's* crew thread their way in a tight group down the narrow Governor's Lane, heading back to the harbour, still animatedly talking together about this latest, to them, inexplicable turn of events.

'The way things are going,' Morehouse despaired as Callaghan searched for Colleen but saw no sign of her, 'we'll soon be facing the rope. If only I knew Desiah and the kids are safe, I could explain what really took place. What do you think's happened to her? And what,' he confronted Callaghan, 'is your General useless Smith doing to find her–'

He stumbled, jostled from behind. Recovering his balance, he held out a crumpled piece of paper. 'Someone pushed this in my hand!'

Aware of Deveau looking over his shoulder, Callaghan read the pencilled message:

Leave on Gratia when ship's orders received. Arrive Genoa 15 January.

'Martens!' the First Mate snarled, turning and scanning the sea of heads around them.

Leaping on to the courthouse steps, Callaghan saw a man in a cowled black robe forcing a path through the crowd.

'Over there!' Deveau yelled, running after the figure.

'No!' Callaghan shouted. The last thing he wanted was for the German to be caught.

But Deveau was closing on his quarry. Callaghan chased after the First Mate and slammed into him as Deveau grabbed the hooded man. All three fell to the ground. Before Callaghan could stop him, Deveau pulled back his captive's black cowl, revealing the frightened face of a Moor.

'Where is he?' Deveau grabbed him by the throat. 'Tell me or by hell I'll make you talk.'

The Moor clawed at his neck, trying to tear Deveau's hand away.

'Where is he?' Deveau repeated. 'The man who gave you the message?'

'Not know,' the Moor rolled his eyes. 'He paid money. Said give paper. Then run fast.'

Callaghan prised Deveau's fingers loose and yanked him off the Moor. The man scuttled into the curious crowd.

'You tried to stop me!' the First Mate accused.

'Sure I did.' Callaghan kept his voice low, aware of startled people around them, 'If it had been Martens, where would that have left Desiah?' He pulled the First Mate to his feet. 'Let's get back to David.'

Deveau hesitated, then curtly nodded.

Morehouse was standing by the courthouse wall, the note in his hand. 'What ship's orders?' he questioned, brandishing it. 'The *Gratia*'s confined to Gibraltar.'

His anger dissipating, Deveau scanned the note again and looked at Callaghan.

'The fifteenth? That's three weeks away. Genoa's no more than a ten-day voyage. What's the bastard up to now?'

'More to the point,' said Callaghan, 'how will the British Admiralty react after we've left? Will they wire Genoa and have the police waiting to send us straight back?'

Morehouse stared at him with disbelief. 'You're not suggesting we sail! We've been ordered not to leave port!'

'The threat still hanging over Desiah and the children gives us no choice, David.' Callaghan reminded him.

'Oh, God!' Morehouse groaned, 'Talk about being impaled in a cleft stick.'

Callaghan turned to Deveau. 'I've been expecting Sweeny to do something for days now, but I didn't anticipate this.'

'From what you've told us about him,' Deveau said, 'maybe we should. Okay, let's work out when we sail. I say late Christmas Eve when everyone will be off guard.' He ignored Morehouse staring at him. 'You and I have given evidence, Michael, as have John, Gus and Johnny. What if we go, taking Orr, Higgins and Willie with us,' he now turned to Morehouse, 'but leave you here, Captain, to explain to the court.'

'Explain!' Morehouse protested. 'Explain what, for hell's sake?'

'Just tell them you had no choice but to order us to sail,' said the First Mate, 'or you'd have been bankrupted if the cargo had stayed tied up here any longer.'

'Then that's what we must do, David,' Callaghan said. 'And add that we'll return as soon as the cargo's been unloaded.'

'We?' Morehouse grated. 'You don't mean you intend returning, too?'

'Okay. Oliver and the others.'

'And how will I explain your absence when they get back?'

'Tell them I was taken ill in Genoa,' Callaghan said. 'Or even better, fell overboard.'

Morehouse was silent, wrestling the conflict in his mind.

'Okay,' he finally surrendered. 'But Sir James Cochrane's not going to like it. Nor Flood. This is a British court of law we're flouting.'

'Damn their court' said Callaghan, yet realising that should he succeed in capturing Martens – and Sweeny, too – it would put end to any resumption of the Inquiry. 'And damn Solly Flood!'

- 53 -

Horatio Sprague stood in the window of the American Consulate, looking up at the blanket of mist hanging over the top of the Rock. On days like this, Gibraltar felt like a prison and he was always glad when the fog lifted and he could see the sky above.

He turned back to Callaghan in the room.

'Things look black for you, Callaghan. If only you'd tell them your true identity, and Police Commissioner Smith wired the Admiralty, confirming the New York murders you're investigating, they might believe in the innocence of the *Dei Gratia's* crew and end the Inquiry.'

Knowing he would soon be gone, Callaghan felt guilty keeping up the pretence with Sprague, but he had no alternative. 'I dare not, sir. Flood would have to be told, and having seen what kind of man he is, I doubt he'd keep it confidential.'

'He would have no choice, not if the Admiralty ordered him to.'

'That's assuming they believed what happened on board the *Celeste*, sir. But even if they did, Flood seems to have a flair for leaking information.'

'Very true,' aaid Sprague and sat down. 'So what do you intend?'

'Mr Pisani is going to keep representing us. We still hope to win.'

'I don't know whether that's wise,' said Sprague. 'Pisani looked quite angry as he left court. It's no good having an advocate who's no longer on your side.'

'I'll discuss it with David and Oliver,' Callaghan said. 'Your message referred to a wire?'

Sprague handed him a new cable. 'It arrived an hour or so ago.'

Callaghan hid his relief as he read it:

GENOA, 21 DECEMBER 1872

AMERICAN CONSUL, GIBRALTAR

SWEENY, COTTONE HERE. HOTEL DE GENES.

O M SPENCER, CONSUL

'So, Genoa is Sweeny's destination after all. But the name, Cottone, keeps cropping up. Is there any way I can find out who he is?'

'I could wire Mr Monti, our Consul in Palermo,' Sprague replied, 'and ask him to send me brief details on him?'

'If you would, sir. But more a dossier than brief details And maybe a copy to Mr Spencer?'

'Mr Spencer?' Sprague queried.

'Just in case, sir. Call me an optimist, but I've a feeling we'll be on our way to Genoa sooner than everyone thinks.'

- 54 -

Tuesday, December 24, 1872

Callaghan and Colleen were standing at the hotel balcony watching the street below rapidly empty of people as the shops closed, and the wares on display in the market place were packed up on assorted mules and carts. The Spanish vendors had long since left, to return across the border before the evening gun fired at half past five and Gibraltar's fortified gates closed for the night. A sudden quietness descended over the previously bustling town, and a chill breeze blew in from the harbour.

Colleen shivered and went inside. Callaghan closed the casement windows as he followed her. She returned to her chair by the fire. Callaghan sat facing her. She extended her hands to the warming flames. 'Are you sure Flood hasn't placed a guard on the _Dei Gratia?_' she asked.

'He hasn't so far. He's so taken up with bringing us to a trial, the thought of our absconding seems not to have occurred to him.' He gave her a rueful smile. 'It didn't occur to me either. I was expecting Sweeny to do it legally – transfer both cargoes to other vessels with new crews. I should have realised that acting within the law is not Brains way.'

'There's going to be a great furore when they realise you've sailed. What if the Genoa police are waiting for you – as they're almost bound to be?'

'I'll face that if and when it happens,' said Callaghan. 'I'm more worried that Sprague could cancel his request to Palermo for the dossier on this Cottone, Brains' new associate, or that Consul Spencer in Genoa will refuse to give it to me.'

Colleen had been pondering the same possibility. 'Why not write Mr Sprague a letter, saying that when Captain Morehouse ordered the *Dei Gratia* to sail, you decided to sail with her to get to Genoa, but for obvious reasons couldn't tell him beforehand. I'll have it delivered to him after you sail, once I'm sure you're safely away.' She stretched a hand to him, he held it. 'Meanwhile, I'll book a sleeping compartment on a train from Algeciras to Genoa, and be waiting for you when you arrive.'

'I like your letter idea,' Callaghan said. 'But when you get to Genoa, don't forget the promise you made in New York, about staying away from Sweeny until I get there.' He paused, expecting her to protest, but when she didn't he continued. 'Even though your Baedeker's hotel is far enough from his, knowing you, I want you to promise me again. Don't,' he stressed, 'go searching for him.'

'I promise,' Colleen agreed, too quickly for Callaghan's peace of mind, but before he could say anything more she continued. 'It's still possible that the diamonds are headed for Palermo, and Sweeny's only in Genoa to ensure his barrels remain on board, and aren't taken off with the rest of the cargo.'

'Another three weeks, we'll finally know,' Callaghan said. 'If it *is* Genoa, then Palermo still makes good sense as an arsenal. And as somewhere from which to distribute the arms by sea.'

They sat in silence a moment, realising they were parting company, neither wanting to and wondering what lay ahead of them both. Colleen broke it. 'Have you thought any more as to why Sweeny has added two weeks to your sailing time? Twenty four days for a voyage that should take no more than ten?'

'To give himself time to organise the selling of the diamonds?' Callaghan speculated. 'And rather than risk the *Dei Gratia*'s cargo being searched in Gibraltar, he thinks it's safer for her to get clear away, but delay arriving in Genoa until everything's in place?'

'Yes, that fits.' Colleen rose from her chair, knelt by his side and rested her face against his thigh. 'It will be Christmas Day tomorrow.' Her green eyes looked up into his. 'Instead of our being together, you'll be at sea again, and I'll be on a strange train.'

'There'll be plenty of other Christmases,' Callaghan replied, equally serious. 'We've a whole lifetime of them ahead of us.'

'Provided nothing goes wrong,' she said, her voice little more than a whisper.

'Trust me,' Callaghan pledged. 'Nothing will.'

- 55 -

Midnight, Tuesday, December 24, 1872

With Deveau at the helm, the *Dei Gratia* slipped her moorings and sailed silently out of Gibraltar harbour. The moon was hidden behind dark clouds and her departure was unnoticed.

Once safely out into the bay, Deveau ordered full sails raised. Minutes later they rounded Europa Point and set course for Genoa, some 850 nautical miles away.

Callaghan stood on the prow, wondering which was journey's end for him?

Genoa? Or Palermo?

Lying awake in her sleeper on the train to Genoa, Colleen was staring up at the ceiling, wondering how far Michael and the *Dei Gratia* were out to sea at this moment.

She had no doubts but that he was well away. "Determination" was Michael's middle name, which had seen him rise to Major in the 8th New York Cavalry, less than six months after enlisting, and a "hero" too, the way he'd led his men from the front in General Custer's charge against Jubal Early at Rockfish Gap. The charge that saw him badly wounded, but so providentially brought them together.

That same determination would ensure he'd find Sweeny. As for what would happen when he did – she forced all thoughts from her mind of how Michael would exact his vengeance – just as long as he first made Sweeny sign the affadavit clearing her father's name. But if Michael thought she was going to stay cooped up in her hotel, twiddling her thumbs until he arrived in Genoa, he was mistaken.

Okay, so she'd assured him she would, but he'd forgotten her trick of crossing her fingers whenever he asked her to make a promise she had no intention of keeping. Not only was she going to keep a daily eye on Sweeny, but just in case Mr Sprague withdrew his request to Palermo for a dossier on the mysterious Cottone, she was determined to find out as much as she could about him, too.

She was still convinced he was a revolutionary, but the more she could discover the better. It might even be she could assemble her own dossier on him. And just to see the look on Michael's face when she gave it to him – Colleen smiled to herself at the thought – would make the risk of it more than worthwhile.

Seated on a slatted wood bench in a dark corner of an almost empty third class carriage, Father Shaw's killer was brooding about the young woman sleeping in her berth two coaches back.

Sweeny's neice.

As he well knew, two months earlier, back in New York, she'd been trying to find her uncle's whereabouts in Europe. She must have succeeded and sailed to Gibraltar, where both ships were ordered to call, to await Sweeny's instructions, and was now on her way to Genoa, the same as the *Dei Gratia*. And Genoa was but a ferry distance to Palermo to meet up with him.

Too many coincidences.

Father Shaw's killer did not like coincidences.

The only thing to do with coincidences was eliminate them.

Five minutes before the train arrived in Genoa would be the ideal time to knock on her door pretending to be a porter, wait for it to open, clamp his hand over her mouth before she could scream and push her inside, force the strychnine pill into her mouth, wait for her spine to snap, and quietly exit her compartment, locking the door behind him as the train pulled into the station.

That should give him at least half an hour to reach the palazzo before her body was discovered and assumed to be a natural death, leaving him free to proceed with his plan without fear of the Genoa police hunting for anyone connected with her demise.

A woman she might be. And maybe even innocent of any complicity with Sweeny.

But that mattered for nothing in his greater scheme.

The end always justified the means.

Genoa

The moon was hovering above the Hotel de Genes out of a cloudless, midnight-blue starry sky as Don Salvatore Cottone stood at his bedroom window, smoking a corona, and looking down at the deserted Piazza Carlo Felice.

He was thinking about Sweeny. The man did not appeal to Don Cottone.

From the first moment of their meeting he had taken a dislike to the New Yorker. Uncouth in speech and mannerisms, Sweeny grated on Don Cottone's sensibilities. His preference was for people of refinement, a trait inherited from his Norman ancestors.

Thirty-eight years ago, when he was but twelve, this quality had been recognised by his father's *amico*, Baron *Inglese* and, as a consequence, he had made himself responsible for young Salvatore's education, teaching him to read and write, including English, paying for him to attend college, and encouraging him to enter a Dominican seminary to train for the priesthood.

Life was strange, Cottone reflected.

Had it not been for the death of his father curtailing his studies, followed a year later when his uncle also died and he himself then become head of the family, he would today have been a priest, like Guilamo. And probably content to be one.

His thoughts returned to Sweeny, in his room down the corridor, no doubt in one of his dark moods, brooding as to how, when Kaufmann reached Genoa, he could inflict greater pain on the German than any of the retributions he'd thought up so far – all involving Nino and his stiletto.

But as to the vulgarian's concept, Don Cottone had to admit it was brilliant, offering untold rewards. Nor was there any denying Sweeny's razor-sharp intelligence, or his peculiar talent for devising an almost limitless pool of money-making schemes.

Also to be considered were Sweeny's meetings, past and future, with Father-General Beckx, which the uncultured East-Sider was prone to boast about – another unpleasant trait – but which would ensure the downfall and death of the *usurpatore* Victor Emmanuel, with Sicily returned to Sicilians. As it should be.

A different people. A different language. A different culture. A different way of life.

And so, taking Guilamo's advice rather than Carlo Maranzano's, his son-in-law, Don Cottone had kept his distaste for Sweeny hidden behind an impenetrable mask. Not once during their negotiations had he allowed the filisteo to suspect how near he was to being separated from his cargoes, and their proceeds utilised to set up the operation without him.

But the die was now cast. Back in Monreale, with Guilamo left behind to arrange the sale of the diamonds, he had shaken hands with Sweeny. And the hand of Salvatore Cottone was more binding than an impressed seal – it was a matter of family honour. As head of the family he would never disgrace that honour. Nor was he a man who would ever break his word.

Having taken an entire floor of the *Hotel de Genes*, Sweeny was pacing his bedroom, chomping a cigar. Not for nothing, he brooded, had he earned the moniker "Brains" back in New York.

He'd stolen a march on Boss and Oakey leaving them behind to face the music. He'd paid Dick Connolly a measly $5 million to flee the States, rather than have him in the dock facing trial, and revealing all he knew as City Comptroller, about how each scam, every jack one of them, were *his*, Sweeny's, brainchild.

Well, it was gonna be the same over here.

Salvatore Cottone, the family's so-called *padrone.*

Father Guilamo Cottone, his duteous nephew priest.

Carlo Maranzone, Salvatore's son-in-law, his assumed heir apparent.

Three more to get his upper hand on, just like back in New York.

Okay, so he and Salvatore had shaken hands on the deal.

Except, there was nothing in writing.

Big mistake, Cottone.

It was now time to start thinking up more scams to syphon off the profits into the new bank accounts he'd opened up in Paris and Zurich – all in different names of course.

Leaving just enough to keep Cottone happy.

But maybe not Maranzano, Sweeny pondered. He'd picked up on his sly eyes. Not someone to be trusted. A man to keep his own eyes on. And if he put a foot wrong, he'd be taken care of. Good and proper.

Brains intended leaving nothing to chance.

Carlo Maranzano, was lying in bed in his room further down the corridor. The sheets were still warm from the supple body of the young Genoese girl – she couldn't have been more than fifteen – smuggled up the backstairs by Guido, one of his two bodyguards.

His physical needs having been sated, Maranzano was staring up at the ceiling, thinking how differently things would be done if he was Don. Frustrated by his father-in-law's constant state of self-discipline – instilled in him during his years in a Dominican seminary and encouraged by Guilamo's priestly guidance, resulting in his silent, brooding analysis before deciding on any course of action – Maranzano wanted to take advantage of the simmering mood of rebellion now existing in Sicily and get the people on the streets again, just like six years ago. Admittedly many had died when Emmanuel sent in the gunboats and shelled Palermo. But if only his father-in-law had persevered, rather calculate the cost in human lives, calling a strategic halt and reverting back to guerrilla warfare, they would have regained their freedom, and Sicily would not now be ruled by a rabid cur of a Piedmontese outsider.

As for Sweeny, the man from New York was a foreigner and as such their code of honour did not apply. He should be disposed of, his diamonds used to liberate Sicily, and not a franc given to any other cause. If he was Don, Maranzano brooded, none of it would go to freeing mainland Italy. Or to liberating the Pope.

Let the Church find its own solution.

And Sicily return to its old ways of doing things.

Palermo

At first, Carlo Maranzano's mafioso had refused to talk.

But bound to a chair, the point of Guilamo's stiletto pressed to his throat, he had forgotten his vow of omerta and revealed all, to be paid by the stiletto pushed in deeper, severing his artery.

His mind now concentrated on how to send warning to his Don, Guilamo turned away from the blood-soaked body, unconcerned as how to dispose of it. One his men could bury it somewhere, or dump it in a Palermo back alley.

A telegrafo to the Hotel de Genes was the swiftest way. But should it fall into Maranzano's hands, his uncle would remain oblivious of the danger hanging over him.

A risk Guilamo was not prepared to take.

The only other way was by ferry. It would take days, stopping at Reggio, Sapri, Napoli, and Livorno before reaching Genova. But, he calculated, with both New York vessels still days from reaching Kaufmann's yet unexplained change of destination, it gave him just enough time.

Genoa, Italy

January 15, 1872

- 56 -

Wednesday, January 15, 1873, Genoa

Callaghan stood with Deveau on the *Dei Gratia's* deck as Genoa drew nearer across the water. A shaft of sunlight broke through the grey winter sky of early morning, framing the ancient port like a painting. Built into an amphitheatre of hills encircling a wide bay, the city was a jumble of red, green, ochre rooflines, scattered with white church domes and round cupolas. Villas with hanging gardens and wooden terraces dotted the slopes above. Higher still, silhouetted against the skyline, stood Genoa's age-old fortress walls, interspaced by tall watchtowers.

Riding at anchor in the outer harbour were four steamships and a spanking new steam yacht. Beyond them, on the other side of the protecting mole, the inner harbour was full of all manner of sailing vessels; brigs, barks, schooners, ketches, tied up alongside quays, loading or unloading cargoes, and fishing boats of every colour discharging their overnight catches.

The familiar shape of a pratique boat appeared from behind the port-light at the end of the mole and headed towards them.

'The pratique boat, John,' Deveau called to Wright. 'Lower sails. Drop anchors.'

Under arrest again! Callaghan thought to himself, then turned away to lend a hand with the sails. But the only matter concerning the grandly uniformed Genoese official was their clean bill of health, and having satisfied him of this the *Dei Gratia* was guided into the inner harbour and to an empty berth, finally tying up at journey's end, 4060 nautical miles from New York.

There was no sign of any authority waiting for them on the quayside either. Nevertheless, not knowing what action Gibraltar had instigated after their flight, Deveau was anxious to register the *Gratia's* arrival and start the unloading. And being that this wasn't likely to be until tomorrow, Callaghan was impatient to see Colleen. 'I'll see you later, Oliver.'

'Take care, Michael,' said Deveau, scanning the busy dockside. 'I can see no sign of him, but I'd bet my last dime the son of Satan's out there somewhere, watching us with those evil eyes of his.'

Pulling his jacket collar up as if shielding himself from the winter chill, Callaghan walked down the gangplank on to the quay and threaded his way through the hectic activity. Finding the nearest gate in the high perimeter wall into the city, he showed his seaman's papers to a blue-uniformed Custom guard with a red-cockaded hat, and was allowed through.

He hailed a passing cab. 'Hotel Savoia'.

Settling back into his seat and watching the historic city pass by the window, Genova was certainly a city of contrasts, Callaghan brooded. Modern-day coaches and cabs, wagons, carts of archaic design, all mingling together, filling cobbled streets dominated by tall ancient buildings, mediaeval palazzos with jutting balconies tiered one above the other, alleys so narrow, blotting out the sunlight, that only pedestrians and sedan-chairs could enter.

Ten minutes later, he paid-off the cab-driver and entered the hotel.

Crossing the black-marbled foyer – quiet apart from a few loitering guests – he approached the reception-desk. A young male clerk, wearing an immaculate suit, frowned at Callaghan's rough seaman's appearance. 'May I help you?' he queried in a disapproving voice.

'My wife is staying here. Mrs Colleen Callaghan–'

'She is not here,' the clerk interjected in an even more inhospitable tone, 'though I remember the name.' He produced a wire from under the desk. 'This is her telegrafo from Gibraltar, requesting we reserve her a room. She never arrived, nor send us a cancellation,' he looked at Callaghan with a sour expression as if holding him responsible for such a lack of courtesy, but not surprised by it, coming from the wife of such a rough looking man. 'We held the room for a day before freeing it.' His tone hinted that Callaghan should consider compensating them for the loss of income, but not holding out much hope of it.

Callaghan was too thunderstruck to pay it any heed. Instead, despite it being obvious the clerk was telling the truth, he still challenged him.

'Are you sure? She's from New York. Young, five foot six, slim, extremely pretty.'

'I am positive signor. We have no American guests staying here at the moment. Nor have there been for some weeks.'

Not even thanking the man, Callaghan exited the hotel, his mind whirling. Why hadn't she arrived? Where was she? What the hell had happened to her?

His mind instantly turned to Martens, with the terrible thought that after having probably watched the Moor give Morehouse the note for the *Dei Gratia* to jump Gibraltar harbour and sail to Genoa, he himself would have to get here ahead of the vessel…

And the next train to leave Algericas was the one Colleen had taken.

If Colleen's theory about the German being Reikel's strong arm protector was right, what if he'd seen her in New York, maybe in St. Francis Xavier, asking Reikel about Sweeny, seeking his address, and so knew her to be his niece?

But even if he had, so what?

He wouldn't regard her as a threat to him?

Or to Sweeny?

Surely…

In desperation, Callaghan realised that standing outside the *Savoia* was getting him nowhere.

He leapt into a cab standing outside the hotel. 'Porto Franco.'

Dismissing the cab outside the customs gate, Callaghan ran for the *Gratia*'s berth. As he neared it, he saw that unloading had already started.

Two loaded wagons were heading toward the port's ancient warehouse area. A third had four dockers waiting to receive what looked like the wagon's last net of barrels being lowered by a horse operated hoist on to those already stacked. And three more with patiently seated wagoners were waiting their turn to be loaded.

Oliver was on the quayside, clearly arguing with a tall man with a black dispatch case and wearing a dark overcoat. As Callaghan drew near to them, he saw the man was in his late thirties, and heard his English accent above the surrounding din.

'I repeat, Deveau, that by leaving Gibraltar in contravention of Sir James Cochrane's ruling, both you and Captain Morehouse have violated the Admiralty Court's authority.'

'And I repeat we had no choice,' Oliver snapped back. 'I had to get the cargo to Genoa in time, or Captain Morehouse would have been ruined.'

'Hardly on time, Deveau. You are ten days overdue.'

'The *Gratia* sprang a leak,' Oliver fabricated. 'We had to call in at Palma for repairs.'

'You are having an adventurous voyage, Deveau.' Deep sarcasm was clearly evident in the Englishman's tone. 'Be that as it may, the Inquiry is suspended until your return. Unless, that is, Sir James tires of waiting and announces his verdict without you. In which case, your flaunting of the Admiralty Court's authority will most certainly be taken into consideration, and you and your Captain could find yourselves facing grave charges. Extremely grave charges, I trust I am making myself clear.'

'Crystal. It so happens I'm setting back as soon as we've finished unloading. As you can see, I've engaged extra wagons to speed things up.'

'Then the sooner you sail the better. I am only sorry that Italian law does not empower me to send you back under armed escort. But if you have any regard for your captain, you will return in less time than it took you to get here. I will wire to say you are on your way, and trust this will prevent Sir James from re-convening without you. I bid you good day, Mr Deveau.'

Turning, the man marched away stiff-backed, with the walk of an ex-military officer.

Callaghan crossed to Deveau. 'I take it that was the British Consul?'

'Mr Montague Yeats high and mighty hyphenated Brown. But forget about him. What about you? You're looking worried stiff.'

'It's Colleen. She didn't check into her hotel. Tell me she's waiting on board?'

'Sorry, Michael. But I'm sure she's okay. Have you tried the American Consulate?'

'That was my next call, hoping she's called in there. But it looks like unloading's well under way.'

'Over half done. I was about to send Willie to bring you back.' Deveau indicated at the third cart which was now fully loaded and following the first two towards the warehouse district. 'As it is you're in time, there's three still to be loaded. But if you're right about the same strategy being used as with the *Celeste*, the extra barrel will kept back until the last one – or left in the hold.'

But Callaghan's mind was still with Colleen. Despite praying she'd booked into another hotel, what if the reason for her not arriving at the Savoia was more sinister?

What if she was in danger? At this very moment?

The destination of the barrel was of no importance until he knew she was safe.

'Here's another kingfish heading toward us,' Deveau cut into his conflict.

Callaghan turned. Forcing his way along the quayside, clearly in a hurry, dabbing his tanned bald head with a handkerchief, was a middle-aged man of medium height carrying a leather brief case. Wearing a light grey, waist-coated suit, he was tubby with a round face.

'Are either of you with this brigantine, Dei Gratia?' he indicated their vessel. His accent was American, New England, and maybe Harvard or Yale.

'I'm Deveau, her First Mate, acting as master,' Oliver replied.

The American held out his hand. 'Oswald Spencer, American Consul in Genoa. I read about you in a report from Consul Sprague, Deveau. Sorry to hear about your troubles. You should be commended for bringing the *Celeste* into Gibraltar, not face an Inquiry. Typical of the British. Punctilious to the nth degree and then some. I'm looking for a Michael Callaghan of the New York Pol–'

'I'm Callaghan,' Michael cut across him.

Grabbing hold of Callaghan's arm, Spencer pulled him aside. 'Is there somewhere we can talk? In private? It's mighty urgent!'

Deveau had overheard. 'Use the Captain's cabin, Michael.'

'Thanks, Oliver.'

'I'll let you know when the last wagon's being loaded.'

Callaghan nodded. Following Spencer as he hurried up the gangplank to the Main Deckhouse, down the companionway and across the salon into the cabin, the Consul subsided into Captain Morehouse's chair. 'Close the door,' he instructed.

Callaghan shut it with an instinctive gut fear. 'Is it my wife?'

'You've answered my question, Callaghan,' Spencer said grimly, placing his briefcase on the floor. 'I thought the same surname was too much of a coincidence. I've got bad news.'

Callaghan's heart plummeted. 'She's not—' He left the rest unspoken.

'Sweeny's holding her,' Spencer blurted, 'in exchange for information. He's given me forty-eight hours to reply, and a warning not to contact the police. It arrived at the Consulate two hours ago, only minutes after I got the news that the *Gratia* had finally docked.' He glared at Callaghan. 'Took your damn time getting here. Three weeks!,' Then, heeding the look on Callaghan's face, he hurriedly continued. 'Knowing from Mr Sprague about your mission and seeing Sweeny's hostage had the same surname, I came straight here to tell you.' He pulled out his watch. 'There's less than forty-six hours left, Callaghan. Time's fast running out for her.'

Though his mind was racing with questions – mingled with relief that he at least knew where Colleen was, and she was alive – Callaghan asked only the vital one, 'What information is Sweeny demanding? – sir,' he added.

'Some details from Mr Sprague.'

Sprague. It was obviously to do with the *Celeste*, still in Gibraltar. But what the hell could Sprague tell Sweeny that he hadn't already been told by Martens, when the killer arrived in Genoa and reported in to him?

'What details?' Callaghan pressed.

'I'll be told when I agree. I'm then to wire Sprague, pass on his reply to Sweeny, and your wife will be released. But if I refuse, or – to repeat – contact the police, she won't be seen again.'

'Not seen again!' Callaghan flared. 'Sweeny wouldn't dare—'

'No, but Cottone would.'

'Cottone? Sweeny's new associate? He's not that ruthless? Surely?'

'Ruthless! And some!'

'A revolutionary?'

The Consul looked puzzled. 'Cottone a revolutionary? What gave you that idea?'

'You mean he's not?'

'Anything but.'

'Then what is he?'

'Mafia.'

It was Callaghan who now looked mystified. 'Mafia? Who or what in the hell is that?'

'Like no other organisation you've ever heard of.' Spencer pushed a finger under his stiff collar to loosen it as if it had suddenly become too tight. 'It's only since Victor Emmanuel took over Sicily that the world outside the island has come to hear of them. Leading Italian newspapers have recently been publishing articles on them, but for the most part their activities are shrouded in secrecy. But having served a year in our Palermo Consulate, I know just how ruthless they can be. Hardly a week goes by without a body being left on the street as a warning to others, with no one – not even the police – daring to remove it until they say so.'

Callaghan dropped down hard onto the bed. 'And that's who this Cottone is? Some sort of leading Mafia figure?'

'More than that.' Spencer loosened his collar again. 'He's the supreme boss – the capomafia – of the entire island, seemingly the first in Mafia history.'

'History?' Callaghan repeated, latching on to the word, but with his thoughts on Colleen and how to deal with this unexpected development.

Spencer nodded. 'They've been around for centuries. In fact, for you to realise what we're up against, it would help you to know something about them.'

'I'd prefer to talk about freeing my wife – sir.'

'Did you fight in the war, Callaghan?'

'Sure.'

'Then you must know the rule: know your enemy. And it doesn't just apply to the science of warfare, but to every walk of life – especially when you're up against someone as powerful as Cottone, and an organisation as ruthless as the Mafia.' Assuming his right to continue, Spencer leant forward as far as his stomach would allow. 'They date back to the eleventh century, when Norman barons took over the island, forcing its people into serfdom. The more partisan-minded Sicilians fled into the hills to resist – rather like Robin Hood in Sherwood Forest – setting up camps in what they termed mafias. It comes from the Arabic word mafie – who ruled the island before the Normans – and means "a place of refuge".'

His mind still on Colleen, Callaghan tried to cut in but Spencer ignored him.

'But going a step further, many of the resistance groups – *cosche* as they call themselves, their word for "families" – then divided up the island between them, each controlling a particular area, with the father at the head, followed by his sons, then sons-in-law, cousins, nephews, and finally loyal friends, buying the fidelity of the peasants living in their part of the island by sharing their booty with them, but in return demanding their silence. They call it omerta – it means "being a man" – under which the people are not permitted recourse, whatever the circumstances, to any legal authority, or even the slightest co-operation with them.'

Spencer wiped his brow. The man seemed genuinely scared stiff, Callaghan thought, now forcing himself to listen as the Consul continued.

'To give you some idea of the loyalty demanded – then and now – the Mafia has a proverb, which goes something like this. L'omu ch'e omu non rivela mai mancu si avi corpa di cortella. Which means,' he gulped, 'The man who is really a man reveals nothing, not even with a dagger through him.'

'Hardly Robin Hood-like,' Callaghan responded. 'But with respect, interesting though all this is, sir, it doesn't help Colleen.'

'Hear me out first, Callaghan,' Spencer insisted. 'As I stated a moment ago, to discover the enemy's weaknesses, one should first be apprised of all there is to know about them.'

Callaghan hesitated, and abruptly nodded for Spencer to continue.

'Over the centuries their overall control of Sicily – and the people's fear of them – grew to such an extent that they in effect ruled the island. More and more, the land owners were forced to hand over the management of their estates to the various Dons – the name of respect by which the head of a cosca is known…' Spencer paused, then went off on a tangent. 'As for the word Mafia, it's a collective title, given to them by outsiders, which they themselves do not acknowledge. To them, every cosca is a separate family, each opposed to the other, and ruled by a Don as their capocosca – it means "head of the family" – who use every way they can to exercise greater control over their respective territories. Like having a son go into the law. Or enter the priesthood–'

'The damn Church again,' Callaghan cut across him. 'Everywhere I go, it keeps cropping up.'

Spencer looked shocked. 'This is Italy, Callaghan. Here the Church is – or at least was, before Victor Emmanuel abolished it – an integral part of the fabric. And old habits die hard.'

'I don't mean just Italy,' Callaghan said. 'It started back home in New York and has continued ever since. Religion as a whole, that is, and now includes even Islam.'

'You sound very antagonistic towards it?'

'Just making a comment. But to repeat, none of this helps Colleen. Especially as she's being held by some criminal organisation, who likely don't give a damn whether or not she–'

'It so happens they don't consider themselves criminals,' Spencer cut across him, 'more as protectors of the peace. Each cosca has a tiered system of control. Below a Don is a consigliere, an advisor. They, in turn, are followed by the caporegime, the lieutenants. Then come the lower echelon, the mandatari, who carry out the instructions—'

'Are they capable of murder?' Callaghan intruded, returning to his greater fear for Colleen.

Withdrawing a photograph from his case, Spencer handed it to Callaghan.

It showed a mustachioed man standing on a barren hillside, with a foot planted, in the pose of a hunter standing over a dead animal, on the chest of a male corpse. He was wearing a wool-lined jacket, baggy trousers tucked into leather boots. Across his chest were bandoleers of ammunition, and in the crook of his arms he was holding a short-stocked, sawn-off shotgun.

'It's called a lupara,' said Spencer. 'It's a most fearful weapon, designed to be hidden inside clothing. Sprays lead pellets and makes one hell of a mess. Take a closer look.'

Callaghan looked at the corpse, riddled with bullet-holes, surrounded by a pool of blood. 'I've seen worse,' he said, handing the photo back.

Spencer looked momentarily shocked at Callaghan's hardness, but continued. 'That may well be, nevertheless that is the value they place on human life. Murder is an everyday event to them. It means no more than swatting a fly. Even more, they have a practice of making the punishment fit the crime. Betray their secrets and the dead offender's tongue is severed and forced into his mouth. Rape, or seduce a female member of the family, and it's his testi—'

'You've made your point, sir. So they're killers. At least with men. What about women?'

'No…' Spencer hesitated. 'They deal differently with women?'

'How different?'

'Houses of ill-repute.'

'Brothels!' Callaghan felt as if he'd been struck.

Spencer's expression was sombre. 'It's one of their many sources of income. They have them right across the island. Palermo. Messina. Catania. All the major towns.'

Callaghan sprang to his feet. 'Then we've no choice but to agree. Provided Sweeny keeps to his side of the bargain.'

'Why shouldn't he?'

'Brains! He's never kept his word in his life, not even if he swore it to the Virgin Mary.'

'Surely, if he gets his information?'

'That would be no guarantee. And what if Mr Sprague doesn't have it?'

Spencer rubbed his bald head, perplexed by the whole predicament.

'But I have a suggestion.' Thinking on his feet, Callaghan was now only concerned about Colleen, capturing Sweeny was no longer important. 'It will require your help, sir?'

The Consul's eyes narrowed warily as he waited for Callaghan to proceed.

'If we can discover where they're keeping Colleen, then maybe I can break her out. The only way to do this is for you to continue negotiations with Sweeny, and insist on seeing her to ensure she's alive. They'll either have to bring her to you; or more probably you to her.'

Seeing alarm on Spencer's face, Callaghan hastily reassured him. 'I'll be outside the consulate.'

'Callaghan!' the Consul protested, once more loosening his collar. 'I evidently didn't make myself understood. You don't have the slightest conception of the kind of people we're dealing with here. Your East Side criminals are children by comparison. Cottone is constantly shadowed by two bodyguards. Worse, his son-in-law, Maranzano, also has his own bodyguards. They've taken over an entire wing of the Hotel de Genes in the Piazza Carlo Felice, and are protected around the clock by even more guards, every one of them having sworn blind obedience to Cottone by cutting their wrists for their blood to drip on to a paper replica of some blessed saint or other, and reciting a sacred oath to sacrifice their lives to Cottone, if he so orders them to.'

Spencer stressed his next words for Callaghan to comprehend the reality of the situation.

'This is what we'd be up against. They may not be fanatics in the visionary sense of the word, but they come pretty damn close. *Not* the sort of people to tangle with.'

'Maybe not, sir, but we've my wife's life at stake here. And with respect, the worst you'd be facing is a bumpy coach ride. They're going to need you alive to wire Sprague. The risk is all mine and Colleen's.'

Massaging his furrowed brow as he wrestled between his instinct for self-preservation and a desire not to be thought cowardly, Oswald Spencer blurted, 'I think it best we call in the police.'

'No police. If Cottone's the kind of man you say he is, his warning has to be taken seriously.'

Gulping, the Consul surrendered with an air of resignation. 'Okay, Callaghan. I'll contact Sweeny at his hotel as soon as I get back to the consulate.'

Removing a folder from his brief case, he handed it across. 'But it may help you to read this dossier first. Mr Sprague wasn't too pleased about you leaving Gibraltar without confiding in him, but understood your reasons and as you see, here is the information you asked for on Cottone.'

Taking the folder, Callaghan sat down again and read the page inside:

SALVATORE COTTONE

BORN: MONREALE 1811.

FATHER: GABELLO (ESTATE MANAGER) TO BARON INGLESE.

COLLEGE EDUCATED, PAID BY INGLESE, THEN DOMINICAN SEMINARY TO STUDY FOR PRIESTHOOD.

SPEAKS ENGLISH.

LEFT SEMINARY AT 23 ON FATHER'S DEATH. SUCCEEDED HIM AS GABELLO.

MARRIED. ONE DAUGHTER. NO SONS.

MONREALE. THE MOST IMPORTANT SICILIAN COSCHE AND SEAT OF CATHOLIC BISHOPRIC, WITH HISTORY OF CLERGY PROTECTING LOCAL COSCA IN RETURN FOR FINANCIAL SUPPORT.

COTTONE BECAME DON OF MONREALE COSCA AT 30, ON KILLING OF UNCLE BY RIVAL COSCA.

AFTER AVENGING UNCLE'S DEATH, COTTONE BEGAN A BURRUSCA (MAFIA POWER WAR) TO CONTROL PALERMO AND WATERFRONT. TOOK OVER NORTHERN PALERMO AND SURROUNDING VILLAGES (CONTROLLING ROADS FROM THE WEST) MONTELEPRE AND MISILMERI (CONTROLLING ROADS FROM THE INTERIOR) VILLABATE AND BAGHERIA (CONTROLLING ROADS FROM THE EAST). DEMANDS AND RECEIVES PIZZO (PROTECTION MONEY) ON ALL GOODS ENTERING AND LEAVING PALERMO.

COTTONE BROUGHT CASTELLAMMARE COSCA UNDER HIS INFLUENCE BY MARRYING DAUGHTER TO CARLO MARANZANO,

SON OF CASTELLAMMARE DON. ONE SON (BORN 1868) NAMED SALVATORE AFTER COTTONE.

COTTONE NOW SICILY'S CAPOMAFIA (SUPREME BOSS) FIRST IN MAFIA HISTORY.

MARANZANO THOUGHT TO BE COTTONE'S HEIR-APPARENT.

So this was Sweeny's new crime partner, Callaghan thought. Salvatore Cottone, ex-religious student, now capomafio not only of Palermo, but the whole of Sicily. A powerful ally for Brains to have chosen. Which reminded him of Colleen's theory.

'Sir, would Cottone have anything to gain by getting rid of Victor Emmanuel?'

'Everything to gain and nothing to lose,' Spencer replied. 'Emmanuel's doing his level best to stamp out the Mafia, sending in troops – quoting his words – to purge the island. There's a bloody fight for control taking place there at the moment, with the army holding on the spot tribunals and executions, and the Mafia retaliating with political assassinations.'

That confirmed Colleen's theory, Callaghan thought. Sweeny. Cottone. Martens. An unholy trinity of men with a multiplicity of purpose. Restoring the Church to power. Regaining control of Sicily. And Sweeny accruing a hefty profit by financing the counter revolution.

Spencer handed him two photographs. 'The top one's Cottone.'

Callaghan looked down at the portrait of a handsome nobleman, with silvery grey hair and a small pointed beard. He studied the aristocratic face in detail. It wasn't at all what he'd expected. And yet, there was something disturbing about the dark eyes staring coldly into the camera. Or was it merely the superior pose of a man used to command? Cottone's features, with his imperious nose, reflected the inherited blood of a Norman Baron of old, mixed with the dark, dispassionate gaze of an Arab. A deadly combination.

The second picture showed three men posing together on the steps of a large white villa. The man in the middle was at least six inches taller than the other two, heavily built. The one on the right was thin with a long, mean face, the other was squat, with black hair plastered flat with grease. All three were cradling lupari – the taller man's silver-patterned, presumably to show his elevated position in the Mafia echelon.

'That's Maranzano,' Spencer pointed to the taller man. 'The other two mafiosi – that's the comprehensive name given to all Mafia members – are his personal bodyguards, from his father's Castellammare cosca, and sworn to protect him. All three are ruthless, but be particularly wary of Maranzano. He's reputed to be a sadist, as well as a killer.'

Callaghan studied the face, noting the thick sensual lips, hinting at a cruel nature.

'Michael!' Deveau yelled down the companionway. 'Hold's empty. Barrel's gone. Last cart's moving off.'

Callaghan leapt up. 'I have to go, sir. I'll see you at the Consulate.'

Deveau was waiting on deck with Callaghan's sea-bag and a folded parchment. 'It's a street map of Genoa. Just got it for you from a vendor.' He clasped Callaghan's hand. 'Take good care.'

Callaghan returned his grip. 'Thanks Oliver. And for all your help. Don't worry about Flood. If I come out of this alive, I'll stop in Gibraltar on my way back to New York and explain it all to the court. If I don't, I'll get Mr Spencer to send them a diary that will achieve the same result. And *The Mary Celeste* will then be a thing of the past.'

Running down the gangplank on to the quayside, Callaghan followed after the wagon.

- 58 -

Callaghan kept close to the prows of other berthed vessels, tailing the wagon as it trundled across the cobbled quay and headed for a towering mass of ancient warehouses east of the harbour, their stonework black with centuries-old grime.

The wagon entered a dark alley, depositories looming high on both sides, shutting out the sunlight. Callaghan followed it, keeping a safe distance behind. Ahead of him, the wagon rumbled up the narrow, twisting passage – other alleys leading off in various directions, a veritable maze in which it would be easy to get lost – finally turning into a big warehouse that looked even older than the rest, its arched entrance dark and low like a crypt.

He ran across the alley, rubbed a clear circle in one of the dirt covered panes down the side of the building and peered through. The light inside the building was dim, but he could make out the previous wagon-loads of barrels stacked against a far wall.

The last wagon stood in the middle of the floor. Next to it was a mule-cart, its driver seated. Three warehousemen lifted a barrel off the wagon onto it and secured it with rope. Painted white on the side of the barrel, Callaghan saw a small, crucifix-shaped cross.

The black-suited, black-shirted young driver flicked his reins and drove out of the building and headed for the city, staring straight ahead with a fixed expression as if he was in a trance.

Callaghan let the cart get some fifty yards ahead, then went after it. The dark alley led into another, then another, until one finally entered a high-walled, cobbled square. An arched gateway opened into the city. Not turning his face, the cart driver produced a document. The custom guard glanced at it and waved him on.

Crossing the cobbles, Callaghan showed his papers to the guard and hurried through the gate into a busy street, pavements crowded with canvassed stalls and vendors vociferously exhorting their particular products to the passers-by. Momentarily overwhelmed with all the noise and the bustle, Callaghan searched for the cart and saw it a short distance up the street. He pushed his way through the press after it, drew level with the driver and again noted the way the young man was staring fixedly ahead, as if he was oblivious of everything around him.

Entering an even busier street, with a plaque reading Via San Lorenezo high on the wall of a corner building; the cart trundled along it then turned left, into another dim alley.

Callaghan waited a moment for it to open up a gap, ran across the street and found himself in a dark mediaeval city, where, despite the passing of centuries, time had seemingly stood still. A cobbled labyrinth of silent, intersecting byways twisting in every direction between tall gloomy tenements, all seeming to be leaning toward each other, hiding the sky. But other than the rumble of its wheels, the cart had gone.

Callaghan hesitated, not knowing which way to follow.

The rumbling ceased.

An alley with a low archway at its far end seemed to draw him. He ran through it and around a corner, into a small, deserted piazza with cramped exits leading out from its other three corners. Choosing the alleyway to his left he sped down it, but it humped over a stone bridge, narrower than the cart. Doubling back, he tried the next exit, but after a couple of turns it led to a dead end. Despairing now, he ran back to the still deserted piazza and down the last alleyway, around a corner, and saw it led into an arcaded passage between two buildings – but wide enough for a cart. Embedded into an ancient stone arch above the entrance to it, was a black, marble tablet with a carving – almost worn away by the passing of time – of a man in a loin-cloth with seven swords impaled in his body: three in his back, one in his chest, two in his stomach and one into his groin.

Callaghan stared up at it. Seven swords. The emblem of the Black Knights?

His hand went to his sheath for his seaman's knife. Clutching it, he crept to the end of the long dark tunnel and peered out at a closed courtyard full of weeds pushed up through cracked slabs.

Across the quadrangle was a large, crumbling U-shaped palazzo. Centuries old, built of yellow sandstone now grey with grime, its ornate capitals and mouldings told that it must once have been magnificent, but it was now a decaying ruin of flaking stonework, broken windows, and old doors hanging off their hinges. Completing the horseshoe of buildings was a dilapidated stable-block, its roof falling in.

The mule cart was tied to a post outside, but the barrel was gone.

Callaghan looked at the palazzo, wondering how many men were inside? The pale driver for one. Martens and other Black Knights? Sweeny, gloating over his diamonds? Cottone, Maranzano, protected by their four bodyguards, and maybe more *mafiosi*?

His gaze swept the courtyard. It was too open to chance going any nearer. And with Colleen's life at stake, the risk was too high.

Weighing up the odds, he decided it made more sense to get to the American Consulate and wait there for Sweeny to contact Spencer.

Sheathing his knife, he turned back up the tunnel.

From a dark room on the palazzo's first floor, slate-blue eyes looked down on Callaghan retreating up the alley. Clasping the hilt of a dagger with one hand, the other gripped the blade so tightly that blood slowly oozed from the watcher's cut fingers.

Six weeks back, on board *The Mary Celeste*, he'd held his rapier to the man's throat. One thrust then would have killed him. He should have done so. Whoever the man was, he was no seaman.

This was the second thing to go wrong. The first was killing Sweeny's neice. Nearing Genoa, he'd gone to her compartment to force her to swallow the strychnos pill. She was standing out in the corridor with two porters and her luggage, and he'd had to let her live.

Her presence on the train may have been a coincidence.

But all coincidences should be eliminated.

Sweeny's neice should have been eliminated.

And now the man who had found the palazzo.

He could be working for Sweeny.

Right from the very beginning. All the way from New York.

The watcher's hand clasped the blade tighter.

Blood slowly welled in his cupped palm.

What if the man now telegraphed Sweeny? Palermo, by boat, was only days away.

The palazzo was to have served as his base until the diamonds were sold.

They would now have to be moved to the castle. His Alamut.

And his own conspiracy, far beyond Father-General Beckx' planned counter-revolution, must be delayed.

All because of one man.

Whoever he was, he would not escape the next time.

The watcher's grip on the blade tightened. He held out his hand.

Red globules slowly fell onto the diamonds glinting below him in an open chest.

Purchased by blood.

- 59 -

Fiesole

The sun had long since fallen behind the hills of the Arno Valley.

The room was in darkness, save for the dim light of a single candle on the desk. Whenever he was reading Saint Ignatius's Spiritual Exercises, Beckx preferred it this way. It helped him to imagine all manner of demons and evil spirits lurking in the blackness of the corners, and gave him the terror-feeling of Hell that Loyola's manual demanded.

Since receiving Father Reikel's telegraph he had followed Blessed Ignatius's example, and remained in silent contemplation to prepare for the re-emergence of the Society, once Emmanuel had been overthrown. He returned to his copy of the Exercises, a 250-year-old, black leather-bound Latin translation, now faded, of Loyola's original, Castillian edition, which he treasured above all other books in his library, including the Bible.

Beckx particularly liked its strict discipline. Before Loyola's miraculous conversion while recovering from battle wounds, he'd been a soldier, his whole upbringing until then had been about the bearing of arms. The feeling of military discipline was in every page of the book. Beckx approved of discipline. It created efficiency. He also agreed that in the same way the body was strengthened by physical exercise, so could the spirit be infused by spiritual training.

He also approved of the way Loyola had divided the Exercises into weeks.

During their training, Jesuit novitiates were completely isolated, allowed access only to their confessor and director of the retreat. The manual's procedure was imprinted on Beckx' memory.

Week One: The purgative week, when the novitiate is to exercise his imagination to seeing and experiencing for himself the terrors of Hell and impress on him the supreme folly of mortal sin.

Week Two: The ultimate contrast, when the novitiate concentrates his imagination to be living with Christ in Galilee, feeling himself to be walking the same dusty roads, to the point where he can feel the dirt on his feet, and then entering the same villages and towns to preach to the people.

Week Three: When the novitiate is to exercise his imagination to experience the anguishes of Christ, transporting himself to be sitting at The Last Supper, sweating drops of blood in the Garden of Gethsemane, suffering the pain of being scourged, then the dreadful agony of the Crucifixion.

Week Four: When the imagination is exercised to actually smell the immeasurable fragrance and sweetness of the Godhead, the purpose of which is to make the novitiate realise his ultimate reward for accepting his vocational call will be eternal union with God.

This was the point at which the novitiate entered into the true state of sanctity. Sadly yet inevitably, there were those who condemned the Exercises, claiming their effect on susceptible minds could lead to madness. One living American writer had recently even gone so far as to call them "a psychological masterpiece". That was absurd. Such people did not appreciate the care that went into the selection of candidates. Only healthy young men of sound mind were chosen. Men like Father Reikel – well able to submit to the intensity of their ten-year training.

The American's blasphemous judgement only displayed his ignorance of why and how Ignatius had been guided to write The Exercises.

The why was because it was the time when the heretical anti-Christs, Luther and Calvin, were spreading their false doctrines. Telling people that the only way to God was by faith and faith alone – and not by belonging to God's one and only true Church on Earth, the Church of Rome.

Heresy.

As for how – this was further proof of God's approval of the Society's formation. Seeking isolation away from the world and all its pleasures, the Blessed Saint had found a cave outside Manresa in Southern Spain. With him he had a copy of Garcia de Cisneros' Exercises of the Spiritual Life, written when Cisneros was abbot of the monastery at Montserrat.

Reaching for his own copy of the book, always on his desk, Beckx opened it to the descriptive and well-thumbed passage that appealed to him most.

Picture to yourself the torments of Hell, as well as Hell itself: A desolate place deep under the Earth, like a fiery crater blazing with dreadful flames, shrouded in terrible darkness. Cries and lamentations which pierce to the very marrow fill the air. The unhappy inhabitants whose pain and torments no human can describe, are eternally burning in raging despair.

No wonder it had inspired Ignatius to subjugate his body to the same plane as his spiritual mind – praying on his bare knees seven hours a day, wearing a vest interwoven with sharp pieces of iron next to his skin, and a crucifix of nails against his breast, so that if the need for sleep tempted him to lie down on the damp cave floor, the vest and crucifix pierced his body, drawing blood and reminding him of the weakness of the flesh.

But Saint Ignatius's self-discipline had been rewarded. When the time came for him to write the Exercises, the Blessed Virgin appeared before him in a vision and dictated every word for him to write down. Together, Mary, Mother of God, and Ignatius, had divided the manual into weeks, and then specified the exact nature of each exercise. Beckx especially favoured those for the first week, the purgative week, when the novitiate's mind was most receptive.

Turning back to his copy of the Exercises, Beckx opened it at the exact page:

The first point consists in this: that I hear, with the eye of the imagination, those enormous fires, and the souls, as it were, in bodies of fire.

The second point consists in this: that I hear with the ears of the imagination the lamentations,

cries, howlings, and the blasphemies against Christ, Our Lord, and against all His Saints.

The third point consists in this: that I smell with the smell of the imagination the smoke, brimstone, refuse and rotting things of Hell.

The fourth point consists in this: that I taste with the taste of the imagination the bitter things: the tears, sorrows, and the worms of conscience in Hell.

The fifth point consists in this: that I feel with the sense of touch of the imagination, how those fires fasten upon and burn souls.

It was masterly, thought Beckx. Having completed his work, Ignatius journeyed to Rome and showed it to Pope Paul III, who gave it his papal blessing. Thus it was that the Society of Jesus – the greatest teaching Order known to man – came into being. And with what success, turning back the tide of the falsely named "Protestant Reformation", repressing its heresies, and taking the true gospel of Rome to the four corners of the globe.

What Mother Church needed today, he brooded, was someone with the same zeal, the same selfless dedication of Saint Ignatius himself.

Staring into the darkness, Beckx thoughts turned again to the emissary he had sent to New York. The one he had entrusted with the holy mission to restore Holy Church to power.

Father Karl Reikel was such a man.

- 60 -

The United States Consulate, Genoa

Spencer was sitting at his green leather-topped desk, writing by the light of a red-globed, brass oil-lamp, as Callaghan entered the study from upstairs. Seeing a warm inviting fire in the white marble fireplace, he crossed to the hearth and stood with his back to the flames.

The Consul raised his head. 'Did you sleep?'

'Rested. My mind's with Colleen. When will Sweeny's carriage be here?'

'At ten.' Oswald Spencer's voice was strained.

'You'll be fine, sir,' Callaghan tried to again reassure him. 'Sweeny needs you alive to send the wire to Sprague.'

The Consul forced a smile. 'So I keep telling myself, except it doesn't help any.' He indicated the paper on his desk. 'I thought I'd make my will, just in case. Would you witness it for me?'

'Of course, sir. But I don't think you need worry about it for a good many years yet.'

'Always wise to be prepared for the worst, Callaghan.'

Spencer indicated to a telegraph on the desk. 'The message you've been hoping for has come through from Mr Sprague. The Canadian Police have found Mrs Morehouse and children safe and well; staying with relatives on Prince Edward Island.'

'That's a load off my back.' Callaghan felt relief flow through him. 'I can now take Sweeny on with no holds barred. Cottone, too. Which reminds me, sir. Do you have a revolver?'

Spencer nodded. 'A Colt.45. A keepsake from the war. Locked in my desk.'

'Bullets?'

'Box of six.'

'May I borrow it?'

'Certainly.' The Consul unlocked a drawer, produced an oilskin wrapped bundle and a small cardboard box from it, and gave them to Callaghan. 'I should have thought of it myself. It will help knowing you're not only behind me, but that you're also armed.'

Callaghan unwrapped the revolver from the oilskin, inserted a finger through the trigger guard, tested the Colt's balance, spun the cylinder to make sure it was unloaded, held the barrel to the light and peered into it, relieved to see no rust. He pocketed one bullet, loaded the other five – ensuring the hammer was over an empty chamber – and thrust the gun under his trouser-belt.

'Time to be off, sir. But first, if I'm not back in forty-eight hours, there's a diary upstairs in my sea-bag. Would you send it to Henry Pisani in Gibraltar, Captain Morehouse's advocate? Now that Mrs Morehouse and the children are safe, Pisani can use it as evidence to end the Inquiry.'

Spencer frowned. 'All very mysterious, Callaghan. Why wasn't it produced before?'

'Because of the threat against them, in case it turned out to be for real. But now we know they're being protected, will you do it, sir?'

'Of course. Although I would still like to be told more about it–'

'Sir, it's nine forty-five,' Callaghan cut across him, heading for the door. 'I'd like to be well hidden before the coach gets here, just in case they have someone following.'

Spencer rose somewhat reluctantly from his chair, then remembered his will. 'Wait a moment, Callaghan.' He held up the document. 'Your signature.'

'You'll need two, sir.'

'You're nearest the door. Call my housekeeper.'

- 61 -

From behind bushes in the Villa Negri gardens, Callaghan watched the black coach stop outside the Consulate, black curtains drawn over its windows, hiding whoever was inside. No one descended and the dark-suited driver remained seated.

The consulate door opened and Spencer appeared, framed against the light inside the building. Pulling the door closed behind him, he hurried down the path, no more than a dark outline as night closed in, and climbed into the coach. The driver flicked his reins and the coach pulled away.

Despite the late hour, the streets were busy and it was forced to proceed at a crawl. Callaghan remained hidden until it turned for the city centre and he was sure it wasn't being followed. Scanning Oliver's map, he ran across the gardens, crossed a small piazza and down a side-street, finally emerging in a wide avenue leading to the Piazza Carlo Felice as the coach was passing.

Still restricted by traffic, it entered and crossed the Piazza, exiting into the Via Sellai. Turning right at the statued Palazzo Ducale, the Palace of the Doges, it headed down the Via San Lorenzo, in the direction of the harbour, then veered left and entered a dark alley. Keeping close to the walls of the buildings, Callaghan followed. At the end of the alley was a high brick wall with an arched gateway. Beyond, the tall shapes of warehouses stood outlined against a cloudy night sky

A customs-guard emerged from an inset door in the gateway. He exchanged brief words with the driver. Moments later, the wide gate swung open. Keeping the coach between himself and the guard, and using the darkness of the surrounding buildings for further cover,

Callaghan walked alongside the coach through the gateway and kept abreast of it across a cobbled square, into a dark narrow alley.

With the iron-rimmed sound of its wheels resounding and bouncing off the walls of the empty alleys, Callaghan again let a small gap open up as the coach continued down one black byway after another, and finally entered a blind alley at the end of which was a low archway. Trundling through it, into a walled yard of an ancient warehouse, the coach wheeled in a tight circle and finally stopped alongside a small door in the side of the building. A faint, flickering light penetrated through the warehouse's grime-covered windows.

Callaghan stole into the compound and pressed into a dark corner to watch.

A man, Maranzano's height, descended from the coach. Spencer followed, blindfolded. He felt for each rung with his feet until they touched the ground. The man thrust a lupara into Spencer's spine and prodded him into the warehouse. A dim light from inside gave Callaghan a glimpse of crates and casks scattered across a stone-flagged floor as the big man removed Spencer's blindfold and the door closed. The coach driver remained seated, not moving.

Minutes passed, the door opened and Spencer reappeared, blindfolded again. The big man loomed behind him and thrust him back to the coach. As the Consul climbed in he coughed.

One cough. One guard.

The coach rolled away, through the archway, and faded into the labyrinth of byways.

Callaghan settled back to wait.

An hour or more passed before he decided it was safe to emerge. Creeping to the side door he pressed slowly down on the latch, making no sound.

He sensed, rather than heard, someone behind him. Before he could turn, an explosion of pain flashed through his head, and everything went black.

- 62 -

Callaghan came to from blackness to dark light, to grey shade, as if rising out of a bottomless pit, only to slide back into blackness. Fighting against it, he neared the surface, aware now of his head resting on something soft, and fingers gently stroking his forehead and lightly brushing his hair.

Recognising Colleen's perfume and realising his pillow was her lap, he opened his eyes. Though all around him was in gloom, her face was silhouetted against a dim light flickering from somewhere behind her, highlighting the tawny shades of her hair.

Feeling around him, the floor beneath was covered in straw. He tried to lift himself up but the movement was too sudden. A sharp pain stabbed behind his eyes forcing him to close them again. He lay back down.

'Stay still,' Colleen whispered, and her fingers returned to stroking his brow.

Slowly reopening his eyes, Callaghan made out her features more clearly, her beautiful face and high cheekbones, her green eyes full of concern for him mirroring the dancing glow of the reflected light. He pulled her down to him. They held each other in silence for a long moment. He could feel her heart beating against his chest.

'Thank God you're alive,' he whispered back. 'Having lost you once, I wouldn't have wanted to live a second time without you.'

'Nor me you,' she said.

Another long moment passed before she broke their embrace and Callaghan saw they were in a walled corner of the warehouse, behind a hastily erected L-shaped barricade of crates with a top row of casks.

The reflected light dancing on the high ceiling came from its other side.

He slowly sat up. The whole of his head was a dull ache. Gingerly touching his neck, he drew a sharp breath at the tenderness there.

'Lie still a while longer.' Colleen gave her reason for whispering by pointing to whoever was on the other side of the barrier.

He tried a reassuring smile, but his facial muscles were too numb to hold it.

'It's easing by the second,' he whispered back, reaching down to his belt – his revolver and seaman's knife were gone. 'I must be getting past it. I should have realised they'd have someone outside, but whoever he was he was good. I waited at least an hour. He never made a sound.'

'It was the thin one. With a mean, ferret-like face.'

'I'll remember that.' Callaghan recollected the photograph Spencer had shown him. 'He's a man named Maranzano's bodyguard–'

'Maranzano!' Colleen grimaced. 'The man gives me the shivers. Looks at me like he's trying to undress me with his eyes.'

'I'll remember that, too,' Callaghan promised.

After three weeks apart, there was so much he wanted to say, but this was neither the place or the time. 'Are you okay? They've not hurt you?' he asked.

Colleen gave him a rueful smile. 'Only my pride at getting caught.'

'Same here.' Keep talking Callaghan told himself, the best antidote to keep Colleen's mind from of any panic she might be feeling, and himself to ignore his pain.

'What happened?'

'My own stupidity,' she replied, hesitating before she explained. 'When I promised you in Gibraltar that I would remain in my hotel until you arrived–'

'You checked into another hotel nearer Sweeny's to keep watch on

him,' Callaghan cut across her. 'Or was it his new partner in crime –
Don Cottone – you thought you'd try to find out about?'

'So Sprague didn't withdraw his request to Palermo for the dossier,
as I thought he might,' Colleen ignored his accusation.

'It was sent to Consul Spencer. Cottone's the head of a Sicilian
organisation called Mafia. I'll explain more about them later. But what
happened? How did you get caught?'

Colleen took a moment to collect her thoughts. 'You're right my
motive. From the first day I checked into the other hotel, I almost
took up residence in the de Genes' lounge, sitting behind a palm
watching Sweeny coming and going, mostly with an aristocratic-
looking man–'

'Early sixties, grey hair, pointed beard?'

'Yes.'

'Cottone.'

'But how do you know what he looks– '

'Spencer showed me his photograph. But finish your account first.'

Colleen pulled a wry face. 'I know it was foolish of me, going there
day after day, but I wanted to be doing something, and thought I'd
kept myself hidden. But then, one morning, Sweeny entered the room,
walked straight to my table, sat down and asked–'

'What are you doing here in Genoa, in all of the places, in all of the
hotel lounges?'

'I panicked. Next thing, I was telling him Father had died – though I
managed to refrain from saying Tweed had hired someone to kill him
– and I was touring Italy again to try to get over his death, and
happened to be passing the hotel in a cab when I saw him coming out
of it and guessed he was staying there–'

'To which he replied: "Some likelihood".'

'Adding "great as it was to see me, being there I must want him for
something – what was it?"'

I compounded it by saying it was an affadivit clearing Father's name, to which he replied by lighting one of his foul cigars, blew smoke in my face, said he'd sign it "the day pigs learn to fly", and walked off.'

'Still the same charming Brains we both love.'

'I was so shaken, I stayed in my hotel for days. But yesterday I chanced going out for a walk. A short distance from the hotel a coach stopped alongside me. I was bundled into it and since then I've been kept here, guarded by the same two men, with no visit from Sweeny, only Maranzano; and no explanation from him as to what they want from me – not that Maranzano could tell me anyway, being he speaks no English. But then, just before you were seized, Consul Spencer was brought in, blindfolded. Maranzano removed them. Mr Spencer told me I was being held in return for information, asked if I was unharmed, assured me I'd soon be free, and was blindfolded again and taken away.' She grasped Callaghan's arm. 'But he didn't say what information…' Her voice tailed off.

Drawing her head on to his shoulder, Callaghan placed his arm around her and held her tight. 'Like you, I don't know. But don't worry, everything will be okay.' The promise was made with a confidence he was far from feeling.

'No, Michael,' Colleen insisted, pulling away from him and fighting to prevent her voice from breaking. 'You must tell me exactly what's happening.'

Callaghan hesitated, then realising she had a right to know, he proceeded to update her.

'But what information?' Colleen repeated when he had finished. 'It obviously has to do with *The Mary Celeste*. But won't Martens have told Sweeny everything that's happened?'

'That's my thought, too. Still, Spencer's wire to Sprague requesting whatever it is, should be well on its way by now.'

'I still don't understand it,' Colleen insisted.

'Nor do I,' Callaghan said. 'Which means we must be missing something. Something vital.'

'Not that it's of any help, but when we met in his hotel, Sweeny seemed very edgy.'

'Maybe starting to wonder, now he knows all about Cottone, whether he can be trusted. It can't be everyday a Mafia Don gets to safeguard a hundred million dollars of your diamonds.'

'Not if Sweeny's crediting him with his own particular brand of ethics,' said Colleen. She gripped his hand. 'What will happen should Sprague not have the information, or refuses to give it?'

'Hopefully, we won't be around to find out.' Callaghan got to his feet and made for the barricade. Peering through a gap in the crates, he could see Maranzano's squat and greasy mafioso sitting on an upturned crate, whittling a piece of wood with a stiletto, his lupara propped up against another crate on which stood a glowing oil lamp. Next to the lamp was Spencer's Colt.45 and his seaman's knife. There was no sign of ferret-face but, Callaghan reckoned, the odds against him getting over the barrier and reaching any of the weapons first must be less than zero.

Nevertheless, should he try? Chance the element of surprise? As he pondered, another sharp pain shot through his head and that decided it for him.

Stretching out again on the straw, he reached out for Colleen to lie beside him. 'I think I prefer you without a beard,' she whispered, placing her arm around his chest. 'Head still hurting?'

'A little. There's only squat-and-greasy on duty. Where's ferret-man?'

'He'll be somewhere nearby, resting. What are you planning?'

'Our escape.' He drew her to him. Looking through the grimy window, he saw dawn wasn't far off. 'Just give me an hour to get my strength back and by then I'll have thought of something.'

- 63 -

Friday, January 17, 1873

From the dim light seeping into the warehouse, Callaghan saw it was dawn. He looked around their improvised prison, from the centuries-old stone paved floor scattered with pieces of rusted iron hoops, to thick planks of wood stacked against the walls.

Alongside him, Colleen stirred and turned to face him, 'How is your head?'

There was some stiffness and soreness as he sat up. 'Fine.' He reached for a broken hoop. The rust was on the surface, but the metal underneath was still strong.

'What are you planning?'

'To paraphrase Archimedes: "Give me a lever and I will move the earth with it." I only hope he was right.'

Crossing to the barricade, he saw that ferret-face was now on guard, sitting on the box, honing his stiletto on a stone. Eying the lupara on the floor close to the mafioso's feet, Callaghan crouched down and examined the stone slabbed floor. The mortar surrounding the flags looked brittle with age. Choosing a slab behind one on which rested a crate, he inserted the hoop into the surrounding mortar and prised at it, making no sound. A chunk of mortar came loose in his hand.

'I'll keep watch,' Colleen whispered. She stole to the barricade.

Carefully picking away until he'd removed enough mortar to insert his hands under the flag, he tried to slowly lift it. It wouldn't budge. Straining, he heard it grate as it came loose.

Colleen spun around. 'Ferret-face!' she mouthed.

Callaghan scattered straw over the slab. They moved swiftly back, lay down again and closed their eyes, heard the mafioso approach and felt the laden silence as he peered through the barrier at them. Colleen moved in false restlessness, rustling the straw. It must have satisfied ferret face they were asleep and they heard the box scrape the floor as he returned to it and sat down.

'We must try again,' Colleen whispered.

'Give it a minute.'

They waited. Callaghan nodded. They crept back to the barricade. Colleen peered through, nodded "okay". Raising the flag inch by slow inch, Callaghan cautiously manoeuvred it across the square of earth exposed underneath, and lowered it down on to the slab behind.

'Squat-and-greasy's taking over,' Colleen whispered. 'Ferret-face is going to lie down. No, he's not! Someone's come in–' She turned to Callaghan, fear in her eyes. 'It's Maranzano.'

Joining her, Callaghan watched Cottone's son-in-law approach his two bodyguards. In the light of day, Maranzano was even taller than his photograph suggested; over six feet of bulging muscle, with dark olive skin and black, wavy hair. Opening his coat, he removed his silver-filigree lupara, propped it against a crate, indicated to the barricade and said something to ferret face.

Expecting Maranzano to check up on them, Callaghan half turned away to again scatter straw over the flag's removal. But satisfied with ferret-face's nod that all was well, Maranzano upturned another box and sat facing his two Castellammare mafiosi. The three began talking in low voices.

'For a moment there, I thought he was here to check on you.' Colleen whispered.

'So did I.' Callaghan pulled her away from the barrier. 'And from the size of him, and what Spencer told me about him, I wasn't looking forward to his way of going about it.'

Quietly covering the exposed earth with straw, they lay down again. Colleen placed her head on his shoulder. Holding her close and staring up at the roof high above them, Callaghan was suddenly aware of hunger pains in his stomach and realised it was must be all of fifteen hours since he'd last eaten in the Consulate with Oswald Spencer.

'I assume they're feeding you? I could eat the proverbial horse.'

'Mid-morning, mid-afternoon. Bread, cheese, cheap wine.'

'At this moment that sounds like a feast.' He tried to make light of their situation for her. 'But while we're waiting to be served, what's the first thing you're going to do when we get out of here?'

'A bath,' Colleen said, longingly. 'I'd give anything for a long, hot soaping.'

'Tonight in the Consulate,' Callaghan promised. 'Its marble one is the last word in luxury.'

'Big enough for two?' asked Colleen, joining in the pretence.

'Enough to swim in.'

'Mmm. Can't wait. Just the thought of having my back sponged. Bliss.'

'Your request will be my command,' Callaghan promised. Holding her tight, they watched the sun's slow ascent as midday approached and passed, with Maranzano and his two bodyguards still muttering on the other side of the barricade.

Callaghan felt his eyelids getting heavy, when the warehouse door opened and closed, and footsteps crossed the stone floor. Exchanging querying glances with Colleen, Callaghan and she crept to the barrier and peered through to the other side.

Sweeny.

- 64 -

Though it was a year and two months since Callaghan last saw him, Brains hadn't changed. Still the same squat shape wearing his habitual black topcoat, thick black hair escaping from under a black silk tophat, black walrus moustache, long thick sideburns hiding much of his plug-ugly face.

Preceding him, flanked by two bodyguards, was Cottone. Silver-haired, slim, about five foot ten tall, wearing a long dark overcoat but no hat, his face was leaner than in his photograph, his nose more hawk-like, increasing the impression of a cruel nature, while his whole attitude denoted detachment and superiority.

His two bodyguards were short and burly, faces cold to the point of being expressionless. One had Moorish features; the other a flattish face with Asiatic eyes. Both carried a lupara.

Maranzano and his men stood up as Cottone approached them. He asked his son-in-law a question. Maranzano picked up Spencer's Colt.45 and indicated towards the barricade.

Callaghan noticed the scene was enacted with a minimum of words and the briefest of gestures which, he decided, must be a peculiarity of the Mafia.

Removing a cigar case from his inner overcoat pocket, Cottone selected a corona. The Asiatic-eyed mafioso produced a box of vestas and lit it. Cottone drew on it, exhaled a wreath of smoke and nodded. Just once. His and Maranzano's two mafiosi made for the barricade.

Placing a protective arm around her shoulder, Callaghan drew Colleen back into the shadows of their restricted prison space.

A top cask was removed, revealing all seven men on the other side of the barrier. They in turn looked at their two prisoners. Cottone's appraisal was dispassionate, Maranzano's scrutiny hostile. But Callaghan's focus was on Sweeny, who was studying his bearded face with narrowed eyes.

The Asiatic-eyed mafioso gestured with his lupara for Callaghan to approach the barrier. As he obeyed, stepping out of the prison's gloom, Callaghan saw recognition dawn on Brains face. His bushy eyebrows knitted in a vicious scowl. 'Michael!' he snarled.

Cottone's facial expression stayed unchanged, seemingly undisturbed by Sweeny's knowledge of the prisoner. Maranzano, however, pointed his lupara at Callaghan and looked at Sweeny for him to explain.

'Buon giorno, Uncle Peter,' said Callaghan.

Brains' scowl deepened. 'First, Colleen. Now you. What d'hell's going on here, *Mikey?*

'Missing you, Uncle *Petey*. You were in such a hurry to get away we never got to say goodbye.'

'Cut the humour, Mikey, you're in no position to act the funny guy. How come you knew I was in Genoa? And don't give me a dumb answer like Colleen. Something peculiar's going on here and I don't like the smell of it.'

'You know this man?' Cottone asked.

'Sure. Name's Callaghan. He's married to my niece over there, got some personal vendetta against me. But more than that – he's a cop.'

Cottone's only reaction was a hardening of his impassive gaze. Callaghan felt the capomafia coldy appraise him. Sensing the tension, Maranzano questioned his father-in-law. Despite speaking Italian, Callaghan understood none of the Sicilian's curt reply, apart from polizia. Maranzano angrily sliced a hand across his throat, telling Cottone what he should do. Cottone ignored him.

Maranzano's eyes flared at this rebuff in front of the four lower echelon mafiosi. Callaghan saw his grip tighten on his lupara, but he controlled himself and lowered the shotgun.

Sweeny stepped nearer. 'You ain't answered my question, Mikey? I'll ask you one more time, count to three, then get Nino to persuade you,' he gestured towards Cottone's two bodyguards, though which was Nino was impossible to guess, since neither reacted to hearing the name. 'He's ace with a shiv,' he threatened, lapsing into his East Side vernacular, 'the Apaches back home got nothing on him, peels yehs skin off in strips.'

Colleen cried out, stepped to Callaghan's side and clutched his arm. Brains gave an evil smirk. 'Or maybe yehs'll talk quicker if we work on Colleen? That should loosen yehs tongue.'

Callaghan suppressed his angry response. His thought now was to secure Colleen's release. 'I see you've not changed any, Uncle Petey. But okay, I'll tell you all you want to know. Except, Colleen's not involved in any of it, so first I want her taken to the American Consulate—'

'No, Michael,' Colleen protested, 'not without you.'

Callaghan kept his eyes on Sweeny. 'And confirmation on its letterhead that she's arrived there safe and unharmed.'

'Yehs surely not trying to negotiate,' Brains' East Side accent broadened with disbelief. 'Yehs obviously not listening. I've only got to let Nino work on her and yehs'll be begging to talk.'

Still thinking a move ahead, Callaghan held himself in check. 'I also want a letter from you saying that Colleen's father was never involved in any of your scams—'

'Scams! Say that again, Mikey, and I'll have Nino cut yehs tongue out as well as strip yehs—'

'In return, I'll wire Consul Sprague in Gibraltar, authorising him to send Consul Spencer here whatever information you're—'

'How d'yehs know about them?' Sweeny exploded. 'Or me wanting information from them? And what d'yehs mean – yehs'll do the authorising? How come yehs tied up in all this?'

Callaghan glanced at Cottone, the capo's face remained unreadable. Maranzano was looking as if he was burning to know the reason for

331

Sweeny's reaction, but having had one rebuff, was restraining himself from asking Cottone. As for the four mafiosi, they were obeying the omerta: hearing nothing, seeing nothing, obeying their Mafia code of silence.

'I've been tied up from the day you caused my father's death, Sweeny. I swore I'd track you down and get even–'

'Yeh? Well yehs might have tracked me down, Mikey, but from where I'm standing yehs a long ways off getting even.'

'Signor Callaghan,' Cottone intruded. 'You have not yet explained why you're in Genoa, or how you knew we were here?'

'Because, Signor Cottone,' Callaghan deliberately used the capo's name, 'I got lucky when a John Doe was found murdered in an alley off South Street, a stiff that turned out to be – just for you to know what a cheap, lying, double-crossing skunk you're dealing with – Sweeny's diamond merchant Joseph Kaufmann.'

'Kaufmann!' Sweeny's swarthy skin paled. 'Kaufmann's dead?'

'Oh, please, uncle dear,' Colleen exclaimed, 'You know damn well he is. Killed, as was Father Reikel, in the most vicious way, by your psychopathic–'

'Reikel!' Sweeny protested. 'Father Beckx' emissary? Yehs telling me he's dead, too?'

'You know my name, Signor Callaghan. How?' Cottone intruded again, his voice was now menacing. 'But I suspect that you and your signora have more revelations to make than the killing of a diamond merchant and a priest.'

Callaghan glanced at Sweeny, looking shell-shocked. All put on, of course, but what was he hoping to gain?

Unless he had a hidden agenda he didn't want Cottone to know about.

In which case, now was the moment to stir things up even more. Saying enough, but not revealing all his cards. He gripped Colleen's arm, silently asking her to let him do the talking.

'Sure. Kaufmann and Father Reikel were both murdered, mutilated, by a psychopathic killer named Arian Martens, who Sweeny hired to—'

'What d'hell yehs talking about, *Mikey?*' Sweeny snarled. 'I don't know any Martens.'

Whatever he was up to, Brains' acting couldn't be faulted, thought Callaghan, ignoring him and addressing Cottone. 'He ordered Kaufmann's death to prevent him turning police evidence. Reikel was killed to prevent him persuading the captain of one of the brigs carrying the barrels—'

'*Brigs?*' Sweeny almost screamed at him. '*Barrels!* Yeh saying yehs know about my *ships?* And about the barrels—'

'Why are you persisting in this, uncle dear?' Realising what Michael was up to, Colleen joined in. 'Sure we know about them. *The Mary Celeste* and the *Dei Gratia.*'

'You telling me they're my ships?' Sweeny looked poleaxed. 'What d'hell's happening here? I was reading about them only yesterday. Both under arrest by the damned Limeys, with Limey snoops going over them inside out—'

'I hope they are,' Colleen blurted with spirit, her tone sounding almost vindictive. '*The Mary Celeste's* at least. And that they've found the diamonds—'

'Shut yeh mouth,' Brains snarled across her, 'or I'll get Nino,' he indicated to the Asiatic eyed mafioso, 'to shut it for yehs—'

'Signor Callaghan,' Cottone interjected. 'Tell me why—'

'I ain't finished,' Sweeny snarled.

Cottone curtly nodded to Nino. He prodded Sweeny with his lupara. Brains looked down at the weapon with horror.

'When Kaufmann failed, as we now know why, to telegraph the Hotel de Genes with the names of the vessels,' Don Cottone continued, still addressing Callaghan, 'it forced us into using your signora to — shall we say — persuade Consul Spencer to telegraph Gibraltar. The information we required were the names of all sailing ships from New York awaiting orders there, and thus identify our vessels.'

He turned to Colleen. 'With my gratitude to you, signora, we now have them. You also said that only one of them is being searched. Why is the other not also being searched?'

Maranzano stepped nearer, as if hoping to maybe understand some of Colleen's reply.

Callaghan again gripped her arm, for her not to answer.

Now even more bemused than ever, his mind raced as he tried to work out why Sweeny had withheld the vessels' names from Cottone...unless, he suddenly thought...unless Brains was hedging his bets about taking Cottone on as his new partner in crime, and was holding back on him in case he decided to double-cross him as he had with Boss Tweed back in New York?

If so, Brains was playing a more dangerous game this time, which made this the ideal moment to really stir things up between the two.

'I don't understand why you're asking, Signor Cottone,' he replied. 'Sweeny's the one with all the answers. He's the one Martens reports in to–'

'Yehs ain't poxing listening, Mikey,' Sweeny raged. 'I don't know any Martens.'

Callaghan ignored him. 'And gets his orders from. Wiring Martens to have the *Dei Gratia* jump Gibraltar with the second barrel of diamonds. She docked here yesterday–'

'No!' Sweeny yelled, like someone in torment. 'It can't have.'

'The vessel is in Genoa?' Cottone's voice was suddenly ominous.

'No more. By now it's on its way back to Gibraltar. But the cargo's unloaded. I followed the wagon to a warehouse and saw the diamonds barrel put on a mule cart, then taken to a palazzo–'

'Nino!' said Cottone. The Asiatic-looking mafioso moved his stiletto to Sweeny's throat.

Brains stared at it, the blood draining from his face.

Still with his gaze fixed on Callaghan, 'What palazzo?' Cottone asked.

- 65 -

How much to say, what to omit, Callaghan mused, eyeing Bruno's stiletto held to Sweeny's throat. Having been told by Spencer all about Cottone's ruthlessness, he didn't want Sweeny killed. Not until he'd secured Colleen's release. And found out what was going on.

'The palazzo?' Cottone repeated in a low monotone full of menace.

Colleen grasped Callaghan's hand, letting Cottone know that whatever he was planning to do to them, they were in this together.

'In an alleyway off the Via San Lorenezo. I assumed Martens was handing the diamonds over to Sweeny and you were all inside checking them. So I thought I'd play safe and follow Consul Spencer to wherever you were holding Colleen, except,' he said ruefully, 'I got caught. Anything else you want to know, ask Sweeny, not me.'

Cottone nodded to Nino. The mafioso pricked Sweeny's throat, drawing blood. Brains wiped his neck and looked horrified at his reddened hand. Colleen tightened her grip of Callaghan's hand.

Cottone said something to Sweeny in a low voice. It clearly held an unpleasant threat of what would happen to him should his answer not satisfy the capomafia, and Brains' legs buckled under him. He fell to his knees babbling, 'I swear in the name of Mary, Mother of God, and all that's holy, I don't know any Martens.' Raising a gold crucifix hanging on his watch chain to his lips, he desperately kissed it. 'And may God strike me down dead right here and now if I'm lying.'

He paused, as if to prove to Cottone that because God hadn't struck him down dead, he must be telling the truth, then ranted on, his forehead damp with perspiration. 'Whoever he is, he must have found out about the stones and forced the vessels' names out of Kaufmann before he killed him, changed their destinations and sailed on board the first one. For himself,' Brains blubbered, *'not for me.* Because I ain't never heard of him before now.'

He looked up pleadingly at Cottone. 'Would I be so brainless as to sail across the Atlantic to put a deal to you, when all the time I was going to renege on it? Would I? I ask you? But we know where he is, right?' he grovelled. 'And the diamonds. Some palazzo off the Via San Lorenezo.'

Cottone signalled Nino. He lowered his stiletto. Clearly unhappy Sweeny was being allowed to live, Maranzano angrily challenged Cottone, repeating his gesture of slicing a hand across his own neck. Again, Cottone ignored him. A flush of anger darkened Maranzano's face.

Sweeny, the strength returning to his legs, slowly rose to his feet.

Reeling from knowing that all his and Colleen's theorising had been so wrong, Callaghan desperately tried to think how he could manipulate this new development to buy Colleen's release.

Cottone cut into his thoughts. 'Is there anyone else who knows about the diamonds?'

'No one,' said Callaghan. 'Only Martens.'

'We will find him,' said Cottone. 'If not at the palazzo, then when he tries to sell the diamonds.'

'And he's sure gonna pay for all his meddling,' Brains snarled, incensed that Callaghan and Colleen had witnessed his humiliation, wanting to show he was still someone to be reckoned with. 'Slow, real slow. One cut of Nino's stiletto, one strip of his skin, for every stone we lose out on if those Limeys find the *Celeste's* before we get her bills of lading from him—'

'I can get the *Celeste's* cargo released to you without Marten's lading bills,' said Callaghan seizing the opening, hoping that what he was about to offer them would be believed.

'Oh, yeah?' Brains snapped. 'How you gonna do that, Mr Clever Dick?'

Cottone fixed his eyes on Callaghan, waiting for any sign he was lying.

'Sprague. He's been made power-of-attorney by the *Celeste's* underwriters for her cargo to be released. The British won't refuse, they're interested only in what happened to her captain and crew.'

This was the lie they had to believe, especially Cottone. The truth was that Winchester, the *Celeste's* major shareholder, had instructed the Board of Underwriters in New York to refuse Sprague's request, and was on his way to Gibraltar to represent himself before the Inquiry.

'Sprague's getting a copy bill-of-lading from Genoa, for him to accept tenders for her cargo to be transferred to another ship. A wire from me,' he held Cottone's gaze, 'he'll award it to you. Your ship can then head straight to Palermo. A week later the diamonds will be yours to count.'

'You mean you've not told Sprague about my stones being on board?' Sweeny's brows met in a suspicious scowl.

'No, otherwise he'd have had no option but to tell the Inquiry. Imagine the sensation that would have made. Every major newspaper would have carried the story. You'd have read all about it and gone to ground. And any hope of my finding you would have gone.'

'Signor Callaghan? Why should Consul Sprague be influenced by a wire from you?'

'It's what we agreed with the New York Police. He won't release the cargo until he gets a wire from me that I need it sent to Genoa to check it here, rather than in Gibraltar. And I wasn't going to wire him until I had Sweeny under lock and key and on his way home to face trial.'

'In your dreams, Mikey,' Brains sneered.

'And what is to stop us sending the wire in your name?' Cottone questioned.

'It has to include a codeword, known only to Sprague and myself.'

'No problems,' Sweeny grated. 'Five seconds with Nino you'll be screaming out the word.'

'And how will you know I've given you the right one?' Callaghan challenged him.

'I didn't say anything about him killing you. Just peeling you. All we have to do is keep you alive to see if you're levelling with us. If not, you'll wish you'd never been born–'

'What if Consul Sprague telegraphs Consul Spencer to confirm your message?' asked Cottone.

'He won't. Not if mine's got the codeword. But should he, Spencer would co-operate to effect my release.'

'Release!' Brains snarled. 'Other than a slow painful journey to Hell, yehs not going anywhere, Mikey. *I can promise* you that.'

'I know that, but Spencer won't. So, Signor Cottone,' Callaghan faced the capomafia, at the same time gripping Colleen's hand for her not to make any protest. 'A wire to Consul Sprague in return my wife's release. And your guarantee that Sweeny will give her the affidavit, clearing her father's name. Are we agreed? As I understand it, the word of a Don is never broken.'

Cottone studied him a long moment before replying: 'You have my word.'

Callaghan's heart leapt with relief.

'Hey!' Sweeny protested.

Ignoring him, Cottone fixed his impassive gaze on Callaghan. 'With the proviso that you will both be sent to Palermo until the cargo arrives there. The signora will not be released until it has been checked for the diamonds. You, I regret, will not be released.'

Colleen's finger nails dug into Callaghan's palm.

'We have no materials here for you to write the telegraph to Consul Sprague,' Cottone added. 'Signor Sweeny will return to the hotel for some and be back within the hour.'

'And maybe you'll make sure he brings my wife's affadivit with him?' Callaghan said. 'I trust your word, but I wouldn't trust his in a million years.'

Cottone turned his gaze to Colleen and gave her an almost imperceptibe bow. 'You will have your document, signora,' he said. 'Meanwhile, should you require anything?'

'Breakfast,' said Colleen. 'We've not eaten since yesterday.'

Don Cottone snapped his fingers.

- 66 -

'Despite Cottone's word, I doubt that Sweeny will write the affidavit,' Colleen said as she tore off a hunk of bread to go with her cheese. 'But thank you for trying.'

'Oh, I think he will.' Callaghan accepted the loaf and cheese from her and broke off his own pieces. 'Now he knows what Cottone is capable of, he won't have the courage to refuse.'

She looked across at him, 'Do you think Martens has stolen the diamonds for himself, or do you think he's still a Black Knight, a Totenbund, dedicated to their cause? If so, was Kaufmann in on it? Double crossing Sweeny? Being German and a Catholic, he was probably just as much opposed to Bismarck's Kulturkampf policy as Father Reikel.'

'That's a lot of questions to answer at once,' Callaghan smiled. 'But to answer the first two, no, I don't think Martens has deserted the cause. Everything we know about him, especially that Knights Templar tableau on board the *Celeste*, point to him still being Totenbund.'

'And Kaufmann?'

'Again, no. His diary memos to wire Sweeny suggest otherwise.'

Callaghan swigged some wine and passed the bottle to Colleen.

'As I see it, after skipping New York, Sweeny's original instructions were for both brigs to sail to Marseilles. But whether by chance or not he met Cottone, and it resulted in them making some deal—'

Poised to drink from the bottle, Colleen cut in. 'It must be really big to interest Sweeny.'

'For sure it must be. But whatever it is, and despite altering the destinations to Palermo, Brains still played it safe by having them call into Gibraltar for another possible change of orders, in case he and Cottone couldn't agree terms.'

He paused to break off some more bread and cheese. Seated on the straw laid floor, ankles crossed, knees akimbo, Colleen continued for him. 'Meanwhile, Reikel arrives in New York to raise finance for a Jesuit-led counter-revolution to oust Victor Emmanuel and Count von Bismark. He meets Kaufmann who tells him – either in the confessional or seeking his guidance – about Sweeny's diamonds.'

She swigged some wine. Callaghan took over.

'Reikel tells Martens, his *Totenbund* protector, and together they plot to steal them by forcing Kaufmann to divert both ships to Genoa – with the *Dei Gratia* sailing ten days behind to wait in Gibraltar until the *Celeste* reaches her journey's end and her cargo is safely unloaded, at which they'd then send instructions for the *Gratia* to follow on–'

'Except,' Colleen hitched on to the explanation, 'Kaufmann was planning to outwit them by wiring Sweeny after the *Celeste* had sailed–'

'For Brains to meet the *Celeste* in Genoa and deal with Martens, then discharge the exact number of barrels as per the bill-of-lading, leaving the vessel free to sail to Palermo with the diamonds still in the hold–'

'And the *Gratia* to sail from Gibraltar straight to Palermo without even calling into Genoa.'

Callaghan helped himself to more bread and cheese. 'Unluckily for Reikel, Martens wanted Kaufmann killed in order to ensure his silence. Reikel refused to agree to the killing of a fellow Catholic, especially a Jesuit, so Martens killed them both.'

'Except,' Colleen screwed up her face – delightfully thought Callaghan – as she pondered another problem, 'that brings us back to Cottone. If he and Sweeny aren't involved in Martens' counter-revolution, what sort of scheme have they agreed? What has a Mafia Don got to offer Sweeny? And what has Sweeny got to offer him back in return?'

'That's baffling me as well,' Callaghan confessed.

'Unless...' Colleen speculated, '...unless Cottone's planning to steal...' Her eyes filled with sudden conviction. 'That has to be it! Cottone's not interested in Sweeny. Or any deal he has to offer. Only his diamonds!'

'That's just one of my new theories,' Callaghan replied. 'But who knows. What's more, I get the feeling it's not over yet.'

He broke the remainder of the bread and handed half to Colleen. 'We'll have to wait for Sweeny to return for me to write him the wire, before we can get back to testing Archimedes. But as soon as he, and then Maranzano leave...' He paused, not wanting to cause her more alarm, then decided to share his unease. 'All this talking between Maranzano and his mafiosi is making me edgy. They've been huddling together again ever since Cottone and Sweeny left–'

'Michael,' Colleen diverted across him. 'When we get out of here, shouldn't we just report everything to the authorities and return home? Let others deal with it all? Let New York know where Sweeny and their money is, and apply to have him extradited? Tell the Italian military what Martens and his Totenbund are planning and leave it all to them? And call in at Gibraltar on the way back, go over Flood's head, and tell the British Admiralty what really happened to *The Mary Celeste*? Being realistic, you've no hope of any retribution against Sweeny now, surrounded as he is by Cottone and his Mafia, and as for my affidavit–'

The warehouse door opened.

They heard a familiar voice growl something to Maranzano.

'Sweeny,' both said at the same time, turning to face the barrier.

A top cask was removed from the barricade and Sweeny glowered at them from above a crate, rolling an unlit cigar between his moustache-hidden lips as Maranzano's two mafiosi returned to Cottone's son-in-law. Brains raised a pistol to show he was armed, placed a sheet of paper and a pencil on the crate and stepped back,

342

removed his cigar, spat away dry pieces of tobacco stuck to his lips, and gave Callaghan an unpleasant leer. 'I hope for your sake this telegraph works, Mikey. I wouldn't like to be in your skin, or stripped of it, if it doesn't.'

Callaghan picked up the pencil. 'What's your vessel called?' he asked, making himself stay calm.

'The *Santa Rosalia*.'

'When can she leave?'

'Tomorrow.'

Callaghan wrote the message, giving Sprague the go-ahead to accept a tender from a Palermo company named Cottone for the *Celeste's* cargo, and have it transferred to the Santa Rosalia.

Sweeny signalled him back with his pistol and extended his hand for the wire.

'In exchange for Colleen's affidavit,' Callaghan reminded him.

Sweeny pointed the pistol at Callaghan's head. 'Give it me.'

Callaghan held the paper in both hands, threatening to tear it. 'The affidavit.'

Sweeny bit through his cigar, trying to control his spleen. Spitting the bits away, he produced a sheet of paper with his unmistakable scrawl, slammed it down on the crate and snarled, 'Take it.'

Callaghan read it. Tersely worded, it was nevertheless sufficient to clear Colleen's father of any suspicion of involvement in The Ring's activities. He handed Sweeny his written telegraph.

Brains grabbed it and read it. 'What's the code-word?'

'Come on, Sweeny. You don't expect me to fall for that?'

'Worth a try,' Sweeny growled, pocketing the wire. 'You could have slipped up.' Lighting another cigar, he took a long puff and studied the lighted end. 'We searched that palazzo. Place was empty. But you should have told me about the emblem, Mikey.'

'The Black Knight crest?'

'Is that what you thought it was?' Brains sneered. 'You went to the wrong school, Mikey.' He took another pull at his cigar. 'Still, give us a couple of days and this Martens guy of yours will be paying long and slow for trying to outsmart me. The *Gratia*'s diamonds will be back in my possession. And the three of us, you, me and Colleen, will be on our way to Palermo to play happy families and get ready for your funeral. Afraid it'll have to be a quiet one, though, Mikey, and burial in one of Cottone's vineyards – except I can promise you a great view across the bay.'

'And I hope you enjoy your retirement in Sicily, Uncle Petey,' Callaghan retaliated, hoping his weakness for boasting would loosen his tongue. 'Assuming Cottone allows you to keep a few of the diamonds.'

'Retirement!' Brains snarled. 'You sure as hell don't think this is all about me sheltering out to grass in Palermo? Listen up, Mikey. Twelve months from now I'll be back in New York. And not just me, but Cottone and his Mafia as well. This King Victor Emmanuel's making things a little too hot for him on the island at the moment, so rather than fight the guy...' calming down, Sweeny dragged out his final punch for him to enjoy it all the more, 'we're moving his business, or should I say our new partnership, right across the big pond–'

'New York!' Callaghan exclaimed, aghast at the thought of it. 'New York wouldn't have you back – not in a million years!'

'Not have me back!' Sweeny hurled his cigar to the floor. 'Yehs couldn't be more wrong, Mikey. They're begging me back. My Paris attorney's already negotiating the deal, part of which includes immunity from prosecution. Not only that, but when I do return, you sure as hell don't think that this next time, I'm gonna be satisfied with just New York.'

He ground the cigar under his heel. 'No way, Mikey! No way! Cottone and me are forming a joint organisation to take over every major city, every city hall, every police department through-out the entire U S of A.'

His savage outburst over, he gave an evil smile. 'What's more, Mikey, with all I now know about…Martens, did you say his name is? Beckx can whistle for the percentage I was going to give him. I'll donate it to the American Church – and have the Vatican moved to Washington instead, with a proper God-fearing Irishman as Pope in place of a creeping Eyetie.'

He doffed his black silk top hat. 'See you in Palermo, Mikey. You too, Colleen. I'll find you some decent widow's weeds for the funeral.'

Crossing over to Maranzano, Brains muttered to him, and both men exited the warehouse.

Callaghan waited for squat-and-greasy and ferret-mean to replace the cask and turned to face Colleen. She looked back at him, her eyes wide open with shock, not even looking at the affidavit in his hand.

'Michael, you don't believe him? New York wouldn't be so stupid as to let him back? They couldn't! Surely! Not after all he did!'

'If they do, they're crazy!' said Callaghan. 'When I said it wasn't over I never expected that. But at least we now know what the damn shyster's up to. Hell's bells – bringing the Mafia into the States!'

He offered her the affidavit. Colleen shook her head, telling him it wasn't important at that moment. He pocketed it.

'We have to get to Spencer for him to telegraph Washington,' she urged, 'Surely Congress can overrule New York and prevent this from happening? It must.'

'More than that,' said Callaghan, 'I think this answers the question of whether we should sail on the next boat home. We have to find Martens before they do, and stop them getting their hands on the *Gratia*'s diamonds. Cut off their funding and their plans will be scuppered at source.'

He looked around. Dusk was already descending. The relit oil lamp was casting fluttering shadows across the ceiling. Now was the best chance to escape. There was no time to lose.

He checked through the barrier. Squat-and-greasy was sitting on his own, whittling at another piece of wood. Ferret-face was presumably resting.

He knelt by the patch of earth left by the flag's removal. Colleen crossed to the barrier and resumed her watch. Digging a cavity under the stone slab on which the crate was resting, he chose three planks from the corner of their prison, placed two as a fulcrum across the flag behind the hollow, slid the third plank into the cavity and lowered it on to the fulcrum. He checked the angle. He would have preferred it steeper, but it should still create enough upthrust to topple the crate forward and hopefully leave enough of a gap for him to get through. Another uncertainty was the element of surprise. Would it startle squat-and-greasy enough, or would his reaction be instant? His lupara was less than an arm's length away.

Finding a piece of timber to use as a club, Callaghan stood over his makeshift lever.

Colleen glanced through the gap, nodded and moved clear. Bending his knees and poised to land the full weight of his body on the plank, he froze as he heard the warehouse door open.

Colleen peered back through the barrier,' It's Maranzano,' she whispered urgently over her shoulder. 'There's someone with him.' She spun around. 'Blindfolded! His wrists tied!'

Callaghan crossed to her side, to see Maranzano prodding a dark-suited man between the shoulders with his silver filigree lupara, towards squat-and-greasy. In the dim light from the oil lamp, the prisoner appeared to be young, slim, with dark hair and olive skin.

Grabbing his lupara, squat-and-greasy stood up. Maranzano made his captive kneel and took off the blindfold. Holding his lupara's muzzle to the young man's head, Maranzano asked him a question. The young man shook his head.

Ferret-face entered the circle. Maranzano uttered one word to him.

Placing his lupara against a crate, the mafioso looped a coil of what looked like wire around the prisoner's neck and pulled it tight, choking him. The young man's head rocked as he tried to loosen the garotte with his bound hands. Signalling ferret-face to relax the wire, Maranzano rested his lupara against the crate and repeated his question. The captive again refused to answer. Ferret-face reapplied his garrotte.

This time, the young man's struggles were less violent, the strength sapping out of him.

'Michael,' Colleen clutched his arm, 'we must do something!'

Callaghan crossed to the plank, flung himself up and landed on it with both feet, tilting the slab. The crate slid forward. The cask above it tilted and crashed to the floor, splintering open, splashing its contents over the three mafiosi and their prisoner.

Callaghan hurled through the gap left by the crate. Squat-and-greasy was nearest. Clawing at his eyes, he'd dropped his lupara. Grabbing it by the barrel, Callaghan swung it, smashing the mafioso's skull, then turned to ferret-face who was scrambling on his knees for his weapon. Bringing the butt down on the nape of the man's neck, Callaghan heard the bone snap, then threw himself sideways, cocking the lupara's hammer as Maranzano grabbed his own lupara and swivelled around, arcing the twin-barrels at him. Callaghan pulled his trigger first. The shot tore a hole in Maranzano's chest, hurling him backwards and flattening the upturned crates. His eyes stayed open, staring sightlessly up at the warehouse ceiling.

Callaghan picked up squat-and-greasy's stiletto and severed the prisoner's ties. The young man got to his feet and crossed to Maranzano's body. He looked down at it, knelt, made the sign of the Cross, recited something in Latin, then spat, once in Maranzano's right eye, once in his left.

Hearing Colleen's cry of horror behind him, Callaghan turned and saw her staring at the young man with open disgust. Then she gave a warning cry: 'Michael!'

Callaghan spun around. The young man was pointing Maranzano's lupara at him. He backed towards the door, then out of the warehouse.

Colleen ran to Callaghan's side. 'Michael! He was a priest! What he did was revolting! And why did he hold a gun on you? What does it all mean?'

Callaghan was silent for a moment, then gave a wry smile. 'I should have seen it all sooner, Colleen. The emblem. Sweeny worked it all out with one look, while the answer's been staring me in the face for two months and I never saw it.'

'Saw what?'

'Who Martens is.'

'Who he is! He's a Totenbund, a political assassin, a Black Knight. We might have been wrong about Sweeny, but not about Martens.'

'Except he's more than Totenbund. Infinitely more. I'll explain it all when we get to the Consulate, but the sooner we're away from here the better. Cottone's going to want revenge for the death of his son-in-law.'

Pausing only to pick up a lupara and bandoleer, and thrust squat-and-greasy's stiletto in his sheath, Callaghan hurried Colleen out of the warehouse.

- 67 -

'You may leave it with me, Callaghan,' said Spencer. 'I will write Washington a full report and have it despatched by the first available steamship. Rest assured, neither Cottone, nor his Mafia, will be allowed to enter our great country. Nor will Sweeny be readmitted – other than extradition to stand trial, that is, and pay for his crimes.'

'Thank you, sir.'

The Consul brooded, swirling his brandy around his glass. 'Now, about this Martens?'

Increasingly concerned by Callaghan's and Colleen's non-appearance, he'd not waited to read Head's diary. Horrified by the account, getting more and more convinced they'd become two more of Martens' victims, he was about to call the Genoa police when they arrived at the Consulate. He was now fully informed of the entire affair.

Colleen looked up from her chair by the the fire. 'Yes, Michael. What did you mean by saying he was more than Totenbund?'

Placing his empty brandy glass on a side-table, Callaghan began explaining.

'Sweeny started me thinking when he told me I was wrong about the shield over the palazzo gateway. But it wasn't until I realised Maranzano's prisoner was a priest that everything fell into place. The design is nothing to do with any Death League, Black Knights, Totenbund, Carbonari, call them what you will...' He paused. 'It's a Jesuit emblem – I once saw it as a boy in school and forgot all about it as kids do – illustrating the seven deadly sins, the swords placed in the parts of the body they identify with each of the seven greatest temptations: pride, wrath, envy, gluttony, avarice, sloth, and lust.'

'You saying it's a Jesuit building?' Oswald Spencer protested. 'And nothing to do with any politico Freemasonry movement?'

'Yes to both, sir. Guessing, I'd say it was once a seminary.'

'But damn it, man—'

'Well, it confirms Martens' connection to Father Reikel,' Colleen cut across the Consul.

'Except not in the way we thought, Colleen.'

'What other way could there be?'

Callaghan held her puzzled expression as Spencer also waited his answer.

'Martens and Reikel are one and the same man.'

'But he can't be,' Colleen stared back at him. 'Father Murray identified Father Reikel's body, and conducted the internment service.'

'That blinded me too. I can only guess that despite all he said, Murray must be ultramontane and not only knew what was happening, but deliberately misled me, to put me off the scent. The body under the Brooklyn Bridge was that of the real Arian Martens. If I'm right, he was a German seaman who just happened to resemble Reikel, especially his almost white hair. Reikel murdered him for his papers—'

'If I'm following you correctly,' Spencer cut in, 'you're now saying the killer's a Jesuit *priest*.'

'I'm afraid so, sir. On the *Celeste*, I saw him kneeling in front of a sword and assumed he was carrying out some form of ritual ceremony. Colleen later identified the hilt as that of the Black Knights. But looking back on it now, he was using it as a substitute Cross.'

'And he's not a Black Knight after all?'

'On the contrary, sir, he's very much one. It's my guess he joined them in Berlin to help fight against Bismark's Kulturkampf policy against the Church of Rome – maybe to the point of even forming some sort of underground resistance of his own—'

'But, damn it, man—'

'I'm having to guess much of this, sir, but it all ties in with the facts.'

Callaghan re-gathered his thoughts. 'In the meantime, from what he inferred in the warehouse, Sweeny was going to donate part of his stolen two hundred million, say the biblical ten percent – or ten percent of ten percent, knowing Sweeny, two million dollars, still a hell of a lot of money – to help the Jesuits restore the Church in both Italy and Germany, and free the Pope from house-arrest in the Vatican. Sweeny mentioned Father General Beckx in the warehouse. So, knowing Reikel's extreme views, Beckx sent him to New York to liaise with Kaufmann and ensure that the stones – including Sweeny's donation – would soon be on their way to Europe.'

Spencer looked as if he wanted to ask another question, but Callaghan continued.

'But on reaching New York, Reikel got greedy and decided to divert the entire two hundred million to the cause, forcing Kaufmann to co-operate, probably by threatening the life of his wife, as he did with Morehouse…and the rest you know.'

Spencer frowned 'I'm sorry, Callaghan, you must be mistaken. It's inconsistent for a man to be both priest and killer.'

'Not really, sir. We're all of us part good and evil, but the separation's more extreme in Reikel. Having worked in the College of Propaganda, he's probably a hyper ultramontane and regards Victor Emmanuel's disestablishment of the Church, his imprisonment of the Pope, and von Bismarck's Kulturkampf policy, as akin to blasphemy. It's more than likely he considers both to be instruments of Satan, and would regard their removal as a holy victory in the fight against The Devil.'

'A bit beyond me, all this,' Spencer muttered, 'I'm a lapsed Espicopalian, especially since I came over here.'

'Just think of him as a fanatic, sir, a latter-day Ignatius Loyola, whom I rather suspect he's trying to emulate.'

'Come,' Spencer objected. 'That's a bit much, comparing a killer to a Saint.'

'Maybe so. But there are many parallels between the two. Especially the situation facing their Church, both now and when Ignatius came to its rescue.'

'Such as?'

Beginning to tire of the Consul's questions, Callaghan determined to keep his answers brief.

'It was during the time – as I'm sure you know, sir – when the Catholic Church was losing ground to the Protestant Reformation. Its prestige had sunk to an all-time low, partly through a succession of corrupt popes, with people leaving it in growing numbers, when Ignatius arrived on the scene to stop the rot. Before his conversion he was a soldier, and I guess it was inevitable that his way of reversing the trend was more military than spiritual–'

'In what way, miltary?' the Consul demanded.

'The Jesuit manual he devised, known as the Spiritual Exercises, with its concentration on the terrors of Hell and eternal damnation–'

'Yes, but damn it, man,' Spencer objected, 'that was hundreds of years ago, when people still believed in hell-fire, and demons with horns and tridents. Modern thinking is quite different.'

'Not Jesuit thinking,' Callaghan replied. 'I once had to research the Order for an article in my father's newspaper. Their indoctrination methods are still unchanged to this day. Reikel will have undergone the same intensive training. Over the years, their maxim, "The end justifies the means", has been used by some Jesuits to justify even regicide–'

'Oh, come!' Spencer exclaimed. 'I cannot accept that!'

'It's not an opinion sir, it's historical fact, including a Pope according to Colleen's librarian friend back in Gibraltar. And more recently, our own Abraham Lincoln–'

'Okay,' Spencer hastily conceded. 'In which case, it seems we're dealing with a killer who possesses considerable intellect, and makes him infinitely more dangerous than a common assassin.'

'And with stronger motive,' Callaghan stressed, 'when you consider the way the Jesuits have been persecuted of late, thinking he has right on his side. There's nothing worse than a fanatic, especially a religious one. What with the militant speeches the Pope's been making recently, he probably can't wait for the revolution to start. I have a more than strong hunch he's set up his own body of Jesuit militants, rather like Loyola, except that in Reikel's case, he's training assassins not missionaries.'

'Trained assassins!' Spencer jerked upright. 'What makes you think that?'

'Some papers I found in his sea chest. Colleen had them translated. They referred to an ancient Persian sect called the Assassins. Reikel has clearly been studying their methods–'

'I've read about them,' said Spencer. 'Islamic killers. Their leader indoctrinated them by using drugs, then tested their obedience by ordering some of them to leap off a cliff to their deaths.'

'Yes, sir. Their methods of killing were with the sword and poison. And as you know from Head's diary, two of Reikel's victims had their throats slashed, Briggs and the two in New York were killed with strychnine pills, each strong enough to kill ten men.'

'Okay, Callaghan,' Spencer pursed his lips tight, 'you've convinced me. In which case, it would seem we're not only dealing with a religious fanatic, but a psychopath, too.' Pausing, he pondered aloud. 'I wonder which side of his nature is more predominant? Jesuit? Black Knight? Or Assassin?'

'Maybe all three existing together within one body?' Callaghan suggested. 'A split personality, if that's possible.'

'Dubious,' the Consul frowned. 'But letting that be as it may, what made him copy an Islamic sect, of all things? It seems a strange thing for a Jesuit priest to do?'

'Again, sir, I'd say he was trying to emulate Loyola.'

'In that way?'

'According to the sceptics, Loyola's Spiritual Exercises with their emphasis on experiencing Heaven and Hell, were taken from Islam, rather than the Virgin Mary as he claimed. It's sometimes described as the Jesuits' Koran. At the time of his conversion, Southern Spain was emerging from eight hundred years of Muslim rule. He'd have been fully conversant with their training methods, many of which are similar to ones found in his Exercises.'

'So Reikel decided to follow him? On the principle of what was good enough for Saint Ignatius was good enough for him?'

'Except that in his quest, he unfortunately found the Assassins. Unlike Loyola, Reikel doesn't have ten years in which to train his recruits. He wants them ready yesterday. And with their short-cut methods of indoctrination by drugs, the Assassins were exactly what he was looking for. Which is why I'd lay ten against one that somewhere out there, he's got a training camp for young and susceptible Jesuit priests, run on the same lines as the Shi'ites Alamut.'

'With that precise aim?' asked Spencer, perplexed.

'I know this will sound far-fetched, sir,' Callaghan replied, 'but I suspect his main objective is to assassinate leading Italian and German politicians, the primary targets being Victor Emmanuel and von Bismarck.'

'Great heavens!' Spencer got to his feet and paced the room. 'If you're right, Callaghan, this is serious, damned serious. It may be the lesser of evils to let Cottone find him.'

'Except that may not solve it,' Colleen said. 'Not with Sweeny in the equation. He considers himself to be religious. And Reikel's a priest. Sweeny's only concern is to retrieve his diamonds, then continue his plans of infiltrating the Mafia into the States. If Reikel's found, I suspect that once Sweeny's anger has cooled down, he could try to persuade Cottone to let him go rather than kill him. It might even suit

Cottone if Reikel continued his plans. Assassinating Victor Emmanuel would leave Sicily free once again.'

Spencer massaged the top of his bald head. 'That's a point,' he conceded. 'So where do we go from here?'

'As we've already agreed, sir. Get the Genoa police to help find Reikel. And also have them confine Sweeny and Cottone to their hotel until he's safely under lock and key.'

'But of course,' said Spencer. Returning to his desk, he selected a sheet of Consulate headed paper and picked up a pen. 'I will also write to my colleague in Florence asking him visit Father-General Beckx to inform him that his trusted emissary has turned into a renegade, but this,' he started writing, 'obviously takes priority.'

'Sweeny said he knew how to find him,' Callaghan brooded. 'But will the police?'

'They'll undoubtably start with the city's churches,' Spencer commented, scribbling away. 'Especially the Jesuit ones. In the hope of finding some priest in the know.'

'But I thought they were all closed, taken over by the State?'

'For worship,' the consul glanced up. 'But many are rich in paintings and treasures. In their cases, clerics have been retained as paid guardians – and there are a number of wealthy churches here in Genoa. Some of their priests may have heard a whisper.'

'How long will it take the police to get started?'

'At a guess, a day or so – give or take.'

Callaghan stood up. 'That's too long. Sweeny has already got a head start. Things could start happening before then.'

Colleen looked sharply up at him. 'Michael, what do you intend doing?'

He smiled to reassure her. 'Only keep watch on the hotel until the police arrive.'

'But what if something should transpire before then?'

His smile faded. 'Let's just hope nothing does.'

She stretched out her hand. 'Be careful, Michael. Cottone's probably looking for you as well – to avenge Maranzano.' Her grip tightened. 'I won't feel safe until we're back home again.'

'I'm afraid Cottone won't be stopped by an ocean, Mrs Callaghan,' the Consul said, looking grim. 'Unless we find some evidence to put him away under lock and key, he won't rest until his family honour has been satisfied – in your husband's case, a life for a life – even if it means sending his best mandatari all the way to New York.'

Seeing stark fear in Colleen's eyes, Callaghan pulled her to her feet and drew her to him. 'Don't worry,' he assured her, despite a knot in the pit of his stomach. 'Fate has been kind to us so far. It's not going to deal us a losing hand now.'

'Of course it won't,' Colleen whispered, holding him tight. 'You'll be back with me before you know it.'

- 68 -

It was just gone eleven o'clock, an hour to midnight, as Callaghan entered the Piazza Carlo Felice.

A line of coaches, carriages and cabs standing outside an imposing building in the right corner of the piazza, with a colonnaded entrance from which men and women were exiting, many in evening clothes, placed it as the Teatro Carlo Felice. Which meant, according to Spencer's directions, that the Hotel de Genes was the well-lit building in the opposite corner.

Finding a narrow recess opposite, Callaghan wedged into it. He glanced across the piazza at the darkened facade of a large church. Standing outside it, waiting to drive across the piazza and join the line of vehicles waiting outside the Teatro, was a black coach. Its driver was a silhouette in the darkness and remained so, despite some of the church's stained glass windows suddenly reflecting the flickering light of a moving candle.

A caretaker priest entering the main chapel, Callaghan thought, and one of the many soon to be questioned by the Genoa police.

He refixed his eyes on the Hotel de Genes.

Inside *San Ambrogia*, Nino watched a black-cassocked young priest cross to the altar, holding a gold candlestick in front of him, hand cupped over the flame to prevent it blowing out. Despite its dim glow, it revealed the ornateness of *the church's* interior. Mosaicked walls, ceilings in richly coloured frescoes, the high altar with four monolithic black marble columns, many large paintings.

The pale faced priest knelt before one of Saint Ignatius healing a demoniac, placed the candlestick on the floor, crossed himself and bent his head to pray.

Nino stepped out of the shadows. Putting his stiletto to the priest's throat, he forced him to his feet and thrust him to the main doors.

Before emerging into the night, Nino glanced out at the piazza. Most of the people about were exiting from the *Teatro Carlo Felice* and entering vehicles and being driven away, others preferring to walk and talking amongst themselves, too engrossed to pay him any heed. Prodding the priest with his stiletto, Nino forced him down the steps and into the waiting coach.

Bruno flicked the reins and headed for the de Genes, trundling slowly across the piazza so as not to draw the attention of the escaped American, hiding in a dark cleft opposite, his eyes fixed on the hotel.

Driving past the front of the de Genes, Bruno turned into the tunnel leading to the rear courtyard and the back stairs up to his padrino's room.

It didn't take long for Nino to make the priest talk. No longer than it took to insert the needle-sharp point of his stiletto under the the young man's right index finger nail and slowly prise it off. Had it not been for the cloth stuffed into the priest's mouth, his screams would have woken up the entire hotel.

Throwing cold water over the unconscious cleric's face, bringing him around, Nino inserted the stiletto under his left index finger. The young priest babbled out where Reikel was hiding.

From his chair by the fire, Cottone looked across at Bruno.

The Moorish-looking mafioso peered through the curtains, across the piazza. 'Si, padrino, he is still there.'

In a chair opposite, Sweeny chewed his unlit cigar. 'Why don't we send Nino across to finish him off?' he urged, with the right amount of calculated deference in his voice.

The glow of the fire shone on the silver filigree of Carlo Maranzano's lupara, lying across Don Salvatore Cottone's lap.

'Because it is a matter of family honour,' he said in a voice devoid of emotion, 'which only I can satisfy.'

358

- 69 -

The light of another dawn broke through the white flecked clouds hanging over Genoa and crept into the narrow recess. Callaghan stamped his feet on the floor to restore his circulation. It had been a long cold night, but across the piazza the hotel was coming to life. Lights were showing in the staff's attic windows, most of the ground floor, and some of the guests' rooms.

Thinking longingly of a hot bath and a savoury meal, he saw the Moorish-looking mafioso and a black-cassocked priest emerge from the de Genes rear tunnel and head across the piazza. The priest's two index fingers were bandaged. As they came nearer, Callaghan recognised him as the young man who had driven the mule cart to the palazzo.

Callaghan hesitated. Should he follow them? Or stay watching the hotel until the Genoa police arrived? Seeing the priest's bandages, the man had likely been tortured. Forced to reveal Reikel's hiding-place? Was the priest being made to take him there, to prove he was telling the truth, before Cottone and Sweeny ventured out of the hotel? Or was the *mafioso's* being with him just a decoy?

The *mafioso* and the priest entered a street leading out of the south east corner of the piazza.

Callaghan decided. Checking the lupara and bandoleer hidden under his jacket, stiletto in his belt, he moved out of the recess and followed.

From his first-floor window Cottone watched Nino exit from the de Genes' tunnel, cross the piazza and follow after the American. The man would never know he was being followed. And Nino would obey his *padrino's* orders to the letter of his law.

In his native Sicilian, he instructed a mafioso standing behind him. 'Inform Guilamo and Signor Sweeny that Santa Maria sails within the hour.'

'Si, padrino,' the mafioso said and left the room.

Cottone inserted two bullets into the empty chambers of a revolver. One for Reikel. One for the American.

Tailing the *mafioso* and the priest down the street – the Via Stefano, according to a plaque high on its corner wall – they turned into a stable-yard. Callaghan slipped into a shop doorway. Despite the early hour, Via Stefano was starting to fill with people and horse traffic. The rising sun was swiftly dispersing the grey-flecked winter clouds.

Callaghan saw the young priest and the *mafioso* drive out of the yard on a mule-cart – the one used to collect the barrel of diamonds from the warehouse, he recognised the markings – the priest at the reins, the *mafioso* sitting beside him. The cart turned left, making for a narrow gateway in a fortified wall at the far end of the street.

He exited the doorway and, from a distance, followed the cart through the archway, along a curving street and through another gateway in a second fortified wall.

Crossing an old stone bridge over a wide river, the road turned to dust, climbing above the city and out into the country, leaving its white villas and palaces all huddled together far below. The early morning sun had driven away most of the winter clouds and the sky was now a brilliant azure. To Callaghan's right, the wide bay stretched to a hazy, distant horizon.

There were many on the road, some going in the same direction, but most were making for the city. Farmers with wagons full of produce; drovers herding animals or packed mules; peasant women with baskets on their heads, still-tired children awoken too early lagging behind them, and every once in a while, the more fortunate in a carriage and pair.

The cart lumbered on, the *mafioso* looking straight ahead and the priest sometimes jigging the braces, but the mule refusing to move any faster.

The road continued on through the most breathtaking scenery Callaghan had ever seen; cliffs climbing so precipitously it was sometimes forced through dark, jagged tunnels hewn out of the rock, before emerging back into the sunlight and the luxuriant vegetation of chestnut, palm and coniferous trees: firs and pine, the Mediterranean appearing between their branches, its rugged coastline indented with coves, its waters reflecting the blue of a now cloudless sky.

Sometimes passing an old watch-tower, and once, the ruins of an ancient castle, the road continued toward a distant, tree covered headland jutting out into the sea.

The sun had passed its zenith before they reached it. Turning on to a dirt track, the mule-cart trundled across open ground, making for a forest of chestnuts and pines covering the whole of the peninsula. Far below, the Mediterranean stretched away into the distance, its white crested waves breaking against the rocky shoreline.

From behind the trunk of a large chestnut tree, Callaghan watched the cart enter the trees and disappear from sight. Alongside the track was a deep, dry ditch. Running to its cover, he crept along it until he reached the forest's edge, and followed the dirt track deeper into the forest, taking care not to tread on any fallen twigs as he slipped from tree to tree, until the path dipped into a glade and ended. The mule, with its cart, was tethered to a low-hanging branch, but there was no sign of the priest or the *mafioso*.

From a slope above, he heard stones clattering down. Climbing toward the sound, he crested the brow and, through the trees, glimpsed the two men heading deeper into the forest. Using the trees as cover, he followed them, zigzagging up slopes and down into hollows, shafts of sunlight breaking through the branches and creating patches of light across the forest floor. From up ahead he heard the distant sound of waves crashing on rocks. It grew louder. More light filtering through the trees told him they were nearing the end of the headland. It was time to make his move.

Ahead of him, the priest led the *mafioso* along a faint track skirting around the left side of a rocky hillock. Callaghan ran to the right of the knoll, weaving through trees and reaching the other side of the mound ahead of them. Hiding behind a thick shrub, under an overhanging outcrop of rock, he placed his lupara on the ground, unsheathed his stiletto and waited.

The two men appeared around a corner of the hillock, the young priest still leading. In that same instant, he lifted up the skirts of his cassock and fled down the path.

In one swift movement a stiletto appeared in the *mafioso's* hand, his arm drew back, the knife flashed through the air. The young priest fell, the blade embedded in his back. His body rolled down a steep bank and against a tree. The Moorish-looking *mafioso* looked down at the corpse. Callaghan crept up behind him, put his left arm around his throat and thrust the stiletto up under his ribcage. The *mafioso's* body sagged to the ground. Callaghan nudged it with his foot down the slope. It rolled to a stop against the dead priest.

Wiping the stiletto clean of blood on the grass, he went back for the lupara. A large piece of rock had fallen off the outcrop on to it, bending the barrel. Callaghan swiftly crouched down. His eyes searched the surrounding undergrowth. He had an uneasy feeling he was being watched, but nothing moved. Dismissing it as an unfortunate stroke of fate, he stood up, discarded the bandoleer and retreated backwards, clutching the stiletto, eyes flickering from one bush to another, and from one tree trunk to the next. Still nothing stirred.

He reached the treeline and glanced over his shoulder. Backdropped by the mainland he saw a wide shimmering bay. Beyond it, through the branches of huge chestnut trees draping the hillside, a panoramic sweep of the blue Mediterranean extended to a far horizon. At the edge of the headland overlooking a large cove, almost hidden by lush vegetation, rose the stone walls and battlements and rounded watchtower of an ancient castle.

Reikel had chosen well, Callaghan thought. If Alamut had been the most beautiful spot since the Garden of Eden, this was surely its successor.

Still glancing down at it, he saw that the spreading branches of one majestic chestnut tree standing near its western wall, were overhanging the battlements below the tower.

Calculating it would be dusk in about two hours, he sat down with his back against the trunk of a tree, embedded the stiletto in the ground by his side and settled down to wait, still searching the forest's undergrowth, poised to react should someone emerge from it.

Nino stared impassively from behind a large pine tree at the castle, then back to the American. By dropping a rock on the lupara, he had succeeded in disarming the man, thus obeying his padrino's command, but he'd also thought he had given him no reason to suspect he was being followed. The man's watchful position, his darting eyes, the stiletto by his side ready to be be used, clearly told that he had the senses of a hunted animal. But as for him now killing Bruno, as well as Carlo Maranzano, this was for his *padrino* to avenge.

Realising that the American was waiting for dusk to descend, Nino turned away and headed through the forest for the cove, to be there waiting for his Don.

- 70 -

Callaghan dropped the few feet from the branch to the battlement. The heavy wooden door to the tower was unlocked. He slipped through and found himself on a wide stone landing halfway up a spiral staircase, lit by torches in iron sconces. At the top was a solid wooden door with heavy iron hinges, studded with large nail-heads. He climbed up and listened with his ear to it, but from inside there was only silence. He turned away and crept down the stone steps, pressing against the curving inner wall, until he reached a long, arched gallery, again lit by torches, with dark wooden doors, each with a solid, eye-level hatch.

From behind the first door he could hear wailing and moaning. Inching the hatch open, he peered through. Inside the room were nine young men in brown homespun robes, all in various stages of paroxysmic agonies. Three were writhing on the floor. Four were huddled against the walls, faces turned away from some horror too terrible to witness. And two were staring terror stricken into space.

Closing the hatch he moved to the second door. The voices from inside this room were very different. Softer, like the sighing of people in ecstasy. Again inching the hatch open, he saw six men, young like the others but wearing white robes, all kneeling on the floor, arms stretched out in adoration to someone only they could see. The look on each face was of bliss.

Hearing a door open behind him, he turned and saw five young men wearing black robes with red sashes exit from another room on to the gallery. Under their sashes were open swords. They stood still, staring zombie-like at him, then drew the swords and advanced on him, blocking the way back to the battlement.

The only escape was down. He ran along the gallery to the stairs, hearing them in pursuit, but only the sound of their feet, no voices and therefore all the more eerie. Tearing down two torch-lit flights, he found himself in a large hall on the ground floor. The arched main double doors had a thick iron lock but no key. He tried to open it, but it was fast.

Behind him stretched a long, stone-flagged corridor. He ran along it, the five sworded men following him, still making no sound, and saw steps leading down to another door. He fled down them, threw the door open, and in the light of the moon shining through a barred window found himself in a large scullery. The door was thick and heavy, with a sturdy, wooden locking beam. He slid it across. It would buy him precious minutes.

In the corner was another flight of stone steps. He raced down them into a stone walled cellar. The faint light filtering in through two slits in the walls revealed a large stack in the middle of the floor, covered with tarpaulin.

But there was no way out.

Above him he heard the pounding of something solid being battered against the scullery door. Remembering the broken, twisted bodies of Reikel's two New York victims, he was under no illusions as to what the Jesuit priest would do to him, and felt a cold shiver crawl up his spine. Determined not to succumb without resisting, and hoping to find something more than his stiletto to use as a weapon, he lifted the tarpaulin.

Under it was a huge cache of explosives: firearms, boxes of dynamite, detonators, rolls of fuse wire, boxes of vestas, all proof of Reikel's revolutionary intentions – but also the way to maybe prevent him, Callaghan thought, staring at the cache. Even more, if he used a whole coil of wire to delay the explosion, it might buy him time to attempt an escape.

He found what looked to be the longest coil of fuse wire, connected one end with his stiletto to a detonator, lit the other end with a vesta, replaced the tarpaulin, ran back up the steps to the scullery and closed the cellar door. The door to the corridor was still resisting the battering but the beam was splitting.

Clutching his stiletto he stood in the middle of the floor and waited.

The door burst open. Swords drawn, the five priests advanced on him. He dropped his stiletto in a fake gesture of surrender.

Indicating with their swords, the priests forced him back up the two flights of stairs to the gallery and up the spiral steps to the room at the top of the tower.

Knocking on the iron studded door they were bidden: 'Herein!'

He was pushed inside. From his earlier study of the castle he knew it to be the uppermost room, high above the battlements. Its inner wall, broken by a full window to a stone balcony, was rounded, following the shape of the circular tower. The furniture was austere, a simple, narrow bed on bare floorboards, a bookshelf full of leather-bound books. And a plain table behind which sat Reikel wearing his black robe and red sash.

The Jesuit looked up from reading a large, black Bible. On the table, in a plain pewter holder, was a single candle, its flickering yellow flame lighting the bones of his face, leaving the hollows in shadow. With his albino white hair the visual effect was one of evil.

In the stone wall behind him was a recessed hearth with an iron brazier, full of grey ash, that looked as though it hadn't been lit for many years. Higher up on the wall was a rude wooden Cross bearing the broken figure of the crucified Christ.

On the stone floor to one side of the hearth was an open chest from which a hundred million dollars worth of diamonds glinted in the glowing light of the candle, tinting some of them red as though reflecting all the blood that had been shed over them.

366

'How did you find me?'

Reikel's slate blue eyes, intensified by mirroring the candlelight, were almost hypnotic as they fixed on him. Returning the priest's gaze Callaghan tried to oustare him, but then tore his eyes away and looked back around the room, focusing on four engravings similar to the ones he'd seen in the library of Saint Francis Xavier in New York.

The first was of screaming men and women with terror-stricken faces, clawing at a thick iron grating barring their escape out a fathomless pit, with the fires of Hell flaring up out of it to engulf them, and a bolt of lightening from the heavens above flashing down on them.

In the second, a young man, an arm held by an angel, the other by a demon, was being urged to choose between a twisting path leading up to Heaven, or a straight easy path down to Hell.

The third depicted Christ surrounded by His followers and holding His Cross in front of Him like a standard bearer entering battle as He confronted Satan and his army of demons.

Callaghan turned to the last engraving.

It showed a stairway filled with men who had chosen to fight for Christ, each bearing a Cross as they ascended up to Heaven to claim their eternal reward.

And this was how Reikel regarded himself, Callaghan thought. As chosen to fight some holy war. Seeing himself earning the same eternal reward.

'Are you alone?'

The Jesuit priest's cold eyes bore into Callaghan's. Receiving no reply, his voice became more muted, yet more threatening: 'How much do you know?'

'Everything,' Callaghan replied, conscious of the seconds ticking away as the coil sparked toward the detonator in the cellar below, full with boxes of dynamite. If he could just keep the psychopath talking until the explosion tore through the castle, the balcony and topmost branches of the chestnut tree were only feet away.

'You're a psychotic Jesuit priest, Karl Reikel. Back in New York you killed Jacob Kaufmann and a seaman, Arian Martens, and taken the lives of the entire complement of a brigantine, *Mary Celeste*. Nine innocent people, including a young woman and child. For two barrels of diamonds. All to remove King Emmanuel and Count Bismarck, restore the Church, and release the Pope from house arrest in the Vatican.

'Tell me,' Callaghan deliberately challenged, intent on dragging time out, 'aren't you going against all Christian teaching? The Bible says that all earthly governments are ordained of God, and those who use force to usurp them are rebelling against His holy will?'

Reikel continued to stare at him, then suddenly stood up, crossed the room and opened the long window.

Hanging low in the sky, a pale full moon shone through the trees, casting dark shadows across the balcony. From far below came the sound of waves crashing on rocks.

'Kommen hier,' Reikel whispered, stepping outside.

Callaghan followed him. The balcony protruded high above the castle, with a sheer drop down the cliffs to the cove. The moon was casting a silver glow across the dark waters of the larger bay beyond, bathing the panoramic scene as clearly as daylight. The night-blue sky full of stars, and the faraway mainland speckled with a myriad of flickering lights, gave Callaghan the strange unearthly feeling of being suspended high above it all, in space. He stepped back.

'I see you feel it,' Reikel murmured. 'What does it say to you?'

Still feeling as though he was falling, Callaghan remained silent.

With his gaze still fixed on the moonlit panorama, Reikel whispered the answer to his own question, quoting from the Bible: 'And The Devil took Christ up into an exceeding high mountain, and sheweth him all the kingdoms of the world, and the glory of them.'

Surely, Callaghan thought, recognising the passage from Satan's Temptation of Christ in the wilderness, and realising from the look in Reikel's eyes that his spirit was elsewhere, the madman wasn't identifying himself with the Son of God?

'And The Devil saith unto Him,' Reikel continued. 'All these things I will give Thee if Thou wilt fall down and worship me. Then said Christ unto him, Get thee behind me, Satan, for it is written: Thou shalt worship the Lord thy God and Him only shalt thou serve.'

Reikel turned his face, his eyes burned feverishly into Callaghan's. 'Thus you have your answer. Having refused to bow the knee to the Evil One, Christ took up His Cross and became the victor over him. And following the example of our militant Lord, I also refuse to bow the knee to those who seek to destroy His Church.'

Wondering when those damned explosives were going to blow, Callaghan argued back.

'But surely, didn't Christ also say: Blessed are the merciful for they shall obtain mercy, and blessed are the peacemakers for they shall be called the children of God?'

'But first must come the *victory* over evil!' Reikel returned, exultant. 'This our militant Lord foretold when He warned: Think not that I come to send peace on earth. I come not to send peace, but the sword.'

'But that's a false interpretation.' Callaghan was genuinely aghast by the Jesuit's reasoning. 'As a priest you must know the rule for obeying scripture. Add nothing to it, take nothing from it, change nothing in it. Christ wasn't saying he was the instigator when He said that. He was telling His disciples that by preaching His Gospel they would incur Satan's wrath, and The Devil would resort to every means to oppose them, even the sword.'

Despite realising he was defending what for years he'd been denying, Callaghan continued.

'The religion of Christ is based on love, not enmity for those whose views do not agree with your own? With your twisted reasoning you've killed an innocent mother and little child, as well as all the other lives you've taken.'

Giving Callaghan a thin smile of contempt for one who could not be expected to understand, Reikel responded with another quote: 'Blessed are those whom men shall revile and persecute and say all manner of evil against falsely, for the sake of Christ,' then continued with his twisted reasoning. 'The child was sacrificial in the greater cause, as were the children of Bethlehem slain that the Christ child might live, fulfilling the words that in Rama, there was heard lamentation, and great mourning,' *he again quoted.* 'Rachel weeping for her children.'

The man's quite definitely deranged, Callaghan decided, looking into Reikel's burning eyes.

Without warning, the Jesuit suddenly pushed Callaghan back into the room and came right up to him, his slate-blue eyes now icy cold again.

'But we are not here to argue doctrine.' His voice reverted to a threatening whisper. 'Apart from yourself, who…else…knows?'

'God?' said Callaghan.

Reikel studied him, face showing no emotion, then he crossed to the table, opened a wooden box and removed three cloth bags; one grey, one brown, and one black. Untying the grey sack, he withdrew a pinch of grey powder.

'Halt ihn fest!'

Dragging Callaghan to the floor, four priests pinioned his arms and legs, the fifth held his head firm and squeezed his nostrils tight. Reikel knelt alongside him and whispered: 'Ololiuqui from the seed of the Ipomoea violacea. Mixed with black henbane it produces a foretaste of Hell and can persuade the most stubborn to talk.'

Out beyond the window, unseen inside the room, the dark shape of a large, unlit steam yacht slowly glided into the cove, its engine running silent, and anchors ready to be lowered.

Forcing Callaghan's mouth open, Reikel poured in the powder.

It was very bitter. Callaghan felt himself begin to shiver. Then came giddiness and a feeling of numbness, a sensitivity to even the dim light of the candle. He closed his eyes, only to find he was falling, falling down a dark pit that was blacker than the darkest night. From its bottomless depths emanated the most terrible sounds, the cries of the eternally damned wailing with the pain of souls in torment. As he fell, twisting, turning ever deeper into the void, he tried to raise his hands to his ears to shut out the dreadful howls, but he was unable to move them. The pit opened into infinity, flaring up towards him was a consuming fire. In its centre were the inhabitants of Hell, gaunt faces pleading upwards and sinewy arms outstretched in desperation, while dancing around them oblivious of the flames, talon-like fingers seeking to grab him, were cackling fiends and demons, creatures more monstrous than imagination could conjure. In their midst, Callaghan saw his own face, the skin slowly peeling off layer by layer from the heat, until only an eyeless skull remained as the flames now started on his body.

Through it all he felt his heart pounding, his mind being deprived of all reason, and heard a faraway voice whispering: 'Who else knows? Tell me and you will be released from the fire.' As his flesh parted from his body, leaving only a skeleton, a part of Callaghan screamed to tell Reikel everything. But his stronger half fought back, not allowing him to speak.

Slowly the visions grew fainter, floating away as though on a cloud. Then they were gone.

He surfaced in the room, his clothes soaked with perspiration. Reikel was kneeling over him, a pinch of brown powder between his fingers.

'Extremely resistant,' said the Jesuit. 'But having survived Hell, we will see what a taste of Heaven can achieve.' Again forcing Callaghan's mouth open, he poured powder in a thin stream out of his hand. 'Peyote, from the cactus peyotl of the genus Laphophora.'

In moments, Callaghan felt a wonderful sense of anticipation, an overwhelming exhilaration, combined with a feeling of rapture. The walls of the room dissolved into a wide, yet inaudible river of glorious colours, so indescribably beautiful they could not be of this earth. He felt himself smile in pure joy at the feeling of sheer bliss. He tried to fight it but the sensation was too strong. Bathed in a silvery light, he was floating through air that was both scintillating and purifying, towards a distant golden glow. From the heavenly music emanating around it, he knew without a doubt, it must be eternal, holy, the ultimate. Beneath him, the shining river meandered slowly towards the most beautiful garden he had ever seen. With gentle rolling hills, it was covered in lush vegetation, dotted with trees heavy with fruit, a garden of paradise, the Eden of God's first creation, where man would want for nothing, where there would be no sorrow, no suffering, no pain, only joy. As he approached it, he saw that the golden glow was radiating from a sylvan glade lapped by the river's shimmering waters. In the glow's very centre stood a mighty golden figure. A figure that could be only God Himself, standing there, His arms lovingly outstretched to welcome him, to willing forgive him – him, Michael Callaghan – for his harsh words, his sarcastic comments, his unkind thoughts. He wanted to experience Him more than anything he'd ever known.

'Tell me who else knows,' he heard God ask, in a voice so gentle, so full of love, he wanted to cry. 'Tell me and you will enter my Kingdom.'

Tears streaming down his face, Callaghan held nothing back, telling God everything. Colleen waiting in the Consulate. Sweeny and Cottone in the Hotel de Genes.

The glow faded. Callaghan stretched his arms toward it. But it was now no more than a distant speck. And then it went out.

Finding himself back in the room, Callaghan felt physically drained, yet mentally alive, with none of the after-effects associated with drugs. Everything he'd felt was still clear in his mind. Was there a Heaven out there somewhere, or had it been no more than a hallucinatory experience?

'Bring ihn hier!' he heard Reikel command, then felt himself being raised to his feet.

Looking across the room, he saw Reikel out on the balcony, a black pill in his hand.

The strychnine pill! Oh, God, if ever I need You to answer my prayer, now would be the right moment for the explosives to blow!

The priests pulled him to his feet. Callaghan tried to fight to free himself, but he hadn't the strength. They dragged him through the open window out on to the balcony, and he heard the sea pounding against the jagged rocks below.

Was this the last earthly sound he would ever hear?

'Heaven?' Reikel asked. 'Or Hell? You've seen both. Which will you find yourself in?'

He paused. 'I think…'

O, please, God! Callaghan's plea came from the very depth of his soul. Save me! Save me!

'Hell!' said Reikel, raising the strychnine pill.

Please! O, God, please, please help me!

The pill touched his lips.

Callaghan heard a shot.

Reikel clutched at his chest, blood seeping through his fingers, then he staggered back over the balustrade and plunged down into the black depths below.

Callaghan turned around.

Standing in the window, a revolver in his hand, was Don Cottone. Behind him, leering with anticipation, was Sweeny. Deeper into the room was the Asiatic-eyed *mafioso*.

Looking emotionless at Callaghan, the capomafia raised his revolver and pointed it at him.

'A life for a life,' he said, no inflexion in his voice.

The barrel moved upwards until it was aimed straight at Callaghan's head.

Cottone pulled the trigger.

The bullet whistled past Callaghan's ear into the darkness beyond.

Throwing the gun at Callaghan's feet, Don Cottone walked out of the room.

- 71 -

'Why didn't he kill me?' Callaghan asked. Still weak in his legs, he was sitting on the balcony, his back against the balustrade, and Sweeny standing in the open window, having at last stopped drooling over the diamonds, still glistening in their chest against the fireplace wall.

'He sure gave you a helluva fright,' Brains grated. 'It was worth it just to see the look on your face.' Cottone, he'd already gloated, was overseeing the priests carry the arms cache up from the cellar, then down to the cove where boats would ferry it to Cottone's steam yacht, the *Santa Maria*, and taken to Palermo. As for why the dynamite hadn't exploded, a mafioso sent down to the cellar to check, had found the fuse only half burnt, a fault in the wire having extinguished the spark.

Providence, Callaghan wondered to himself? Who knew? Only someone infallible. And no human born could ever be that.

Sweeny gave Callaghan a rueful grimace, clearly disagreeing with Cottone's decision, and now answered his question. 'To satisfy some stupid Mafia debt of honour, that's why. Guilamo, the priest whose life you saved in the warehouse, is his favourite nephew, his dead brother's son.'

'Nephew? He wasn't one of Reikel's men?'

'Hell, no! Did you think he was?'

'Something like that,' Callaghan affected a grudging admission of his error, realising Sweeny was in a puffed-up, elated mood, and hoping to get him to reveal more.

Brains gave him a scornful look. 'Yehs sure been getting it wrong, Mikey. Guilamo's a priest right enough. I met him in Notre Dame

375

Cathedral. That's in Paris, France, in case you didn't know. He's the one Cottone's chosen to succeed him, not Maranzano, which is why Carlo was plotting to croak the Don and take over. Guilamo found out what he was up to, and rather than risk Carlo intercepting his wire, he got the first ferry to Genoa. But a pal of Carlo's chanced wiring him, and he was waiting for Guilamo at the dockside. He was grilling Guilamo to reveal all he knew, when you saved him by killing Carlo, stopping Carlo from putting his plan into action. So, according to Cottone's stupid code, he owed you two lives. His own – which he paid off by killing Reikel. And his nephew's–'

'By deliberately missing me?'

'Crazy ain't it?' Sweeny growled. 'Me? I'd still have plugged you. But what the hell,' he shrugged, 'it means we're all even and can all go home – except for one last thing.'

Picking up the Bible and lighted candle from the table, he walked out onto the balcony. 'I cast this man out from the fellowship of the Church,' he intoned, opened the Bible and slowly, ceremoniously, closed it, then threw the candle over the balustrade at the point where Reikel's body presumably still lay sprawled on the rocks below.

Callaghan recalled a scene from his childhood, of a ceremonial service at his church to excommunicate a member who'd fallen from grace. After pronouncing the dreadful sentence, the priest had closed the Bible, symbolising the book of life, extinguished a candle by throwing it to the floor, to show that the light of the soul had been removed from the sight of God, and finally tolled a bell as a death-knell for one who had died. He'd had terrible dreams about it for nights after.

By the Bell, Book and Candle, he thought. Was it that easy to erase a renegade priest from the Church's roll call? If there was a final Day of Judgement, would it be that easy then?

'I'll ring the bell when I get to Palermo.' Brains added. Lighting a cigar, he inhaled and slowly exhaled the smoke. I was gonna give the

Church a percentage from the sales of the stones to get it restored and the Pope freed – two million, that's a helluva lot of dough – and when I get back to New York, I may still give it to the Church back home instead.' He brooded about it. 'But I'll give it some thought first.'

'You surely don't still think you're going to be allowed back into the States?'

'Nothing's more certain, Mikey. Not just me, but Cottone, too. And when we are, the Sicilian operation will be peanuts to what we're gonna make over there. Especially Reikel's drugs idea. After seeing those priests high on his heaven powder, that's gotta be the biggest money-spinner of them all.'

'Forget it. When this story gets out, you've as much chance being allowed back in–'

'What story?'

'*The Mary Celeste.* You. Reikel. Cottone. The whole thing.'

Sweeny exhaled smoke. 'Who's gonna publish it?"

'*The Times.*'

'Who in the hell's gonna believe you, Mikey? A psychotic Jesuit priest. Smuggled diamonds. Deserted castles. Indoctrinating drugs. Renegade novitiates. A plot to assassinate the King of Italy and Germany's Chancellor. A Sicilian organisation called Mafia no one back home's ever heard of. Yet,' he stressed. 'Can you really see *The Times* printing such a cockamamie story?'

'I've got the evidence to prove it. Including the occupation of this castle.'

'We've almost emptied it. By the time the Genoa police get here there'll be no sign of any occupation. The priests will be taken to Palermo until the effects of the drugs have worn off, then sent back to the mainland. Bruno's gonna get a proper burial. As for Reikel's body – weighted and thrown overboard once we're into the Mediterranean–'

'Head's diary will back me up.'

'And who's Head?'

'The *Celeste's* steward.'

'Is it authenticated?'

Callaghan knew where this was headed.

'Because if it's not, who's to say you didn't make up the story and got someone to forge the diary for yehs?' Taking a long and self-satisfied inhalation on his cigar, Sweeny exhaled a wreath of smoke. 'If I was you, Mikey, I'd forget it. Publish it and you'll be laughed to scorn.'

He stood there a long moment, exulting in his victory. 'See yehs in Noo Yoik, Mikey,' he rasped and gestured at the open chest. 'I'll send some of Cottone's men up for my stones.'

And with a last laugh, Sweeny walked through the open window and exited the room.

- 72 -

Callaghan stared into the room. Through the open window the diamonds glinted in the silver moonlight reflected by the panes.

Yehs ain't gonna get your hands on them, Uncle Petey, he muttered to himself. Not without yehs finding thems scattered on the rocks below, and having to pick thems up one by bleeding one.

He tried getting to his feet, but the strength hadn't fully returned to his legs. Turning on to his hands and knees, he crawled across the balcony. Reaching the window, he was forced to sit again, his back against the jamb, half out on the balcony, half in the room.

The moon's rays shone on the outer wall of the tower, casting the inner wall in shadow inside the room, making it look as though the more the wall circled, the more it thickened. A peculiar optical illusion.

Or was it?

Callaghan's eyes followed the two curving lines. The concave circle formed by the inner wall seemed to be smaller than the convex circle formed by the outer wall – like a lesser circle within a bigger circle. The tangent point where they almost touched, was the window, the wall's thickness there was about two feet. The thickest part of the wall seemed to be at the hearth.

Callaghan narrowed his eyes, trying to work out the two diverging curves.

The thickness at the fireplace looked to be at least nine feet. Maybe more.

What was it that Colleen said in Gibraltar? The way Mr Turner told the story was like hearing some lurid novel. Hiding in castle priest holes.

His mind raced. Okay, this wasn't medieval England. But Lombardy had once also had its share of historical intrigue...

He crawled across the room. Ash from the brazier covered the hearth floor. He brushed some away and saw scrape marks, made almost indistinct by ash having been rubbed into them, heading from the back of the fireplace toward the diamond chest only feet away.

His eyes searched the recess for a hidden catch. Brazier. Iron tongs. But both freestanding.

He looked up the chimney. As far as he could see in the moonlight, its soot-caked stones were rough hewn, with some protruding further out than others, leaving dark hollows between them, one in particular, a foot or so above his shoulder.

He reached up. There was a stone missing. Inside it was a metal bar. A lever? He touched it. Well-greased, and recently if he was any judge. Reikel? He pulled it down.

With a grating sound the back of the hearth slowly lifted until there was a gap of some three feet under it. Behind it was a cavity, some seven feet wide, four foot deep, and six feet high. Its floor, thick with dust, showed where the chest had been dragged inside. Thin beams of moonlight filtered in through ancient air-holes bored through the outer wall, revealing two pulley chains, both with iron weights and another lever. All also greased.

Grabbing the chest's handle, Callaghan dragged it inside the hearth, manouevred it into the cavity, lay on his back and pushed it all the way in with his feet. Scooping up ash from the brazier, he rubbed some into the new scrape marks, entered the cavity backwards, spread more ash across the hearth floor, took hold of the inside lever...

And hesitated.

Had Reikel ever entered inside the cavity himself and tested this inner lever? Maybe.

But maybe not.

He'd clearly used it as a hiding place for the diamonds. But he'd have had no cause to use it for anything else.

Tomorrow morning, when the moonlight now seeping through the air-holes was replaced by the first rays of the sun, signalling that enough hours had passed for him to chance re-entering the room...what if the inner lever no longer worked? Would he be entombed inside, fated to die a lingering death from starvation, his cries for help ringing through the empty castle? With neither Colleen or Spencer knowing where he was, there would be no one with any idea where to start searching for him. Though the chains and lever had been recently greased, was it worth risking his life, just to outsmart Sweeny?

Callaghan pulled down the lever.

One of the iron weights descended, a chain rattled over its pulley, the wall rumbled down.

Sitting by the chest, his back against the outer wall, shafts of moonlight filtering in through the air holes now his only connection with the world outside, he fought off a wave of claustrophic panic.

He heard the sound of footsteps enter the tower room...then hurry back out.

Minutes later, running feet reached the top of the tower's stone steps and into the room.

'It was there! Right there!' Sweeny's anguished voice, muted by the hearth-back, reached his ears. More footsteps entered the room. Sweeny's despair grew louder. 'It can't have vanished into thin air!'

'Yet it has.' Don Cottone. Voice flat, still in control of his emotions. 'Together, it would seem, with your nemesis.'

'But they can't have.' Sweeny was now almost wailing. 'Not from up here. The only way is down the stairs and through the door, where we were all standing. And the chest's too heavy for one man to carry.'

'Which suggests he had others with him,' Cottone reasoned.

'Like who?' Sweeny howled.

'Consulate soldiers?' a third voice suggested.

'Yes, sure, Guilamo,' Brains sounded close to tears. 'Then they musta had wings!'

'The balcony?' said Cottone.

Two sets of footsteps crossed the room to the window, one scurrying – Sweeny. There was a pause, then one set returned into the room.

'They must have been waiting on the forest edge for his signal,' Guilamo stated. 'Climbed the tree on to the battlement and up to this room, lowered the chest from the balcony with ropes, and by now they'll be heading back to Genoa.'

'Then we gotta get after them,' Sweeny yowled from further away. 'They can't have much of a head's start. The chest's gonna hamper them.'

His feet again scurried across the room and faded away down the stone stairs. Cottone and Guilamo exited after him.

Folding his arms on his knees and resting his head on them, Callaghan settled in to wait for morning, praying the lever would work.

'No matter how many times you intend looking, there is no sign of anything here.'

Guilamo's voice woke Callaghan up with a start. He felt stiff.

He'd tried to stay awake, but two days with no sleep had caught up with him and sometime during the night he'd finally succumbed. Now, from the thin rays of the sun slanting in through the air-holes, he guessed it to be early morning.

'I can goddamn see that,' Sweeny's voice grated. 'But I can't see how they got away from us in the forest, not carrying that chest. I want to check around from up here, in case the stinking rat saw something we can't see from the ground – like maybe a hole in the rocks leading to a cave or something. I've still got a queer feeling he's hiding somewhere near.'

Footsteps crossed the room. From out on the balcony, came the murmur of their voices as they surveyed and discussed the scene stretched below them, then re-entered the room.

'Nothing,' Sweeny snarled. 'Not a goddamn thing.'

'I think it's time to accept he got clean away,' said Guilamo.

'The rotten louse,' Sweeny snarled. 'Your uncle should never have spared his life, even it was to satisfy his code of honour. But he was always trouble for me, right from when I first met him. And now the thieving sonofabitch has gone and stolen my diamonds. I worked damned hard for them. Earned them fair and square.'

'We still have the other barrel,' Guilamo prompted. 'The American Consul in Gibraltar will have received our telegraph by now. His reply accepting the tender will be waiting for us in Palermo. Santa Rosalia is ready to sail, and the *Celeste's* diamonds will soon be in our possession. Their sale will easily finance our new American operation.'

'Maybe,' Brains rasped. 'But when I get back to New York, Mikey's gonna be at the top of my hit list.'

And with that the two men left the room.

Callaghan heard the distant clanking of the Santa Maria's anchors being raised and the sound of her engines come on, then fade as the yacht steamed out of the cove.

Now was the moment of reckoning, he thought, placing his hand on the lever.

Would the second chain lift? Or would he be doomed to die here in this dark cavity, his body never discovered, his only company a hundred million dollars of diamonds...

Or had Cottone outwitted him and left Nino behind, waiting for him to emerge from wherever he was hiding, as the Santa Maria seemingly left the scene?

He raised the lever back up.

Nothing happened.

His heart seemed to stand still.

Then the chain rattled as the second iron weight slowly descended.

And the back of the hearth grated up.

Callaghan crawled out of the cavity into an empty room.

He stood up, stretched his aching body, then walked out on to the balcony.

The Santa Maria had cleared the cove and was sailing across the larger bay, heading out to sea. He watched it get smaller until it disappeared over the horizon.

What would be Sweeny's fate, Callaghan wondered, when Consul Sprague replied to Cottone he didn't have power-of-attorney and the *Mary Celeste's* cargo was not his to negotiate? Deprived of both diamond barrels, would the capomafia allow Brains to live, or would he administer Mafia retribution, with Sweeny's bullet-riddled body dumped in a Palermo alley, or buried away in an unmarked grave in one of Cottone's vineyards?

Whichever.

If anyone deserved it, Sweeny did.

- 73 -

Colleen and a clean-shaven Callaghan were sitting at dinner together in the Hotel de Genes.

With the diamonds safely in the vault of the Consulate's Genoa bank, he was ending his account, explaining that the Castello Portofino, a military garrison stretching back to the time of the Romans, had been demilitarised only five years ago and left deserted. Reikel must have heard about it after fleeing Berlin to Genoa to escape Bismarck's persecution of the Jesuits in Germany, and realised its position on the tip of the lonely promontory made it an ideal centre in which to indoctrinate his selected band of assassins.

'They were all priests and novitiates who followed him from Berlin,' he concluded. 'When they reached the castello, Reikel used the drugs to win them over to his cause, just like the Shi'ite Assassins.'

But Colleen was still not fully over not hearing from him for over forty eight hours and returned to it. 'I thought you must be dead. That I'd lost you.'

'You won't get rid of me that easily,' Callaghan quipped. 'Not until I'm a hundred.'

'And a day.' She held his hand across the table. 'What about *The Mary Celeste*? Are you still giving Jennings the story?'

'I've thought much about it. Despite what Sweeny says, I still think I could prove the diary's authenticity. But when all's said and done, maybe it's best left a mystery. Otherwise, the very fabric of the church could be undermined, all because of one fanatic. But thinking back to the castello, when I found myself defending the principles of the Sermon on the Mount,' Callaghan gave a wry smile, 'I now realise that

God's existence is neither proved, nor disproved, by the actions of His believers, who are all human and subject to temptation.'

He felt his throat dry. He glanced at the two carafes. Water, or wine? He poured wine, sipped some and continued.

'And when someone falls, then as well as the so-called sinner, we also hold God guilty by association, to the point that critics, and again I confess I was one of them, argue that the very existence of sin is proof there is no God. But to quote your Mr Turner; and I'm looking forward to meeting him when we reach Gibraltar – but only *after* a resumption,' he grinned, 'of where we left off the last time we slept there.'

Colleen squeezed his hand.

'But God didn't make us puppets. He gave us free will. To choose either good – or evil, as Reikel did. The reason those poor kids on the streets back home go hungry isn't God's neglect but man's selfishness. As for proof of His existence, we have only to look beyond man, to the wonder of Creation. The Sun, Moon, stars, the very universe itself, revolving in order rather than disorder, and it's all enough to make one realise there must be a Creator behind it all.'

Colleen's bare foot caressed his leg under the table. He succeeded in fighting on.

'So, rather than for one man's actions causing the Church to be unfairly criticised, I think *The Mary Celeste* is best left well alone. Let her pass into history. And her mystery remain a mystery.'

'But what about David and Oliver, still stuck in Gibraltar?'

'That shouldn't be too much of a problem. Solly has only got fabricated evidence, but nothing concrete. And once he knows the threat against Desiah and his kids was only a bluff, David will take the stand. So, thinking it through, I don't think there's any need for me tell it to the Enquiry after all. I was also going to involve Mr Sprague in recovering the *Celeste's* diamonds, but again after giving it more thought, I think it's best we keep it all to ourselves and Mr Spencer, don't you, and let the *Celeste* continue on to Genoa and unload the barrel here for him to deal with? He's promised to keep what happened a secret, and knowing him as we do I believe he will.'

'I couldn't agree with you more. And when we ourselves return home?'

'I'll take you up on your offer. But rather than sell your father's house, let's borrow against it and sell the mews-house instead. Lumped together, we should be able to raise enough to buy back the Despatch from the receiver.'

'I think Father would approve of that,' Colleen smiled. 'As he would also thank you for the affidavit.'

'You thanked me for that last night. With some enthusiasm as I recall.'

'That was because I was glad to have you back safe.'

'Sure it was.'

He gripped her hand and continued. 'You know, I keep remembering what Father Murray said about the United States one day becoming the leader of the English-speaking nations, and I think I agree with him. But there's much to be done first. The fight against corruption in high places, like Tweed's Ring. The need to reconcile North and South once again into one nation. We can only assume the mantle of world leader when all this is done and we are truly "united states".'

He smiled at her. 'It promises to be exciting, and we can be a part of it, Colleen. Working together on our own newspaper. And I rather think my father would also approve.'

Colleen smiled back at him. 'Nothing would please me more. And we can also use it to help keep Cottone and his Mafia out. Uncle Petey too, assuming Cottone lets him live.'

'If he does,' Callaghan said grimly, 'let him live, that is – Sweeny still needs to be brought to trial. The shyster's still gotten away with too much – despite losing out on the diamonds – without him returning to Noo Yoik and setting up another crime empire.'

He paused as a dark-suited hotel manager approached the table. 'Signor Callaghan?'

Callaghan nodded.

The man handed him a sealed envelope. 'From the American Consulate.'

Callaghan opened it and read the brief note.

'What is it, Michael?'

'It's from Mr Spencer. His colleague in Florence has been to Fiesole. Father-General Beckx denies his Society have a priest by the name of Karl Reikel.'

Colleen frowned. 'What do we make of that?'

Callaghan shrugged. 'Based on all we know, I guess we can take it with a pinch of salt.'

'Is there any reply, signor?' the dark-suited manager questioned.

'No, thanks.'

The man still hesitated, 'I am sorry to trouble you, signor, but as I approached your table, I overheard you mention the name Sweeny. May I ask if you are acquainted with him?'

'Vaguely,' replied Callaghan, guardedly.

'May I also ask whether you know his forwarding address?' The man looked embarrassed at having to ask the question. 'I'm sure it must be an oversight, but when he and his guests left two days ago, he omitted to pay his account.'

Colleen arched her eyebrows at Callaghan. 'What was it you said a moment ago, Michael? About Uncle Petey having gotten away with too much?'

Epilogue

The secret panel opened and Father-General Pierre Beckx entered "The Room of the Popes".

The Holy Father was seated, wearing white robes, on an ornate chair on a raised dais at the far end of the room. Beckx slowly approached him, leaning heavily on his cane. The Pontiff held out his right hand. Lowering himself to his knees, the Jesuit reverently kissed the papal ring.

Pius indicated a chair placed below the dais. 'How is your health, my friend?' The customary warmth was missing from his voice.

'My mind is well, Holiness. The flesh less so. But my spirit grieves I was not able to fulfil your trust before the Act became law.'

'God must have His purpose in allowing it,' Pius said, looking down on Beckx. 'Although I confess that despite much prayer, His reason remains obscure. Holy Scripture tells us that man is subject to sovereigns. But as Christ's appointed Vicar on Earth, my sovereignty is above all others. If I were to accept this usurper's conditions, then in the eyes of the world, I would be his subject, and, by implication, be acknowledging him as head of Holy Church.'

'That is clearly not God's will, Holiness. Your mission must be to resist, and continue to refuse to leave the Vatican.'

'Which I will, my friend, to the day when I am finally called to my reward. But it would greatly encourage me to understand God's design. My only conclusion is that He is deliberately allowing us to go through the fire, and from it we will emerge all the stronger to face the future challenges of this modern age.'

Beckx solemnly nodded his agreement with the Pontiff's reasoning.

'Faced as we are by a common enemy,' Pius continued, 'the process of conciliation from within has already begun. For the first time in four hundred and fifty years, the schism between Ultramontane and Gallican is forgotten. Their claims for separate self-governing churches have been put aside and they join us in decrying this outrage against Holy Church. As a consequence, when the soul of this so-called temporal King Victor Emmanuel is finally cast into the everlasting fire, the Church that emerges will be all the more united, and thus all the more ready to assume its rightful position as the only true Universal Church of God.'

'My spirit is strengthened by your wise words, Holiness,' the Father-General dutifully replied. 'It makes both my crosses easier to bear.'

'Both crosses, my friend?'

'Yes, Holiness. The first was the unexpected withdrawal of a substantial sum to aid our cause, promised by an American businessman currently on a cultural tour of Europe. The other was when my emissary to America, who was returning with an even larger contribution, went missing at sea. His vessel was discovered in mid-Atlantic with everyone on board missing and no indication as to how they met their end. God alone knows what terrible fate the Evil One had waiting for him out in the vastness of the cold, grey Atlantic—'

Beckx paused, unable to continue, and evincing a rare glimpse of grief.

'My good friend,' *Pio Nono* sympathised, 'take strength in the knowledge that he, too, is now receiving his eternal reward. What was the name of the vessel?'

'*Mary Celeste*, Holiness.'

'Maria *Celeste*.' Pius made the sign of the Cross. 'Is there no indication as to what happened?

'None, Holiness. Only in Heaven is the answer known. On Earth it will remain a mystery that will never be solved.'

Historical Note

The Mary Celeste has been one of the great unsolved sea mysteries for almost 150 years, the subject of countless newspaper articles, books, television documentaries, with theories ranging from giant squids, to UFOs and the Bermuda Triangle.

Most of the myths surrounding the brig can be attributed to a short story, J. Habukuk Jephson's Statement, published in Harper's Magazine and written by a twenty-five year old doctor named Arthur Conan Doyle, later to become famous as the creator of Sherlock Holmes. His first work of fiction, he misspelt her first name as Marie, thus giving her the name by which she is still mostly known, even in public records. Among his story's main "claims" was that "the lifeboat was intact and slung upon the davits", a fact refuted by Gibraltar Consul, Horatio Jones Sprague, in his report to Washington, dated December 13, 1872, in which he stated: No ship's papers were found on board, except the log book, which has entries up to the 22nd or 23rd ultimo, nor were any boats found on board.

I began tackling the mystery in the British Library, discovering a book, "*Mary Celeste*, the odyssey of an abandoned ship" by Charles Edey Fay – an ex-president of the Atlantic Mutual Insurance, New York, the *Celeste's* insurer's, still in business to this day – which was a mine of information. But even this account, as with all others on the subject, concentrates most of its attention on the *Celeste*, and gives very little about the *Dei Gratia*.

Turning my attention to this vessel, I started with the Maritime History Archive, Memorial University of Newfoundland. In response to my application for a copy of the *Dei Gratia*'s crew list for 1872/73, I received the following reply:

> Thank you for your letter of December 7, requesting information on the *Dei Gratia*. We do not have the crew list or official log book for the vessel for 1872. I would suspect that it was not handed to the Registrar General as it does not show on our index, although we have the locations of about 95% of existing crew lists.

For the records relating to this particular voyage not to have been handed in, made me sense I was on to something. Deciding to find out all I could about David Morehouse, the *Dei Gratia*'s captain, my next letter – to the Peabody Museum, Salem, Massachusetts – led me first to the Maritime Museum of the Atlantic, Halifax, Nova Scotia, and from there to the Volunteer Admiral Digby Historical Society (the town of Digby, named after the Admiral, was the *Dei Gratia*'s port of registry).

Here I struck gold in the person of Hilma Woods, the Society's Secretary, who not only told me that a member of the Morehouse family, Inez Morehouse, had written a book entitled, "330 years of Morehouse Genealogy, 1640-1970", but also sent me 30 photocopied pages on David Morehouse. Among them was a summary from an interview with Captain Morehouse's widow, Desiah, published in the Boston Sunday Post, August 15, 1926, in which Desiah stated:

> My husband knew Captain Briggs of *The Mary Celeste* well. In fact, they were friends for many years. Now here is a strange coincidence that the Briggs family is evidently unaware of.

> The *Dei Gratia* and *The Mary Celeste* were loading in New York at the same time. My husband frequently told me that on the night before *The Mary Celeste* sailed, he and Captain Briggs had a

farewell dinner together at the old Astor House in New York. As both of their vessels were destined for Genoa, Italy, they parted with the friendly assurance that they would have another meal at that port.

The mystery now took on a new dimension. Before this, every article, book, documentary, had taken it for granted that the *Gratia* had simply chanced on the *Celeste* in mid-Atlantic. But now, the knowledge that the reputedly deserted brig had drifted nine days on one of the world's busiest sea-routes without being discovered by another vessel, then had been happened upon by the *Dei Gratia* – which did not leave New York until ten days after the *Mary Celeste*, and whose captains had met at the Astor House, the evening before the *Celeste* set sail – was, to put it mildly, somewhat coincidental.

My next step was to obtain copies of the Gibraltar Inquiry transcripts, but they contained only the replies of the witnesses, with few full stops and commas to show where one sentence ended and the next began, nor the questions put to them by the Admiralty's "prosecutor", Solly Flood, and the *Dei Gratia*'s "defence counsel", Henry Pisani. Solly Flood's grilling, and the punctuation of the replies of the *Gratia*'s crew, included in the Inquiry scenes in this book, are therefore based on the suspicions and temperament of the British advocate, as reported in the newspapers of the time.

However, in reading the transcripts, my earlier suspicions were even further aroused by the fact that Captain Morehouse in the *Dei Gratia*, the heavier of the two vessels (transcripts, p.52) was able to enter Gibraltar harbour, yet Deveau, in the lighter *Celeste*, was forced "to run up the Spanish coast, 30 miles after leaving Cape Cueta, or 40 miles that was after leaving Cueta at 6am, in sight of land" (transcripts, p.10) despite the *Celeste* having "kept sight of the *Dei Gratia* until we arrived in the straits, when we lost sight of her". (transcripts, p.20)

The Inquiry papers also revealed many other interesting facts, including:

1. James Henry Winchester, *The Mary Celeste's* major shareholder, who sailed to Gibraltar to give evidence, stated under oath: "I was in New York when the *Celeste* sailed on her last voyage. I know what cargo she had on board. It consisted of 1701 barrels of alcohol, 1 barrel in dispute." When asked about the sword found under Briggs' bed, his reply was: "I know nothing of the Captain having a sword, nor of any sword being on board at all."

2. Justice Sir James Cochrane, on being informed that the *Gratia* had jumped harbour and sailed for Genoa with First Mate Deveau and the rest of the crew, while the Inquiry was still in progress, leaving Morehouse behind in Gibraltar, stated: The conduct of the salvors in going away as they have done, has, in my opinion, been most reprehensible, and may probably influence the decision as to their claim for remuneration for their services; and it appears very strange why the Captain of the *Gratia*, who knows little or nothing to help the investigation, should have remained here, whilst the First Mate and the two men who boarded *The Mary Celeste* and brought her here, should have been allowed to go away as they have done.

3. Deveau, on his return to Gibraltar, did not endear himself to Sir James by revealing that the *Gratia* had taken twenty-four days to sail to Genoa, a journey that should have taken no more than eleven days. Nor was Sir James pleased when Deveau informed the Court: I was obliged to leave one of the two men in hospital at Genoa, in consequence of his having injured himself from over-exertion whilst bringing *The Mary Celeste* to Gibraltar. His name is Charles Lund.

"Charles Lund", whoever he was, "disappeared" in Genoa – and was never heard of again.

4. When the *Gratia* returned from Genoa, Captain Morehouse, who had previously refused to give evidence, now took the stand and the Inquiry resumed. Stating under oath that the *Gratia's* cargo consisted of "refined petrol, 1735 round barrels, and 1 in dispute", he did not however volunteer that he and Briggs knew one another, nor that they had dined together the night before *The Mary Celeste* sailed.

The scrape marks on the *Mary Celeste's* bows and the cut in her rail, were examined by John Austin, Surveyor of Shipping at Gibraltar, but not explained. In Para 47 of his Affidavit, he states that a "length (of canvas) cut off with a knife" had been used to cover the windows of the Captain's cabin. As for the sword, he stated: I observed in this cabin a sword which the marshal informed me he had noticed when he came on board for the purpose of arresting the vessel. It had not been affected by water, but the blade appeared to me to have been smeared with blood and afterwards wiped. (Affadivit, para 44).

The report of Gibraltar's Dr. J Patron stated that the sword and "red-brown spots of wood, about half an inch in diameter and dull in aspect, which were separated with a chisel" (from First Mate Richardson's cabin) were subjected to various tests but found, "according to present scientific knowledge", to contain "no blood." (But what would today's forensic tests have made of them? Author).

The contents of the sea chest marked "Arian Martens" were never properly examined, only its items listed in the inventory of the *Celeste's* effects, made by the Admiralty Court.

On February 5, 1873, the USS Plymouth, arrived in Gibraltar on a routine visit. At Consul Sprague's request, its commander, R Shufeldt examined *The Mary Celeste*. The following day, February 6, he submitted a report to the Consulate. On February 7, the day after the Plymouth left Gibraltar, Consul Sprague handed the report to the Court. It concluded with the following extract:

> *I am of the opinion that she (Mary Celeste) was abandoned by the master & crew in a moment of panic & for no sufficient reason. She may have strained in the gale through which she was passing & for the time leaked so much as to alarm the master, and it is possible that, at this moment, another vessel in sight, induced him – having his wife and child on board – to abandon thus hastily. One day I hope & expect to hear from her crew. If surviving, the master will regret his hasty action. But if we never hear of them again, I shall nevertheless think they were lost in the boat in which both master & crew abandoned The Mary Celeste.*

Captain Morehouse's claim was finally accepted on March 14, 1873, some three months after reaching Gibraltar, but rather than the usual one-half of the value of ship and cargo, he was awarded only one-fifth – £1,700 ($8,300) – a figure regarded by the insurance and shipping world at the time as being "totally incommensurate with such a hazardous salvage".

According to Maritime Registers, the *Dei Gratia* and *The Mary Celeste* were allowed to leave Gibraltar on March 10 – four days before the verdict – with Deveau again commanding the *Gratia* (leaving Morehouse behind to collect the award). After picking up a return cargo from Livorno for the voyage home, he returned to Gibraltar for Morehouse on May 13. The brig finally reached New York on June 19, 1873.

The *Celeste* arrived in Genoa on March 21 (a voyage that took 11 days) under a new master, Captain Blatchford, where her hull was surveyed and found to be in perfect order. On March 26, Consul Oswald Spencer wired Washington: There were landed 1701 barrels.

The cargo came out in excellent condition. (Might it be he was confirming the safe receipt of the diamonds? Author).

The *Celeste's* instructions to sail to Palermo for a return cargo of fruit were cancelled. She left Genoa on June 26 with a cargo for Boston, arriving September 1, leaving September 13, and eventually reached New York on September 19, 1873. Her subsequent career was an unhappy one. For the next thirteen years she went from owner to owner, seventeen in all, none succeeding in making her pay her way. Her last owners deliberately wrecked the vessel on a reef off Haiti in a vain attempt to make a false insurance claim. This escapade made her a total loss.

As for the *Gratia*, she sank at her moorings in Cork Harbour, Ireland, in 1913. Her timbers were still showing up to 1947, but with the expansion of a dry dock she was buried out of sight.

Solly Flood never succeeded in returning to London. He died in Gibraltar, May 13, 1888, three months short of his 87th birthday.

Meantime, in Germany, on July 13, 1874, seventeen months after the *Celeste* Inquiry was closed, Bismarck was driving in an open carriage through the streets of Kissingen, when a man in the crowds fired a pistol shot at him from point-blank range. At that exact moment, Bismarck raised a hand to acknowledge the people's cheers, thereby deflecting the bullet. Kullmann, the would-be assassin, was a Roman Catholic. Defending his act, he claimed that Bismarck's Kulturkampf policy was threatening the very existence of his religion. This gave Bismarck the ideal excuse to launch a furious attack on the Church of Rome. Returning to Berlin, he charged all German Catholics in a speech from the Reichstag:

"Though you may try to disown the assassin, he nonetheless clings to your coat-tails. Moreover, you will never be able to shake this murderer loose".

He now increased his war on the Church. More bishops were thrown into prison, priests were deprived of their parishes, until half Germany's Catholic population had no spiritual leaders. But his violent reaction created a backlash of opinion and he was forced to withdraw his anti-Catholic measures and, loath to admit defeat, said he was giving up the fight against "Black International" (the Church of Rome) to instead fight the threat of "Red International" (the Socialist movement).

Because Pius IX, Pio Nono, had kept them out of Italy for so long, the citizens of Rome did not share the rest of the Catholic world's regard for him. He died in the Vatican on February 7, 1878, but his tomb in San Lorenzo Fuore le Mure wasn't ready. On its completion three years later, when his body was moved there, it was done at night for fear of demonstrations. Nevertheless, the people got to hear of it and turned out in their thousands, hurling bricks and stones at the coffin.

Four succeeding popes – Leo XIII, Pius X, Benedict XV, and Pius XI – also willed to remain as "prisoners of the Vatican". The latter, Pius XI (who, because of his Jesuit confessors, was said to be a secret Jesuit) was appointed Pope in 1922, the year the Fascists marched on Rome.

Seven years later, February 11, 1929, the Fascist leader, Benito Mussolini, signed the Lateran Agreement with a gold pen that Pius had just blessed, giving the Holy See complete sovereignty over a new Papal State, known as Vatican City, and a subvention of 750 million lire, plus interest on 1,000 million lire of State Bonds, as a "definite settlement of its financial relations with Italy in connection with the events of 1870".

Pius asked banker Bernardino Nogara, an Italian Jew who had converted to Catholicism, to advise him. Nogara recommended that two-thirds of the settlement should be invested; and one-third ($30 million) converted into gold and deposited at Fort Knox, USA, where it remains to this day, with a current value of well over a billion dollars.

Father-General Pierre Jean Beckx remained in Fiesole until 1883, when he finally retired because of ill-health. He was succeeded by Anthony M Anderledy, a Swiss. Beckx returned to Rome, where he died in 1887. But the atmosphere in the city was so anti-Jesuit, the Society's temporary headquarters remained in Fiesole until 1895, and its Congregation three years earlier, in 1892, had to assemble at Loyola, Saint Ignatius' birthplace in Spain.

A military fortress was first built on the site of Castello Portofino by the Romans in about AD 400, and extended in the 16th century by the military engineer, Olgiato. There were no roads into the promontory until 1876 (four years after the events in this story) when one was built from Santa Margherita, and even Napoleon, when he attacked the castle more than seventy years earlier, had to do so from the sea. Demilitarised in 1867, it stood empty for seven years and a year after this story was bought as a residence for 7,000 lire by Montague Yeats-Brown (the British Consul who ordered the *Dei Gratia* to return to Gibraltar). He renamed it Castello Brown after himself, and it is still known by this name today. Now owned as a museum by the town of Portofino its views are still as breathtaking. It can be seen by Googling: "Castello Brown, Portofino".

Louis Jennings retired from The New York Times in 1876, and returned to England with his wife, Madeline, daughter of the eminent David Henriques of New York. He became the Conservative Member of Parliament for Stockport, and died at Elm Park Gardens, London, on February 9, 1893, aged fifty-six.

"Boss" Tweed was brought to trial on 55 charges of defrauding the City of New York. Found guilty on a total of 102 counts, each punishable by a year in prison, he managed to escape to Spain, but was caught, extradited, and died of pneumonia in Ludlow Street jail, New York, in April 1878. He was buried in white lambskin, "the emblem of innocence".

Mayor "Elegant Oakey" Hall remained in office to the end of his term, despite appearing in court four times, indicted on the same charges as "Boss" Tweed. He was finally *acquitted* on Christmas Eve, December 24, 1873, and spent his remaining years as a newspaperman, and an attorney. On March 25, 1898, he was baptised into the Church of Rome.

"Slippery Dick" Connolly remained abroad. He spent his days wandering from one country to another, "a lonely man, shunned by everyone" (New York Times). He was tried and convicted in absentia and never returned to New York.

But Peter "Brains" Sweeny did return, on December 19, 1876, having agreed to refund New York City a mere $400,000 in return for immunity from prosecution. (The archive records of the New York State Department of Justice, Organised Crime and Racketeering, state that Sicilian crime entered the USA, via New York, at the same time.)

Sweeny's settlement was announced on June 8, 1877. He made the payment from his late brother's estate. The New York Telegraph said that by negotiating such a deal, Sweeny should be called the Metternich, Talleyrand and Pitt of New York. He resumed his worship at the Church of Saint Francis Xavier, and it was he who proposed "Elegant Oakey" into the Catholic Church.

Sweeny lived another 35 years, and died at Lake Mohapac, New York, in 1911, a wealthy man. (Which perhaps suggests that even though Don Cottone was deprived of the proceeds of Sweeny's diamonds, his "expertise" was not only of enough value to the Mafia to let him live, but also that he was well paid for it over the remaining years of his life.)

Though Sicilian crime had spread into most major American cities by the late 1880s, the word "Mafia" did not appear until October 1890, when *The Times* of London used it to report a gangland war for control of the New Orleans waterfront between the families of Matranga and Provenzano. It was won by the Matranga family, with many corpses left on the streets of the city, among them, David Hennessy, a police chief who was "probing energetically" into the affair.

That a connection existed between Sicilian Mafia and New York's Tammany Hall, was claimed by Lieutenant Joe Petrosino, a tough New York cop and bitter opponent of the Mafia. In a report (found in the archives of the Department of Justice) he stated that once a mafioso arrived in the USA, he would join a political gang and thereby receive unlimited protection. 'Nothing we can do against so-and-so', Petrosino was often heard to say, 'he's a Tammany Hall man'".

In 1909, Petrosino sailed to Palermo to find out how many Sicilians were emigrating illegally.

The Mafia were waiting for him. On the instructions of Don Vito Cascioferro, Sicily's then capomafia, Joe Petrosino was shot dead in the *Piazza Marina*, the very centre of Palermo.

However, the Mafia did not become a national threat until the 1920s. After much fighting with the Neapolitan Camorra – ruled in Chicago by Al Capone – the largest emergent family was the Castellammare, headed by Don Salvatore Maranzano.

Born 1868 in Castellammare del Golfo, Sicily, and christened Salvatore after his grandfather, Maranzano was college educated and studied to become a priest. He arrived in New York in 1918 and thirteen years later, 1931, declared himself to be the supreme Capo dei Capi – the "boss of all bosses", ruling over an area stretching from New York, Buffalo, Boston, Chicago in the north, to Miami, New Orleans in the south, San Francisco, Los Angeles in the west. He held his council meetings in a hall in the Bronx, festooned with religious pictures and a crucifix over the platform.

On September 10, 1931, on the orders of Salvatore "Lucky" Luciano, four mafiosi – "Bugsy" Seigel, Albert Anastasia, "Red"

Levine, "Three Finger Brown" Luccese – killed Maranzano in his Park Avenue real-estate office with six knife wounds and four shots.

By the mid-1930s, the Mafia had become the largest and most powerful of the United States' syndicated crime networks. In most cities there was usually only one family in control. In New York, there were five.

Investigations conducted by US agencies during the 1950s-1960s, revealed the structure of American Mafia to be like its Sicilian prototype, and now calling itself Cosa Nostra: "Our Affair".

Richard Rees

Richard Rees is originally from Wrexham, North Wales, where he had an accountancy practice, but became a writer after the deaths of his young wife, Richenda, then his only daughter, Elisabeth, from ovarian cancer. He now lives a quiet life in the seaside town of Llandudno, at the foot of the Snowdonia National Park, doesn't drink or smoke, and so sounds a bit of a bore, but is gregarious, keeps fit, swims, drives fast and doesn't play golf.

For more information on Richard's books, including where to purchase them, or to contact Richard, go to

www.richardhrees.com

Printed in Great Britain
by Amazon